*The Christmas Boutique*

ALSO BY JENNIFER CHIAVERINI

*Resistance Women*

*Enchantress of Numbers*

*Fates and Traitors*

*Christmas Bells*

*Mrs. Grant and Madame Jule*

*Mrs. Lincoln's Rival*

*The Spymistress*

*Mrs. Lincoln's Dressmaker*

*The Giving Quilt*

*Sonoma Rose*

*The Wedding Quilt*

*The Union Quilters*

*The Aloha Quilt*

*A Quilter's Holiday*

*The Lost Quilter*

*The Quilter's Kitchen*

*The Winding Ways Quilt*

*The New Year's Quilt*

*The Quilter's Homecoming*

*Circle of Quilters*

*The Christmas Quilt*

*The Sugar Camp Quilt*

*The Master Quilter*

*The Quilter's Legacy*

*The Runaway Quilt*

*The Cross-Country Quilters*

*Round Robin*

*The Quilter's Apprentice*

# THE CHRISTMAS BOUTIQUE

*An Elm Creek Quilts Novel*

## JENNIFER CHIAVERINI

WILLIAM MORROW
*An Imprint of* HarperCollins*Publishers*

THE CHRISTMAS BOUTIQUE. Copyright © 2019 by Jennifer Chiaverini. All rights reserved. Printed in the United States of America. No part of this book may be used or reproduced in any manner whatsoever without written permission except in the case of brief quotations embodied in critical articles and reviews. For information, address HarperCollins Publishers, 195 Broadway, New York, NY 10007.

HarperCollins books may be purchased for educational, business, or sales promotional use. For information, please email the Special Markets Department at SPsales@harpercollins.com.

FIRST EDITION

*Designed by Fritz Metsch*

Library of Congress Cataloging-in-Publication Data has been applied for.

ISBN 978-0-06-284113-1

19 20 21 22 23   LSC   10 9 8 7 6 5 4 3 2 1

FOR

MARTY, NICHOLAS, AND MICHAEL,

*with all my love*

*The Christmas Boutique*

# *Sylvia*

THIN, PALE SUNBEAMS shone tentatively around the edges of curtains drawn tight against the winter cold in the windows of the master suite of Elm Creek Manor. Although Sylvia Bergstrom Compson was eager to get up and seize the day, she lingered in bed, reluctant to jostle her dear husband, slumbering peacefully by her side.

Throughout the summer and into the autumn, Andrew had risen first. He had often been settled at his favorite fishing spot, a large, round, flat rock beneath a willow tree on the bank of Elm Creek, before Sylvia even opened her eyes. But after winter descended upon central Pennsylvania, more often than not, he pulled the bedcovers up to his chin and slept in long after Sylvia and the manor's other permanent residents had finished breakfast and were going about the business of the day. How amused Sylvia had been to discover her new husband's surprising seasonal preference, and after she thought she knew him so well! She suspected that in the years to come—may they have many together—they would discover more intriguing, unexpected quirks and contradictions within each other.

Perhaps they would discover less endearing traits too, but she and Andrew were both too grateful for their second chance at love to fuss over trivialities.

Sylvia smiled fondly as she watched Andrew doze beneath the

beautiful bridal sampler they had received as a wedding gift only a few months before. The Elm Creek Quilters had surprised her by collecting quilt blocks from her friends, quilting students, colleagues, and admirers from around the world, sewing them together into an exquisite expression of their warm wishes and affection. Sylvia and the other Elm Creek Quilters worked so closely together that it was a marvel how her friends had managed to collaborate on such a complex project without her suspecting a thing. Then again, she and Andrew had surprised them all the previous Christmas Eve when they had come to Elm Creek Manor expecting a festive holiday party, only to discover that they were attending a wedding. Naturally their friends would want to tease Sylvia and Andrew just a little by surprising them in return.

Now, after nearly a year full of surprises, it would soon again be Christmas Eve, Sylvia and Andrew's first anniversary. She had been so preoccupied with other matters—wrapping up another successful season of Elm Creek Quilt Camp; bidding farewell to friends departing for distant locales, from Philadelphia to Maui; putting the last stitches into a new quilt, her contribution to her church's annual fund-raiser for the county food pantry—that she hadn't had a moment to spare for holiday plans. Perhaps her young friend and colleague Sarah McClure had already typed up a spreadsheet or two delineating arrangements for meals, decorations, and entertainment, but Sylvia thought she and Andrew should plan their anniversary celebration themselves.

And Sylvia and Andrew's marriage was such an unexpected blessing that it surely ought to be celebrated in fine style.

Although they had first met as children, their lives had taken them down different paths, winding ways that had led to and from Elm Creek Manor over the course of several decades. Sylvia had first known Andrew as her younger brother's classmate, a shy, scrawny, badly neglected boy whose family had recently moved into a ramshackle house on the outskirts of Waterford.

At school, most children eyed Andrew's tattered clothes, bruised limbs, and haunted expression and kept their distance, but a few older boys bullied him cruelly until Sylvia's younger brother put a stop to it. Richard was clever, athletic, and popular, and after he insisted that Andrew be allowed to join in their games, the other boys grudgingly accepted him.

Andrew and Richard soon became good friends. One afternoon when Sylvia and her elder sister, Claudia, met their brother at the schoolyard gate to walk him home, Sylvia spotted Andrew wearing a jacket Richard had recently outgrown. Later that night, when she told her father what she had seen, he nodded thoughtfully and questioned her about the boy.

"I don't know much," she admitted, embarrassed, but she told him the little she had observed and inferred.

The next morning at breakfast her father told Richard that he looked forward to meeting his new friend. "You may invite Andrew to come home with you after school any time you like," he added.

Richard's face lit up. "Really? Can you drive him home after? He lives out in the country."

"*We* live out in the country," said Claudia loftily, "and we walk to and from school."

Richard frowned. "Andrew lives way out in the other direction, so he'd have to walk to school and then more."

Their father raised a hand to end the argument before it escalated. "Richard, I'm happy to drive your friend home. You may tell him I said so."

After that, Andrew came home with Richard nearly every day. Sometimes Sylvia asked about his family in a casual, conversational way so it would not seem like an inquisition. Andrew said little in reply, but it was enough for Sylvia to conclude that he was miserable at home and that he worried about his little sister, who was often ill.

Sylvia wished her compassionate, generous mother were there to advise her, but she had passed away four years before, leaving the family irreparably bereft. She thought maybe they could invite Andrew and his little sister to live at Elm Creek Manor, but she reluctantly abandoned that scheme as impossible. Andrew's parents probably wouldn't allow it, even though, as Sylvia and Claudia had noted in a rare moment of agreement, they didn't seem particularly interested in being parents and weren't very good at it.

"Maybe they'd be nicer if not for the Depression," Claudia mused aloud.

"You can't blame the Great Depression for everything," said Sylvia. "Father says lots of people in Waterford are out of work, many families are going hungry, but hardly any kids show up at school with bruises and messy clothes all the time."

The Bergstroms were considered one of the wealthiest families in the Elm Creek Valley, but even they had to watch every penny. Their entire savings had vanished overnight in October 1929 when the First Bank of Waterford had gone under after a larger bank in some far-off city called in its debts. The family business, Bergstrom Thoroughbreds, had earned almost nothing for years. Most of their former customers had lost their fortunes in the stock market crash, and those days hardly anyone could afford to squander money on expensive, impractical luxuries like champion horses. Sylvia's father assured her that their family would get by. They owned their own land and had no mortgage, and they grew some of their own food. Their forests would provide wood to burn if they ran out of coal. The manor was full of lovely things acquired in more prosperous times that they could sell to pay bills or barter for whatever they could not make or grow themselves.

As poor as they had become, the Bergstroms were far better off than most of their neighbors. Sylvia knew her mother would have urged them to share what they had with the less fortunate, including Richard's new best friend. Especially him.

When the weather turned colder, Sylvia gave Andrew warm, sturdy clothes Richard had outgrown but not worn out. Every morning she filled her brother's lunch box with enough food for two hungry children, and once she discreetly slipped a toothbrush and a comb into the pocket of Andrew's jacket while the boys were off playing. Gradually Andrew began to fill out, and as the first winter snows began to fall, whenever Sylvia and her sister met the boys at the schoolyard gate, she observed that his face and hands were clean, his smile shy but bright, his hair no more tousled and tangled than any other boy's.

In December, Sylvia's father invited Andrew to spend Christmas at Elm Creek Manor, ignoring Claudia's protests that he would feel out of place among all the aunts and uncles and cousins returning to the ancestral estate for the holidays. Sylvia was annoyed at her sister and fiercely glad her father had included the boy. His eyes shone with joyful delight as he beheld their traditional Christmas feast—tender *Jägerschnitzel*, grilled pork loin with mushroom gravy; sweet potatoes; creamed peas; and for dessert, Great-Aunt Lucinda's *Lebkuchen*, *Anisplätzchen*, and *Zimtsterne* cookies, as well as apple strudel made from the recipe Great-Great-Aunt Gerda Bergstrom had brought over from Germany. Afterward, Andrew gazed, awestruck, upon the glorious Christmas tree in the ballroom, adorned with candles and precious German glass ornaments Sylvia's great-grandparents had received as wedding gifts ages ago. Sylvia knew this would be a Christmas he would never forget.

If Sylvia needed any more proof of the boy's happiness, his reluctance to go home after the celebration convinced her. Her father had to coax him into the car by likening it to Santa's sleigh and reminding him of the wrapped box he had found beneath the Christmas tree bearing his sister's name, a gift Santa surely intended Andrew to deliver.

Later, Sylvia was in the kitchen drying and putting away dishes when she heard her father return. "Do you know what Andrew said to me as I drove him home?" she overheard him tell Great-Aunt Lucinda, who had met him at the back door. "He said that this was the best Christmas he had ever known. We've compared these past few Christmases to those of the twenties and rue how we've come down in the world, and yet this little boy was overwhelmed by our abundance."

"That's a lesson for us all."

"I can't help thinking how much more we could do for Andrew and his sister if—"

"No, Fred. I know your heart's in the right place, but you can't take children from their parents."

"If you saw their home, you'd feel differently."

"There's much more to a home than material comforts."

"That's precisely my point. From what I've seen, the children don't receive many spiritual comforts either."

Worried, Sylvia stole closer to the doorway, but even though she held her breath and strained her ears, her father and great-aunt had walked off down the hall, their conversation fading until she could no longer hear them.

In the months that followed, her father's worries proved prescient. Richard and Andrew were eight years old when Andrew ran away from home. Richard hid his friend in the wooden playhouse their father had built near the stables and exercise rings, setting him up with warm blankets and comic books and smuggling him food at night while the rest of the family slept. Sylvia discovered their secret one autumn night when she woke to the sound of her brother creeping past her bedroom door. She followed him to the kitchen, where he filled a bag with leftovers, crept outside and across the bridge over Elm Creek, and unwittingly led her to the hideout.

The boys begged her not to tell her father, but she thought she had no choice. He contacted the authorities, who conducted a brief investigation and immediately removed Andrew and his sister from their parents' custody. Sylvia's father offered to take the children in, but the law gave preference to relatives, and the children were sent to live with an aunt in Philadelphia.

After Andrew's sudden departure, an angry and bewildered Richard missed his best friend terribly. At first he wrote Andrew numerous letters, but their father did not know where to send them. It was a long time before Richard forgave Sylvia for betraying them.

For years thereafter, Sylvia thought of Andrew and his little sister at Christmastime and hoped they were celebrating somewhere warm and safe, that they were happy, cared for, and loved. Now, at last, she had no doubt Andrew was.

SYLVIA FELT HER breath catch in her throat as she gazed upon her husband while he slept, remembering the small, frightened child he had been. Even now his lined face was almost boyish in repose, his brow furrowed slightly as if in concentration, his breathing steady and even. Sylvia wished with all her heart that she could reach back through time, embrace that little boy, and assure him that one day his unhappiness would be behind him. He would know sorrow but also great joy, and after many years, Sylvia and Andrew would rediscover each other.

But before then, they would have another meeting, and another parting.

From the time he was quite young Richard had longed to explore the world beyond the Elm Creek Valley, and when he turned sixteen, he convinced their father to enroll him in a young men's academy in Philadelphia. A few days into the term, he discovered that one of his new classmates was none other than his long-lost friend Andrew Cooper, a scholarship student, one of the brightest young men in the class. This happy news helped Sylvia bear her brother's absence a little better, but she still missed him terribly and wished he had not been so impatient to leave home. But except for the occasional lament to her closest friends in her quilt guild, she kept her feelings to herself. It was autumn of 1943, the entire world was at war, and with so many families losing brothers and sons every day, she felt ashamed to complain when her brother was merely away at school.

That year she looked forward to the holidays more eagerly than ever because Richard would be coming home for semester break. On the day of his arrival, the manor fairly hummed with anticipation as young cousins darted about laughing and playing, aunts and wives cheerfully worked in the kitchen, sending delicious aromas wafting through the halls—baked apples, cinnamon, vanilla, and nutmeg. Sylvia and Claudia bustled about, getting in each other's way and on each other's nerves as they finished preparing rooms for their overnight guests and putting up the last of the decorations. Sylvia chose tasks that kept her near the front windows, and whenever Claudia was not around to scold her for idleness, she paused to gaze outside through the falling snow, hoping to glimpse a taxicab approaching.

She was in the dining room folding napkins when a cousin raced downstairs from the nursery shouting that a car was coming up the drive. Sylvia hurried to the foyer, steps ahead of a veritable stampede of cousins and aunts and uncles, her heart pounding with anticipation and joy. Her father reached the tall, double front doors first and flung one open. "Welcome home, son," he called out, but then he halted in the doorway, his smile turning to puzzlement.

Sylvia ducked beneath his arm and stepped outside. "Richard," she cried, and then she too abruptly paused at the sight of a small figure lingering cautiously behind her brother. Blue eyes peered up at her from beneath a white fur hood, but the rest of the face was concealed behind a thick woolen scarf.

"Well, sis?" Richard inquired merrily, relishing her astonishment. "Are you going to let us in or keep us standing out here in the snow?"

His words roused their father to smile broadly, step aside, and gesture for them to enter. Dumbfounded, Sylvia backed into the house and out of the way as Richard guided his companion into the warmth of the foyer. He gave Sylvia a grin and a quick peck on the cheek in passing, but he was quickly surrounded by aunts and cousins sending up a chorus of greetings as they helped him and the young woman out of their wraps. Sylvia glimpsed porcelain skin, a flush of roses in the gentle curve of a cheek, luxurious dark hair spilling over the girl's shoulders nearly to her waist.

"Everyone," said Richard, raising his voice to be heard over the cheerful din, "I'd like you to meet my— I'd like to introduce you to Agnes Chevalier."

"Hello," said the girl, looking shyly around the circle of expectant faces, her voice trembling slightly.

"Welcome to Elm Creek Manor, Agnes," said Claudia, stepping forward to take their coats and scarves. She passed them on to a responsible younger cousin with instructions to hang them up to dry, then turned back to Agnes and placed an arm around her shoulders. "Let's get you two in front of a warm fire, shall we?"

As Claudia led Richard and Agnes across the foyer toward the parlor, Sylvia exchanged a quick glance with her father, enough to confirm that he had not expected Richard's traveling companion either.

As they warmed themselves by the hearth with hot tea and cozy quilts, Richard explained that Agnes was a student at his academy's sister school, and that they had met while volunteering for a joint community service day. In his usual offhand way, Richard explained without a hint of boastfulness that her father was a successful attorney, and that her mother descended from a wealthy and prominent political family whose name Sylvia immediately recognized, rendering her momentarily awestruck.

Unfortunately, in the days that followed, aside from Agnes's lineage and her undeniable beauty, little else about their unexpected holiday visitor impressed Sylvia very much. Agnes was exasperatingly naive and she tried too hard to please. She knew next to nothing about farm life or quilting or anything else practical. Worst of all, Richard seemed thoroughly besotted with her.

"I'm beginning to understand why Agnes's family didn't object to her spending the holidays far from home," she murmured to her great-aunt Lucinda as they peeled sweet potatoes for their Christmas Day feast. "They probably find her as tiresome as we do."

"That's unkind, especially at Christmas," her great-aunt chided. "And speak for yourself. The rest of us like Agnes very much."

Sylvia stifled a groan, but she could not deny that her father seemed to find Agnes utterly charming. Claudia was going overboard to make the girl feel welcome, and Claudia's reticent beau, Harold, was surprisingly warm and friendly in Agnes's company. Even James, Sylvia's otherwise wonderful husband of three years, seemed oblivious to the faults and annoying quirks all too evident to Sylvia.

"You might want to try to get to know her better," James cautioned on the day after Christmas. "You should find some common ground, just in case she becomes a permanent member of the family."

"Heaven forefend," Sylvia declared, but she resolved to conceal her disdain for the sake of family harmony. Eventually Richard's infatuation would prove to be nothing more than a passing fancy, and next Christmas, they would again celebrate with only the Bergstrom family, and Harold, since he always joined them. If Richard wanted to bring a friend home from school for the holidays, he should choose Andrew next time.

In early January, Richard and Agnes returned to Philadelphia, and Sylvia began counting the weeks until he would return—alone, she hoped—for summer break. She tried not to make too much of a new tone in his letters, expressing not only his increasing affection for Agnes, but also his outrage and indignation for the rising animosity toward German Americans that was spreading throughout the country. By springtime, he resolved to enlist in the military and prove his patriotism by fighting the Nazis. Andrew, ever his loyal best friend, decided to join up with him.

James and Harold raced to Philadelphia to stop them, fervently hoping that the young men would be sent away from the recruiting office with a handshake and a suggestion to return when they were eighteen. But Richard and Andrew were determined, and when Richard lied about his age and went unchallenged, Andrew did too.

James and Harold arrived in the city too late to intervene—
too late as well to prevent Richard and Agnes from marrying in
haste, like thousands of other young couples faced with separa-
tion and an uncertain future. Agnes's parents must have given
their consent under duress, for they did not attend the courthouse
ceremony and disowned their daughter before the ink dried on
the marriage license.

With two weeks to go before Richard was due to report
for basic training, he escorted his young bride—beautiful but
tremulous with joy and worry—home to Elm Creek Manor.
Andrew and Harold accompanied them, with James as the
group's resigned and watchful leader. When the two young soldiers crossed the threshold, their innocent pride and excitement
brought fresh tears to Sylvia's eyes. "What have you done?" she
cried, flinging her arms around her brother, barely hearing his
spirited reply.

That night as James and Sylvia prepared for bed, exhausted
and drained by the week's tumultuous events, he took her in his
arms. "Sylvia, darling, there's something I need to tell you."

"James, you mustn't blame yourself," she said, unsettled by the
regret and apprehension in his eyes. "You tried. I know you would
have prevented this if you could have. It's in God's hands now."

"Sylvia . . ." He sighed heavily against the skin of her neck, his
embrace tightening. "I'm going too."

For a moment she couldn't breathe. "What do you mean?"

"I enlisted. Harold too. It was the only way we could be sure
we would be placed in the same unit."

"James, no." The room spun. Sylvia pressed a hand to her lips
and sank down upon the edge of the bed. "You couldn't have. You
promised me you'd wait to be drafted."

James sat beside her and took her hand. "I had to do it. I can't
protect Richard from home. Now I'll be able to look after him.

I swear we'll all come back to you safe and sound. You have my word."

She would have protested that it was beyond his power to promise her that, but the words stuck in her throat. What good were her protests now? He had enlisted; he could not undo that decision even if he wanted to.

The next morning, Harold and Claudia announced that he had proposed, and she had accepted. Sylvia assumed that they would marry at the county courthouse before Harold departed, but Claudia said they would wait until he came home. Sylvia nodded, murmuring congratulations and feigning delight, marveling at her sister's certainty that Harold would return from the war. So many other young men they knew never would.

The men's last days at Elm Creek Manor flew by with terrible swiftness. All too soon they reported for duty, and after eight weeks of basic training, they were sent to the Pacific, a cruel irony considering Richard had enlisted to fight the Nazis.

Soon thereafter, Sylvia realized she was pregnant.

Months passed. Letters from the men were infrequent and precious, despite heavy censoring that sometimes rendered them barely comprehensible. Sylvia and Claudia had dedicated themselves to the work of the home front since the war began, but now they redoubled their efforts, organizing scrap metal drives, buying war bonds, enlarging their victory garden, contributing Grandmother's Flower Garden segments to the Waterford Quilting Guild's raffle quilt for the war effort. Their work kept despair at bay and would hasten the end of the war, or so they desperately hoped.

As the lonely, anxious weeks passed, Sylvia began to develop a grudging respect for her new sister-in-law. From time to time, Sylvia surreptitiously read over Agnes's shoulder as she wrote to Richard, and she was surprised to find not one word of complaint in her letters, only loving encouragement and light-hearted descriptions of how she spent her days. Agnes joined Sylvia and Claudia in their volunteer activities, and although she couldn't sew to save her life, she could knit with impressive speed, darning socks and mending sweaters so well that her repairs were nearly invisible. If she found a garment that had shrunk in the wash or could not be mended, she unraveled the stitches, wound the yarn into balls, and knit socks and wash-cloths for the Red Cross to give to soldiers.

Perhaps this was the side of Agnes that had won Richard's heart.

Sylvia prepared for the arrival of her unborn child, praying that the war would end and James would return in time for the birth. But summer passed, and then autumn, and with each pass-ing week it seemed less likely that their loved ones would come home to them soon.

"Don't worry," Claudia told her. "Just this morning I heard on the radio that the Allies have made so many gains in Europe that the war will be over by Christmas."

Sylvia prayed she was right.

December came, but while victory seemed increasingly likely, it remained elusive, impossibly distant. The first snows fell, soft and gentle, and before Sylvia knew it, the holidays were approach-ing. The joyful family celebration she had envisioned the year before was not to be; with the men away and her father recovering from influenza, their aunts and uncles and cousins had decided to stay home to conserve fuel and other scarce rations.

It was a subdued, wistful season, and for a while that suited Sylvia's melancholic mood, but two days before Christmas, her longing for her husband and brother became too much to bear. She sat in the front parlor listening to carols on the radio, strok-ing her rounded abdomen and brooding. Agnes sat in the chair closest to the fireplace, diligently knitting while Claudia cut templates for her bridal quilt and mused aloud about her wedding gown. Agnes nodded along, but for Sylvia, her sister's chatter barely registered as she tried to imagine what James, Richard, Andrew, and Harold were doing at that moment, and then tried very hard not to imagine it.

As the lyrics of "I'll Be Home for Christmas" broke into her reverie, Sylvia suddenly felt tears rising, anger surging. "Turn that off," she ordered shakily. When Claudia and Agnes merely paused in their handwork to stare at her uncertainly, Sylvia hauled herself from her chair, crossed the room, and snapped off the radio. "I can't listen to that anymore. They aren't coming home for Christmas, so what's the use of dreaming about it?"

"Sometimes dreams are all we have," said Agnes.

Sylvia clenched her teeth to hold back a bitter retort. She could not bear platitudes, and she needed more than dreams. She needed James beside her. She needed Richard home and safe.

"What we need is a Christmas miracle," said Claudia. "For the war to end. If ever we ought to pray for peace on earth, this is the time."

"The war will end when we win," said Sylvia sharply, despondent. "However long it takes, however many lives it takes."

Agnes shuddered, her pretty features pinching up as if she might burst into tears. Ashamed of herself, Sylvia looked away and was about to turn the radio back on when Claudia said, "We've done nothing to prepare for Christmas around here."

"We sent the men their packages," said Agnes.

"I know, but we've done nothing for ourselves."

"No one's coming to visit," Sylvia reminded her.

"Yes, but we're still here." Claudia set her paper and scissors aside. "We should bake Great-Aunt Lucinda's cookies and make Gerda's apple strudel."

Sylvia shook her head. "We don't have enough sugar rations."

"We might have enough, and even if we don't, we could still decorate." Claudia rose. "Come on. We need something to remind us of the joy and hope of the season."

Dubious, Sylvia nonetheless felt a faint spark of interest. Their orchard had yielded an abundant harvest that autumn, so she knew they had plenty of apples. When she surveyed the pantry, she found that they had just enough of the other necessary ingredients to make one strudel. She went to tell Claudia and Agnes, only to find them in the foyer unpacking boxes of decorations they had brought down from the attic. Sylvia lent a hand, but first she returned to the parlor to turn on the radio, leaving the door open so they could listen to carols as they worked. A quiet happiness filled her as she unwrapped the familiar accoutrements of the holidays—Richard's soldier nutcracker, the paper angels she and Claudia had made in Sunday school, Great-Aunt Lucinda's Santa Claus cookie jar, and something unexpected: a pillowcase filled with segments of a quilt in rich hues of red, green, gold, and cream sewn by several Bergstrom women through the years but never completed.

As she examined the pieces, marveling at the handiwork of her mother, her great-aunt, and her sister, Claudia and Agnes suggested she work on the quilt. Tempted, Sylvia nonetheless hesitated. "But the decorations, and the baking—"

"We can handle the decorations," Agnes assured her, "and the strudel can wait until tomorrow, can't it?"

"You should be sitting with your feet up anyway," added Claudia.

Sylvia was about to retort that she was pregnant, not ill, but it was the perfect excuse. Although she couldn't possibly complete the quilt by Christmas Day, stitching a few blocks might lift her spirits. Perhaps she could plan to finish in time for next Christmas, when James would be home and they could snuggle their

child in the quilt's soft folds in the warm glow of the lights on
the Christmas tree.

Lost in reminiscences of Christmases past and dreams of the
Christmas future she yearned for, Sylvia spent the hours in sewing and reflection. Later, when hunger beckoned her from the
parlor, she discovered her home transformed by the loving attention of her sister and sister-in-law. All the old, familiar, beloved
decorations adorned the foyer, the ballroom, and other nooks and
corners where so many fond memories lingered. Candles glowed
softly in the windows, and wreaths of holly and ivy graced the
doors and banisters.

Early the next day, Christmas Eve, Sylvia and Claudia taught
Agnes how to make the traditional Bergstrom apple strudel from
Great-Great-Aunt Gerda's recipe. Perhaps enticed by the familiar,
delectable aroma, Sylvia's father insisted he felt strong enough
to leave his sickbed and join them for lunch. "How wonderfully
festive," he declared as he descended the grand oak staircase, admiring their decorations from above. "I believe we'll have a merry
Christmas after all."

The following morning, he felt well enough to accompany Sylvia, Claudia, and Agnes to church. The mood of the congregation
was more subdued than celebratory, more longing than joyful.
Sylvia knew that nearly every person gathered there yearned for
a brother, father, husband, or son overseas, or was grieving for
someone lost to the war. Even the pastor had a brother serving in
France, and before long his sermon turned to their absent loved
ones and their longing for peace.

"We must not give in to despair," the pastor said, his gaze earnest and imploring as he looked out upon the worshippers. "We
must have faith that the Lord who loves us will not abandon us.
Though far too many of us have sewn gold stars on the service
banners displayed in our front windows, though so many of us

mourn, we must not believe that God has ceased loving us. He has not forgotten us. In our moments of weakness, we may fear that we walk alone, but we must never forget that God has sent us the light of his love and mercy. The light shines in the darkness, and the darkness shall not overcome it."

Sylvia fought back tears, longing for her husband and brother so desperately that she almost could not draw breath for the pain in her heart. If James and Richard did not return to her, she did not know how she could endure it. She knew that she could not.

"Today, my dear brothers and sisters," the pastor continued, "we are confronted by darkness—the darkness of war, of tyranny, of oppression, of loneliness, of evil manifest in the world. Today, with the entire world at war, this darkness seems very deep indeed, but we must not forget that Jesus Christ brought the light of peace, and hope, and reconciliation into the world, and no darkness shall ever quench it. Each of us must bring light into the world, so that the darkness will not prevail."

Head bowed, Sylvia pressed her lips together to hold back a sob. She wanted the light the pastor described to shine through the darkness of her life, but she was afraid, and she had never felt more alone. The darkness surrounding her was so opaque she feared no illumination could penetrate it.

Suddenly a hand clasped hers—Claudia's. After a moment Sylvia reached out her other hand to Agnes, and only then did understanding dawn. Claudia and Agnes were lonely and afraid too. They had to be light for one another.

The three women held hands for the rest of the sermon. They held hands still as they rose to sing the final hymn. As the last notes of the song faded away, Sylvia felt peace settling into her heart, and she whispered a prayer of thanks for her sister and her sister-in-law, whom she too often took for granted. They must sustain one another, whatever came, whatever darkness threatened them.

Later, at Elm Creek Manor, Sylvia, Claudia, their father, and Agnes gathered in the parlor to exchange gifts, most of them homemade garments or heirlooms now passed down to one who had long admired them. Afterward, in keeping with Bergstrom family tradition, they read aloud letters from absent loved ones, none dearer than those from their brave soldiers, saved for this occasion so they would feel as if the family had reunited on Christmas Day. Sylvia had drawn upon her every ounce of willpower not to open James's letter as soon as it had arrived a week before, but now she was grateful she had waited.

The men had been promised a hot Christmas dinner instead of the usual rations, James had written, turkey with dressing, cranberry sauce, mashed potatoes, green beans, and apple pie for dessert. "I'd give my last dollar for us all to be gathered around the table at Elm Creek Manor instead, enjoying our traditional Bergstrom Christmas feast," he admitted, "but our little celebration will make us feel closer to home, and no king in his castle will savor his Christmas dinner more."

Other letters shared more news. Harold complained of a mild stomach ailment but assured Claudia that otherwise all was well. Richard sent his love and proudly announced that he was learning how to drive a tank. Andrew had written one letter for the whole family, thanking them for the pictures Sylvia's father had taken of Claudia, Sylvia, and Agnes standing on the back steps of the manor. "I don't have a sweetheart to write home to," he confessed, "so I especially welcome your letters." He promised to look after Richard and thanked Sylvia's father for the memories of the best Christmas he had ever known. "Those memories are a comfort to me this year as I spend the holidays in the heat of the South Pacific, far from the snowy forests and fields of home."

"Next year we will all be together again," said Claudia, with such resolve that for a moment they all shared her certainty. "Next Christmas, the war will be over and the boys will be home."

Sylvia prayed it would be so—but only part of her heartfelt prayer was answered.

The war did end before Christmas came again, but only Andrew and Harold lived to see it.

When the telegram arrived to inform Sylvia that her worst fears had come true, she was so staggered by shock and grief that she miscarried. Soon thereafter, her father succumbed to a stroke. So it was that one terrible incident on a remote Pacific island claimed the lives of four members of her family, several days and thousands of miles apart.

Later, months after Imperial Japan surrendered, Andrew paid an unexpected visit on his way from Philadelphia to a new job in Detroit. Anguished, he confessed to Sylvia how her future brother-in-law had been complicit in James's and Richard's deaths. Haltingly, every word paining him, he described the terrible scene he had witnessed from a bluff overlooking the beach, how Richard had come under friendly fire, how James had raced to his rescue, how he could have saved his brother-in-law with the help of one more man. Andrew had run down the bluff to the beach where his friends lay wounded, knowing that he would never reach them in time, while only a few yards away, Harold had cowered in the underbrush rather than risk his own life.

Andrew had left early the next morning without telling anyone else what he had confessed to her. When Sylvia confronted Claudia with the terrible truth and Claudia rejected it as a cruel lie, a chasm split open the fragile ground between the two sisters, compelling Sylvia to flee her beloved home, never to return.

Or so she had thought, all those years ago.

*     *     *

SYLVIA REACHED OUT a wrinkled hand and gently stroked Andrew's cheek, lightly stubbled before his morning shave, the face dearer to her than she could have imagined when she had fled Elm Creek Manor in anguish, when he and her brother had gone off to war so full of pride and anticipation, when he had been a small, hungry boy longing for the sanctuary of a loving home. They had both found their happy ending, but she would have done so many things differently if only—

Andrew's eyes opened, and a slow smile spread across his face. "Good morning, sweetheart," he said, clasping his hand over hers. "That's a very serious frown for so early in the day."

"It's not as early as you think, sleepyhead," she said lightly.

He was not fooled. "What's troubling you?"

"Oh, it's nothing. Just the Ghost of Christmas Past nagging me again."

"Sylvia, honey." He moved her hand to his lips and kissed it. "If you brood over the past—"

"Yes, yes, I know. If you brood over the past, you can't enjoy the present or dream about the future." She bent closer and kissed his cheek. "Your sister's old saying rings true, at the holidays perhaps more than any other time of the year. Don't worry about me. A good breakfast is all I need to put things right."

He smiled, a bit uncertainly, but as they rose and made ready for the day, he let the matter rest.

Perhaps to convince Andrew that she was taking his sister's advice to heart, when she dressed, Sylvia paired a cheerful red cardigan with her ivory blouse and comfortable black slacks. "My, don't you look dapper," she said, admiring the figure he cut in his freshly ironed charcoal slacks and red-black-and-white-plaid flannel shirt, neatly tucked in. His steel-gray hair was parted on the side, his eyes such a rich, clear blue that they seemed to shine for her even when he wore his glasses, which at the moment were tucked into his shirt pocket. Despite his limp, a remnant of his wartime service, he carried himself with almost military precision, but though his bearing gave him a stern and measured air, he was the kindest and gentlest of men.

He smiled, pleased by the compliment, and reached for her hand. Together they left their suite and walked down the hall to the grand oak staircase that descended to the foyer. At the second-floor landing, Sylvia paused for a moment to savor the brief, reverential hush that enveloped Elm Creek Manor on particular mornings when the guest rooms were vacant. It was peaceful, and yet Sylvia always sensed an undercurrent of expectation and delight, as if something wonderful might happen at any moment. In a few months, the gray stone manor would bustle and hum with the sounds of dozens of lively quilters enjoying a week of quilting, friendship, and fun. Even sooner than that, the couple would host Christmas for nearly two dozen family and friends.

"We need to begin decorating for the holidays," Sylvia remarked, taking in the scene from above. "Some garland and lights and ribbon-tied evergreen boughs will give our guests a warm, festive welcome."

"They'll be expecting something amazing, you know," Andrew teased, squeezing her hand. "We set the bar pretty high last year with our surprise wedding."

"I don't see how we could top that. Our friends and family will just have to settle for merry and bright."

"At least we have plenty of snow on the ground. Even if some of it melts, we're sure to have a white Christmas. Kayla and Angela will be thrilled."

Andrew's granddaughters lived in Southern California, so they never had the chance to play in the snow during the winter holidays unless Andrew's son and his wife drove them up into the mountains, or flew them across the country to visit Andrew's daughter, Amy, and her family in Connecticut. But this year, at Amy's suggestion, Andrew's children and their families were coming to Elm Creek Manor so they could spend Christmas together as a proper family. Sylvia and Andrew had plenty of room for all, and it made sense for the West Coast and East Coast families to meet somewhere in between.

Andrew's family, as numerous as they were, made up only half of the guest list. Sarah McClure's mother was coming in from Erie, her father-in-law from Uniontown in southwestern Pennsylvania. Most of the Elm Creek Quilters had promised to drop by either on Christmas Eve or Christmas Day, whenever they could break away from their own family celebrations. Rounding out the party, of course, were Sylvia, Andrew, and the manor's four other permanent residents.

Perhaps eventually they would number five, Sylvia mused, thinking of Anna Del Maso, the wonderfully gifted chef who had joined the staff a few months before. Sylvia inhaled deeply, certain she detected the tantalizing fragrances of ginger, molasses, and nutmeg wafting on the air from the kitchen. Although Anna was a frequent overnight guest, she had kept her apartment in downtown Waterford even after accepting the position on the staff of Elm Creek Quilts. She was not obliged to cook for the household in the off-season, but she often did, waving off their rather feeble protests with assurances that she needed to test a new recipe and they were actually doing her a favor.

When Andrew sniffed the air, sighed with contentment, and threw her a grin, Sylvia knew he smelled breakfast cooking too. Suddenly ravenous, they descended the staircase, Sylvia grasping a banister worn smooth by the hands of generations of Bergstroms who had inhabited the manor before her and the many friends and guests who had resided within its gray stone walls in the decades since.

Side by side Sylvia and Andrew crossed the black marble floor and turned down the older, west wing of the manor, built by her great-grandfather in 1858. The new, grander wing, including the three-story foyer, banquet hall, and ballroom on the first floor, the vast library on the second, and the nursery on the third, had been added by her grandfather decades later after Bergstrom Thoroughbreds had become more successful than its immigrant founders could have imagined. As Sylvia and Andrew made their way to the kitchen, she wondered what her great-grandparents would have thought of the changes their descendants had brought to the farm they had founded in the fertile Elm Creek Valley in central Pennsylvania so many decades before.

And to think Sylvia had once abandoned her beloved home, determined never to return.

More than fifty years before, after Andrew's stunning revelations, she had fled Elm Creek Manor without explanation, without bidding anyone farewell, although as she strode away clutching a suitcase in each hand, she thought she glimpsed Claudia and Agnes watching her from an upstairs window. She was halfway to Harrisburg before she realized she had made no plans beyond boarding that bus.

She sought refuge with James's parents on their six-hundred-acre horse farm on the Chesapeake Bay about twenty-five miles southeast of Baltimore. The Compsons had aged years since Sylvia had seen them at James's funeral, but they welcomed her with open arms and open hearts, understanding her devastation and never troubling her with the obvious questions of why she had come so unexpectedly and how long she intended to stay.

As the months passed, Sylvia found solace in the familiar rhythm of life on a farm, in the Compsons' benevolent company, in the routine of the days and the satisfaction of the harvest, for they raised crops for the family's use as well as horses. Summer blazed and ripened, the rich colors of autumn faded, and soft snowfalls dusted the fields and riding trails that had become almost as familiar to her as those of home. Almost imperceptibly, the rawness of her grief dulled, but sometimes she would find herself swept up in a wave of sorrow so sudden and powerful that it took her breath away.

On Christmas morning, Sylvia woke wondering how she would endure the day. Memories of Christmas Eve gatherings around the luminous, fragrant evergreen in the ballroom of Elm Creek Manor, of the happy clamor of a houseful of friends and relatives, and of the Bergstroms' famously delicious Christmas Day feasts haunted her as she helped her mother-in-law prepare for the Compson family celebration. And yet, to her grateful surprise, the warm embraces of James's loved ones, the children's laughter, the melodies of cherished carols, and the other sights and sounds and fragrances of the holiday gently bound together her shattered heart. The Compsons had not forgotten their sorrow, but on that holy day they found happiness in one another and in hope for the future. Sylvia sensed James's presence in the midst of his family, and for the first time since his passing, she understood that although he was gone, their love endured.

The warm glow of hope and love lingered until three days after Christmas, when Mrs. Compson told Sylvia that she and her husband had received a letter from Claudia. She had asked if Sylvia was with them, and if not, if they knew how to reach her. "Sylvia, dear," she added kindly, "Charles and I are very happy to have you here with us, but eventually you're going to have to move on with your life."

Taken aback, Sylvia merely looked at her. What was she doing if not living? Her aching heart told her all too clearly that she was alive.

"I believe your place is at Elm Creek Manor, but if you don't feel you can go home . . ." Mrs. Compson sighed. "Well, if not that, you must choose something. You can't continue to go through the motions of living. You have to truly live. James loved you. Don't choose a life of perpetual grieving for his sake. That's no way to honor his memory."

As the winter passed, Sylvia mulled over her mother-in-law's words until she could no longer deny their truth. James would have wanted her to live a full, rich life. Richard would have been thoroughly disappointed with her if she forgot how to laugh, to enjoy life, and to embrace adventure.

The last snowfall had not yet melted when she decided that as her first bold step into the future, she would earn her college degree. Over the past few months she had taught several of Mrs. Compson's friends to quilt, and she had discovered she had a knack for teaching. By midsummer she decided to attend Margaret Morrison Carnegie College and study to become an art teacher.

The years passed. Sylvia graduated summa cum laude and began teaching in the Allegheny Valley School District. She shared her knowledge of quilting and her passion for the traditional art form with anyone who wanted to learn. As she accumulated numerous awards at national juried quilt shows and her renown as a master quilter grew, she was invited to lecture and teach at quilt guilds, folk art museums, and university domestic-arts programs across the country, including her alma mater. She visited James's parents whenever she could, although that became more difficult as the responsibilities of her work steadily increased. Mrs. Compson honored her promise not to disclose her whereabouts to Claudia, but from time to time her sister still wrote to them, as did Agnes, and Andrew too. The Compsons would share news from Elm Creek Manor with Sylvia, perhaps hoping to pique her curiosity so much that she would finally return home.

Sylvia never succumbed to temptation. Over time, the flow of details about Elm Creek Manor slowed to a trickle, and with Mr. and Mrs. Compson's passing, it stopped altogether.

In the autumn of 1995, fifty years after Sylvia fled Elm Creek Manor in anger and despair, a lawyer from Waterford rang her at her home in Sewickley. His careful, apologetic announcement that Claudia had died staggered her. To Sylvia, her sister remained a young woman, trapped in memory's amber exactly as she had been in 1945. Sylvia could not imagine Claudia with wrinkles and silver hair like her own, or the intermittent aches and stiff joints that had crept up on her over the decades. It was even more impossible to believe that her estranged sister was gone.

Harold had preceded Claudia in death and they had no children, so the manor, the grounds, and all the old family heirlooms were Sylvia's alone. She was not sure she wanted them. She had made a life for herself in Sewickley, and she could not bear the thought of rattling around the manor alone, not at her age, not when none of her friends remained nearby.

Regardless, it was her duty to dispose of the estate properly. She hired a private detective to find a more suitable heir, for surely one of her many cousins yet lived. When the detective failed to locate a single distant relation, Sylvia wondered if he had searched as thoroughly as his fees merited—a suspicion that years later would prove to be well founded. But at the time Sylvia believed herself to be the last Bergstrom, and she returned to Elm Creek Manor as the sole heir of her ancestral home.

The lawyer had warned her that Claudia had not maintained the estate well even before her decline, but in late September when Sylvia finally made the trip through the rolling hills of central Pennsylvania to the Elm Creek Valley, she was unprepared for what she found. She could scarcely breathe as her taxicab turned off the main highway onto the narrow, gravel road to the residence, through dense forest and over the old stone bridge across Elm Creek. When the taxi emerged from the woods, Sylvia discovered that the sweeping front lawn had become patchy in some places and overgrown in others. Beyond it, however, the gray stone walls of the manor stood tall and whole at the top of the rise—but Sylvia's momentary relief faded when the cab pulled to a stop in the circular driveway and she beheld peeling paint, broken windowpanes, and crumbling mortar.

The worn exterior, disheartening though it was, could not fully prepare her for the disaster awaiting her inside. Claudia had sold off many family heirlooms to make ends meet after she and Harold had driven Bergstrom Thoroughbreds into bankruptcy, but as Sylvia made her first tentative survey of her inheritance, the empty spaces where valuable antique furniture and fine art had once enjoyed pride of place dismayed her at every turn. As if to make up for ridding the manor of its treasures, Claudia had stuffed rooms full of worthless clutter—junk mail, yellowing newspapers, tattered mesh vegetable sacks from the supermarket, mason jars full of rusty nails and stripped screws. Sylvia could not fathom why her sister had hoarded so much useless rubbish. Perhaps this was one last spiteful jab at her estranged sister, whom Claudia must have known would be responsible for cleaning up the mess she left behind.

Resigned, Sylvia got started.

She began with the kitchen, but after several backbreaking hours of hauling and scrubbing, the once cozy, efficient room seemed no cleaner than before. When twilight descended, she spread quilts on the sofa in the west sitting room and sank into sleep, exhausted and ineffably sad. In the morning she woke, stiff and disoriented, and when she remembered where she was and why, she felt immobilized by the sheer weight of the enormous task awaiting her. But she could not lie there stewing in resentment. The manor was hers now, as well as the remaining acreage that Claudia had not sold off. She had to meet with the lawyer and pay her sister's debts. Every room of the manor had to be cleared, the rubbish sorted from items worth keeping. There were details and entanglements to sort out, papers to sign, accounts to reconcile.

For weeks Sylvia toiled alone, but for all her effort she made little headway. Frustrated and weary, she closed up the manor and returned to Sewickley to spend the holidays in the company of friends, gratified by how overjoyed they were to see her. Everyone offered condolences for her loss, and some volunteered to help her tie up the loose ends of Claudia's estate, but Sylvia demurred, reluctant to reveal just how much work was involved. Although she wanted to blame her sister for the manor's disrepair, she had come to realize that she too was at fault. She had abandoned home, family, and business, knowing that Claudia and Harold were not fit stewards of the Bergstrom legacy. She was as much to blame for what had befallen Elm Creek Manor as her sister was, perhaps more.

Two days after Christmas, Sylvia returned to Elm Creek Manor with a renewed sense of purpose. The legal matters of Claudia's estate were nearly resolved, and after months of deliberating the fate of Elm Creek Manor, she had at last decided what to do.

After reserving a few precious family heirlooms for herself to cherish always, she would finish clearing the manor of Claudia's detritus, bringing in a forklift if necessary. She would hire a contractor to make repairs and get the grounds in decent shape. Then, when the manor was no longer an embarrassment to the Bergstrom name, she would sell it and return to her home and friends in Sewickley.

She had expected to feel relieved once she made up her mind, but if anything, she felt worse than before. She knew she had chosen the most sensible path forward, and yet it pained her to think of selling the estate to a stranger when it had belonged to the Bergstrom family since the day Hans, Anneke, and Gerda Bergstrom had set the cornerstone in place.

Chin up, she ordered herself. She had done without Elm Creek Manor for decades. She could do without it again. But she would not entrust the Bergstrom legacy to just anyone. It was her duty to wait until she found the ideal steward, someone who would restore the manor to its former glory, filling the halls with love and laughter once more. She could afford to be patient. She had been absent from Elm Creek Manor so long that she didn't care to hasten her final parting.

Yet a great deal of work remained to be done before she could hope to get a fair price for the estate, and she could not do it all herself.

In June 1996, Sylvia hired a young woman named Sarah Mc-Clure to help her clean out the manor and prepare it for sale. One prospective buyer had spoken of turning the manor into an apartment complex for students of Waterford College, and Sylvia had been tempted to accept his offer. In all the months the estate had been on the market, no one else had suggested a more appealing plan, and as a retired teacher, it pleased Sylvia to imagine students enjoying such a beautiful, comfortable home.

To Sylvia's everlasting gratitude, Sarah became suspicious of the developer's plans and secretly investigated his company. When Sarah learned that the developer intended to raze Elm Creek Manor and build condos on the property, Sylvia immediately broke off negotiations. At a loss for what to do next, she asked Sarah to help her find a way to bring the manor back to life. Sarah's ingenious and unlikely suggestion was to turn Elm Creek Manor into a retreat for quilters, a place for them to stay, to learn, to find inspiration, and to enjoy the companionship of other quilters.

How fortunate it was that Sylvia had accepted Sarah's proposal, or her beloved home would now be rubble in a demolition landfill, and the local quilters she and Sarah had invited to become founding members of the faculty would not have become her dearest friends. What a blessing it was that Elm Creek Quilts had prospered, or Sylvia might have been forced to sell the manor anyway, and she would have been a hundred miles distant when Andrew pulled up in his motor home for the surprise visit of a lifetime. She had been astonished to discover that he had not forgotten her, and they had quickly resumed their old friendship. Soon their feelings grew deeper, and before long, they fell in love and married.

A warm, calloused hand closed around hers. "Sylvia?"

She gave a start. "Andrew?" Her reverie faded, and she realized she had come to a halt in the middle of the hallway. "Yes, dear?"

He studied her, brow furrowing in concern. "Are you all right? You seemed worlds away."

"Nonsense. I'm right here." She squeezed his hand and smiled up at him. "Precisely where I ought to be."

AS SYLVIA AND Andrew continued on to the kitchen, the sounds of conversation grew louder, the tantalizing aromas of molasses and spice more irresistible.

Sylvia entered the kitchen just ahead of Andrew and paused to admire the cheerful scene. It was fair to say that no other place in the manor had undergone a greater transformation since Sylvia's return than the kitchen. In addition to the rubbish Claudia had left behind, she had found dated appliances, not a single one of which had come off the assembly line post-1945 except for a tiny microwave on the counter, possibly the first ever invented, by the look of it. Poor lighting, clogged pipes, broken stovetop burners—the list of essential repairs and recommended upgrades had gone on for pages, but after the launch of Elm Creek Quilt Camp, Sylvia had settled for making the place clean and functional. For several years, the Elm Creek Quilters had managed to feed dozens of quilt campers three meals a day by adapting to what Sylvia euphemistically called the kitchen's charming quirks, but conditions were far below professional standards. When the time came to add a chef to the staff, Sylvia was not surprised when Anna made the promise of a total remodel a condition for accepting the job.

Sylvia knew that drastic improvements were long overdue, so in early September after the camp season ended, she had arranged to fulfill Anna's wish list. Contractors transformed the kitchen by gutting the space, knocking out a wall and expanding into the adjacent sitting room. They installed state-of-the-art appliances, marble counters, efficient workstations, a central island, spacious cabinets, a walk-in pantry, and eight cozy booths perfect for faculty and campers alike to catch up with friends over a cup of tea and a decadent dessert.

The blank wall above the nearest booth awaited the quilt Sylvia and Anna were making together from scraps of fabric from Great-Aunt Lydia's collection of feed-sack aprons. They had set the quilt aside recently to work on holiday projects—Sylvia, her promised contribution to the Christmas Boutique; Anna, a Hanukkah gift for her friend Jeremy. They planned to resume their collaboration after the holidays, and when their quilt was finished, it would boast an appliqué still life of fruits and vegetables framed by blocks that reminded them of the kitchen: Broken Dishes, Cut Glass Dish, Honeybee, Corn and Beans, and several yet to be decided.

Now, Sarah sat at another booth, her back to the doorway, an empty plate at her right hand, a file of what appeared to be camp documents lying open on the table before her. Sylvia muffled a sigh. Sarah ought not to be sitting alone. One of the manor's other permanent residents should be seated across from her—her husband, Matthew. But on the day after Thanksgiving, he had told Sarah that his father, Hank, needed him to take over the family construction company while Hank recovered from a flare-up of an old back injury. He could not afford to turn down jobs during such poor economic times, nor could he manage without someone he trusted on site to supervise the work. Sarah had been surprised and hurt to discover that Matt had already agreed to go.

"Without discussing it with you first?" Sylvia had exclaimed when Sarah had confided in her afterward. He should have consulted Sylvia too, as his employer, but it seemed unkind to mention it.

Sarah had nodded, disconsolate. "That's what hurts the most."

"But Uniontown is a three-hour drive away—and you're thirty weeks pregnant!"

"Thirty-one on Monday."

"But what about your childbirth classes, and your preparations for the nursery?" Sylvia had forced herself to pause and take a breath. This was no time to compound her young friend's distress. "We can figure that out together, I'm sure."

"Gretchen offered to step in as my labor coach."

"Gretchen?" What she wanted to ask was why she would choose a relatively recent friend, the newest member of the Elm Creek Quilts faculty, instead of her own mother? Carol lived some distance away, but she was a nurse.

"She has more experience with this than you'd expect. She nominated Joe to take care of babyproofing the manor."

"Andrew would be happy to assist, I'm sure."

"As for the rest of it, I'll manage somehow." Sarah had shrugged, but her eyes brimmed with tears. "What else was I supposed to do? If I asked him not to go, he'd probably stay, but he'd blame me if his father's business failed. I just—I don't want that on my conscience."

Sylvia had squeezed her hand and murmured encouragement, but Matthew's choice mystified her. And what was Hank thinking, putting his son in such an impossible position? Privately Andrew agreed with her. Though he usually kept his opinions to himself unless he was asked to offer them, he could not conceal his disapproval of Matt's decision. He appreciated filial loyalty as much as the next man, but he thought it irresponsible of Matt to leave Sarah during her pregnancy, since it wasn't absolutely necessary. "It's not like he's in the service or something," he had said to Sylvia, incredulous and disappointed, after Matthew had loaded his pickup truck and departed for Uniontown on the Monday after Thanksgiving.

Matthew had returned as promised for the weekend, but the tension between the two expectant parents was evident in their strained smiles, in the new, stilted politeness in their conversation. Now another Monday morning had come. He must have left for Uniontown already or Sarah would not be seated alone, engrossed in camp work. Sylvia decided to sit with Sarah while she ate her breakfast and try to cheer her up. Andrew would understand, and he had other friends there to keep him company.

One relic of the olden days remained in the newly modernized kitchen—a long wooden table and benches placed squarely in the center of the dining area. The Bergstroms had considered it an antique even when Sylvia was a child, and it was too full of sentimental value and family history to discard.

Two more of the manor's permanent residents sat across from each other at the far end of the table. Gretchen Hartley, the newest member of the faculty, had taken her first quilting lessons from none other than Sylvia herself, as a high school student in

Ambridge, Pennsylvania. Gretchen wore a thick navy cardigan buttoned over an ivory blouse, but the formality of her tan corduroy skirt was offset by her comfortable fleece slippers, their size exaggerated by her thin ankles. She was in her sixties, with steel-gray hair cut in a pageboy and a frame that seemed chiseled thin by hard times, but Sylvia was pleased to see that her careworn look lessened with each week she spent at Elm Creek Manor.

Across from Gretchen sat her husband, Joe, a former steelworker who had lost his job years before after an accident at the mill left him with a broken back. His inherent determination and Gretchen's unwavering support had compelled him to work tirelessly to regain his mobility, and in the years since, he had built a second career as a skilled carpenter and expert restorer of antique furniture. He and Andrew had become good friends, and when he and Sylvia entered, Joe looked up from the newspaper spread on the table and grinned in welcome, his weathered, calloused hands cupped around a steaming mug.

"Good morning," Sylvia sang out, returning Joe's smile. "What is that marvelous smell?"

"Gingerbread waffles with apple-raisin compote," said Anna, smiling too as she deftly turned two golden-crisp waffles from the iron onto a platter. Tall and robust with dark, sparkling eyes, she wore her long, dark hair in a French braid beneath her white chef's toque. Her white apron was smeared with whole-wheat flour and molasses, but her sleeves were immaculately clean. "Are you hungry?"

"You bet," said Andrew, making his way to the coffeepot on the nearby counter. "Coffee would hit the spot too."

"Then you're in luck, because I just brewed a fresh pot," said Gretchen.

"Sylvia, the kettle's on for your tea," said Anna, inclining her head toward the gleaming eight-burner gas stove on the far wall.

Sylvia thanked her, helped herself to a waffle and a hot cup of Earl Grey, and made her way around the long wooden table to Sarah's booth, while Andrew joined the Hartleys. "Good morning, dear," Sylvia said, setting down her breakfast and easing herself into the seat across from her young friend. "Did you sleep well?"

Sarah smiled wanly and rested a hand on her abdomen. "More or less. Barnum and Bailey woke me a few times with their gymnastics."

Sylvia laughed lightly, amused by the image and the whimsical names. Sarah and Matthew did not know whether their twins were boys or girls or one of each, and they didn't want to know until the babies were born. Most of their friends understood and respected their decision, but some of the Elm Creek Quilters hoped they would change their minds because, they said, it would be easier to make quilts and other gifts if they knew whether the babies were girls or boys. Diane Sonnenberg was the most persistent in her complaints, as she was about most things. Convinced that Sarah and Matt had glimpsed the truth during one of Sarah's ultrasounds, she scrutinized the couple's words and actions for clues. To tease her, Matt began calling the babies various paired names, usually silly phrases that drove Diane crazy and amused everyone else. Sylvia's favorites included Sugar and Spice, Zig and Zag, and Needle and Thread.

"Did Matthew set out early?" Sylvia inquired casually, cutting a small bite of waffle.

"He heard that snow is on the way and he wanted to beat the storm." Sarah pushed her folder aside and rested her arms on the table. "That's what he said, but I think he wanted to get away before we had another argument."

"Oh, Sarah, surely not."

"I'm annoyed with him for being away and I took it out on

him when he came home." She glanced away, blinking as if warding off tears. "If he's trying to avoid me, it's my fault."

"What? Why would you think such a thing?"

"I made him promise that regardless of any other consideration, he won't miss the birth of our children."

"A perfectly reasonable request."

"I also warned him that if his father insists he can't manage without him after the twins are born, and if Matt agrees to stay on, I'm not leaving Elm Creek Manor to go with him."

For a moment Sylvia was speechless. "How did he take it?"

Sarah gestured to the window between them, where a few flakes of snow drifted lazily down upon the rear parking lot. "He left early."

"I see." Sylvia took a careful sip of tea, thinking. "Try not to make too much of that. He probably wanted to beat the storm, just as he said."

Frowning skeptically, Sarah titled her head toward the window. "What storm? All I see are a few flurries."

Before Sylvia could reply, Joe spoke up. "Are you two talking about the nor'easter?"

"What nor'easter?" Sarah repeated, with a pointed look for Sylvia.

"I know it doesn't look like much now, but I heard on the radio that we're supposed to get up to fourteen inches of snow."

"Again?" Anna lamented. "Didn't we get our share over Thanksgiving weekend?"

One could not blame her for thinking so. The Elm Creek Quilters had come to the manor the Friday after Thanksgiving to enjoy their own special holiday, a marathon day of quilting to work on holiday projects, with a potluck lunch made from Thanksgiving leftovers. Sylvia had made excellent progress on her quilt for the Christmas Boutique, a striking combination of

Star of the Magi, and Chimneys and Cornerstones blocks in rich shades of green, red, gold, and ivory. The party had unexpectedly turned into a sleepover when the storm worsened and the roads became impassable.

"Fourteen inches of snow," marveled Gretchen, shaking her head.

"After the storm passes, temperatures are expected to plunge," said Joe, remarkably cheerful given his dire report. "Three days of subzero temps with wind chills near forty below."

"Goodness," said Sylvia, shivering at the very thought of it. "And when is this storm expected to arrive?"

"By late morning."

Sarah inhaled shakily. "Maybe Matt was right to leave early," she said, for Sylvia's ears alone. "Maybe I'm overthinking this."

Sylvia reached across the table for her hand and smiled encouragingly. "I'm sure that's so."

"I hope no one was planning to go out today," said Andrew. "Sounds like we should all just hunker down and wait out the storm."

"The pantry's well stocked," Anna remarked. "We'll be fine even if the roads are closed for days. Sarah, could I borrow some pajamas again?"

"Of course, and you can take your pick of the guest rooms."

"But I do have plans to go out," said Sylvia. "I need to drop off my quilt for the Christmas Boutique at Good Shepherd Church."

"Must you do that today?" asked Gretchen. "I thought the sale began next week."

"It does, but they need our donations ahead of time so they can take inventory and arrange the displays." Sylvia sighed, considering. "I suppose it can wait. Likely the volunteers who would be collecting the donations have heard the same forecast and will be staying home too."

Sylvia turned her gaze toward the window. Perhaps it was her imagination, but already the flurries seemed to be thickening.

She decided to heed Andrew's sound advice and deliver the quilt when the weather improved. In the meantime, she would enjoy the comfort of her beloved ancestral estate, the company of good friends, and the picturesque view of the snowfall through the window. She knew how extraordinarily fortunate she was to have them.

# 2

# Mary Beth

GLANCING UNEASILY AT the low, mottled gray sky, Mary Beth Callahan dug her keys from her coat pocket and hurried across the parking lot to her car, a Fabric Warehouse shopping bag dangling from her arm. She had run out of delft-blue thread the previous evening, and she could not finish her last quilt for the Christmas Boutique without it. If the approaching storm turned out as bad as expected—and in Mary Beth's experience, grim forecasts tended to be the most accurate—she was not about to be stuck at home without the supplies she needed. Her holiday prep schedule was so packed that even an emergency as ostensibly minor as running out of thread could utterly ruin all her carefully crafted plans.

The oncoming blizzard had already wreaked enough havoc on her day, obliging her to squeeze in errands she had meant to complete later in the week into these fraught few hours before the storm forced her to take shelter at home, waiting anxiously for her husband to make his precarious way back from work, hoping that her son and only child was safe in his dorm at Penn State. She understood why Melanie Tibbs had moved the Good Shepherd Church facilities committee meeting from tomorrow evening to that afternoon, for they had many time-sensitive matters to discuss, but the change raised the stakes on an already challenging day. Still, serving the church and the community allowed her to atone for past mistakes, and she was determined to follow through, even if it left her feeling perpetually distracted and pulled in twenty different directions at once.

Fabric Warehouse took up an entire wing of a strip mall on the northwest fringes of Waterford, where nearly every tenant was a big-box store and all the restaurants chains. The vast acreage of parking was ominously full, more likely due to anxious citizens preparing for a wintry siege than holiday shoppers unwilling to let a little blizzard come between them and a bargain. A dark tan minivan stalked Mary Beth all the way back to her car, but she ignored the driver as she stowed her purchases in the trunk, climbed in, adjusted her rearview mirror, and checked her seatbelt twice before pulling out of her parking spot and heading toward the exit.

A light dusting of snow on the highway whirled in icy cyclones in the wake of passing traffic, both of which grew heavier as Mary Beth approached the downtown. The fastest route to Good Shepherd Church would take her along Main Street between the college campus and the town, but she hesitated before taking the proper off-ramp. In recent months she had deliberately avoided those particular blocks—not because the area was often congested when classes were in session or because distracted student pedestrians with no instinct for self-preservation were annoying, although both offered reason enough, but because the sight of a certain empty storefront made her head throb and her heart plummet with guilt and remorse.

Some wrongs simply couldn't be put right, no matter how desperately she wanted to.

Steeling herself, she drove on, resisting the temptation to take a roundabout way, one easier on her conscience. Part of her self-imposed atonement was to bear witness to the harm she had caused others. That she had never meant for it to happen and would give anything to undo it mattered not at all. That she had not personally rendered the final blow was irrelevant. That the one who had suffered the most had offered forgiveness did not lessen her culpability.

Her heart thudded as she reached the busiest intersection on Main Street, where the main entrance to the Waterford College campus faced the town's most popular retail and entertainment district. As fate would have it, a red light brought her to a halt right in front of the building she most dreaded to see.

She forced herself to look.

The upper levels of the three-story redbrick building were almost unrecognizable behind a framework of scaffolding, the doors to the ground-level businesses inaccessible behind rubbish bins and construction equipment. Those shops and offices were empty now, the former tenants persuaded by the new landlord's exorbitant rents to relocate.

One small-business owner had resisted, but eventually she too had been forced to close the doors to her beloved shop, not merely until she could reopen elsewhere, but forever. And although she apparently did not blame Mary Beth for her misfortune, she would not be wrong to do so.

Mary Beth pressed her lips together as her gaze took in the dismayingly altered storefront, and the large window that had once boasted an enticing display of quilts, fabrics, books, and notions, which changed with the seasons, now darkened and covered with construction permits. Her heart cinched at the sight of the faint discoloration of the stone above the door where the red-and-gold GRANDMA'S ATTIC sign had hung proudly for so many years.

She had once enjoyed shopping at Waterford's only independent quilt shop, her step quickening with anticipation the moment she put hand to doorknob. A bell on the door would tinkle merrily overhead as she entered, and the owner, Bonnie Markham, would glance up from the cutting table or the cash register and smile in welcome. Warm folk music—hammered dulcimer, guitar, violin, and flute—played softly over hidden speakers, and the faint aromas of cinnamon and coffee wafted on the air, perhaps from an office in the back. Mary Beth had found great pleasure and inspiration wandering the aisles of Grandma's Attic through the years. It was impossible to count how many of her favorite quilts owed their existence to a new technique she had observed Bonnie demonstrating or to a particularly evocative fabric that sparked her imagination.

But then, inexplicably, Bonnie had hired Diane Sonnenberg to work at the shop—Diane Sonnenberg, of all people, Mary Beth's next-door neighbor and archnemesis, a quilter of marginal talent and abrasive personality who had somehow managed to befriend some of the most prestigious quilters in the Elm Creek Valley. Although their sons had been best friends since the second grade, and Mary Beth's husband got along well with Diane's husband, Tim, a chemistry professor at Waterford College, Mary Beth and Diane had a history of enmity, the result of disputes over property boundaries and noise ordinance violations that had turned bitterly personal. Mary Beth didn't trust Diane to cut her fabric accurately or to withhold snide remarks about her color choices, so if she glanced through the front window and saw Diane inside, carrying on as if she actually deserved to be there, Mary Beth would walk on by and come back another day. Diane's presence was inconvenient and annoying, and it was difficult not to take it personally that Mary Beth herself had submitted a résumé soon after the shop opened and had received nothing more than Bonnie's promise that she would keep it on file.

Bonnie must have hired Diane out of pity. Why else would

she have overlooked Mary Beth, the infinitely more qualified applicant? She had won scores of ribbons at the Waterford Summer Quilt Festival through the years and at the time had recently been reelected as president of the Waterford Quilting Guild. Diane was only an ordinary member of middling ability who had served on the refreshments committee once but seemed disinclined to seek a more demanding leadership role.

If only Diane had never joined the guild, how much better everything would have worked out for everyone.

Mary Beth would never forget how shocked and dismayed she had felt when Diane had first shown up at a guild meeting, strolling into Meeting Room C of the Waterford Public Library as a guest of longtime member Agnes Emberly. Afterward Diane had submitted a registration form, but since nothing in the bylaws permitted the president to veto applicants at will, and since Diane was apparently Agnes's protégé, Mary Beth had had no choice but to grit her teeth and accept her application. The guild was large enough that they could avoid each other without drawing attention to their mutual antipathy, and after a few weeks passed and Diane remained well outside the periphery of Mary Beth's inner circle, she was satisfied that her obnoxious neighbor knew her place and would keep to it.

How wrong she had been.

Mary Beth had barely let down her guard when Diane announced her intention to challenge her for the guild presidency, showing no respect for more than a hundred years of tradition in which incumbents were allowed to run uncontested, retaining their posts until they voluntarily stepped down or died in office. Worse yet, Diane actively campaigned at guild meetings, buttonholing members as they arrived and departed, haranguing others with a stump speech throughout the refreshment break.

"The guild desperately needs change," Mary Beth overheard

Diane tell Gwen Sullivan and her auburn-haired daughter, Summer, a student at Waterford College, as they helped themselves to cookies and coffee at the snack table. "Under the current regime, it's become cliquish and moribund."

"Has it?" asked Gwen, raising her eyebrows, but she seemed amused rather than offended.

"'Current regime'?" Summer echoed. "That seems kind of harsh."

"Harsh but true," said Diane. "The officers invite the same handful of local speakers every year. They run the same block swaps. They hang the same quilters' quilts at the Waterford Summer Quilt Festival. The guild's creativity has stagnated so much that I can predict within a tiny margin of error which guild members will bring what dishes to the holiday socials and potluck picnics."

When Gwen laughed, Mary Beth felt the blood rush into her face. "Hello," she said sharply. "Standing right here. You know I can hear you, right?"

Gwen and Summer had the decency to look chagrined, but Diane merely shrugged. "Sorry, Mary Beth, but I've pointed out these problems before and you haven't done anything to solve them. Maybe you can hear me, but I'm not sure you're listening."

Furious, Mary Beth strode back to the podium to call the meeting to order. She was too disconcerted to respond properly that night, but at every subsequent meeting, she made sure to promote her own candidacy whenever she could slip it unobtrusively into the program. She had the microphone and the bully pulpit; why not use them? Naturally Diane complained that this wasn't fair, and when she had the nerve to demand equal time, the guild voted to allow both candidates to make a speech to the entire group on election night before ballots were cast.

The decision stung and smacked of disloyalty, but when

Mary Beth vented to her husband, Roger sighed wearily and said, "They're probably just trying to be fair to both sides."

"Or they want to give the *appearance* of fairness." Perhaps Mary Beth's friends were so confident she would win that they saw no harm in letting Diane speak her piece.

The night of the election came. Mary Beth had her hair styled and wore her most flattering professional outfit. Diane, unfortunately, looked as she always did—slim, tall, gorgeous for her age, with curly blond hair that fell effortlessly in place and a sense of fashion that her peers admired and even their teenage daughters complimented. Fortunately, in that particular forum, substance was far more important than style.

Diane was allowed to speak first. She used her time onstage to spout platitudes she had probably picked up watching presidential election coverage on local television. New leadership would bring a change of pace and fresh ideas, she said. If she were elected, she would invite better speakers, arrange new workshops, spend members' dues more frugally and with more accountability, and so on and so forth. It was all nonsense. Anyone who had lived next door to that woman as long as Mary Beth had—and that was too long—knew that Diane had the attention span of a puppy and couldn't possibly deliver on any of her promises.

But, she realized bleakly, she was the only person in that room who had ever lived next door to Diane.

Hiding her sudden fear as the applause for her rival faded, Mary Beth realized her only hope was to be concise, focused, and merciless. She took the podium and, after the preliminary niceties, she launched into a description of the achievements of her previous administrations, but only the most important, in the interest of brevity. "For the benefit of my opponent," she continued, holding up her own well-read copy of the official guild handbook, "who may not be aware of what is required of the president, I will now read the president's official duties from the bylaws."

A ripple of surprise passed through the audience. Diane had returned to her seat, and Mary Beth noted with satisfaction that she glanced to her friends for reassurance, but did not seem to find any.

"'The president shall prepare the agenda for and preside at quilt guild meetings and shall direct such meetings in a pleasant and professional manner,'" Mary Beth said, and then bit her lower lip and winced. Everyone knew Diane's default mode was virulent sarcasm.

"'The president shall appoint committee chairpersons and coordinate the activities of all the committees.'" With a sharp intake of breath, she glanced up from the handbook and frowned, feigning worry. Diane could barely keep her purse organized.

"'The president shall be authorized to cosign checks on behalf of the guild.'" Mary Beth arched her eyebrows in warning, for Diane rarely managed to pay her own member dues on time.

"'The president shall appoint an ad hoc committee to help coordinate all necessary activities for producing a quilt show.'" Mary Beth set down the guild bylaws and shook her head. "Oh, honestly, ladies, need I go on? Would any of us feel comfortable entrusting our beloved Waterford Summer Quilt Festival to someone who has never won a ribbon?"

A murmur of dismay swept through the audience. One of Diane's friends squeezed her shoulder, a brief gesture of encouragement, but Mary Beth felt a surge of triumph, knowing she had won even before the first ballot was cast. When the votes were tallied and her reelection confirmed, relief flooded her with such force that she did not trust her trembling legs to support her weight. She had to accept her friends' congratulations perched on a chair. Afterward, Diane left the meeting hall so quickly that Mary Beth barely had a chance to enjoy watching her go.

She savored her victory, but only briefly, because Diane ruined that too. Diane dropped out of the guild, which would have been glorious except that she took her closest friends with her, which included some of the guild's most talented and dedicated members. Bonnie owned the only quilt shop in town, Gwen published academic research on quilt history, Summer was regarded as a quilting prodigy who represented the guild's future, and Agnes was a master of appliqué who unfailingly contributed the work of four quilters to the guild's service projects. As a distraction, Mary Beth encouraged her own friends to spread rumors that Diane had blackmailed them into leaving. In the frenzy of speculation that followed, everyone forgot the ludicrous claims Diane had raised in her campaign about the so-called problems that allegedly threatened the guild's long-term survival.

After that, things should have settled comfortably back to normal, but they hadn't. Mary Beth never forgave Diane for stirring up so much conflict and threatening her position. She wished the Sonnenbergs would move far away and leave the neighborhood in peace, but apparently she was cursed with Diane the way other people were stuck with miserable allergies or chronic lower back pain. She could not get rid of Diane permanently, but could only try to keep the symptoms from spreading.

That proved more challenging than she anticipated, especially after Diane and her friends teamed up with the renowned Sylvia Bergstrom Compson to create Elm Creek Quilts. Factions existed in the guild—small and fragmented, but a significant presence nonetheless—who thought the burgeoning company was a wonderful addition to the local quilting community and spoke reverently of events they had attended at the manor. When Elm Creek Quilt Camp was in its third year, Mary Beth and her vice president considered adding a guild-wide boycott to the bylaws, but others on the executive board pointed out the rule would be difficult to enforce and might upset a sizable voting bloc. Because now, thanks to Diane, they had voting blocs, and in addition to her great many other concerns, Mary Beth had to worry about satisfying an electorate.

Since declaring a boycott of all things Elm Creek would probably backfire, Mary Beth had settled for passive resistance, ignoring invitations to events at Elm Creek Manor and taking her business to Fabric Warehouse and mail-order companies rather than Grandma's Attic. Fortunately, since all guild correspondence was sent to the Callahan home, she could filter out flyers and invitations from Elm Creek Quilts before the other members discovered their existence.

Eventually the tumult subsided and Mary Beth was able to restore order. All was well for several years, and would have remained so if Diane had learned her lesson and had kept her distance instead of sneaking into a guild meeting and luring Mary Beth away from the podium just long enough to make that wretched announcement that had thrown everything into chaos—

Mary Beth inhaled deeply, shakily. She was doing precisely what she could not allow herself to do. She could not blame Diane for what had happened next, for the way things had gone so shockingly, tragically wrong, or why.

The stoplight turned green. Gaze fixed on the road ahead, Mary Beth drove on, past the former quilt shop and future location of University Realty's new offices. No wonder the real estate company had raised the rents after they had purchased the building; they had coveted that prime location for themselves. Mary Beth knew the interior designer they had hired and had heard that they were sparing no expense in their remodel. Out with the warm and cozy quilt shop; in with the finest furnishings and state-of-the-art integrated technology. Although Mary Beth had stubbornly, spitefully taken her business elsewhere for the past few years, she ached with longing for Grandma's Attic now that it was gone.

If only she had made it clear that her argument was with Diane, not with all the Elm Creek Quilters. If only she had not spoken so disparagingly about Elm Creek Quilts so often around the dinner table, when really her biggest gripe with the company was that they allowed Diane to be a part of it. If only Brent had not absorbed her carelessly contemptuous words and acted upon them in ways she never would have imagined possible—

She blinked her eyes furiously to clear away tears. It pained her that she could pinpoint the precise moment when she had steered events inexorably toward disaster, and yet could do nothing to change them.

It all came down to that letter from Elm Creek Quilts.

IN JANUARY—HAD IT really been almost a year?—the Elm Creek Quilters had sent out letters asking Sylvia Bergstrom Compson's friends, family, former students, and admirers to contribute blocks to her wedding quilt. Six-inch blocks were requested, patchwork or appliqué, in cotton fabrics from a palette of green, rose, lilac, blue, and ecru. The submission deadline was April 1, and participants were encouraged to "choose any pattern that represents how Sylvia has influenced you as an artist, a teacher, or a friend."

It was a wonderful idea, the sort of project quilters eagerly embraced, especially when the intended recipient was as universally beloved and admired as Sylvia. If Diane had not been involved, Mary Beth would have read the letter aloud at the next meeting of the Waterford Quilting Guild and would have encouraged everyone to participate. She would have sewn a block herself—Wedding March, perhaps, or Bride's Bouquet. But when Mary Beth spied Diane's name in the letter, her instinctive reaction was indignant outrage. How dare those Elm Creek Quilters expect their members to contribute to this quilt when not one of them deigned to join the guild? How dare they contact the Waterford Quilting Guild *at all* after quitting in a huff in the aftermath of Diane's failed coup?

"Those Elm Creek Quilters think their time is more valuable than ours," she fumed to Roger and Brent that evening over a dinner of broccoli, cheese, and rice casserole. "They think we have nothing better to do than sew blocks for some stupid bridal quilt. Don't they know we make a quilt a year for a real charity? They ought to try giving back to the community for a change, but with them it's just take, take, take."

"They make quilts for hospitals," said Brent. "I heard Mrs. Sonnenberg talking about it once. They make quilts for the kids' cancer ward at Hershey Medical Center and for the neonatal unit at the Elm Creek Valley Hospital."

Mary Beth bristled, but as ever, she instinctively softened her tone when she spoke to her son. "Then they ought to understand how much work is involved in a project like this."

"They're just asking for one quilt square," said Roger, without looking up from his plate. "It doesn't sound like that much effort."

Mary Beth glared. "It's not the effort. It's the principle." How could he not see that? Her glare relented when she turned to her son. "Honey, I'm sure you know better than to mention this conversation to Mrs. Sonnenberg."

Brent shrugged and nodded. Of course he would never tell tales on her to that conniving shrew next door, even though she was the mother of his best friend.

What a difference it would have made if Mary Beth had allowed her temper to cool; if she had reflected upon the bride and groom and the good intentions behind the Elm Creek Quilters' request; if she had considered the many members of her guild who adored Sylvia and would have been eager to contribute to her bridal quilt. Then she might have set aside her personal issues with Diane, put the letter in her satchel with the other guild business, and read the request for blocks aloud at the next meeting. But instead she tucked the letter into a filing cabinet in her quilt room.

Even then, if she had just left it there, it would not have been too late to avert disaster. Why hadn't she just let it go? But although Mary Beth had put the letter out of sight, it had remained firmly fixed in her mind. She fumed whenever she saw Diane, which was far too often, an inescapable consequence of living next door. She was tempted to send Sylvia an anonymous letter spoiling the surprise, but although that might give Mary Beth a moment of satisfaction, it would do nothing to establish clear boundaries between her guild and the Elm Creek Quilters. Eventually, after finding it impossible to simply let the matter drop, Mary Beth decided to return the letter to the sender and explain that in the future they were to regard her guild as strictly off-limits.

She waited until the first day of March, exactly one month before the quilt blocks were due—too late for the Elm Creek Quilters to contact guild members individually for them to make the submission deadline, but just early enough to make them feel obliged to make the attempt.

Mary Beth had remained on relatively good terms with Bonnie, so she decided to return the letter to her at Grandma's Attic, a safe, public place if not quite neutral territory. To her dismay, when she entered the shop, the only employees in sight were Diane and Summer, who were sorting a bin of mail on the cutting table but glanced up at the sound of the door chime. Stalling for time, Mary Beth removed her hat, smoothed back her platinum-blond pageboy, and, addressing neither of them in particular, asked, "Isn't Bonnie here today?"

"No," Diane said abruptly. Turning her back, she sat down on a stool and resumed her work. Summer murmured something to her, probably a reproach, and Diane muttered a response. Mary Beth couldn't make out the words, but the disparaging tone was unmistakable. Drawing closer, she spotted several large padded envelopes torn open and lying empty in a stack just within Diane's reach, and on the cutting table between her and Summer, several quilt blocks were arranged in two neat rows.

Summer smiled pleasantly at Mary Beth to make up for her rude companion. "Bonnie's not here, but may I help you?"

"I suppose so," Mary Beth said, resigned. She would much rather deal with Bonnie. "You're Summer, right? Summer Sullivan?"

"That's right."

"Your name is in the letter, so I guess you'll do." Mary Beth took the Elm Creek Quilters' request letter from her purse and gave it to the auburn-haired girl. "I believe this was sent to me by mistake."

Summer skimmed the page, nodding. "We definitely meant to send this. You're listed as the contact for the Waterford Quilting Guild, and we hoped you would announce it at your next meeting."

She tried to return the letter, but Mary Beth waved it away. "Oh, no, I couldn't."

"Why not?" asked Diane.

"I couldn't impose on my fellow guild members like that. They'd probably feel obligated to participate, and that isn't fair. It's not like this is for charity. If I endorse your project, where does it stop?"

"We're not asking you to endorse it, just announce it," said

Diane. "Just tell them about the quilt and let them decide whether they want to help."

"Many of your guild members have known Sylvia for years," said Summer, bewildered. "Don't you think they would want to know about her bridal quilt?"

"Don't you think once they see the finished quilt they'll be ticked off that you kept them from participating?" Diane added.

Mary Beth regarded her sourly. "If those few members of my guild are such good friends of Sylvia's, I'm sure you have their addresses and can contact them individually. Our guild happens to be very busy, so regardless of their feelings for Sylvia, we would appreciate it if non-members didn't come around begging for blocks."

"How would you know if you never ask them?" Diane protested. "If they don't want to participate, fine, but you won't even give them the chance to refuse for themselves!"

The consternation and outrage on Diane's face were priceless, but Mary Beth had completed her errand and refused to waste time in debate. "Make sure to take our address off your mailing list," she told Summer over her shoulder as she turned and left the shop. The chime rang again as the door closed behind her. From the safety of the sidewalk, she stole a glance through the front window in time to see Summer throwing the invitation into the trash where it belonged.

Later, over supper, she glowed as she shared the story of her triumph with Roger and Brent. "It felt so good to put Diane in her place," she said. "I'm sure those blocks scattered all over the cutting table are supposed to be for Sylvia's bridal quilt."

Roger and Brent nodded and continued eating.

"The ones I saw weren't anything special," she mused aloud. "I guess those Elm Creek people aren't the wonderful teachers they consider themselves to be. Or the people who sent the blocks didn't send their best work, which doesn't say much for how they regard Sylvia."

"Or they were beginners," said Roger, reaching for another piece of chicken, "and that *was* their best work."

"That couldn't possibly be the case," said Mary Beth. "Beginners know better than to ruin a group quilt with their sloppy blocks."

"It's a gift to congratulate a bride and groom, not a masterpiece to display in a show. If beginners want to express their good wishes, they shouldn't be criticized for the number of stitches per inch they use."

"Stitches per inch refers to quilting, not piecing," snapped Mary Beth. "Which just shows you don't know anything about it."

"Mom, you've been going on about this stupid quilt for months," said Brent. "You should really just forget about it. It's not that big of a deal."

"It *is* a big deal. Diane and those Elm Creek Quilters think they're the best thing that ever happened to quilting in Waterford. They dismiss everything my guild has done for this town as inconsequential, as if quilting didn't exist in the Elm Creek Valley before their ridiculous quilt camp."

Only then did Mary Beth realize that this was what bothered her most—not that the Elm Creek Quilters included Diane in their circle, because for all she knew they kept her around for comic relief, but that they excluded *her*—and not just Mary Beth but her closest friends and the organization to which she had devoted countless hours and immeasurable energy. The Elm Creek Quilters held themselves aloof and superior up in that grand old manor, snubbing the Waterford Quilt Guild—except for paying customers—until they needed a favor.

She knew Roger would disagree with her interpretation, so she didn't share it with him. Anyway, the matter was settled. The Elm Creek Quilters would have to stitch that bridal sampler for Sylvia without help from Mary Beth or her guild, and with any luck, she would never hear another word about it.

But luck was not on her side, and Diane proved to be as unwilling as Mary Beth to let things go.

A little more than two weeks later, at the guild's monthly meeting, Mary Beth's cell phone went off in the middle of her introductory remarks. Since all of her friends were present and Roger and Brent were under strict orders never to interrupt a meeting, she could only assume it was an emergency.

Heart racing, she turned the program over to the vice president, dashed into the hallway, and accepted the call even though she did not recognize the number. She heard only silence. "Hello?" she said. "Who's there?" Still nothing.

She held on for a moment just in case it was a bad connection, but eventually she hung up and returned to the meeting—only to find Diane at the podium reading the block request letter to a very attentive audience.

Horrified, Mary Beth wrested the microphone away, but after Diane blurted out a few last taunts and made a hasty retreat, she struggled in vain to restore order. The guild turned on her, demanding to know why she had not told them about the Elm Creek Quilters' request, shouting down her attempts to explain, protesting that it was her fault they had barely enough time to sew a block for Sylvia, which, apparently, every single quilter in the room wanted to do. Distressed, realizing that she had irrevocably lost control of the meeting, she handed the microphone to her vice president and fled.

She drove home in a daze. In the safety of her living room, she clung to Roger and sobbed out her tale of woe. The commotion drew Brent downstairs from his bedroom. He sat beside her on the sofa, wide-eyed and incredulous, as the story of her humiliation spilled from her.

Roger stroked her back and sighed. "I guess maybe now you'll finally drop this silly feud with the Sonnenbergs."

"Dad," protested Brent. "She's upset."

"That's your response?" Mary Beth pulled away from her husband and reached for the box of tissues on the end table. "Your wife is dishonored in front of all her friends, and that's how you respond?"

"What do you want me to do? Run next door and challenge Tim to a duel?"

"Don't be ridiculous. This is between me and that—that evil witch. How can you call it a silly feud? It's much more than that, and that woman's behavior tonight proves it."

Dabbing at her eyes, she told Brent that she did not want him to spend time with Diane's son anymore. He protested that none of this was Todd's fault, and they had midterms coming up, and they always studied together. "We're partners for the physics project," he added. "Not to mention he's been my best friend since the second grade."

Mary Beth sniffled into her tissue. She hated to disappoint her son. "Well—"

"Please, Mom. This way, I might overhear her if she plans anything else."

"By all means," said Roger, exasperated. "Let's spy on the neighbors."

"If she tries anything else, I'm pressing charges." Still, Brent had a point. "All right. You can still be friends with Todd under one condition. If that woman says a single word against me, you'll defend me." Unlike her husband. She glared at Roger, but he had collapsed against the sofa cushions and was shaking his head at the ceiling.

"I promise," said Brent solemnly.

And that, she later realized, had been the point of no return.

MARY BETH SWALLOWED hard, fighting back the all-too-familiar taste of remorse and shame. Why had she made defending her honor a condition of Brent's friendship with Todd? She had only meant for him to speak up for her, certainly nothing more than that. She should have been more specific. She should have taught him better so that she would not have needed to clarify, as one would to a toddler, that he should use his words, not his hands.

No. She should have left her son out of it entirely, as Diane had.

As Mary Beth later learned, Diane had never drawn Todd into their escalating conflict. He had not known that his mother had disrupted the guild meeting, or even that she and Mary Beth disliked each other, until Brent told him several days afterward, blurting out an accusation like opening a release valve on pressurized anger and resentment. How much worse Brent had felt when Todd's utter bewilderment proved that the hostilities tormenting his mother were so inconsequential to Todd's mother that she had never even mentioned them.

The snowfall was steadily increasing, the small icy crystals on her windshield giving way to thicker, wetter flakes. Mary Beth switched on her wipers as she turned onto Church Street and drove uphill, leaving campus and the defunct quilt shop behind. When the news first broke of the incident at Grandma's Attic, she assumed that Bonnie and her staff would clean up and restore order, and everything would go on as before. She had not known that the store had been struggling for years. She never would have guessed that one act of thoughtless cruelty could push it over the edge.

On the morning of April 2, one day after the deadline to submit blocks for Sylvia's bridal sampler had passed, Mary Beth was eating breakfast with her family before Roger left for work and Brent for school. "Here's something you'll enjoy," said Roger, folding the front section of the newspaper and sliding it across the table to Mary Beth.

"What is it?" asked Mary Beth, dubious. She rarely read more of the news pages than the headlines; the national stories were always so depressing and the world news inscrutable.

Roger reached across the table and tapped the weekly police report. "What?" Mary Beth said, and then words leapt off the page: One week before, Grandma's Attic had been robbed and vandalized. The cash register had been emptied and the previous day's receipts, which the proprietor usually deposited in the bank after closing but had failed to do on that day of all days, had been taken from the office. Although more had been damaged than stolen, assorted tools and equipment were missing, as was a carton of quilt blocks.

Mary Beth gave a start. The police report was deliberately vague, but the missing quilt blocks surely were the contributions for Sylvia's bridal quilt.

"I heard it was a real mess," Brent offered, watching her intently as she read.

"This is the first I've heard of it." She should have been informed immediately. Bonnie was no longer a member of the guild, but this crime was relevant to the Waterford quilting community, and Mary Beth was the center of the Waterford quilting community. She slid the paper back to her husband. "Why on earth would you assume I would enjoy reading this?"

He feigned innocence. "Bonnie Markham's one of those Elm Creek people, right?"

"Yes, but that doesn't mean I'd celebrate her misfortune." She frowned when her husband and son exchanged a look of surprise. Honestly, what did they take her for?

Brent shook his head, baffled. "You never shop there anymore. You're always talking about how much you hate them."

"And now they'll be too busy to interfere with your quilt guild," said Roger.

"And that quilt for old Mrs. Compson," Brent added. "Now they won't be able to bother you about that stupid quilt anymore."

There was that. Still, she liked Bonnie, and it was unsettling that the criminals had targeted a quilt shop. Why a quilt shop, when robbers usually focused on convenience stores and gas stations? It was unnatural, a strike at the heartland, at home and family and all that quilting represented.

And what did it say about her that her husband and son assumed she would find any robbery and vandalism in their small town a cause for celebration?

ALTHOUGH SHE HAD not realized it, the pieces were falling into place.

First, there was the break-in.

Next, Brent surprised her with an early Mother's Day present—a new Bernina, the sewing machine of her dreams, with a computer touch screen and all the features and attachments she would ever need. He claimed he had bought it for fifty dollars at a garage sale.

Then, soon thereafter, Diane phoned to ask if Brent knew anything about the incident at Grandma's Attic. Diane's key to the shop had disappeared from her purse after Brent had spent the night at their house, the day before the break-in. And since the police had found no signs of forced entry—

"How dare you!" Mary Beth snapped.

"I'm sorry. I know this is a terrible thing to suggest, but—"

"My son was here at home that entire night. What about *your* son?"

"Todd was—"

"Not Todd. Michael. He's the troublemaker in this town. Everyone knows his reputation. I bet this wouldn't be the first time he took your keys."

A careful pause. "You would be right, but he assures me he had nothing to do with it."

"He assures you. Oh, that's rich."

"Please, Mary Beth, just talk to Brent."

"I'm hanging up now."

She slammed down the phone and clutched the back of a chair for support, head spinning. That nasty, spiteful, vicious woman! She knew for a fact that Brent had been asleep in his own bed that night; not that it mattered, because he absolutely could not have been involved, he was always home on weeknights. Except . . .

Mary Beth felt a chill. The robbery had occurred during spring break. Brent and a friend had spent the night of the break-in at another friend's house.

That was what he had told her. Why shouldn't she believe him? She did believe him, but just to be sure, she invented an excuse to phone the other boys' parents.

Brent's alibi quickly fell apart.

That still didn't prove he was involved—and yet. The new, very expensive sewing machine. The missing blocks for the bridal quilt Mary Beth had spent weeks denouncing.

Apprehension and uncertainty plagued her, but she dared not ask him outright, so deeply afraid she was of what he might say, what truth he might confess or implausible lie he might invent.

And what of poor Bonnie? Mary Beth had learned through her few remaining quilting friends that Bonnie's insurance claim had been denied because the police suspected it was an inside job. She was holding a special sale in hopes of raising enough cash to pay off her debts and avoid bankruptcy, but rumor had it that little salvageable inventory remained. Even if she sold every item on the shelves and then sold the shelves as well, she could not possibly earn enough.

Could Brent have played a role in inflicting this misery upon Bonnie? Surely not. He was just a boy.

And yet.

In her last official act as guild president, Mary Beth sent out an email to all members, soliciting donations of fabric, notions, books, and other like-new items for Bonnie to sell at her shop. Then she sent out another email, a copy of the Elm Creek Quilters' request for contributions to Sylvia's bridal quilt, to which she added her apologies for failing to tell them sooner and her hopes that the guild would be well represented in the finished quilt despite the late notice. Then she gathered up the guild's files, turned them over to the vice president, and submitted her resignation. She heard later that the sale had been a great success, thanks to the enhanced inventory.

Eventually the police came calling.

Although the other two boys' parents cooperated with the investigation, Mary Beth balked. She insisted that Brent had been home at the time of the incident, even when the officers informed her that his friends disputed that claim. Brent refused to answer any questions about that night, not for the police, and not for his parents. Tearfully Mary Beth begged him to tell her something, anything, that she could use to disprove the accusations, which could not possibly be true. "I don't care if you were drinking beer in the arboretum," she choked out, for she suspected he and Will and Greg spent many summer nights doing exactly that. She had always looked the other way.

Brent gave her one long, bleak, wordless look, dragged himself upstairs to his room, and shut the door.

"Mary Beth, honey." Roger came up from behind her and took her in his arms. Tears glistened in his eyes. "He doesn't have another explanation to give. He did it. We both know he did it."

She nodded, unable to speak. They held each other and wept. Then they calmed themselves, dried their eyes, and called the police.

Soon thereafter, realizing his mother would no longer support his lies, Brent confessed the truth. The new evidence allowed Bonnie to dispute the insurance company's ruling, and they soon overturned their original decision and paid her in full. But although their decision kept Bonnie from bankruptcy, it came too late to save Grandma's Attic.

While their classmates were celebrating the end of senior year, Brent, Will, and Greg were meeting with detectives and lawyers and court mediators. Brent sat for his final exams, but he was in court on graduation day and would not receive his diploma for weeks, by mail. The boys were accepted into a program for first-time, non-violent offenders. At their sentencing, Bonnie asked the judge for leniency. They had never been in trouble before, she said earnestly, and all three intended to start college in the fall. She couldn't bear to think that their future prospects were ruined because of one very bad choice.

"They threw those futures away when they broke into your shop," said the judge, who clearly had expected Bonnie to demand justice and restitution. Yet, impressed by her pleas, he relented and sentenced the boys to probation and community service, which they would serve at Elm Creek Manor. He would consider the terms fulfilled after the boys worked the equivalent number of hours to earn back every cent they had caused in damage.

"But that will take years," exclaimed Mary Beth, rising. "Anyway, her insurance will pay for everything."

The judge regarded Mary Beth over the rims of his glasses.

"What an astonishing sense of entitlement, given the circumstances. I'm beginning to see why your son is here today. If it takes years, so be it. They can work every summer and every semester break until the debt to the community is paid."

Chagrined, Mary Beth sank back into her seat and uttered not another word. Bonnie was satisfied with the decision, and Sylvia agreed to her part in seeing to it that the young men fulfilled their sentences. But judging by their grim expressions, the other Elm Creek Quilters thought that the young men had not been sufficiently punished.

Perhaps no one had told them that the prestigious universities the young men had planned to attend had been informed of the crime, the plea bargains, the sentences. Brent had set his sights on the Ivy League as a ninth grader, and he had worked hard throughout high school to earn top grades and accumulate achievements. His acceptance to Yale had been the fulfillment of a dream. In mid July, Yale informed him by certified mail that his admission had been revoked.

After Mary Beth and Roger recovered from their shock, they desperately scrambled to have Brent reaccepted into Penn State, a college he had turned down months before. Somehow Roger managed it. It wasn't the Ivy League, but, as Roger emphasized in the new, firm manner he had adopted since the disaster, Brent would get an excellent education there if he applied himself and stayed out of trouble.

Soberly, Brent assured them that he understood.

He and his two friends worked hard all summer long at Elm Creek Quilt Camp, probably harder than they had ever worked in their lives—mowing lawns, clearing brush, waiting tables, doing laundry, hauling suitcases, scrubbing trash cans. Diane's two sons also spent the summer working at the manor, as they had for the past few years, earning an enviable sum for their own college expenses. Yet whenever Mary Beth glimpsed them returning to the house next door after a long day, they never seemed as exhausted, sweaty, and filthy as Brent was when he dragged himself over the threshold, famished and too tired to speak.

When Mary Beth first noted the difference, Roger replied sharply, "They're probably more used to hard work." Indignant, she said nothing more about it, but she suspected the Elm Creek Quilters saved the worst, dirtiest, and most tedious jobs for Brent and his friends, and didn't suffer a single twinge of conscience.

If she were brutally honest, that was what she would have done in their place.

Compounding Brent's humiliation, Diane's eldest son had been appointed foreman of the crew of teenage employees. If Brent put in only a halfhearted effort, it was Michael who ordered him to do the task over. If he showed up late, it was Michael who informed him that he could skip his lunch hour or stay after, but he *would* make up the time.

Todd was going to Princeton and Michael was Brent's boss— and would be, every summer and school holiday, until their sentences were completed. Mary Beth could only imagine how Diane must be gloating over their stunning reversal of fortune.

"I can't believe our son has to answer to that juvenile delinquent," Mary Beth griped, watching through the window one morning as Michael hauled his family's trash and recycling cans to the curb. She had let Brent sleep in, and he was still upstairs, racing to get ready for another difficult day.

"Who are we to call anyone's child a delinquent?" asked Roger, incredulous. "Mary Beth, don't you get it? Don't you understand how lucky we are? Bonnie could have demanded much worse and that judge would have been glad to comply. Brent is eighteen, an adult. He could be in prison right now!"

His words struck Mary Beth with almost physical force.

Shaken, she turned away from the window, brushing past Roger in her haste. Upstairs in her sewing room, she listened for the sounds of her husband and son departing. Only when she knew she was alone did she break down in tears.

Roger's words rang all too true. Brent had been granted a second chance, not because he deserved it, but because Bonnie had chosen forgiveness and mercy. Brent had been subdued and withdrawn ever since the sentencing, which Mary Beth had interpreted as an understandable reaction to an unjust punishment. She realized now that she'd entirely misunderstood. Brent wasn't indignant or resentful, but stunned and relieved that the judge had been lenient.

In the third week of August, the Callahans packed up Brent's clothes and supplies, loaded up Roger's car, and drove to University Park, where they settled Brent into his room in Geary Hall and checked in for orientation. After walking around campus to postpone their inevitable parting, they stopped by the Berkey Creamery for ice cream before saying their farewells with tearful hugs and last-minute advice in front of Old Main.

"I'm not going to mess up here," Brent told them, pulling out of an embrace that Mary Beth wished could endure for at least another minute. "I'm going to work hard. I'm going to make you proud of me again, the way you used to be."

Mary Beth and Roger immediately protested that they *were* proud of him, that they knew he would do brilliantly in school, but Brent frowned, shook his head, and wiped his eyes with the back of his hand. "I mean it," he said, backing away. "I will. You'll see."

He turned and walked off toward his dormitory. Mary Beth and Roger watched him go. If he had turned around, Mary Beth would have run after him for one more embrace, one more word of encouragement, but Brent had fixed his gaze straight ahead and did not even glance back over his shoulder.

"He'll be fine," said Roger, a faint tremor in his voice. "He'll be fine."

Mary Beth had no words. Roger took her hand—she could not remember the last time they had held hands—and they walked back to the car in silence.

The sun was setting by the time they reached home. They drove over two desiccated newspapers at the foot of the drive-way, pulled into their garage, and sat without speaking as Roger pressed the button and the door shut behind them, plunging them into gloomy dusk.

Roger heaved a sigh. "I'll take the suitcase inside."

"I'll get the papers and the mail," said Mary Beth, ineffably weary.

She climbed out of the car, stretched, and made her way to the side door while Roger opened the trunk. Her legs were stiff from too much sitting, and as she staggered slowly down the driveway, whom should she see but Diane in her front yard watering the hostas.

*Please don't let her notice me*, Mary Beth silently begged the universe as she retrieved a few envelopes from the mailbox and stooped to pick up the newspapers. Naturally, when she straight-ened, she found Diane watching her. "Back from vacation?" she called, twisting the nozzle of the garden hose to adjust the spray to a fine mist.

Mary Beth halted, arms full of sun-yellowed newsprint. "No," she said flatly, "from taking Brent to school."

"Oh, that's right. Penn State follows the same schedule as Waterford College."

Mary Beth slowly flipped through her mail—bills, notices of

back-to-school sales, a credit card application. "Actually, Waterford College follows the same schedule as Penn State."

"Oh. Right." Diane turned off the spigot and began coiling the hose. "Is Brent excited about the first week of college?"

"Not really." Mary Beth fixed her with a baleful look. "You know very well that he graduated in the top one percent of his class. He's convinced that the classes won't challenge him."

"I'm sure that won't be the case, especially once he gets all those freshman requirements out of the way."

"He won't have many of those, thanks to his AP credits. No one can take those away from him." Then, almost as if she were thinking aloud, she said, "I told him to seek out other ways to enrich his curriculum—research projects, independent study. After graduation, he'll be up against kids with degrees from Ivy League schools. He's going to have to work ten times harder just to compete."

"You know, Penn State is an excellent university. Tim often collaborates with professors in their chemistry department, and he's had nothing but praise for their facilities and faculty and the students he's met. In fact, I think he's a little jealous. And everyone knows Happy Valley is a great place to be a student. I know Penn State wasn't Brent's first choice—"

"It was his last choice." Fatigue took the edge off Mary Beth's retort. "It was his safety school. He's had his heart set on Yale since the ninth grade. I'm sure your son told you that Yale revoked Brent's acceptance because of his legal troubles."

Diane shrugged, clearly uncomfortable. "Todd didn't give me any details."

"Well, now you know, so let the gloating commence."

"Brent's going to be fine. He'll get a great education. None of this will hold him back, not in the long run."

"I hope you're right." She fixed Diane with a look of smoldering, helpless anger. "I want to blame you for this, but I can't. I know I can't. For weeks after it happened, at the shop——" She inhaled sharply, still incapable of admitting aloud what her son had done. "I kept thinking that if only you hadn't humiliated me at the quilt guild meeting, Brent wouldn't have lashed out. But that wasn't where it all began. Maybe if I hadn't reported you to the zoning commission about that skateboard ramp in your backyard, you wouldn't have humiliated me at the quilt guild meeting. And back and forth, tit for tat, going all through the years, for as long as we've been next-door neighbors." Mary Beth looked away, fighting back tears. "You know what keeps me up at night?"

Diane shook her head.

"Knowing that if it weren't for me, and my bad choices, Brent might be settling into a residential college at Yale right now instead of a dorm at Penn State. My bitterness for you poisoned my child. What he did in that quilt shop he learned from me."

"You're acting as if Brent has no future," Diane protested. "He has to finish his community service and he'll attend Penn State instead of Yale. Granted, that's not what he wanted and it's not what you wanted for him, but it's not the end of the road. He still has the whole world open to him. He could take any path, go anywhere."

"That's easy for you to say. Your son's going to Princeton."

"My son didn't wantonly destroy a woman's livelihood."

"Right." Ashamed, Mary Beth inhaled deeply and ordered herself not to lash out again. "It's hard to break the habit of blaming you."

"Brent's going to be all right. It might be hard to see that now, but he'll be all right."

Mary Beth felt her eyes welling up with tears. "I didn't know he could be so cruel, so destructive. But now——" She took a deep, shaky breath. "But now we know, and maybe it's not too late to root out what I planted there, every time I was vindictive to you."

"I can't let you take all the blame," said Diane, a faint flush rising in her cheeks. "I chose to retaliate each time. I could have ignored you. I could have responded like an adult. I didn't. I never tried to make peace."

Mary Beth shook her head. "I've hated you for so long I don't know how to relate to you any other way but with anger."

To her astonishment, Diane looked genuinely hurt. "We don't have to be friends. All we have to do is stop being so stupid."

Mary Beth stared at her, and then managed to laugh. "At least ten bitingly sarcastic remarks come to mind, and yet I can't bring myself to say them."

Diane rolled her eyes. "I'll use my imagination."

They stood in the driveway watching each other, each waiting for the other to make the next move. Suddenly Mary Beth realized that Diane had shaped the woman she had become, with terrible consequences. She had allowed her worst enemy to define her for far too long.

A WEEK LATER, Mary Beth was moping around the house after Roger had left for work, wishing she could think of a good excuse to drive down to Penn State to check in on Brent, when a knock sounded on the front door. To her astonishment, Diane stood on the doorstep looking profoundly uncomfortable. "Lemon squares?" she said, holding out a white plate loosely draped in plastic wrap.

As Mary Beth accepted it, a memory stirred. "You brought us a plate of lemon squares when we first moved in, to welcome us to the neighborhood. I should have invited you in for a chat."

"I didn't take offense. I knew you were busy."

Mary Beth closed her eyes and sighed. A few days afterward, she had dug up a row of forsythia bushes that, according to the lot survey the former owners had shown them, were on the Callahan side of the property line. That was what she told her new neighbor when Diane stormed over, close to tears, to demand an explanation. Diane had called the county and had paid for a new survey that confirmed the property line was precisely where the Sonnenbergs had always thought it to be, but the damage had been done.

"I never did apologize for those forsythia bushes," Mary Beth said, ashamed. "Just for the record, I honestly did think they were on my property."

Diane sighed. "Considering the way those evergreens are aligned, I can see why you would have."

An awkward silence descended.

"Do you want to come in?" Mary Beth asked. "I could make some coffee or tea to go with these lemon squares."

Diane hesitated a moment, but then she smiled. "I prefer coffee, as long as it isn't instant."

ON THE LAST day of August, a Saturday, Diane invited Mary Beth and Nancy Reinhart, the newly elected president of the Waterford Quilting Guild, to join the Elm Creek Quilters and their campers for breakfast at the manor. Sylvia was gracious and welcoming, although it was obvious from her expression that Diane had not forewarned her about the meeting she had arranged between the former rivals.

Sylvia offered them a brief tour of the manor before leading them outside through the older, west wing to the cornerstone patio, where quilt campers were helping themselves to a marvelous gourmet buffet. At Sylvia's urging, Mary Beth and Nancy joined the queue, filled their plates, and mingled among the campers and faculty. At first Mary Beth felt reserved and defensive, like a diplomat who had wandered unwittingly into enemy territory, but when the Elm Creek Quilters approached her and chatted with unfeigned friendliness, she began to relax. She and Nancy had a good conversation about guild procedures, and they agreed to meet for lunch before the next meeting to go over some of the accounts and records, which Mary Beth knew could seem arcane to a novice. She was surprised to discover how good it felt to know that she was helping Nancy and the guild without calculation, without receiving anything in return.

When she wasn't chatting with new acquaintances and former rivals, Mary Beth listened in as the campers reminisced about their week at Elm Creek Manor. She soon learned that although they missed their families back home, Elm Creek Quilt Camp had fulfilled their fondest wishes and exceeded every expectation, and they couldn't bear to see the week come to an end.

She too could have enjoyed an experience like theirs, Mary Beth thought wistfully, every summer for the past several years, if not for her obstinacy and prejudice. Why had she wasted so much time making enemies of these smart, funny, talented women who loved the art and history of quilting as much as she did?

It was a question she was determined to answer, no matter how painful the soul-searching.

As she drove home afterward, Mary Beth mulled over all she had observed that morning and discovered one common thread: the Elm Creek Quilters and their campers seemed happiest when they felt free to express themselves artistically, and when they shared their gifts with others—offering encouragement, passing along knowledge, helping friends learn from their own mistakes.

Perhaps if Mary Beth emulated them, in time she could find some peace and contentment of her own.

IN ALL THE weeks since, as summer faded into autumn and cold winds blew in from the northwest, Mary Beth had sought peace in atonement, deeply remorseful for how her envy and spite had provoked her son's destructive acts. Although she was too ashamed to attend quilt guild meetings, she helped behind the scenes by answering Nancy's questions whenever she called or emailed, day or night. When her newly empty nest and her withdrawal from the quilt guild left her with too many idle hours, she devoted more of her time to charitable works, which included volunteering for the Good Shepherd Church facilities committee and pledging to donate three quilts to the Christmas Boutique rather than her usual one. Two were simple scrap quilts, cozy and colorful, perfect for snuggling beneath on a cold winter's night. The third was much smaller, meant to be displayed as wall art, but far more elaborate—a Dove of Peace quilt, intricately appliquéd and pieced, rendered in fabric but resembling a stained-glass window image of a dove in flight, holding an olive branch. Though it was a complex work, it had come together swiftly, inspired by her yearning for peace in her heart, in her home, and in her community.

And in her troubled son's life as well.

She yearned to see Brent, to take him in her arms as he had not really tolerated since middle school, to offer whatever comfort he would accept. He said he was doing fine and she wanted to believe him, but she would worry and doubt until she could see him and judge for herself. He had not been home since he had left for Penn State. They had spent the Thanksgiving holiday together, but not in Waterford. She and Roger had picked up Brent at Geary Hall, the family had spent the four-day weekend at Roger's mother's house in Johnstown, and they had dropped him off at the dorm on their return journey Sunday afternoon. He would be coming home soon, a week from Friday, after he finished his final exams. But as wonderful as it would be to have him home for the holidays, Mary Beth felt a pang of anxiety, knowing he would not be the same young man who had walked out their front door in August. Her friends had warned her to expect changes: more maturity, a new independence, perhaps frustration or annoyance if they expected him to follow the old household rules that had not bound him at college. Mary Beth would not mind any of that. What she feared to find in her son was a new despondency, insecurity, self-doubt.

He needed rest and unconditional love. The latter she would gladly give, but although he would have weekends as well as Christmas Eve and Christmas, New Year's Day, and the interim free, he would spend the rest of his semester break working off his debt at Elm Creek Manor. Although camp was not in session in the winter, Sylvia and her caretaker, Matt McClure, had assured her that there were plenty of other projects that needed attention on the estate. Privately Diane had told Mary Beth that Matt had fairly routine maintenance in mind, and Brent could expect to be very well fed at lunchtime, but Mary Beth still had misgivings.

"It'll be good for him," Roger assured her. "He'll feel better after he's paid his debt to society."

"You make him sound like a hardened criminal," Mary Beth said, choking up, but she admitted Roger made a fair point.

She longed to accompany her husband when he drove down to Penn State to collect their son, but she had promised to help with the Good Shepherd Christmas Boutique, and the first day of the sale conflicted with the trip. And she could not shirk her duties, she told herself firmly as she pulled into the parking lot next to a red SUV she recognized as Nancy Reinhart's despite the thin blanket of snow that had accumulated on the roof and the hood. Someone had shoveled the parking lot earlier, but evidence of the work was steadily disappearing.

Shivering, she set the parking brake, climbed out of her car, and carefully made her way to the church's side entrance that the custodian always left unlocked for the committee. Inside, she wiped her feet on the mat and shook snow from her hair and coat before joining the rest of the committee in the small meeting room just off the main vestibule. She returned Nancy's nod of welcome and took a seat, exchanging brief greetings with the other women and the lone man on the committee. She was not the last to arrive; she had just settled in with her notepad and pen when Melanie Tibbs hurried in, breathless and red-cheeked. "It's getting bad out there already," she said, shrugging out of her coat but leaving her red wool scarf in place.

"Then we'll keep this brief and to the point," said Nancy, and she called the meeting to order.

They took care of the most essential items on the agenda first: documents that needed official signatures, pending issues that required a vote in quorum. Chairs of various subcommittees spoke next, presenting their reports efficiently since no one wanted to prolong the meeting with questions that could be addressed just as easily via email later. The snow continued to fall thick and fast outside the window, and sudden, strong gusts of wind whistled in the eaves and made the old building shudder.

It was all very distracting, but Mary Beth's attention snapped into focus when the agenda came to the Christmas Boutique. "Everything's coming together beautifully," said Nancy, with great satisfaction, "better than any year in recent memory. Contributions are up, and our volunteer list is nearly full."

"If you still need anyone to take extra shifts, I can manage a few any time Thursday for setup, and for sales or food service Friday and Saturday morning," said Mary Beth, torn between wanting to help and needing to spend as much time as possible with her son.

Nancy smiled. "Thanks, Mary Beth, but our only openings are when you're already scheduled, a consequence of your signing

up for more shifts than anyone else." The others smiled indul-
gently at her.

They were so friendly and kind, one would think they knew
nothing of her family's troubles, of her failures as a mother. "If
anything opens up, let me know," she said. If she could atone for
what she had done and do everything right in the future, perhaps
eventually everyone truly would forgive and forget. All she had
to do was be extremely careful to make no more serious mistakes.

Next, as chair of the environmental-impact subcommittee,
Melanie reported that the church's efforts to conserve energy and
to be more environmentally conscious were yielding promising
results. As an aside, and with a wary glance to the window, she
added, "Since most church events will be canceled due to the
storm, before we leave, we should be sure to turn out all the lights
in the community hall and set the thermostat a few degrees lower.
That'll keep the building sufficiently warm without overheating
empty rooms.

Everyone murmured agreement, and Nancy quickly moved on
through the rest of the agenda as the thick snowflakes fell ever
more swiftly past the window.

Concluding in haste, the committee members rose and began
pulling on their coats even as Nancy was adjourning the meeting. They hastened to the exit, warning one another to drive
carefully, especially when rounding that sharp curve on College
Avenue. Suddenly Melanie called out from the doorway, as a gust
of wind nearly slammed the heavy door closed upon her, "Oh, we
forgot—the community hall. The lights and the thermostat."

Mary Beth was at the back of the group, the farthest from
the exit. Atonement, she reminded herself, although her heart
thudded with dread when she glimpsed the scene beyond the
doorway and she realized just how much snow had accumu-

lated during the meeting. "I'll take care of it," she said over her shoulder as she turned back the way they had come.

Minutes counted, she realized, quickening her pace. She abandoned her plans to return her books to the library, but she absolutely had to stop at the grocery store before she headed home. Her boots echoed on the old wooden parquet floor as she entered the community hall and crossed to the adjacent corner where the control switches were located on the wall. Although the room was bare at the moment, in a few days it would be bright and bustling with dozens of market stands offering everything from handcrafted items and antique collectibles to baked goods and colorful jars of preserves. Her quilts would be among them, all three, now that she had her delft-blue thread to finish the Dove of Peace wall hanging. She hoped it brought in a tidy sum. Every dollar counted and would be put to good use by the food bank.

The grocery store would be mobbed, she thought ruefully, reaching for the switches and dials, turning down the lights and turning off the heat. If only she had started her errands earlier. But how could she have wrung another minute out of that already overscheduled, harried day?

She hurried from the hall and back down the corridor to the exit, gasping as she stepped outside and the full force of the wind struck her. Already drifts had begun to cover the ruts in the snow where the other committee members' cars had been parked. She hoped the weather cleared and the temperatures climbed out of their polar plunge before the Christmas Boutique opened. It would be very bad indeed for many struggling families throughout the Elm Creek Valley if anything prevented the fund-raiser from proceeding as planned.

# 3

## *Gretchen*

FOR NEARLY TWENTY-FOUR hours, snow fell and the wind howled. Safe and snug within the gray stone walls of Elm Creek Manor, Gretchen marveled at nature's fury and waited for the storm to pass. When the driving snowfall subsided, bitter arctic cold descended and dangerous wind chills kept the manor's residents indoors except for the most essential chores. Gretchen layered herself with turtlenecks and cardigans and passed the time binding a crib quilt she planned to donate to a children's charity, discussing plans for the upcoming quilt camp season with Sylvia, or reading by the fireplace while Joe studied woodworking plans. Everyone was content except for Sarah, who rested a hand on her abdomen and brooded, glancing out the windows and occasionally worrying aloud that the roads might not be cleared in time for Matt to return home on Friday evening.

"He'll make it," Gretchen assured her on Wednesday afternoon as she, Sarah, Anna, and Sylvia kept warm in the parlor, where a fire popped and sparked cheeringly on the hearth. "It's bitterly cold, but the storm is over and the snowplows are out in force. Take a deep breath, relax, and think cheerful thoughts. That's best for baby."

"Find some work to distract yourself," Sylvia urged. "What about your new marketing campaign for quilt camp?"

"I finished that yesterday." Sarah sighed and paced the room a bit awkwardly, a hand pressed to her lower back. "I still have to finish the binding on my Christmas gift for Matt's father. I admit I haven't felt inspired to work on it lately."

Gretchen and Sylvia exchanged a look. Sarah's waning interest was perfectly understandable, considering that her father-in-law was responsible for Matt's absence. "I'll get it for you," said Gretchen, setting her own quilt aside. "Where is it? In your bedroom?"

Sarah nodded, but before Gretchen could rise, Anna bounded to her feet. "I'll go. I need to stretch my legs. And after that, I'll make us a batch of mulled cider. That will warm us up nicely."

"Sounds perfect," said Sarah, sighing contentedly as she eased herself into a chair. Gretchen's gaze lingered on Anna as she hurried off on her errand. The young chef seemed restless, and little wonder, considering that she was snowbound at Elm Creek Manor for the second time in as many weeks. Earlier that morning she had joked, half seriously, that she ought to keep a suitcase full of spare clothes and necessities in one of the guest rooms. Sylvia had offered her room and board in the manor when she was hired, the same perk that Gretchen had eagerly accepted, but Anna had declined. Gretchen suspected that she cared less about her apartment in downtown Waterford than about her neighbor across the hall, Jeremy, a graduate student in history at Waterford College. He drove her back and forth to work almost every day even though it was considerably out of his way. Anna referred to him as her best friend, but it seemed to Gretchen that they had recently become much more to each other.

As the newest member of the faculty, Gretchen often felt as if she were still getting to know her colleagues, but in the weeks since she and Joe had come to Elm Creek Manor, she had gradually pieced together a good sense of their strong affinities and friendly rivalries. She barely knew Summer, who had participated in Gretchen's job interview but had left for graduate school at the University of Chicago only a few weeks after she and Joe moved in. Back then, Summer and Jeremy were a couple, and before that they had briefly lived together until a disagreement of some sort had compelled Summer to move out of Jeremy's apartment. Gretchen was not sure how any young couple could rebound and resume a normal dating relationship after living together, but she had seen couples with extraordinary devotion overcome even greater obstacles. For a while, Summer and Jeremy had apparently given it a try, and yet it was evident even to a newcomer like Gretchen that their relationship had become tenuous. It also seemed clear that while the course toward their inevitable breakup may have been set months before, Summer's departure had moved them into a swifter current.

From what Gretchen had observed, it seemed that they had drifted on inexorably until the Thanksgiving holidays, when, amid the fury of a nor'easter and the confusion of canceled travel plans, their romance had finally run aground. And what of Anna, who described Jeremy as her best friend so often and so emphatically that anyone who was paying attention would immediately guess that somewhere along the way, she had fallen in love with him?

Anna would have been a terrible poker player. Gretchen only had to see her smiling and laughing whenever she and Jeremy were together to know she felt much more for him than friendship. Gretchen strongly suspected the feeling was mutual, but Anna and Jeremy were kindhearted and loyal, and neither would have acknowledged an attraction while one of them was involved with someone else. But if Jeremy was single, Anna's restlessness and distraction could mean that she had finally confessed the truth to him. Her eagerness to get home to her apartment suggested that her confession—if there had been one, if Gretchen's romantic imagination was not spurring her to jump to the wrong conclusions—had been warmly received.

When Anna returned to the parlor a few minutes later to deliver Sarah's unfinished quilt and sewing basket, there was a smile on her lips and a flush in her cheeks. Gretchen suspected she had squeezed in a quick phone call to her favorite neighbor on her way upstairs, but of course she would not tease her by saying so. Until Anna brought her burgeoning romance, if that's what it was, out into the open, her secrets were safe with Gretchen.

After seeing Sarah comfortably settled with her work-in-progress, Anna left again but soon returned with a tray of steaming mugs of mulled cider. "Thank you, Anna," said Gretchen, accepting a cup, inhaling deeply the fragrance of cinnamon, anise, nutmeg, cloves, and orange. The first sip was heavenly, the second sublime. "Delicious," she proclaimed. "I could definitely get used to being spoiled like this."

"That's our plan," said Sylvia. "We're delighted to have you here and we hope you never resign—until you and Joe decide to retire, of course."

"But if your retirement looks anything like Sylvia's, you'll be almost as busy as before," said Sarah with a smile, the tension around her eyes relenting for a moment.

"If you keep pampering me like this, I'll be good for another twenty years," said Gretchen. Her new friends laughingly assured her that they were counting on it.

How wonderful if it could be so.

Joining the Elm Creek Quilters had already proven to be a dream come true. A year before, Gretchen never could have imagined herself thriving, able to teach, quilt, and enjoy the work that she loved without worrying about overdue bills and unknown calamities lurking just around the corner. She and Joe had a beautiful new home at Elm Creek Manor, and Joe had set up a workshop in the barn so he could continue his wood-working and furniture restoration, as much a form of artistic expression for him as Gretchen's quilting was for her. In all her life, she had never felt so prosperous, blessed by the riches of good health, fulfilling work, and precious new friendships.

How far she had come from where her immigrant forebears had begun only two generations before.

When Gretchen's grandmother first came to America from Croatia in search of a brighter future, she lived with a cousin's family and worked at a butcher shop in the Strip District in Pittsburgh. Because Marija was pretty, tidy, and good with sums, she was often assigned to ride along on deliveries to the fine houses in Sewickley on the other side of the river. On one occasion a wealthy matron sized her up as a quiet, industrious girl and hired her to replace her second housemaid, whom she had recently fired for theft. The work was hard, but no more so than at the butcher's, and in the Albrechts' house, Marija had her own bed in a small, third-floor room she shared with the other housemaid.

Years later she married the butcher's teamster, the same hand-some Polish immigrant who had shown her all around Pittsburgh on their delivery route. To help make ends meet, she continued to work for the Albrechts until well into her first pregnancy. Years passed, and when her own children were old enough, Marija re-turned to work as a housekeeper for her original employer's daugh-ter, now married with a baby of her own. Marija's eldest daughter left school after the eighth grade to work alongside her, eventu-ally taking over her position when the arduous labor became too difficult. Marija's daughter had married a steelworker and moved into a small house on a hill in Ambridge, where Gretchen was born a year later.

Gretchen was only twelve years old when she earned her first wages minding the Albrechts' six-year-old daughter, Heidi, after school and during summer vacation. It was clear from Mrs. Albrecht's occasional offhand remarks that she assumed Gretchen would enter domestic service like her mother and grandmother before her, and that when Heidi married and started a family of her own, Gretchen would serve in her household. Gretchen had other plans. She was a bright, diligent student, and when she confided to her parents that she wanted to become a teacher, they urged her to save every dollar she earned for her college fund, and they would make up the difference.

At eighteen, she graduated from high school and won a partial scholarship to Margaret Morrison Carnegie College, where she majored in elementary education. Two years into her program, she discovered much to her surprise that her home economics courses were among her favorites. She already knew how to sew, but now she learned to design stylish garments for a fraction of what a similar outfit would cost at the department store. She also enjoyed the creative outlet her quilting class provided. The instructor, Sylvia Compson, an alumna of the college's art education program, spiced her lectures about patterns and stitches with stories of the etymology of quilt block names, the role of the quilting bee in the lives of early American women, and commemorative quilts that promoted justice and social change. Gretchen took to quilting with a passion, ignoring the good-natured teasing of some of her more sophisticated friends, who disdained sewing as an old-fashioned pastime one resorted to out of necessity rather than pleasure, an unwelcome reminder of the limitations of their mothers' and grandmothers' lives.

But quilting was not Gretchen's only passion. By the time she finished her first course with Sylvia Compson, she had fallen head over heels in love with Joe Hartley, a handsome young man she had met at church. He was a machinist at one of the steel mills, a wonderful dancer, polite and respectful to her parents but lively and fun when they were out with friends. He wanted to marry her right away but they agreed to wait until she had earned her degree and had taught for a few years. Sometimes, though, after he walked her home and they had to tear themselves away from each other, breathless and dizzy from fervent kisses, Gretchen considered abandoning her education and marrying him that very night, because the wait seemed unendurable when he held her in his arms.

Leaving college to marry was never more than a fleeting temptation, of course, for she was determined to achieve her goal. In time she earned her degree, found a job teaching at a Catholic primary school, and married Joe in the same church where they had met. Her salary was modest, and Joe took on as much overtime at the steel mill as permitted, but they often found themselves coming up short at the end of the month. Although Joe didn't like it, when that happened, she accepted housekeeping work with the Albrechts to make ends meet. What choice did she have? She and Joe were frugal, but every time they built up a modest savings, the furnace went out or the car broke down or the roof needed to be repaired. So they found their happiness in simple pleasures, and as they gradually saved for their future, which they hoped would include children, they remained hopeful that more prosperous times would come along.

Their dreams were shattered one dreadful morning when the principal came to Gretchen's classroom and gravely informed her that the steel mill foreman had phoned with terrible news. Joe had been rushed to Allegheny General Hospital after a support beam had fallen and pinned him to the floor. His back was broken and he was not expected to live.

Gretchen refused to believe it. Closing her ears to the doctors' warnings that she must prepare herself for the worst, she sat by Joe's bedside and held his hand, alternating between silent prayers and gently spoken reminiscences of their happiest moments together. She knew that if he heard her voice, he would come back to her, no matter how far away he had drifted.

When he survived that first night and regained consciousness the next morning, Gretchen would not allow the doctors' grim predictions to dispel her hopes. When the doctors told Joe he would never walk again, Joe fixed them with a stubborn, steely look until their voices trailed off weakly. Gretchen knew then that he was determined to prove them wrong.

In the long, slow, painful months of his recovery, Gretchen quit her job so she could stay home to care for him. Their modest savings quickly disappeared, but she made ends meet on a small monthly stipend from his union. When that too fell short, she ignored Joe's protests and sought work with Heidi Albrecht, who hired her on the spot as a housecleaner.

Gretchen knew Joe blamed himself for the misfortune that had forced her to give up teaching, which she loved, for dull, exhausting labor in the home of a privileged young woman who felt entitled to her loyal service, thanks to their families' intertwined history, but she never blamed him. It was an accident of fate, no one's fault, but he refused to see it that way. He resolved to regain his mobility and reclaim his old job so she could quit hers.

Within months he could sit up in bed unassisted. Soon he could move from the bed to the chair on his own, and within a year, he could stand. But although Joe defied his doctors' expectations and learned to walk again, he never fully recovered his old strength, and an accidental jolt could make him grimace from pain. Eventually he had no choice but to abandon his plans to return to his old job, his old life. Since he no longer needed her constant attention, Gretchen found a new job as a substitute teacher, and while it was not steady work, it helped pay off some debts and got her out of the house.

Throughout those difficult years, quilting was her solace and escape. She quilted to add beauty to her life, to give purpose to her hours, to distract her from the unfairness of fate, to bind herself to her unknown foremothers who had suffered greater hardships than she had ever borne. Joe often read aloud to her while she sewed. His voice, as strong and deep as before the accident, comforted her, helping her to forget their shabby furniture, her made-over dresses, the diminishment of their expectations. Her scrap quilts brought warmth and beauty into their home, allowing them to turn the thermostat a little lower or to conceal a sagging mattress and threadbare sofa cushions.

In time, impressed by Gretchen's resolve and intrigued by the solace she found in creating objects of comfort and beauty, Joe took up restoring old furniture when, on his daily walk around the neighborhood, he happened upon a discarded antique rocking chair, brought it home, repaired it, and sold it for twenty dollars. Next he restored a bureau and matching chest he had purchased for a few dollars at a yard sale, and sold both for a fifty-dollar profit. Within months, neighbors and strangers alike were stopping by at all hours of the day to browse through the finished pieces on display or to schedule an appointment to drop off worn or damaged furniture for him to refurbish. Eventually Joe made a sign and hung it above the garage door: JOSEPH HARTLEY: FINE FURNITURE REPAIRED AND RESTORED. He worked when he felt able, rested when the strain on his back and legs required. He taught himself cabinetmaking and woodworking from library books and soon began designing and building his own original pieces. An antiques shop in downtown Sewickley began selling his wares on commission, and after the *Pittsburgh Post-Gazette* ran a half-page article on him, customers from as far away as Harris-burg ordered custom-made pieces.

"What a fine pair of artists we are," Gretchen liked to tease him.

"Starving artists," Joe teased back, but it wasn't far from the truth. Even so, they enjoyed a rich, rewarding life. They had each other, and many dear and loyal friends, and fulfilling work that paid the bills, at least most of the time. They were active in their church and shared their time and talents with the community.

And although they were never blessed with children, many children came into their lives nonetheless.

As Joe's reputation as a master woodworker grew, he took on as many commissions as he could handle, but he set everything aside when Gretchen's grandmother made a special request. Her church, a Croatian parish in Pittsburgh, needed a skilled restorer to repair ornate cabinetry in the sacristy, someone who knew how to properly care for the old wood but wouldn't cost them a fortune. Joe promptly accepted the job pro bono, delighting Gretchen's grandmother. "You married a treasure," she exclaimed, patting Gretchen's arm.

"So he tells me," she replied, giving her husband a sidelong smile.

The repairs in the sacristy of Holy Family Catholic Church took Joe several weeks, and whenever Gretchen had a day off from teaching, she would spend the morning with her grand-mother and bring Joe a sack lunch to share at noon. One day, when the restoration was nearly complete, the pastor remarked that he knew of another worthy organization that could benefit from his talents. "They won't be able to pay," he admitted, "but you're a faithful steward of your talents, and I think you'll find the work has other rewards."

Joe agreed to accompany Monsignor Paul to the other site a few blocks away, and Gretchen tagged along, curious.

As they left her grandmother's neighborhood behind, the small but well-kept bungalows gave way to row houses in disrepair— broken windows, trash in the gutters, graffiti on walls and telephone poles, crumbling stoops leading to front doors boarded up with plywood. The monsignor led them to a three-story Victorian house with peeling paint and a front yard entirely taken up by a vegetable garden and a rusty swing set. An elderly man and a woman a few years younger than Gretchen browsed at two card tables set up in the driveway, one stacked with canned goods, the other with used clothing. A neat, hand-painted sign near the entrance announced that they had arrived at Abiding Savior Christian Outreach.

When the monsignor knocked on the front door, a barrel-chested, dark-skinned man wearing a brightly colored tunic opened the door and welcomed them with a broad smile. "This is the man I told you about," Monsignor Paul said, resting his hand on Joe's shoulder. "Joe Hartley, the carpenter who's restoring our sacristy so beautifully. This is his wife, Gretchen. Gretchen and Joe, I'd like you to meet Louis Walker, my good friend and a true servant of Christ."

"I'm glad you can help us," said Louis in a rich baritone flavored with a southern accent. After shaking their hands, he beckoned them to follow him inside, into a small front room with shabby sofas and chairs lining the walls and a table covered in parenting magazines in the center. Upstairs an infant squalled, and from somewhere nearby came the voices of young women engaged in heated conversation punctuated by laughter. The floorboards creaked beneath worn carpeting as Gretchen trailed after the men, past a dining room with a long table set with at least a dozen mismatched chairs and into a kitchen where the smells of fried chicken, scorched oil, and boiled greens lingered in the air.

The tour halted there, and the project requiring Joe's talents was immediately apparent: well-used but poorly constructed cabinetry. Even Gretchen's inexpert eye noted that the doors were too large and banged into each other rather than closing properly. Joe tested one and could open it only a third of the way because the hinges had been set too far from the edge. Gretchen lingered in the doorway as Louis and Joe discussed the project and the priest looked on in satisfaction. At the sound of voices, she scooted out of the way just as three teenage girls, two in the last trimester of pregnancy, one carrying an infant, burst into the kitchen, chatting and teasing one another. Their demeanor became more reserved at the sight of the priest, whom they greeted respectfully, but they bantered cheerfully with Louis as they filled glasses of water at the sink and he queried them about their homework.

As the girls finished their drinks and darted off again, Gretchen realized that Abiding Savior Christian Outreach was a home for girls in trouble, as her grandmother would have phrased it. She wondered where the girls' parents and the fathers of their children were.

While Louis and the monsignor discussed seeking donations of new hinges from a parishioner who owned a hardware store, Joe raised his eyebrows in a silent question to Gretchen. She replied with the barest nod. Of course he must complete the repairs, and not charge a dime for materials or labor. These girls needed a safe, comfortable, functioning home, and Joe would never refuse to help someone in need.

After Joe and Louis worked out the details, Louis gave Joe and Gretchen an appraising look, read the unasked questions in their faces, and explained that he and his wife, Andrea, ran a shelter for homeless girls who were pregnant or had recently given birth. Six girls lived there presently, but they averaged about ten. The most he and his wife had ever cared for at one time was the maximum the house could fit, twenty. "Most of our girls come from Pitts-burgh," he said, "but some run away to the city from small towns in Ohio and western Pennsylvania after their parents throw them out. When they end up on the streets, homeless folks and shelter workers know to send them our way."

"Their parents throw them out?" echoed Gretchen, shocked. "So young, and—and in their condition?"

"A pregnant, unmarried daughter is a bitter disappointment to some families," said Louis. "Their anger gets the better of them and they think throwing the girl out is a suitable punishment. Teach her a lesson."

"What lesson is that?" asked Joe, appalled.

Louis shrugged. "If they break the rules and shame the family, it won't be under their roof. Sometimes homeless girls get preg-nant. Sometimes pregnant girls get homeless."

Gretchen, who longed for a child of her own, could not imag-ine throwing a precious daughter and unborn grandchild out into the world. Family was family, and compassion must always rise above anger.

Sometimes the world seemed broken beyond repair.

The project stretched out over several weeks, since Joe tended his own business in the mornings before heading over to Abiding Savior by mid-afternoon. After Joe mentioned that Gretchen was a home economics teacher, Louis asked if she would teach the girls skills that could help them tend their babies as well as themselves after they left the shelter. And so Gretchen began volunteering at the mission, showing the young mothers and mothers-to-be how to prepare simple, nutritious meals, how to do laundry, how to keep a house clean and safe for a toddler, how to keep a household budget and balance a bank account—something a few of the girls claimed they would never need to know. Unlike her, they would never have enough cash to open a bank account, never enough left over at the end of the month to save.

"Is that what you think?" said Gretchen. "When I was your age, and even younger, very few people imagined a better life for me than to become a housemaid just like my mother and grandmother, but I worked hard in school and earned a scholarship to college, and now I'm a teacher."

"We can't go to school after we have our babies," retorted the smallest of the girls, a fifteen-year-old who wore her hair in tight cornrows with red beads on the end.

"You can find a way," Gretchen said firmly. "Your first duty is to your child, but if you work hard, live frugally, and save, you can make a better life for yourself. I can't do it for you, but I can give you the tools you'll need—and that means learning to balance a checkbook, even if you don't have a bank account yet, because someday you will."

The girls still looked dubious, but they settled down to their studies, and in some of their eyes, Gretchen thought she glimpsed the light of possibility dawning. "A steady job cleaning houses sounds pretty good to me," said one seventeen-year-old with a sigh, absently stroking the head of the baby slumbering peacefully on her lap.

"It is good," Gretchen quickly agreed, chagrined. How thoughtless of her not to realize that the humble fate she had been so determined to rise above could seem to other young women a life to aspire to. For those who had not been blessed with the advantages of a loving home and an education, her starting point was an impossibly distant destination they might reach after a lifetime of struggle.

Education was the key to crossing that vast distance.

As part of her lessons, Gretchen also taught the girls to sew, for she believed every mother needed to know how to sew on buttons, let down hems, and mend torn seams. Most of the girls had never held a needle, so to practice and perfect their stitches, they worked on small, scrap Four-Patch quilts for their babies. Even the girls most ambivalent about motherhood warmed to the project, and as they sewed squares of cotton and poly blends together, they spoke about their hopes and fears for the future. How different their lives were from those of the students Gretchen met as a substitute teacher, girls who were, for the most part, happy and well adjusted, with plenty to eat, decent clothes to wear, and a caring adult at home to love and guide them. And yet she knew that some of the residents of Abiding Savior had enjoyed comfortable, secure, middle-class lives before they had ended up on the streets. Who among the girls who attended her classes and always turned in their homework, she wondered, felt unloved at home and contemplated escape by running away, or sought comfort in a boyfriend's arms?

As the years passed, Gretchen taught an ever-changing group of young women domestic skills and held their newborn babies when they were desperate for a few uninterrupted hours of sleep. Often, frightened and alone when the first labor pains began, they begged Gretchen to come with them to the hospital and stay with them until it was over. So it was that, although she never bore a child of her own, she was granted the great privilege of welcoming many newborns into the world and caring for youngsters who needed every bit of love she had to offer.

Over time, their experiences at Abiding Savior reminded Gretchen and Joe of how richly they had been blessed despite the hardships they had faced, and the hope and optimism of their newlywed years were renewed. Gretchen began teaching quilting to neighborhood girls, and then to their mothers, and then to their mothers' friends, and eventually she founded a quilt guild.

She traveled to other guilds in Ohio, West Virginia, and throughout Pennsylvania to lecture and teach, all the while nurturing a dream to open her own quilt shop. When she was unable to secure a business loan, she agreed to partner with Heidi Albrecht, who had the funds to make Gretchen's business plan a reality.

Their shop, Quilts 'n Things, soon became the most successful quilt shop in the region. They enjoyed a long, successful run until Heidi's controlling behavior and determination to take credit for all of Gretchen's ideas ruined everything. Heidi's ongoing, casually cruel reminders that Gretchen was only a junior partner and her former cleaning lady—spoken in a joking manner in front of customers as well as when they were alone—made Gretchen dread going to work. Just as she was wondering how she could keep her chin up and make the best of it until she could afford to retire, she spotted an intriguing ad in a quilting magazine: Elm Creek Quilts was seeking two experienced teachers to join their elite faculty.

What a dream job that would be, Gretchen thought wistfully, and how wonderful for Joe, who often spoke of retiring to the country, where he could have space for a larger workshop, plenty of fresh air, and a perfect creek for fishing. The more she mulled over whether she should apply, the more she realized that the job had come along at precisely the right time, as if it were an answer to her prayers. And so she mailed off her application packet, traveled to Elm Creek Manor for an interview and tour, and waited anxiously for their decision. It was not long before Sarah called to offer her the job.

Gretchen was thrilled, and Joe almost burst with pride, but as eager as they were to embark on their new adventure, it was difficult to leave behind their longtime neighbors, dear friends, and the people they had met through Abiding Savior. When it came time to say goodbye to Louis and Andrea, Gretchen embraced them both and promised that she would still make quilts for their residents, as she had done for years.

To her astonishment, Louis refused. "Your former quilt guild has volunteered to provide us with as many quilts as we could ever need," he explained. "I'm sure you'll find a worthy cause in your new community that needs your gifts—both material and of the spirit. If you don't find them, they'll find you."

His words soon proved prescient.

Gretchen found a worthy cause for the gifts of her needle— Project Linus, a nonprofit that provided quilts and blankets to children in need, from offering a comforting quilt to a seriously ill child at a hospital to providing a warm blanket to a youngster rescued by the fire department. A few days after Thanksgiving, she had persuaded Sylvia to make Elm Creek Manor an official collection site for local quilters, knitters, and crocheters. And then there was Sarah, a young expectant mother who had suddenly found herself in great need of reassurance and care.

"You're not alone," Gretchen had told her when Sarah tearfully confided how much she regretted Matt's decision to spend most of the winter far from home, how anxious and fearful his absence made her feel. "Agnes has been beside herself wanting to help you decorate the nursery; she would have offered before but she didn't want to intrude. Joe can childproof the manor; he's brought far more treacherous buildings than this up to code. And as for your childbirth classes, I know it's best to have your husband along, but if Matt can't be there, I'll go with you."

"You would? You'd do that for me?"

"Of course." Gretchen had accompanied frightened girls little more than half Sarah's age through the birthing process and had witnessed nearly every possible complication. She knew what to do. "I'm not as handsome as Matt, but I'm far more experienced, and I promise you, you'll be in good hands."

*    *    *

ALTHOUGH THE BITTER cold lingered, the roads were cleared in time for Jeremy to pick up Anna on Wednesday afternoon and take her home. "Not that I haven't enjoyed our extended slumber party," Anna said as she threw on her coat and snatched up her purse, "but, well . . ." She gestured to the back door, where Jeremy waited, and dashed off.

Later that evening, although the winds had picked up, blowing drifts over the road through the woods between the manor and the highway, Gretchen borrowed the Elm Creek Quilts minivan and escorted Sarah to her childbirth class. As they drove to the Elm Creek Valley Hospital, they observed that shopkeepers and apartment superintendents had cleared sidewalks and parking garages in downtown Waterford, and that heavy trucks had hauled countless loads of snow to outlying fields so the eventual thaw would not flood the city streets. In a quiet, comfortable room in the hospital, as they were setting up Sarah's pillows and yoga mat for a lesson on breathing and relaxation techniques, they overheard alarming reports of how other regions of the Elm Creek Valley had weathered the storm. Some neighborhoods were still without electricity after wind-toppled trees had brought down power lines; frozen pipes had burst in a building south of the Waterford College campus, flooding adjacent streets until they were coated in a solid sheet of ice. "We were fortunate," said Gretchen, and Sarah nodded, wide-eyed. They had been cut off from town for a couple of days, but at least they'd had light and heat.

By Friday afternoon, the sun had emerged and the temperatures had risen slightly, easing Sarah's worries about Matt's long drive home. Later that evening, at the sound of his pickup truck pulling into the rear parking lot, Sarah sighed with relief and hurried to greet him. Gretchen and Sylvia broke off their conversation and watched through the kitchen doorway as Matt greeted her at the back door with a hug and a kiss, and then he dropped to his knees and pressed his cheek against her ample belly to tell the babies how much he had missed them.

Sarah had mentioned that she wanted Matt to help her paint the babies' room on Saturday, but by the end of the day, not a single stroke of Sunshine Yellow had been applied to the walls. "He's exhausted from the week on the construction site in the cold," Sarah explained to Sylvia and Gretchen as they tidied the kitchen after supper, although neither of them had said a word of rebuke. "He had to fit a week's worth of his caretaker's duties into the day too, and now all he wants to do is relax. Who could blame him?"

Joe could, Gretchen thought, but she merely murmured something noncommittal and continued wiping down the counters. "Matt has no business taking off when his wife's expecting his babies," he had told her privately just the day before. One quick exchange of glances with Sylvia told her that Andrew had made similar remarks behind closed doors.

On Sunday Matt helped decorate the manor for Christmas, which seemed to restore Sarah's naturally cheerful spirits. That evening, the manor's six year-round residents enjoyed a family-style supper around the long wooden table in the kitchen, but when Sarah offered everyone dessert and coffee, Matt begged off so that he could do laundry and pack his duffel bag. "More cake for us, then," said Sarah lightly, but as soon as Matt left the room, her smile faded.

On Monday morning he left shortly after breakfast. "This week won't be as bad as the last," Sarah said forlornly, watching through the back window as his truck rumbled across the bridge over Elm Creek. "I'll get used to his absence. Each week I'll feel a little less lonely."

"You shouldn't feel lonely," Gretchen said. "Matt's just a phone call away if you need to hear his voice, and you have plenty of company."

"Yes, indeed, dear," said Sylvia, passing by Sarah's booth to pat her affectionately on the shoulder. "How could you be lonely when you're surrounded by such marvelous friends?"

Sarah managed a smile. "You're right. Anyway, I should be grateful for a few quiet moments to myself. Once the babies come, I might not have another until they leave for college."

As if to prove her point, a cell phone rang.

Sarah sat up with a start and reached into her right sweater pocket for the phone, but its screen was dark. Sighing, she set it on the table and quickly retrieved a second phone from her left pocket—vibrating, screen alight—and pressed the button to answer. "Good morning, Elm Creek Quilts," she said, her voice warmly professional.

Instinctively, Gretchen and Sylvia drew closer in case this un-expected bit of camp business required their attention.

"Oh, hello, Nancy." Looking to her friends, Sarah mouthed the last name silently—*Reinhart.* Gretchen needed a moment to re-call a woman she had met briefly at the last farewell breakfast of the camp season in August. She was the president of the Water-ford Quilting Guild, if Gretchen's memory served. "We made it through the storm just fine, thanks, but we're not eager for the next one. How are you?" Sarah's eyebrows rose. "That sounds ominous. What do you mean?" Another pause. "Oh. In that case, you're welcome to come by anytime." She glanced at the clock on the wall. "Twenty minutes? Sure, that's fine. We'll be here. See you soon." She hung up the phone.

"What's going on?" asked Sylvia, taking a seat in the booth across from Sarah. "It sounds urgent."

"Apparently so. Nancy called it a minor emergency, but from the strain in her voice, it sounds more serious than that. She and a friend want to discuss it with us right away, but not over the phone." Sarah glanced at the clock again and winced. "We have twenty minutes. Anna could put together a banquet in that time, but we're on our own."

"I'll get coffee started," said Gretchen, rising. "We have some of Anna's marvelous cinnamon shortbread left. That should do nicely."

"That's our Anna, looking after us even from afar." Sylvia rose and went to the walk-in pantry. "Did Nancy mention her friend's name?"

"Melanie Tibbs, I think? I don't believe I know her."

Sylvia emerged from the pantry carrying a cookie tin and wearing a thoughtful frown. "I knew a Dolores Tibbs, but that was decades ago. She was a friend of my mother, a librarian and one of the four founders of the Waterford Quilting Guild."

"Melanie could be her daughter," said Gretchen, placing a filter into the basket and quickly filling it with scoops of coffee grounds.

"A granddaughter, more likely. Perhaps they need to see us about a quilting emergency of some sort."

"A quilting emergency?" echoed Gretchen, amused.

Sylvia nodded. "You'd be surprised how often they occur around here."

"Whatever it is," said Sarah, climbing awkwardly from the booth and resting a hand on the table for balance, "Elm Creek Quilts must be uniquely qualified to help, or Nancy would have enlisted the Waterford Quilting Guild instead."

They mulled over the possibilities as they went to the banquet hall to set up a table and chairs. Working swiftly, their motions deft and perfectly timed, thanks to many hours spent preparing for quilt camp meals, they placed a cheerful red-and-green-tartan cloth over one of the round tables, arranged chairs all around, and set the table. Sarah had just carried in two plates of cinnamon shortbread while Gretchen followed behind with the coffee service on a tray when the back doorbell rang. Sylvia answered, and by the time she led their two guests into the room, everything was in place.

"Anna would be proud of us," Sarah murmured to Gretchen as they went forward to meet their guests.

"She's taught us well," Gretchen murmured back.

Sylvia made introductions, but while Nancy and Melanie were perfectly cordial, their smiles seemed a bit forced, their expressions strained. Nancy was the elder of the two, in her mid-fifties, with strong, angular features and salt-and-pepper hair cut in an asymmetrical curve that began at her right earlobe and swooped to a point just below her jawline on the left. Melanie was taller and slender, perhaps ten years younger than her companion. She kept her scarf on though bits of snow clung to it, as she no sooner tucked strands of her thick, wavy brown hair behind her ears than they slipped free again.

Sylvia invited everyone to be seated, and Sarah poured coffee while Gretchen invited their guests to help themselves to shortbread. Melanie flashed a quick smile and took a cookie, but Nancy kept to black coffee. Through a bit of small talk as they settled in, Gretchen noticed the two visitors glancing around the banquet hall appraisingly, noting the ample space; the convenient butler's pantry; the floor-to-ceiling window on the western wall; and the two sets of double doors, one leading to the ballroom and the other to the front foyer.

It occurred to Gretchen that they were studying the banquet hall rather purposefully, especially since Nancy had seen it fairly recently, on her tour in August. When she and Melanie exchanged significant, hopeful looks, Gretchen suspected that their emergency required Elm Creek Manor itself as well as the quilters who lived and worked there.

"Thank you for allowing us to impose on you on such short notice," said Nancy, her alto voice firm and calm, as if she were accustomed to taking command in a crisis.

"It's no imposition, but you've certainly piqued our curiosity," said Sylvia. "Please tell us what's wrong and how we can help."

"Melanie and I serve on the facilities committee at Good Shepherd Church," Nancy began. "We're also in charge of the Christmas Boutique. As you must be aware, Sylvia, given that you've been so generous with your donations through the years, the event is our annual fund-raiser for the county food bank."

"Your most important fund-raiser," Sylvia added. "Are donations not keeping pace with previous years'? I'm sure the storm accounts for that. I myself have a quilt upstairs that I made especially for the boutique. I just haven't managed to drop it off yet."

"I have a crib quilt to donate as well," said Gretchen. "Anna, our chef, also plans to contribute some baked goods."

"If they're as tasty as this shortbread, we'll rake in a fortune," said Melanie, helping herself to another piece.

"We'll gladly accept your donations," said Nancy. "I can take them with me today, to save you a trip. But that isn't the emergency I referred to on the phone."

"Although the storm accounts for that too," said Melanie, a tremor in her voice. "But really, it's my fault."

"How is it your fault?" Nancy protested.

"I'm chair of the environmental impact subcommittee. I should have taken care of the lights and the thermostat myself."

"Oh, goodness. Asking someone to turn off the lights and set the thermostat for you is hardly abandoning your responsibilities. If it's anyone's fault, it's—" Nancy shook her head. "Let's not place blame. The point is, our committee met right before the storm struck, and since activities for the next few days had been canceled, Melanie asked the last person to leave to turn off the lights and set the thermostat a few degrees lower in the community hall."

"Just a few degrees," Melanie lamented. "Sixty-four instead of sixty-eight, that's all I meant."

"Let me guess." Sarah sat back in her chair and rested a hand on her abdomen. "That person, who shall remain nameless, instead turned off the heat entirely, as well as the lights?"

"I'm afraid that's so."

"Oh, my," said Gretchen, thinking back to several occasions when the ancient furnace at Abiding Savior had not been able to keep up with the bitter cold of deepest winter. She could imagine the worst.

"The pipes froze and burst," said Melanie. "The community hall was flooded, but since the church was closed and everyone was snowbound, no one realized it until two days later."

Sylvia pursed her mouth and drew in a breath as if to steel herself. "Were the donations for the Christmas Boutique ruined?"

"No, we were spared that, at least," said Nancy. "Only about half of the items we were promised had been dropped off by then, and they were safely out of reach in a storage closet on the second floor. I'm afraid the damage is to the hall itself."

"Wood flooring?" Gretchen guessed.

Nancy nodded. "Mid-century parquet, warped from one end of the hall to the other."

"It looks like it's frozen in waves more than a foot high," said Melanie. "I didn't know a floor could do that."

Gretchen knew it all too well. "It'll have to be torn up and replaced, and the joists beneath it examined for rot. Is the church insured?"

When Nancy nodded again, the Elm Creek Quilters sighed with relief.

"The adjuster has already inspected the damage and approved payment on our claim, but the contractors can't fit us into their schedule until January," Nancy said. "In the meantime, the community hall is entirely unusable."

"The Christmas Boutique," exclaimed Sylvia. "Oh, dear. This *is* an emergency."

Nancy and Melanie nodded bleakly. "So," said Melanie, "after indulging in a minor panic for an hour or two, we thought of you."

"You shouldn't have wasted a moment in panic," said Sylvia. "I know what you're going to ask, and the answer is yes. We'd be delighted to host the Christmas Boutique at Elm Creek Manor. I insist."

"I knew you'd take us in!" Melanie clasped her hands together, eyes shining. "Thank you so much!"

"We have ample space, and camp isn't in session, so why not?" said Sarah. "It's been too quiet around here lately anyway."

"Think it over carefully before you jump in," said Nancy. "We have volunteers assigned to set up the merchandise, handle the sales, and clean up afterward, but keep in mind that there will be crowds of strangers passing through the manor all day long, Friday through Sunday."

Sylvia waved a hand. "We're used to that, but we prefer to call them visitors, not strangers. And let's hope they come in crowds. The more customers the better."

"That's true," said Nancy, "but the larger the crowds, the louder the noise and the bigger the mess."

Gretchen smiled. "I'd imagine that people inclined to support the local food pantry by shopping for homemade and handcrafted goods at a church fund-raiser would be a fairly well-behaved bunch."

"Nancy, what are you doing?" Melanie protested. "They already agreed. Don't talk them out of it."

"I think full disclosure is best." Turning to Sylvia, Nancy added, "As in the past, we'd like to sell refreshments, light meals and snacks, nothing too elaborate. Our volunteers will cook at home, but we'd need to use your kitchen for last-minute preparations, heating some items, keeping other things cold, and so on."

"I'll have to clear that with our chef, but I'm sure it won't be a problem," said Sylvia.

"The problem will be getting Anna to agree to keep it simple," said Sarah. "She may insist upon preparing a lavish holiday buffet."

Melanie's eyes went wide. "Do you think she would? My friends who've attended your quilt camp absolutely rave about the food. I'm thinking of pretending to be a quilter just so I can attend next summer."

"You don't have to pretend. Come to quilt camp and we'll teach you. In the meantime, let's pencil in a yes for use of the kitchen, and a maybe for the buffet. Unless Anna prefers something more à la carte." Sylvia rose and studied the room, turning slowly in place. "If she prefers a buffet, we can collect fees at the door and arrange the serving table along the west wall by the windows, as we do for quilt camp."

"That would work well," said Sarah, nodding.

"On the other hand, if Anna would rather offer counter service, we could use the butler's pantry. And let's be sure to set up all the tables and chairs, because as soon as the smell of Anna's cooking fills the air—" Sylvia broke off, laughing at herself. "Listen to me making plans when I haven't even asked her if she'll do it."

"I think it's a safe bet she will," said Gretchen.

"But . . ." Nancy too rose and looked around the room, wavering between relief and puzzlement. "If you fill this space with dining tables, where will we set up the boutique?"

"Not in here," said Sylvia, surprised. "Don't you remember your tour? I have something better in mind."

Beckoning to Nancy and Melanie to follow, Sylvia crossed the room and opened the double doors on the southern wall. Gretchen and Sarah brought up the rear as Sylvia led their bemused guests into the ballroom, which took up almost the entire first floor of the newer wing of the manor. A carpeted border roughly twenty feet wide encircled a broad parquet dance floor, most of which was subdivided into classrooms by tall, movable partitions. Three crystal chandeliers hung high above from a ceiling covered with a swirling vine pattern of molded plaster. A dais on the far side of the room served as a stage for teachers, lecturers, or performers during the camp season, but during the Christmas season it displayed a tall, verdant, fragrant evergreen tree adorned with the accumulated treasures of three generations of the Bergstrom family—ceramic figurines from Germany, sparkling crystal teardrops from New York City, carved wooden angels with woolen hair from Italy—as well as more recent contributions from Andrew and Sarah. Tall, narrow windows topped by semicircular curves lined the south, east, and west walls. The heavy drapes had been drawn back, and through the glass Gretchen saw a glittering shower of icy flakes swirling in a light wind. She felt a pang of alarm until she realized that the snow had simply blown off the roof, and not that a new storm had swept in while they were engrossed in conversation.

On the wall opposite the dais stood a large fireplace flanked by a rack of fire tools and a newly filled log holder, evidence of Matt's labor at the woodchopping block. He was surely also responsible for the chairs arranged cozily before the hearth and the logs stacked for a fire, awaiting only the touch of a match. Gretchen stole a glance at Sarah and was pleased to see a small smile on her lips. She surely recognized her husband's thoughtful gesture and found reassurance in it.

"This is where we'll hold the Christmas Boutique," declared Sylvia, gesturing with arms outspread. "We'll put our sewing machines and other equipment in temporary storage, arrange the classroom partitions to create aisles, and use our worktables to display the items for sale. We'll deck the halls, serve hot cider by the fireplace, put on some Christmas carols, and make everything so merry and festive that our visitors will browse happily for hours."

"Not only browse, but buy," Sarah added.

Sylvia turned to Nancy and Melanie and peered at them expectantly over the rims of her glasses, which she wore on a silver chain around her neck. "What do you think? Will this suffice?"

"It's absolutely perfect," said Nancy, "but one last caveat—"

"Nancy, no," murmured Melanie. "Not when we're this close to sealing the deal."

"Your generosity is overwhelming," said Nancy, her gaze taking in Gretchen and Sarah as well as Sylvia, "but I feel obliged to remind you that even with our volunteers pitching in, it's going to require a lot of work to pull this off. The Christmas Boutique is supposed to open at ten o'clock Friday morning."

Gretchen knew what the Elm Creek Quilters were capable of, and yet even she felt a tremor of alarm at the thought of all they must accomplish in four days.

But Sylvia did not flinch. "You can count on us," she declared.

Nancy sighed, relieved, and Melanie fairly bounced with delight. A few minutes passed in a flurry of planning and promises, and afterward, Sylvia, Sarah, and Gretchen escorted them to the door, where they put on their coats and gloves and departed in far better spirits than when they had arrived.

As soon as the door closed behind them, Sylvia turned to Gretchen and Sarah, her cheerful confidence vanishing. "Oh, my goodness. What have I done?"

Gretchen and Sarah exchanged a look of alarm. "What do you mean?" asked Sarah. "You sounded so confident that we could do it."

"I was. That is, I am." Frowning briefly, impatient with herself, Sylvia straightened her shoulders and lifted her chin. "A momentary lapse. It won't happen again. We *can* do this, and we will, but we'll need all hands on deck. Let's make some calls and round up our friends. We haven't a moment to lose."

# 4

## *Sarah*

WHILE SARAH AND Sylvia divided up the faculty phone list and summoned the other Elm Creek Quilters to an emergency meeting, Gretchen pulled on her coat and boots and ventured out into the snowy morning to her husband's workshop in the red banked barn to let Joe and Andrew know what was going on. As Sarah rang Gwen's number and waited for her to answer, she wished for perhaps the tenth time that day that Matt was there too. They could use his help. He was the estate's caretaker, a skilled construction worker, and a good, capable, industrious person to have around in a crisis, which this was apparently turning out to be.

But Matt was a three-hour drive away.

She had warned him an unexpected, urgent situation might come up in his absence, but he had brushed aside her concerns. "With the orchard and gardens dormant for the winter and the campers away, this is a slow season for me at the manor," he had said.

"Things may be slower, but they're hardly at a standstill," she had replied. "You've never been a seasonal employee. The newest parts of the manor are about a century old, and there's always maintenance to do. And what about everything else the caretaker is responsible for? Snow removal, tending the furnace, keeping the woodbins filled—"

"Anything essential, I can do on the weekends."

The grin he offered her then was probably supposed to be reassuring, but she was not reassured. Weekends were for baby-proofing the manor, preparing the nursery, discussing baby names, giving her back rubs and foot massages, and for holding her while she slept at night and kissing away her worries. She could do without the pampering if she had to, but how long could he expect to squeeze a full-time job into the weekends?

That would be difficult enough if nothing unexpected came up, and something always did. Today it was the Christmas Boutique; the day before, it was decorating the manor for the holidays.

All of the manor's permanent residents had pitched in to help. While Sylvia and Gretchen had draped the banisters with ever-green garlands and adorned the mantelpieces with fresh pine boughs, Sarah and Matt had gone up to the attic in search of the Bergstrom heirloom Christmas decorations. Matt insisted that Sarah precede him up the narrow, creaking attic steps—the bet-ter to break her fall should she stumble, Sarah supposed, a sen-sible precaution considering she was not exactly agile in her third trimester. At the top, she shivered and hugged herself for warmth as she stepped into the chilly darkness.

"Stay put until I turn on the light," Matt cautioned as he ventured deeper into the space beneath the eaves. He reached overhead for the pull cord, and with one tug, pale light from the single, bare bulb spilled down, illuminating a circle of floor-boards. Stacks of trunks, cartons, and old furniture cast deep shadows in the corners beyond the reach of the light.

To Sarah's right lay the older, west wing of the manor, the original home of the Bergstrom family, built in the middle of the nineteenth century by the first Bergstroms to immigrate to America from Germany. Directly before her stretched the south wing, added when Sylvia's father was a boy. In the attic, the seams joining the original house and the addition were more evident than on the first three stories, the color of the walls subtly different, the floor not quite even. Little visible evidence betrayed that fact, as the belongings of four generations of the Bergstrom family covered nearly every square foot of floor space.

Matt surveyed the attic, grimacing. "We should really help Sylvia get this place organized and cleared out."

"Sounds like the perfect job for our caretaker," said Sarah lightly. "You're right, though. Who knows what precious Bergstrom artifacts are hidden up here, what family secrets await discovery?"

"Maybe that's why Sylvia keeps putting it off."

"Maybe so." Sarah skirted a decrepit armchair and a stack of hatboxes and moved deeper into the attic. "If Joe needs any more furniture restoration projects, I see at least a half dozen pieces in desperate need of his attention." She paused and glanced around. "The trunks should be right around here. I'm sure I left them close to the stairwell when I put them away last year."

"Here," Matt called from several paces away. "A navy-blue trunk and a forest-green trunk, right?"

"And the carton with the Evergleam tree," said Sarah, making her way around a battered pie cabinet to join him. "We can't forget that."

"It wouldn't feel like Christmas without it." Matt threw her a grin as he bent his knees to pick up the green trunk. "Just keep it out of Sylvia's sight. You know the rules."

Sarah knew, but she was tempted to test the rules this year. Maybe Sylvia could learn to love the aluminum tree if she gave it a chance.

Matt refused to let Sarah do any of the heavy lifting, so she limited herself to nudging the trunks and the carton closer to the top of the stairs so he could more easily haul each one down three flights to the foyer. Once there, while their husbands went outside to string lights around the veranda and hang evergreen wreaths on the front doors, Sarah, Sylvia, and Gretchen unpacked and admired the Bergstrom family's holiday treasures: a garland of gold beads and a pair of ceramic candleholders shaped like sprays of holly and berries. A wooden nativity set Sylvia's grandfather had carved, and eight velvet stockings embroidered with the names of Sylvia's cousins. A china angel blowing a brass horn. A wooden music box shaped like a sleigh full of toys that played "God Rest Ye Merry Gentlemen." Boxes of ornaments from around the world, representing the many facets of Sylvia's heritage. Whenever Sylvia unwrapped a relic of great sentimental value, such as the ruby-and-gold-glass star for the top of the tree, she would sigh and smile. Sometimes she would wistfully reminisce about how the family had acquired a particular item, or which of her loved ones had prized it the most.

"Where's the Christmas china service?" she suddenly exclaimed as they reached the bottom of the second trunk. "And our Santa Claus cookie jar? My great-aunt Lucinda kept it filled with *Lebkuchen*, *Anisplätzchen*, and *Zimtsterne* from St. Nicholas Day through the Feast of the Three Kings. Anna was going to revive my great-aunt's tradition as a special holiday treat for me."

"We stored the china in the butler's pantry when we put everything away last January," said Sarah, surprised by her friend's alarm. "You decided that would be safer than hauling such fragile items up and down from the attic every Christmas, remember?"

"Yes, of course," said Sylvia, visibly relieved. "And the Christmas Quilt?"

"Upstairs in my closet, rolled up in a bedsheet to keep it clean," said Sarah. "Where would you like to display it this year?"

Sylvia's gaze went to the railing on the second floor, which began at the top of the grand oak staircase and ran the width of the foyer. "Why don't we hang it above the entrance to the ball-room as we did last year? It's very striking, and it would be one of the first things our guests see when they come through the front door."

"*The* Christmas Quilt?" asked Gretchen as she smoothed the wrinkles from a green-and-red-tartan tablecloth. "With so many quilters in your family, I would have assumed the Bergstroms had many Christmas quilts."

"This particular quilt deserves the distinction," said Sylvia. "Many Bergstrom women collaborated on it, but it took Sarah to finish it."

"We finished it together," said Sarah, "you and me and Agnes."

Sylvia waved a hand dismissively. "Perhaps we helped, but if you hadn't stubbornly insisted that it was possible to assemble a quilt out of all those disparate pieces, they would still be jumbled together in a box in the attic."

"I can't wait to see it, and to hear more about it," said Gretchen. "I'm sure it's quite a story."

"If you help me hang the quilt, I promise to tell you all I know," said Sarah.

"It's a deal."

As the women decked the halls, beginning in the foyer and moving on to the ballroom, Sarah teased Gretchen with tantaliz-ing hints about the Christmas Quilt, which she called *Christmas Memories*, although Sylvia rarely used that title in the stories she had shared with Sarah. From the time the first pieces were cut in the early twentieth century, the longtime work-in-progress had been taken up by a succession of Bergstrom women, each of whom used the rich red, green, cream, and gold fabrics to create blocks in her own signature style.

Sylvia's great-aunt Lucinda had begun the project before Sylvia was born. Her original plan was to make a quilt from twenty Feathered Star blocks, but the intricate piecing required time and persistence, and other household duties often beckoned her away. Each November, Lucinda would take the pieces from her sewing basket and declare, "This year I'm going to finish the quilt in time for Christmas morning."

"You said that last year," one of the younger children would always chime in, usually Sylvia or Richard.

"This year feels like the year," Lucinda would reply, smiling.

For a few weeks she would make steady progress, but it was such a busy season that she never met her deadline, and after the holidays passed, she would lose interest and pack the quilt away. Eventually, reluctantly, she abandoned it altogether. By then her eyes were not as strong as they had once been, and she no longer felt capable of piecing together the tiny triangles as precisely as necessary.

Rather than allow Lucinda's beautiful, intricate handiwork to go to waste, Sylvia's mother decided to finish the quilt by framing the Feathered Stars with appliqué holly wreaths and plumes. Unlike Lucinda, Eleanor worked on the quilt throughout the year, stitching the green holly leaves and deep red berries to ivory squares of fabric with tiny, meticulous stitches. But although she did not put away the quilt at the end of the festive season, she progressed more slowly than Lucinda had, for she could sew only for an hour or two at a time before headaches and fatigue forced her to set the work aside.

Sylvia's mother passed away before she could complete the quilt.

For a very long time it lay forgotten in a trunk among other belongings the grieving family could not bear to part with, but on the fifth Christmas after her death, Claudia unearthed the completed sections and the uncut fabric and decided to finish it herself. Sylvia was skeptical; even though her sister chose Variable

Star blocks rather than the more challenging Feathered Stars or appliquéd holly and berries, Sylvia knew her skills were not up to the task.

All too soon, Sylvia's doubts proved prescient. Claudia judged her seam allowances so inconsistently that her blocks differed up to a half-inch in size, the tips of her triangles rarely met at a precise point, and she frequently lopped off star tips with adjoining seams. Sylvia pointed out these problems with more eagerness than tact, so it was little wonder Claudia rejected her offer to help sew the remaining blocks. "My trouble is that I have an annoying little sister who doesn't have anything better to do on Christmas Eve than criticize me," Claudia snapped. "Great-Aunt Lucinda said I could finish the quilt and that's what I'm going to do. You're just angry because you didn't think of it first. If you had, you wouldn't have let me help you, and you know it."

Claudia was absolutely right, but Sylvia was too proud to admit it. Temper flaring, she rose to storm from the room, but some contrary impulse made her pause in the doorway and retort, "The word 'variable' in your Variable Stars shouldn't refer to their size."

How she regretted her angry words on Christmas Day, when, late in the evening after the family's joyous celebration had drawn to a close, she came upon her sister kneeling on the parlor floor, packing the Feathered Stars, appliquéd holly plumes, and haphazard Variable Stars into a box with the remaining fabric.

"Christmas is over, so you're putting the Christmas Quilt away?" Sylvia inquired, amused. "I see you're following in Great-Aunt Lucinda's footsteps."

"Exactly," said Claudia shortly. "To the letter."

"What do you mean?"

"I mean I'm quitting too. I suppose that pleases you."

Strangely, Sylvia was not at all pleased. "Why quit when you've already made five blocks?"

"Because I've already wasted too much time on this wretched thing." Claudia closed the box and rose, then stood there with the box at her feet, regarding her sister challengingly, as if daring her to continue the conversation.

"Maybe you'll feel differently next Christmas," said Sylvia. "Maybe that's how you'll follow Great-Aunt Lucinda's example, by working on it only during the Christmas season."

"I will never sew another stitch of this quilt," Claudia vowed. "I don't want anything to remind me of this miserable Christmas."

Sylvia gaped at her, astonished and bewildered. While it was true that an inevitable thread of sorrow was woven into the fabric of every holiday since their mother's death, otherwise it had been a happy Christmas. Elm Creek Manor was beautifully adorned with all the familiar heirloom decorations and the charming, whimsical things the children had made at school. The family had gathered together and had enjoyed all their favorite traditions. Granted, the sisters' attempt to make apple strudel from the traditional Bergstrom recipe had not turned out as well as they had hoped, but their aunts had prepared a delicious feast and all the decadent treats they made only during the festive season. It had been a wonderful Christmas, not perfect, but wonderful nonetheless. Sylvia knew it was so, but she also knew that arguing the point would only make matters worse. Their Christmas had been full of blessings, but somehow her sister could not see them.

So the Christmas Quilt was packed away, and was not seen again until Sylvia, Claudia, and Agnes discovered it while the men they loved were away at war. Claudia affirmed her vow never to sew another stitch of it, but Sylvia took it up, piecing several Log Cabin blocks in honor of her dear great-aunt Lucinda, who had adored the traditional pattern. Working upon the quilt brought her a certain peace, a quiet joy amid her loneliness and longing for her husband. That peace was shattered a few months later, and when she fled the manor in the aftermath of Andrew's devastating revelation, she left the unfinished quilt behind.

Decades passed, and she had quite forgotten the Christmas Quilt until Sarah's second winter in Waterford, when Sarah discovered it, coaxed its story out of Sylvia, and resolved to piece all the completed segments together and finish the quilt at last.

She began work at once, and had the top nearly assembled when Agnes and her eldest daughter stopped by on Christmas Eve. It was Agnes who revealed that in Sylvia's absence, Claudia had cast aside her impetuous vow never to sew another stitch of it. "She worked on the Christmas Quilt every year I lived in the manor," Agnes said, lightly running her fingertips over an intricately appliquéd holly plume. "She brought it out on St. Nicholas Day and put it away with the rest of the Christmas things on the Feast of the Three Kings. I'm sure she intended to finish the quilt. Even when she and Harold became estranged and she was at her lowest, she seemed to find comfort in the work."

And yet she had not finished the quilt, but Agnes could not tell them why. She and Claudia had rarely seen each other after Agnes remarried and moved out of the manor. Perhaps like Lucinda, Claudia had abandoned the project when her physical skills failed her. Or perhaps she had abandoned it in anger as she had at age sixteen, or in grief as Sylvia had ten years later. Or perhaps, like their mother, she had passed away before she could fulfill her promise to herself to finish the work.

That was the story Sylvia had told Sarah, who finished the top and quilted it with the help of Sylvia and Agnes. It was complete at long last by the following Christmas.

Sarah passed on that story now, to Gretchen, as they brought out the Christmas Quilt from Sarah's closet, removed the protective muslin sheet, and hung it from the second-floor balcony in the foyer, above the doors to the ballroom and directly across the foyer from the manor's front entrance.

When the men came indoors from hanging the lights on the veranda, they paused to admire the beautiful quilt. "That's quite a work of art," said Joe. "I can't put my finger on it, but it looks antique and modern at the same time."

"You're very perceptive," said Sylvia, impressed.

"There's a good reason you can't pinpoint its age," Gretchen called down to her husband from the balcony. "It's a long story. I'll fill you in later."

"The outdoor lights are up, the Christmas Quilt is hung, and you've really decked the halls," said Matt, gazing around the foyer admiringly. "Does this mean we're done?"

"Not by far," said Sylvia. "We don't even have a tree yet. You and Sarah had better get busy."

Sarah and Matt exchanged a look, puzzled. "Why us?" asked Sarah, descending the grand oak staircase a few steps behind Gretchen. "I mean, we're happy to help, but—"

Sylvia peered at her over the rims of her glasses. "Sarah, dear, you know very well that according to Bergstrom family tradition, the most recently married couple is responsible for choosing the Christmas tree."

Sarah noticed the smiles breaking out on her friends' faces, and she could not keep one from her own. "That's just it. Matt and I may be the youngest married couple here, but we are definitely not the most recently married."

"That would be you," said Matt helpfully, grinning. "You and Andrew."

Sylvia gasped, hand to her heart. "Oh, my goodness. That's right. Andrew, dear, I swear I haven't forgotten our anniversary."

"I know, honey," said Andrew, smiling. He took her hand and

laced his fingers through hers. "I didn't remember that choosing a tree is our responsibility now either."

"I'll help," said Matt. "It's hard work, tromping around in the snow in search of a tree, cutting it down, hauling it back to the manor on the toboggan."

Sylvia looked dubious. "According to custom, the couple is supposed to go alone."

"The Bergstrom family never had newlyweds of our vintage before." Andrew raised Sylvia's hand to his lips for a kiss. "Matt, we'll take you up on that offer, but Sarah, I think you should sit this one out."

Sarah was happy to agree. The twins had been kicking energetically all afternoon, and the very thought of trudging through the snow exhausted her. Besides, she had other plans.

The late afternoon sun was already sinking low in the sky as the newlyweds and Matt bundled up and headed out into the forest with the toboggan and an ax. Gretchen and Joe went to the kitchen to prepare dinner, but when Sarah offered to help, they urged her to sit down by the fireplace in the parlor, put her feet up, and sip a cup of herbal tea. She gratefully accepted, but as soon as she was alone, she slipped off to the banquet hall for some surreptitious decorating. Only after everything was in place did she go to the parlor, sink into the most comfortable armchair, pull a quilt over herself, and close her eyes, telling herself it would be for only a moment.

She woke to a gentle touch on her shoulder. "Supper's ready," Gretchen said, holding out a hand to help her to her feet. As they left the parlor, Sarah looked down the hallway to her left, but although the doors to the ballroom on the other side of the foyer were open, she craned her neck in vain for a glimpse of the tree.

"You can't see it from this angle, but Sylvia and Andrew found a gorgeous balsam fir," Gretchen told her as they turned down the west wing toward the kitchen, from which the rich, mouthwatering aroma of tomatoes and spices wafted. "Matt and Andrew set it up straight and secure in the base, Matt and Joe strung the lights, and Sylvia and I put on the garland."

"And I slept through everything."

Gretchen gave her a quick, encouraging hug around the shoulders. "Don't worry. There's plenty of work left. We haven't hung a single ornament and we're counting on you to join in when we finish up after supper. Just so you know, Matt has already decreed that you're not allowed to climb the ladder."

"I'll stick to the lower boughs, then," said Sarah. "Matt can put the star on top, since he's the tallest."

Although supper was a delight, with everyone in good spirits, Gretchen's chicken chili delicious, and the conversation lively and fun, Matt left before dessert to do his laundry and pack. Sarah's happiness dimmed as she and the others tidied the kitchen and went to the ballroom to hang the lovely Bergstrom heirloom ornaments upon the tree without him. In the end it was Joe, with a makeshift tool he fashioned out of a broom handle and a wire hanger, who placed the ruby-and-gold-glass star upon the highest bough. By the time Matt finally came downstairs, they were returning smaller boxes to the cartons and sweeping up fallen needles.

"I'm sorry I wasn't much help," said Matt.

Everyone protested that simply wasn't so, but his eyes were on Sarah. "You did your share," she said, resting a hand on her abdomen as he crossed the ballroom to join her. "The outdoor lights, the tree—"

"Don't be too easy on him," Joe interrupted, grinning. "He shirked kitchen duty tonight. That'll put him on Santa's naughty list for sure."

Everyone but Matt laughed and chimed in that Joe was absolutely right and Matt would probably find his stocking empty on Christmas morning. Matt accepted the teasing with a grin, but as soon as he was no longer the center of attention, he took Sarah's hand and quietly asked, "Are we okay?"

"Of course." She knew he wasn't talking about the kitchen chores. "We'll always be okay in the end."

He squeezed her hand, but his smile faltered until it was barely distinguishable from a frown.

Night had fallen, and when Sylvia switched on the lights on the tree and the banisters, the effect of color and light and fragrance was so profoundly beautiful that it took Sarah's breath away. Elm Creek Manor was lovely in all seasons, but at Christmas, it became truly magical, the perfect setting for holiday wishes to come true.

But the transformation had required all of them to pitch in, and there was still more work yet to do before they welcomed their out-of-town guests for Christmas. Slow season or not, Matt was needed at Elm Creek Manor. Sarah needed him even if the orchards and gardens didn't.

That had been true before the disaster at Good Shepherd, and it was doubly true now, but Matt was 170 miles away. He would be back in time to help with the second day of the boutique, but Sarah and her friends needed him now. No doubt Hank would argue with equal certainty that he needed Matt too.

Sarah understood that Matt felt caught in the middle, torn between his commitment to her and his need to fulfill his father's expectations. He wanted to please everyone and maintain family harmony—admirable goals, Sarah thought, but too often, in Matt's attempts to treat everyone equitably, he sacrificed her happiness to his father's. That was the path of least resistance, so why shouldn't he take it? He knew Sarah would always forgive him, and would feel bad about feeling bad when he put his father first, and would not pressure him to make her, his wife, his priority for a change. Hank, not so much. He seemed to believe—and would probably always believe—that Matt was his son first, Sarah's husband second.

A secret Sarah had never confided to anyone was that this was why she had changed her last name when she married Matt. She had always liked her birth name. Sarah Mallory was melodic, and it looked pretty written on a page, and it represented her heritage, her late father, her beloved grandparents. She had changed her last name to McClure as a way of staking her claim, as a way to tell Hank and anyone else who might hope that their marriage was a passing phase that she was there to stay.

Afterward, Sarah realized to her chagrin that her defiant gesture had not made the impression she had intended. From everyone else's point of view, she had simply done what was expected, what was traditional. Only in hindsight did she understand that she would have made a bolder statement by keeping her own name, declaring to the world that she and Matt were a modern couple, independent and equal partners, not bound by the conventions of their elders. But even that might have failed, for Hank had never entirely accepted that Matt was his own person rather than an extension of himself.

Sarah had glimpsed signs of his controlling tendencies early on, when she and Matt had first begun dating as students at Penn State, but since they rarely saw him, she invented plausible excuses for his occasional overbearing remarks and let them pass. Sarah had an overbearing parent of her own to contend with, and at the time, she had been more concerned with her mother's disapproval of Matt and her annoying, impossible hope that Sarah would reconcile with her previous boyfriend.

As graduation approached, though, Hank's expectations became impossible to ignore. Matt was majoring in landscape architecture, and Hank hoped, or rather, assumed, that he would put his training to use with McClure Construction, the successful construction company his own father had founded in southwestern Pennsylvania forty years before. Matt had worked for his father ever since he was old enough to hold a hammer, after school and on weekends and during summer vacations. Even as a college student, he had often driven home on the weekends to help with projects that were understaffed or running behind schedule. He wanted to help and he appreciated the extra cash, but he had never intended to take over the family business. When he lost his first post-graduation job in State College and joined a landscape architecture firm in Waterford instead of seeking a permanent role with McClure Construction, it should have been obvious that he meant to pursue his own dreams. Soon thereafter, when he accepted the position of caretaker at Elm Creek Manor, that should have put an end to any speculation about his career plans and all pressure to choose any path but his own.

For years, Hank had watched Matt go his own way without complaint, but the closer he came to retirement, the more frequently he urged Matt to reconsider. When Matt and Sarah had visited him in early September, Hank had told Matt that with two babies on the way, he ought to think more seriously about his future. "A partnership with your old man is as secure a job as you're going to get in this world," he had said, clapping Matt on the back and grinning. Matt hadn't defended his career choice, but merely offered a tight smile. Sarah had bit the inside of her lower lip to keep from blurting out that Matt's job at Elm Creek Quilts would be secure even if he weren't married to the cofounder. He was essential to their operations, but Hank, oblivious or simply indifferent to the pain he was causing, continued to imply that Matt's skills were going to waste and he was one poorly pruned apple tree away from unemployment.

In all the years Sarah and Matt had lived and worked at Elm Creek Manor, Matt's father had visited them only twice. Sarah interpreted his absence as yet another statement of disapproval, but Matt made excuses for him, explaining that he couldn't get away from work with his company so shorthanded. Much to their surprise, in early November, he had agreed to come for Christmas. Blissfully unaware of the conflict that would erupt the day after Thanksgiving, Sarah had convinced herself that his upcoming visit could be a wonderful opportunity to show him how well Matt was thriving at Elm Creek Manor, and what an idyllic place it would be to raise a family. The estate offered acres of forest to explore, a creek for wading, fishing, and tossing stones, a thriving orchard with trees to climb and apples to pluck, gardens for picnics and games of make-believe, and a broad expanse of lawn for running and playing, for crunching through fallen leaves in autumn and building snow forts in winter. As for Waterford, the public schools were among the best in the state, and the college provided many opportunities for educational and cultural enrichment. Most important, the manor was home to Sylvia and other dear, reliable, generous friends who would offer the twins unconditional love and affection. What could give them a better start in life than that?

If this was not enough to bring Hank around, Sarah had decided to make him a quilt as a Christmas gift. She knew she shouldn't expect it to work miracles, but perhaps a quilt of his own would spark his curiosity about, maybe even his appreciation for, the beloved art form that she and her friends preserved, celebrated, and passed on with such dedication. If he thought that Matt was contributing to a worthwhile endeavor on behalf of a company with a promising future, perhaps he would finally understand that Matt had chosen wisely and had every reason to anticipate continued success.

Eager to create something original and unique, Sarah had designed a new block, a Log Cabin variation with a burgundy star in the center rather than the usual solid square, and dark blue, tan, and ivory diagonals instead of the traditional two-part, dark-and-light divisions. She pieced forty-eight blocks, enough for a queen-size quilt, and arranged them in a Barn Raising setting so that the surface seemed to glow with warmth, radiating outward from the center in alternating bands of light and shadow. She had finished piecing the top two days after Thanksgiving, and was thrilled to discover that her design had turned out as beautifully as she had imagined, the cabins underneath the stars reminiscent of snug homes with fires on the hearth, of warmth and comfort on snowy winter nights.

She layered the top, batting, and backing after Matt departed for Uniontown, and she completed the machine quilting during his first week away. The work occupied her thoughts and kept her from brooding too much about his absence, but by the time she began to attach the long strip of binding around the raw edges, her enthusiasm for the quilt had waned. She was determined to push through and complete it in time for Christmas, but she no longer believed that the beautiful gift would help her father-in-law see just how wonderful, rich, and rewarding their lives were.

In hindsight, Hank's unexpected acceptance of their annual invitation to spend Christmas with them at the manor seemed curious, even suspect. Since Matt was in Uniontown more often than not, father and son could celebrate together in Uniontown before Matt returned to Elm Creek Manor, sparing Hank a long drive to a place he had never seemed particularly keen to visit. Why was Hank so willing to visit now? Sarah could not help wondering if he intended to plead his case to her in person, hoping she would acquiesce, give her blessing for Matt to take over McClure Construction, and agree to move to Uniontown after the twins were born. If that was his plan, he was in for a bitter disappointment. She would never give up her home, her friends, her career, and the life she had built for herself at Elm Creek Manor so that Matt could fulfill his father's dream for him, a dream he had never shared.

AFTER SARAH FINISHED her calls to Gwen Sullivan and Anna, she was tempted to phone Matt and beg him to come home to help, but she decided against it. As unfortunate as the damage to the church's community hall was, he would not consider the frenzied scramble to move the Christmas Boutique to Elm Creek Manor an emergency requiring a caretaker's presence. And he would probably be right. The Elm Creek Quilters, Andrew and Joe, and the Christmas Boutique committee's volunteers would manage without him. Sarah just wished they didn't have to.

She had made her calls from the banquet hall while Sylvia used the phone in the kitchen, and they met in the back foyer between the two rooms just as Gretchen came in from outdoors. "Joe and Andrew need to put away a few tools and they'll be right in," she said, slipping out of her coat and hanging it neatly in the closet. She tugged off her boots and put on her slippers, careful not to step on the traces of snow she had left on the mat.

"Diane will pick up Agnes and they'll be right over," said Sylvia.

"Gwen and Anna are on their way too," said Sarah.

They returned to the kitchen, where they tidied up from Nancy and Melanie's visit and prepared to welcome their friends with a fresh pot of coffee, a hot kettle for tea, and the last of Anna's shortbread. Sarah hurried off to collect paper and pencils from her office on the second floor and returned to find Joe and Andrew seated at the long wooden table with their spouses, drinking coffee and apparently debating whether they should see if they were needed to help with the cleanup at Good Shepherd Church.

"You're needed here," said Sylvia firmly. "If they ask for volunteers after the Christmas Boutique, then by all means do your bit, but for now, you're on our roster."

"In that case, put us in, Coach," said Andrew good-naturedly.

"Since we have so little time to prepare," said Gretchen, "maybe Sylvia should explain how they've set up the boutique in the past, and then we can decide how to adapt that to our space."

Everyone agreed that this was a sensible way to begin, so Sylvia described the typical layout of aisles and booths, the assortment of items for sale, the hours and days that tended to be the busiest, and the food service arrangements. "Our ballroom is much larger than the church hall, so we'll be able to have larger booths and more spacious aisles," said Sylvia. "It will be much more pleasant for shopping."

Sarah had been sketching a layout of the ballroom while Sylvia spoke, but a sudden, nagging thought made her set down her pencil. "The church is downtown, just a few blocks from campus on one side and those historic neighborhoods where the professors live on the other," she said. "The boutique probably received a lot of business from people who came in out of curiosity when they passed by and saw all the activity. That isn't going to happen way out here."

"We'll have to publicize the boutique," said Gretchen. "Not only to let folks know about the change of venue, but to convince them the trip out our way will be worth their while."

"Let's underscore that point," said Sylvia. "Although I'm sure

Nancy and Melanie will inform the members of their church, we have to get the word out to the broader community."

Sarah wrote "Publicity" on her notepad and underlined it. If only Summer were there. She would be perfect for the role of publicist, but she was even farther away than Matt.

Just then she heard the back door to the manor open and close, and a moment later, Summer's mother appeared in the kitchen doorway. Gwen had shed her favorite vintage windowpane-check wool coat in the foyer and her cheeks were rosy from the cold. "You started without me?" she protested, smiling as she tucked her voluminous paisley skirts beneath her and sat down on the bench beside Sarah. She wore her long, wavy, gray-streaked auburn hair loose about her shoulders, and as she opened her satchel and took out a yellow legal pad and a pen, her beaded necklaces— seasonally festive in green, red, and gold—clinked faintly in time with her movements. "I take it we don't have a moment to waste."

"We really don't," said Sarah. She had not realized until they had begun working out the details just how much they had to do. Setting up the ballroom and banquet hall, keeping the forest road and parking lot plowed, assisting Anna as she whipped up a dazzling buffet—she was confident they could manage all that, but a publicity campaign too? And what other essential tasks would they discover when the other Elm Creek Quilters arrived with their suggestions?

Gwen arranged her notepad and pen on the table in front of her. "Summer asked me to tell you that she's sorry she can't get here until Friday night, but she has finals. She'll help all day Saturday and Sunday."

"Tell her she'll be greatly missed, but we're grateful for whatever help she can offer when she does come home," said Sylvia, regarding her sympathetically. "I've no doubt you miss her even more than we do."

"Every day," said Gwen, pressing a hand to her chest. "It's like a piece of my heart broke loose. There's an ache where she used to be, and I can't repair it."

"She'll be home soon," said Gretchen. "She'll always come back to you."

"Yes, but never soon enough."

"We're here," a sweet, light voice sang out from the kitchen doorway. Agnes Emberly took in the scene around the table with a smile, her blue eyes eager behind pink-tinted glasses. She was still bundled up in her pink knit scarf and heavy houndstooth winter coat, a pink stocking cap with a fluffy pom-pom atop her short, white curls. "Just let us get out of our wraps and we'll join you."

As she stepped out of the doorway, Diane Sonnenberg took her place. "First things first," she said, pulling off her black leather gloves and tucking them into the pockets of her long, red wool coat. "Who's responsible for this disaster?"

Gwen rolled her eyes. "That's hardly the first thing on our agenda."

"That is *so* like you, coddling criminals." Diane removed her black beanie with one hand and fluffed her short, blond curls with the other. "It shouldn't be too hard to figure out. We just need the names of everyone who attended that committee meeting, and then we can investigate their backgrounds for a possible motive. We can probably eliminate Nancy and Melanie, since they were the ones to seek our help." Frowning thoughtfully, she unbuttoned the top two buttons of her coat and loosened her black-gray-and-red-tartan scarf. "Unless that's part of the culprit's cover—"

Gwen raised a hand, wincing. "Stop right there, Sherlock. What's the point of finding someone to blame? How will that help us prepare for the Christmas Boutique?"

Diane shrugged out of her coat and draped it over her arm. "I guess it wouldn't, but—"

"Then let's not waste valuable time, dear," said Agnes brightly, patting Diane on the arm as she passed her in the doorway and seated herself at the table next to Gretchen. "It was an honest mistake, not a criminal conspiracy to bring down the county food bank. Whoever did turn off the heat that day, I'm sure she or he already feels terrible enough without needing any additional persecution from us. Go on, put away your coat and sit down."

"Am I the only one who's curious?" grumbled Diane, but she did as Agnes said.

Diane had barely taken her seat across from Gwen when they heard the back door open again, followed by the sound of voices, low and earnest. Anna was clearly not alone, but even before she and Jeremy entered the kitchen, Sarah guessed who her companion was. "Jeremy's not an Elm Creek Quilter, but he offered to help," said Anna as she approached them, rubbing her hands together for warmth and glancing hopefully around the table. Her eyes were bright and her cheeks flushed, but perhaps that was just from the cold. "Is that all right?"

"Sure," said Joe, waving them over. "Andrew and I aren't Elm Creek Quilters either, and we're on the roster."

Anna smiled her thanks, darting a quick look at Gwen as she and Jeremy found places at the opposite end of the table from her.

"What did we miss?" asked Jeremy, leaning forward to rest his arms on the table.

"We were just saying that the first order of business is to find out who's to blame," said Diane.

"We were *not* just saying that," said Gwen. "Sarah, I think you have the floor."

Sarah began to rise, but one of the twins kicked her solidly in the ribs, so she thought better of it. "We've got a lot to do and not a lot of time," she said, rubbing absently at the place where a tiny foot had connected with her rib cage. "I've broken down the preparation work into four major categories: setting up the market stalls in the ballroom, publicity, decorating the rooms of the manor that will be open to customers—"

"We've already done a considerable amount of decorating," Sylvia remarked.

"Yes, but I think we should do more, especially in the ballroom and banquet hall," said Sarah. "The fourth category is food service. Anna, we were all hoping you'd be willing to organize a buffet, or counter service meals if you prefer. Nancy has a list of volunteer cooks and bakers ready to prepare whatever you need. If you don't need them, they'll make items for the bake sale instead."

"Of course I'm willing," said Anna, surprised. "Do you really need to ask?"

"We would never presume that you're available in the off-season," said Sylvia. "Especially on such short notice."

"In the future, feel free to presume. The answer will always be yes." Looking around the table, Anna added, "Nancy's volunteers can focus on the bake sale. If one or two of you can help out in the kitchen at peak serving time, I can take it from there."

"I can help you," said Jeremy. "I know my way around a kitchen and I can follow instructions fairly well."

"Wonderful," said Sarah, much relieved. "Remember to save your receipts for any ingredients or supplies you purchase, for the tax deduction."

"You know," Anna mused aloud, "when I worked at Waterford College, we often hosted banquets or dinners for various fundraisers. Sometimes local vendors provided food and supplies as in-kind donations. I could contact some of them and see if they'd be interested in supporting the boutique."

Sarah nodded. "You should probably check with Nancy first, but that sounds like a great idea."

"I'm on it." Anna picked up her pen and began swiftly writing down menu ideas, or so it appeared from a distance.

"We'll have new categories of duties on the days of the boutique, when we'll focus on operational logistics rather than preparation, but for now, this is where we'll get started." Sarah looked around the table. "Any questions? Any volunteers? Anna has food service."

"I'll take publicity," said Diane. "I have contacts in the local media and lots of email lists from the booster clubs at the high school and other boards and groups I volunteer for."

"Sounds good." Sarah noted it on her pad. "Diane will be our publicist."

"Those shoppers will need to park their cars somewhere," said Andrew. "Should we post signs on the forest road directing them to the lot out back?"

"The front entrance is so much grander," said Diane. "It sets the proper tone. That's why our quilt campers use the front entrance on registration day."

"We valet park for the quilt campers on the first day," Andrew reminded her. "They get out at the front door, and we take their cars around to the rear lot."

"We'll need the rear lot and the back door for our workers," said Sarah. "Let's direct customers to the circular drive and the front entrance. It does make a much better impression."

Andrew shrugged and nodded, but he did not seem entirely convinced.

Agnes raised a hand. "May I be in charge of decorating? I don't mean to brag, but I think I have a knack for it." She glanced around the table. "I think it's a two-person job, though. Anyone else for the decorating committee?"

"Sign me up," said Gretchen, smiling. "I had so much fun decking the halls of Elm Creek Manor yesterday. I'd enjoy doing more."

"That leaves setting up the ballroom," said Gwen. "I'll take charge of that. Sylvia, would you join me, since you're the most familiar with the Christmas Boutique?"

"I'd be delighted." Sylvia gestured to the diagram of the ballroom Sarah had sketched earlier. "Sarah, dear, would you mind passing that to Gwen?"

Sarah slid the page down the table, and Gwen studied it thoughtfully.

"Joe and I can join the setup squad," said Andrew. "We can move the partitions, store the quilt camp equipment safely out of the way, and build just about whatever you might need."

"Thank you both," said Sarah, making a few more notes before pushing herself to her feet. "Now that we all have our assignments, should we study the venue?"

Together they crossed the back hallway and began their tour in the banquet hall. The moment they entered, a glittering patch of silver in the far corner of the room caught every eye.

"What on earth?" Sylvia exclaimed. "How did that eyesore get down here?"

"I set it up," said Sarah, abashed, but struggling to keep from smiling. "We've put up the Evergleam every year. You said we could."

"I said if you could bear the sight of it, you were welcome to it, as long as you kept it out of my sight. You always put it in your own suite before."

"Is that an aluminum Christmas tree?" asked Joe. "I haven't seen one of those since the seventies."

"I'm afraid so," said Sylvia. "It should have been recycled ages ago."

"Don't take this the wrong way," said Diane, glancing around the elegant room, "but it doesn't really go with your décor, not to mention the architecture."

"That's what makes it so perfect," said Sarah.

"Oh, hush, dear," said Sylvia, gazing up at the heavens. "That metal monstrosity belonged to Claudia. The rest of my family had much better taste."

"Don't judge your sister too harshly," Sarah protested. "Not for this, anyway. These trees were once the height of holiday fashion. My grandmother had one, and this one brings back fond memories. Everyone, check this out. You haven't seen the best part."

"Please, not the light show," said Sylvia.

Pretending not to hear, Sarah hurried across the room as fast as her ample tummy allowed. With some difficulty, she knelt beside the tree next to a well-worn device that resembled an electric fan, but where the blades should have been was a plastic disk about the size of a dinner plate divided into red, blue, green, and yellow quarters. Sarah flipped a switch on the base, a light bulb illuminated, and suddenly the aluminum tree was awash in projected color, first red, then blue, green, and yellow as the disk slowly revolved. "Isn't it fantastic?" she gushed.

"It's certainly something," said Gretchen, smothering a laugh.

Sylvia shook her head, amused but exasperated. "Enjoy it while you can, but be sure to dismantle it before the boutique."

"Sorry, Sylvia," Sarah replied, all innocence. "We don't have enough time."

"Then at least throw a quilt over it."

Sarah smiled but made no promises.

At Sylvia's prompting, Anna described where she preferred to set up the buffet table—in the center of the room rather than near the windows, as was the custom during quilt camp—with the dining tables arranged all around.

"The setup squad can help with that too," said Joe.

"As will the decorating delegation," said Gretchen, glancing to Agnes, who nodded. "That falls partly under our jurisdiction, I think."

"Very good," said Sylvia. "Shall we move on to the ballroom?"

"Speaking of decorations," said Jeremy as they crossed the room, indicating the Evergleam tree glistening in the corner, "I'm with Sarah. That is amazing."

"It's certainly breathtaking," said Sylvia dryly, opening the double doors to the ballroom. "Like a bad scare."

"Come on," Sarah protested. "It's really not that bad."

Sylvia cast her gaze to the heavens and Andrew turned a laugh into a cough. Jeremy shrugged, his bewildered expression clearly conveying that he shared Sarah's appreciation for antique kitsch. "Wait until you see it at night, when the room is darkened and the color wheel shines," she murmured as they all followed Sylvia into the ballroom, and his face brightened in anticipation.

The group had much more to discuss in the ballroom, which in a matter of days they must transform into an appealing, well-organized, smoothly flowing shopping plaza. Andrew offered several excellent ideas for how to use the classroom partitions to break up the space, while Gwen and Sylvia studied Sarah's sketch and debated how to organize the various items for sale, whether to group similar items together on different tables along the same aisle, or to distribute them evenly throughout the boutique to encourage shoppers to explore. Diane and Anna took seats in one of the classroom spaces and brainstormed, first gathering ideas for publicity, and then for the buffet. Gretchen and Agnes wandered the room together, gazing up at the walls, studying the scene from the dais at the far end, talking animatedly, nodding often.

Sarah too strolled through the ballroom, checking in with

her friends, asking questions, offering suggestions, making notes. When Andrew and Joe asked if they should begin putting away the sewing machines and other quilt camp materials, she thanked them and told them to go right ahead. When Gwen and Sylvia presented their additions to her sketch indicating how they thought the boutique items should be organized, she proposed a few changes to improve traffic flow but otherwise agreed with their plan.

Then Gretchen and Agnes approached the edge of the dais, their faces bright with expectation. "Could everyone gather around, please?" Gretchen called. "Agnes had a wonderful idea for decorating the ballroom."

"I believe we thought of it together, dear."

"No, Agnes, you get the credit. It was your idea; I merely agreed with you."

"That's all well and good if they like it," said Agnes, looking a bit unsettled. "Not so much if they don't."

Curious, Sarah joined the others in front of the dais, wondering if she dared hope Agnes wanted to extend the Evergleam theme to the ballroom. Probably not, she thought regretfully. The aluminum trees seemed to be an acquired taste, one that most of her friends did not share.

"Considering that Elm Creek Manor is the home of Elm Creek Quilt Camp, Agnes thought it would be fitting for us to decorate the ballroom with quilts in holiday patterns and colors," said Gretchen, regarding them expectantly. "I think it's an excellent idea."

"The Christmas Quilt looks so lovely hanging in the foyer," Agnes chimed in. "Why not create an even larger display in the ballroom? It would add such marvelous holiday cheer to the Christmas Boutique, and show our visitors who we are and what we do here."

"We don't have time to make enough Christmasy, holiday-ish quilts to decorate the entire ballroom by Friday," said Diane.

"I'm not proposing we make new quilts, dear," said Agnes. "Let's simply bring out our favorites from our own collections. It doesn't matter if they're not in pristine condition. That just means they've been well used and well loved."

"Hang them high enough, and it's likely no one will notice a faded patch or a loose thread here or there," Andrew remarked.

"Exactly," said Agnes, beaming at her old friend. "I have an antique appliqué quilt that would be just perfect for the wall near the Christmas tree. I'm sure if we all bring a few, we'll have more than enough for the ballroom, and possibly enough to spare for the banquet hall too. Diane, what about that adorable Snowball quilt you made for Michael when he was in high school? Or the red-and-white quilt you were working on for your parents a few years back, or was it for Tim, for Valentine's Day?"

Diane hesitated. "I couldn't get a quilt back from my parents in time, and I can't imagine any quilt Michael has had with him in his college apartment would be suitable for display, even if Andrew hung it from the rafters."

"Perhaps not," mused Agnes, but she brightened as she looked around the circle of friends. "Well, I'm sure the rest of you have quilts in suitable condition."

"I have one or two I'd be proud to show off," said Gwen, nodding. "I love this idea. Let's do it. It would be like a quilt show, and if Diane includes that in the publicity, that could help draw customers to the Christmas Boutique."

"And therein lies the danger," said Diane ominously.

All eyes went to her. "Danger?" echoed Anna, wary.

Diane swept an arm, indicating the entire ballroom. "Have you forgotten we're hosting the Christmas Boutique? If we display handcrafted quilts, people will assume they're for sale."

"I don't think that's a cause for alarm," said Sylvia, peering at Diane over the rims of her glasses. "I believe the distinction between items displayed on the boutique tables and artwork on the manor walls will be apparent."

Gwen eyed Diane with utter bemusement. "You aren't afraid someone will try to buy the wreaths and the Christmas trees, are you?"

"The items for sale will surely have price tags," said Gretchen, the voice of reason and reassurance. "That should clear up any confusion."

"Perhaps we should put a tag on that aluminum nightmare in the banquet hall," Sylvia mused, just loud enough to be heard. Sarah suspected her friend was fighting to hold back a smile, and she did not take the bait.

"I'm telling you, tags or no tags, some people are going to try to buy our quilts," said Diane mutinously. Then she sighed. "But you're right. Holiday quilts hung all around the ballroom would make it even more beautiful and festive, and if people hear there's a quilt show at Elm Creek Manor, they may be more inclined to come and spend their money at the Christmas Boutique. It's a risk worth taking for such a good cause."

"If someone offers to buy one of the quilts hung for decoration, we can just explain that they aren't for sale." Anna shrugged. "Not a problem. Easy fix."

"Let's have a vote," said Sarah. "Everyone in favor of decorating with holiday quilts, raise your hand. Everyone against—" She stopped there, for everyone, even Diane, held a hand in the air. "Okay, then. It's unanimous. Between now and Thursday morning, let's search our quilt inventories and deck the halls of Elm Creek Manor with our favorite holiday quilts."

Everyone chimed in their agreement, and with that matter settled, they resumed their work.

Sarah's gaze traveled around the ballroom, from one cluster of friends to another, her heart overflowing with affection, amusement, and pride. How well they all worked together, even when they disagreed.

It occurred to her—suddenly, startlingly—that she was thoroughly enjoying herself for the first time since Matt had dropped his bombshell and had driven off to Uniontown.

Amid all the hassle and uncertainty, she was having a wonderful time.

She actually loved this. Yes, it was stressful and a bit chaotic, but she thrived on strategizing and hard work. She loved how she and her friends pulled together to solve problems and make good things happen. She relished the challenge of overcoming unexpected calamities—as long as they were relatively minor and harmed no one—and she had certainly seen her fair share in her years with Elm Creek Quilts. How could she give that up? How could she leave it behind for something inevitably duller and less fulfilling?

She couldn't. She loved this happy chaos too much to give it up.

And that, she realized, with an overwhelming rush of hope and relief, suggested that she was just the person to take on the daunting responsibility of raising twins. Elm Creek Quilts had prepared her well. She only hoped Matt would understand why she couldn't imagine raising their children anywhere else.

# 5

# *Agnes*

ON TUESDAY MORNING, Agnes woke to sunlight streaming through her bedroom window and knew it was going to be a lovely day, despite the thick snow blanketing the front yard and dormant backyard garden, despite the bracing cold that made her grateful for her flannel nightgown and warm quilts. "Busy is better than bored," she always told her daughters and grandchildren, and she lived every day as if to prove it.

Dismissing the temptation to linger in bed, she threw off the quilts, shivered in the sudden chill, and hurried to wash and dress. After her usual breakfast of oatmeal and coffee, she headed to her quilt studio, which in its former incarnation had been her eldest daughter's bedroom. She had made it halfway up the stairs when the phone rang. She hurried back downstairs to the kitchen to answer. It was Diane, calling to ask for the names and phone numbers of Agnes's friends in the Waterford Historical Society, the Elm Creek Valley Garden Club, and a few other organizations whose members might discover a keen new interest in attending the Christmas Boutique, now that it would be held at Elm Creek Manor.

"Good thinking, dear," said Agnes. She set down the phone, retrieved her address book from the stack directories on the counter nearby, and got back on the line so she could read off the names and numbers. "Tell them you're a friend of mine and they'll help spread the word to their membership."

"I'll do that, thanks."

"You certainly seem to be making good progress on the publicity front."

"That's not all. I've also learned who was present at the facilities committee meeting at Good Shepherd Church. We have eight suspects, but I think we can narrow down that list by applying a bit of logic."

Logic seemed to have nothing to do with Diane's wholly unnecessary investigation. "Diane, dear, please don't call them suspects. According to Nancy and Melanie, the pastor says no crime was committed."

"He has to be forgiving. He's a minister. It's a job requirement. As I was saying, Nancy Reinhart and Melanie Tibbs were there, but we can rule them out because they're genuinely concerned about the boutique or they wouldn't be working so hard to salvage it. Frank DiSantos was as the meeting too, but he's a volunteer firefighter. If he wanted to ruin the boutique, he would have known how to burn down the hall and make it look like an accident."

"Please take a breath and listen to what you're saying. You're being silly."

"It's not silly to rule out Frank, unless you know something about him that I don't."

"Of course not, but that's not what I meant, and—"

"Then we come to Mary Beth Callahan."

"No, no, no," said Agnes, so forcefully she startled herself. "I will not have you torment that poor woman. I know you two have a rather fraught history, but lately you've been mending fences, and I won't stand by while you tear them down again."

"I wouldn't do that," protested Diane. "Honestly. You act like I have a personal vendetta against her or something."

"Do I?" said Agnes archly. "Don't you?"

"Not anymore. Like you said, we're mending fences. Anyway, I've ruled out Mary Beth. She's been proceeding with caution ever since her son and his gang destroyed Grandma's Attic, and she would never be so careless as to mix up the heating and the lights. She wouldn't have done it intentionally, either. She always contributes a quilt or two to the boutique, and she's not one to squander a chance to brag about how her quilts were so popular they incited a bidding war."

Agnes sighed. "Why don't you rule out everyone? Your inquiries aren't helpful, dear. They won't fix the floor any faster, won't draw crowds to the Christmas Boutique, and won't raise a single dime for the food pantry. Your time would be better spent preparing for the event. For instance, have you dropped off some holiday quilts to help decorate the ballroom?"

Diane hesitated. "Not yet. It's on my list."

"Then it seems you have more important things to do than play amateur sleuth. Get to it, dear. Bye now," she said cheerily, and hung up the phone.

Such misplaced energies, Agnes thought as she resumed her interrupted errand to her sewing room. Opening the closet doors, she glanced at the shelves of fabrics organized by color and then at the bin where she stored works-in-progress, but she quickly turned her attention to her collection of quilts not currently on display elsewhere in her home. Each was carefully rolled around a sturdy, acid-free cardboard tube to prevent straining the fibers and creating crease lines at folds, the pieced and appliquéd sides facing in. She had learned to identify her quilts from the back, not only by the fabric but by the distinctive quilting patterns worked into the three layers, feathered plumes and crosshatches and stitches outlining the geometry of the pieces on the top. Each one was as familiar and precious to her as an old friend.

But one quilt in particular beckoned her that morning.

Its backing fabric print was so subtle, a fine wheat-colored vine on a background of an almost imperceptibly darker hue, that it easily could have been mistaken for a faded muslin. But Agnes knew it by heart. Rising on tiptoe and stretching a bit, she was able to retrieve the quilt without too much strain. It was heavier than she remembered, but perhaps that said more about the strength of her arms than her memory. Anticipation brought a smile to her lips as she spread the quilt upon the bed and stepped back to admire it.

Oh, how lovely it remained, even after all these years.

The design was exquisite, but it was not bragging to think so because she had acquired the pattern from another quilter. The handiwork was all her own, and although her novice stitches were far from perfect, they did not detract from the quilt's faded beauty. It had been no small task to gather those dignified, deep-pine-green, scarlet, and gold fabrics in the postwar years when cheery pastels had been all the rage, but eventually she had found enough bolt ends in bargain bins to complete the top. How amusing it was that a color palette dismissed as old-fashioned when she had sewed the first green curve to the creamy ivory background was now, a half-century later, back in style, just as quilting itself had soared to new heights of popularity.

She hadn't been out-of-date at all, but years ahead of her time.

Cupping her chin with a hand, Agnes studied the quilt thoughtfully, contemplating where she should display it in the ballroom of Elm Creek Manor, which wall would set it off to best advantage without exposing the delicate antique fabrics to direct sunlight. The quilt was about five feet square, with sixteen appliquéd Christmas Cactus blocks arranged in a four-by-four setting, all framed by a graceful, curving border of gold accented by a narrow bias trim of a deeper hue. Making the bias strip and sewing it in place without a single crease or awkward flattened edge had been a painstaking, difficult process. On a few occasions tears of frustration had sprung to her eyes, but she had persisted, determined to finish what she had begun. Fortunately, she had been blessed by the guidance of a wise, patient teacher, and after she had put the last stitches into the binding, her teacher had put an arm around her shoulders, praised her for her hard work, and traced her progress by pointing out the differences between the tentative, hesitant stitches of her first block to the nearly invisible stitches on the last smooth curve of the bias accent. "If you keep this up, I can only imagine the masterpieces you'll be creating when you're my age," her teacher had remarked, and Agnes had nearly burst with pride and gratitude.

What a lovely, generous woman she had been, and how different her gentle, encouraging manner from that of Agnes's first quilting teacher—her stubborn, reluctant sister-in-law, Sylvia.

More than fifty years before, after Agnes and Richard had married in haste and he had brought her home to the Bergstrom ancestral estate before shipping out, Agnes had settled into a strange new life: a bride without an adoring husband by her side, disowned by her own family, an unwelcome interloper caught between two bickering sisters, yet all three women fearing for their loved ones away at war. Agnes soon won over all of the Bergstroms except Sylvia, who was jealous that Agnes had captured her beloved baby brother's heart.

Though the challenge was daunting, Agnes resolved to befriend her disapproving sister-in-law with time and patience, for Richard's sake. Knowing how proud Sylvia was of her quilting, Agnes asked for lessons, thinking that a shared interest might bring them together and that quilting would distract her from her loneliness and worry while her husband was at war. Skeptical but flattered, Sylvia agreed.

Agnes's first assignment was to choose a simple quilt pattern or several blocks in varying styles and increasing difficulty for a sampler. She searched through the Bergstrom women's vast pattern collection for a variety of simple blocks, but before she made her final selections, Claudia told her that a more challenging pattern would help her master a quilter's essential skills more quickly. Trusting Claudia's experience, Agnes decided to make a Double Wedding Ring quilt, charmed by the beauty of its interlocking rings as well as by a superstitious hope that the name would guarantee her and Richard many years of wedded bliss.

Sylvia urged her to reconsider. A sampler had been a tried-and-true project for beginning quilters since time immemorial, and with a unique setting and borders it could be just as charming in its own way as a more complex pattern. But Agnes had her heart set on a Double Wedding Ring quilt and would not budge, especially after Claudia privately praised her for standing up to Sylvia.

All too soon Agnes regretted that she had not taken Sylvia's advice. The bias edges and curved seams of the Double Wedding Ring proved too difficult for her inexpert stitches, and her first half-ring buckled in the middle and gapped at the seams. Every lesson was an exercise in frustration for her and exasperation for her teacher.

She might have improved with practice, but the war intervened.

Richard and James were killed, victims of friendly fire in the South Pacific. In her shock and despair, Sylvia lost James's unborn child, and kindly Mr. Bergstrom was killed by a stroke. Numb and grieving, Agnes took on the task of nursing Sylvia back to health. The work kept Agnes's hands busy and thoughts occupied, a blessing in those dark days. Gradually Sylvia recovered her strength, but she was never the same. Compassion for Sylvia's losses helped Agnes bear her own grief more bravely.

The war ended. Harold came home, and Claudia threw herself

into preparing for their wedding. A few weeks before the ceremony, Andrew passed through the Elm Creek Valley on his way from Philadelphia to a new job in Detroit. Agnes was pleased to see her old friend, although the sight of him brought tears to her eyes as she recalled their carefree student days in Philadelphia with Richard. Andrew limped slightly from the wound he had suffered trying to rescue Richard and James, and although he treated the ladies of the household with the same warm courtesy as always, he shunned Harold. This puzzled Agnes, but she did not pry. Something in the steely gaze Andrew fixed upon his former brother-in-arms warned her that she did not want to know what had happened overseas to cause their estrangement.

One evening after supper, Andrew spoke privately with Sylvia in the library. Agnes was passing in the hall when the French doors banged open and Sylvia stormed out, furious, tears streaking her face. Andrew had followed her as far as the doorway, his own face wet from tears as he looked after her, helpless.

He left early the next morning without telling her or Claudia whatever he had confided to Sylvia. Then, a few days before the wedding, the two sisters had a terrible argument behind closed doors, their voices muffled but their mutual anger unmistakable. That same evening, Sylvia packed two suitcases and fled the manor without telling anyone where she was going or when she might return. Claudia assured Agnes that she would come home when her temper cooled, but Agnes was bleakly certain that she would never see Sylvia again.

Claudia and Harold married, and in the early days, they seemed happy—giddily, recklessly so. They threw lavish parties nearly every week, making up for all the deprivations of the war years by laughing and dancing and feasting themselves and their guests into fleeting oblivion. Agnes looked on in dismay as Harold and Claudia sold off prize horses for a fraction of their value, spending the profits as quickly as they were earned. As Bergstrom Thoroughbreds foundered and the money ran out, Claudia and Harold's marriage disintegrated. The empty halls of Elm Creek Manor echoed with their mutual antipathy. Agnes had never felt more alone. She longed for her parents and siblings, for her friends back in Philadelphia, and most of all, for her beloved Richard. She even missed Sylvia. She fought to preserve what she could of the Bergstrom family legacy until Sylvia finally came home.

Despite her efforts, Claudia and Harold steadily drained their resources throughout their second miserable year of marriage. All too soon the last Bergstrom Thoroughbred was sold off, the last remaining stable hand sent away. Agnes begged the couple to set the profits aside for the future, but they ignored her. Desperate, she sold off antique furniture from the unoccupied rooms. When Claudia refused to help her choose which items to part with, Agnes tried not to imagine that she might be selling off Sylvia's favorite chair or a wardrobe cherished by the mother-in-law she had never met.

Occasionally when Agnes called at the antiques shop in Waterford where she sold the Bergstroms' heirlooms, she found the proprietor engrossed in conversation with Joseph Emberly, a history professor at Waterford College who advised him on the historical context of the pieces he acquired. "I'm a dramaturge for antiques," he told Agnes when Peter introduced them, his smile so cheerfully self-deprecating that she found herself smiling back. Joseph looked to be about six inches taller and ten years older than she, with curly light brown hair with hints of auburn, a short, neatly trimmed beard, and dark blue eyes.

In the weeks that followed, in conversations that began at the antiques shop and often ended at the coffeehouse down the block, Agnes learned that Joseph had enlisted in the army in early 1942 after earning his doctorate from Columbia. His education and fluency in German and Italian prompted the government to assign him to military intelligence. He had served in Washington, then London, and finally Berlin, where he had finished his tour of duty six months after VE Day. His college sweetheart had married another man while he was abroad, so upon his return to the States he had accepted a professorship at Waterford College, determined to resume his dormant academic career hundreds of miles away from the campus where he might accidentally cross paths with the woman who had broken his heart.

"I'm so sorry," said Agnes. "I know something about broken hearts too."

His brow furrowed in concern, and she told him about Richard, how they had met and how she had lost him. Joseph clasped her hand in both of his and simply listened, his sympathetic silence a balm for her heartache.

One day Joseph invited her to lunch, confessing an overwhelming curiosity to know how she came by so many remarkable antiques. Agnes had been without a confidante for so long that before she could think better of it, the story of her miserable existence at Elm Creek Manor spilled from her.

When she finished, she felt strangely lighter for having unburdened herself.

"I wish I could help, and I think maybe I can," Joseph said, his blue eyes meeting hers, his expression profoundly kind. "I have a colleague in New York who could sell your antiques for a higher profit than you could get here in Waterford. I'll put you in touch, but please don't tell Peter. He's a good friend, but he won't stay one for long if he knows I'm steering business to his competition."

"I think Peter would understand, but I promise I won't breathe a word."

"You also mentioned that you regret not graduating from high school."

"I'll never regret leaving school to marry Richard," she hastened to explain. "But now that I find myself in desperate need of a job, I wish I had earned my diploma."

"Would you settle for a bachelor's degree? Waterford College has a scholarship program specifically for veterans, their spouses, and their children—a four-year tuition waver for qualifying students."

It sounded wonderful, but Agnes knew it was not for her. "That rules me out, doesn't it? One has to finish high school to be accepted into college."

"Not if you pass the entrance exams, which someone with a fancy Philadelphia boarding school education ought to be able to manage easily. Unless I misunderstood you, and it was all etiquette and flower arranging?"

Agnes feigned indignation. "Miss Sebastian's Academy is a fully accredited academic institution, offering young ladies a rigorous education in the classics, with additional emphases on the arts and public service."

"Then a few college entrance exams shouldn't give you any trouble." He smiled and finished his coffee. "I have a friend in the admissions office who owes me a favor. He'll help you register."

"Joseph, this is—this is an answer to a prayer." Overwhelmed, Agnes rose from her chair and threw her arms around him. Startled, he laughed and held her, patting her back reassuringly.

True to his word, Joseph spoke with his friend in admissions, and two weeks later, Agnes was sitting in the auditorium of Kuehner Hall, flying through the exams in English literature, composition, mathematics, history, and French. Joseph also arranged for her to sell Bergstrom heirlooms through a dealer in Manhattan, and soon her income from antiques sales nearly doubled. But even then her earnings could not keep up with Claudia and Harold's runaway spending.

In early September, Agnes enrolled in Waterford College and began attending classes, relieved to be away from the manor but nervous to find herself in a classroom again after years away. Often Joseph met her between classes for coffee or lunch, although the first time she addressed him as Professor Emberly, conscious of their altered status and his greater authority, he threw back his head and laughed. "Please call me Joseph," he said. "Otherwise you'll make me feel ancient." She smiled and agreed, and for the first time since Richard went off to war, she felt a glimmer of hope for her future.

Then Claudia and Harold began selling off Bergstrom land.

Agnes fought to preserve every acre, but every time a tract came up for auction, Claudia and Harold argued that they had no other source of revenue. Frustrated, frantic, sick and tired of feeling like a helpless bystander to their self-destruction, she decided she must take drastic measures before nothing was left of Richard's beloved childhood home.

Again she turned to Joseph for help. He engaged an astute, circumspect lawyer who transferred most of the estate to Sylvia's possession, an ingenious and perfectly legal maneuver founded on Sylvia's status as an employee and owner of Bergstrom Thoroughbreds, a role Claudia too had been offered upon her eighteenth birthday but had declined. When the last documents were filed, the lawyer assured Agnes that no one else could sell the manor or the remaining protected acres as long as Sylvia lived.

If Claudia and Harold had investigated, they would have discovered how recently the arrangements had been made, and if they dug deeply enough they would have uncovered Agnes's involvement, but they did not bother. Perhaps they were too angry, or too hopeless, or too reluctant to spend money they did not have hiring a lawyer to sort it out. Whatever they truly felt, they accepted it as an inviolable entanglement of the late Mr. Bergstrom's will, a sign of his preference for Sylvia, which Claudia had suspected all her life and of which she believed she now had proof.

It pained Agnes to hear her kindly father-in-law unjustly maligned, but not enough to compel her to reveal the truth.

Unable to sell off any more land, Claudia and Harold brought their lavish spending to an abrupt halt. In their frustration they turned upon each other, arguing with intensified fury, hurling spiteful insults and bitter accusations. Distressed, Agnes moved from the second-floor bedroom she had briefly shared with Richard to a suite on the third floor, but that was not far enough to block out the sounds of sudden angry shouts, the startling bang of slammed doors, the dull thuds or sharp crashes of objects either thrown or knocked over in their raging.

Then, one day, as if in her misery she wanted everyone else to suffer too, Claudia blindsided Agnes with Andrew's secret, that Richard and James would have survived the attack if not for Harold's cowardice. As horrible as it was, Agnes knew it must be true. Andrew never would have invented such a nightmarish tale. At last she understood why Sylvia had left, and she desperately wished to follow.

Amid the ashes and rubble of their marriage, Claudia withdrew into solitary bitterness. Harold spent his days strolling about the grounds, walking stick in hand, thwacking at underbrush as if to scare up pheasants, making a show of managing the estate for an audience of none. In the evenings he sequestered himself in the library, where the friends of his youth occasionally joined him for cigars and whiskey, drinking themselves giddy until they passed out, slumped over on Mr. Bergstrom's fine leather sofas or sprawled out on the Persian rug. In the morning, Claudia would march into the library, seize an unwelcome guest or two by the collar, and haul them, half awake and stumbling, out the back door.

Agnes tried to lose herself in her studies and by taking up quilting again, determined to learn on her own what Sylvia had failed to teach her. Her classes at Waterford College offered her an escape, and her coffee breaks and lunches with Joseph, immeasurable solace.

When Joseph asked her to marry him, she felt as if the door to her prison tower had been flung open, the portcullis raised, the drawbridge lowered. On the other side stood Joseph, hand outstretched, beckoning her into sunlight and freedom. But although she was very fond of him, she did not feel the same dizzying rush of passion she had felt for Richard. Would fondness and admiration and gratitude be enough to sustain her, to sustain a marriage, for the rest of their lives?

He was too good a man for Agnes to deceive him. "I care for you, very much," she confessed, tears filling her eyes, "but I will never love you the way I loved Richard. I'm sorry."

Joseph looked pained, but he managed a rueful smile. "That's all right. Maybe you'll learn to love me in another way. I know you like me, and that's a start."

"You would still marry me, knowing how I feel?"

"If you'll have me." He thrust his hands into the pockets of his tweed coat and shrugged. "What do you say, Agnes? You have to admit I'd be much better company than that pair up at the manor."

She surprised herself with a laugh, an abrupt, choked sort of sound. "Of course, but I don't need to compare you to anyone to know that you're wonderful company."

Suddenly she realized that indeed, there was no one on earth dearer to her than Joseph. Perhaps that was love, or at least the seed of it.

And so she accepted his proposal.

She needed a week to stoke her courage before breaking the news to Claudia. She found her sister-in-law alone in the parlor with a skein of yarn and knitting needles forgotten on her lap. Agnes cleared her throat to interrupt Claudia's reverie, and then, with little fanfare or preamble, she announced her decision to marry.

Claudia stared up at her bleakly. "How could you have forgotten my brother so soon?"

Stung, Agnes struggled to keep her voice even. "I'll never forget Richard. I'll always love him, but he's been gone almost five years. He would never begrudge me the happiness I've found with Joseph, and I hope you won't either."

Claudia studied her, cheeks flushed, mouth pressed in a thin line. "I suppose you'll need to take different rooms," she finally said. "I know you like the view from the west wing, but the suites in the newer wing are larger and more modern. Joseph might—"

"Joseph and I aren't moving into the manor," Agnes interrupted, startled. "He already has a house, a lovely Cape Cod within walking distance of campus. You can visit us anytime—"

"But that's entirely unnecessary. We have so much room here. Invite Joseph to visit, let him see for himself—"

"Claudia—"

"How could you abandon me? Do you have any idea how I've suffered with—with *him*, how much worse it will be without you?"

"That's not fair. You can't blame me for your unhappiness. You don't have to live this way." Claudia tossed her head, scornful, but Agnes persisted. "Divorce Harold. Throw him out. Let him find a job and make his own way in the world. Write to Sylvia and urge her to come home. Together you can save the estate. The orchard is still thriving. You could earn a living from that, and from renting out the pastures—"

"I don't know where Sylvia is."

"Ask James's parents. Surely they've kept in touch—"

"Sylvia is not coming back," Claudia shrilled. "If she cared about Elm Creek Manor enough to save it, she never would have left!"

Shocked, Agnes regarded her for a long moment, heart pounding. "I don't believe that," she said. "But even so, you can still change your own fate. Harold is no good for you. Separate. Send him away. Make the farm profitable again. It won't be easy but Joseph and I will help you."

"I can't divorce Harold." Claudia bolted to her feet, sending yarn and needles tumbling to the floor. "Don't you understand? He is my penance."

"Claudia, no," Agnes protested, but her sister-in-law fled the room without looking back. Penance for what? For knowingly marrying the man who had refused to save Richard and James? For calling Sylvia a liar rather than accepting the truth, and thereby compelling Sylvia to flee her beloved home? Whatever Claudia thought she was atoning for, Agnes could not see how staying with Harold would accomplish any good.

In the days that followed, Claudia avoided her and barely spoke when they unexpectedly came upon each other in the manor. As for Harold, Agnes saw him not at all, but she knew he was living there still from the sounds of his perpetual arguments with Claudia and of drunken carousing from the library on evenings when his friends met. For Agnes, knowing that her departure was imminent somehow made each day more excruciating. Joseph agreed that they should marry as soon as possible, and as soon as the banns could be announced and the marriage license obtained, they wed at the small Catholic parish on Second Street. The groom's side of the aisle was nearly full of smiling family, friends, and colleagues from Waterford College; the bride's side, nearly empty. Peter, his wife, and two other employees of the antiques shop had kindly sat on the left, where several of Agnes's classmates were also scattered among the front pews, doing their best to create the illusion of a crowd.

Agnes had invited Claudia to the wedding, knowing she would refuse to attend; she had also left an invitation for Harold on the desk in the library, doubtful he would even bother to reply. She had written to her parents at her childhood home in Philadelphia, imploring them to come and asking them to forward the invitation to her brother and sisters and their families, if they had married and moved away. She had sent one invitation to her grandparents at their country estate in Chester County and another to their home in Georgetown, just in case they had decided to remain in the Washington area after her grandfather retired from the Senate. She had written to a few friends from Miss Sebastian's Academy, and their affectionate replies wishing her every happiness warmed her heart, even though each one wistfully regretted that they would be unable to attend the ceremony. At least her friends had replied. Not one member of her family had.

She had expected as much, but their cold silence still pained her. She had hoped her siblings might have broken their mother's embargo, but perhaps she had discarded the invitation and said nothing of it to the rest of the family.

Agnes told herself it did not matter. Joseph's family had welcomed her with open arms. She had already made a few friends in Waterford and looked forward to making many more, now that she would be living in town. A few dozen mostly empty pews would not spoil her beautiful, sacred wedding day.

It was to be the first of many beautiful days by Joseph's side.

How could she ever have worried that she did not love him enough? Within months, she understood that the dizzying rush of youthful passion she had shared with Richard was a brief, dazzling flare compared to the warm, enduring, steady fire she and

Joseph built together. This new, different love did not sweep her away, but rather held her up, grounded her, filled her with certainty and strength.

In those first radiant years of marriage, Agnes embraced her dual roles as college student and professor's wife, attending study groups at the library one day and hosting a cocktail party for the history department faculty the next. Upon completing her degree, she accepted a job with the college library's Rare Books Archive, sorting acquisitions, preserving aged volumes and ephemera, and helping students and faculty with their research.

She also assisted Joseph when Peter consulted him about particularly intriguing antiques that passed through his shop, where the unknown stories behind the furniture and artworks evoked her sympathy and wonder. Had a lovely young woman admired her reflection in the silver hand mirror, or had she lamented over minuscule imperfections invisible to everyone else? Had a doting grandfather carved the intricate circus scene into the lid of the oak toy chest, or had an indulgent uncle with no children of his own purchased it from a master woodworker? Each artifact had been well loved once, or at least well used. How had they ended up in Peter's shop, parted from the families that had left the patina of their lives upon them?

Agnes was four years married and carrying a happy secret she and Joseph had not yet shared with even their dearest friends on the afternoon she made an extraordinary discovery.

It was a blustery, overcast day in late November, when icy raindrops striking the windows warned of winter's swift approach. Joseph and Peter were in the back of the shop examining a cherry armoire recently acquired from an estate sale when Agnes's attention was drawn by an armchair that from a distance seemed to bear identical floral carvings. Curious, wondering if the two pieces separately acquired were somehow connected, Agnes went to examine the chair, but she was still several feet away when she realized the designs were quite dissimilar after all. Turning away, her glance fell upon a maple chest nearly hidden behind a Shaker china closet and an umbrella stand. Moving the umbrella stand aside, she let out a soft gasp of admiration as she took in the chest's fine details, the rich wood burnished to a soft glow, the brass fixtures marred by only a few scattered nicks and dents, the intricate Art Deco floral pattern of inlaid wood on the top and sides.

A memory stirred, the sense that she had once seen something very much like it, and as she knelt before the chest, it suddenly came to the fore: her grandmother's hope chest, which Agnes had last seen as a young girl at her grandparents' estate in Chester County. Perhaps this finely crafted piece had also once held a young woman's quilts, bed linens, tablecloths, even china and silver, as she prepared to manage a household of her own one day, dreaming of her true love, whomever he might be.

There was a latch and a keyhole, but when Agnes tested the lid she found it unlocked, and when she lifted it, the fresh scent of cedar wafted out. Peering inside, she found nothing within but a small iron key, which she assumed fit the chest's lock. As she picked up the key to test her theory, her fingertips brushed against the wooden bottom. Its unexpected roughness gave her a moment's pause. How strange that an artisan who had put so much care into the exterior of the chest would have neglected to sand the inside to a flawless finish. Stranger yet that—she looked again and touched the surfaces to be sure—the interior sides were of smooth, fragrant cedar, but the bottom was of simple plywood.

Puzzled, Agnes sat back on her heels, but as her gaze fixed on the front of the chest, she discovered another curious feature: Either the height of the chest was a clever illusion, or the interior was several inches shallower than it should have been.

Reaching into the chest with both hands, Agnes pressed gently upon the bottom—and the plywood bottom shifted.

Quickly she dug in her purse for her nail file. Mindful of how one careless scratch could diminish the value of an antique, she carefully wedged the file into the narrow crack between the cedar wall and the plywood bottom and applied a hint of pressure.

With a whisper of wood scraping against the grain, the plywood surface rose. Setting the file aside, Agnes slipped her fingertips beneath the plywood and gently tugged.

The false bottom eased free, revealing something hidden beneath, something wrapped in muslin.

Perhaps she should have paused then to call Peter over, but forgetting protocol and caution, she leaned the false bottom against the umbrella stand and removed the object. It was soft and pliant but with some heft to it. Even before she removed the muslin wrapper, she knew she held a quilt.

"Peter," she called, rising, the folded quilt in her arms, "Joseph, come see. I found something."

The urgency in her voice brought them quickly to her side. "What do you have there?" asked Joseph, his gaze traveling from the bundle in her arms to the open trunk and then to the plywood rectangle propped up against the umbrella stand.

When Agnes explained how she had made her discovery, Peter shook his head in amazement. "I've had that chest for years, and I never noticed the false bottom. I never would have guessed something was concealed within it."

"Will you lend me a hand?" she asked, moving into the aisle, holding out the folded quilt so they each could grasp adjacent edges. Shifting position to avoid jostling the merchandise, they stepped apart, unfolding the quilt between them.

"Honey," said Joseph, "this is quite a find."

Agnes nodded, her gaze on the quilt, resplendent in rich greens, reds, golds, and ivory; sixteen identical appliqué blocks framed by a border with graceful curves and a narrow appliqué accent. She was quite sure she had never seen any block exactly like these, although the Bergstrom women's vast pattern collection had included a few with striking similarities. Four branches of dark green reached toward the corners from the center of the square, each with five arced leaves with concave curves along the edges. Dark red, teardrop-shaped buds accented the tips, three for the longest central branch, one apiece for the smaller branches. There were four more red buds in the center of the block, closely placed but not quite touching, their wider curves turned inward, the narrow tips pointing toward the block's edges. Although the pattern had a distinctly floral look, "branches" and "leaves" were not quite the right words, but more accurate terms eluded her. The block's radial symmetry reminded Agnes of the paper snowflakes she and her sisters had made as children, and perhaps that fond memory along with the color palette evoked thoughts of Christmas, of cozy winter evenings with snow falling gently outdoors while a Yule log burned on the hearth.

"It's a work of art," said Agnes, awestruck.

"It's in excellent condition, considering that it's been folded and compressed for years," said Peter, studying it with a more critical eye.

Joseph's gaze went from the quilt to Agnes's face. "How much do you want for it?" he asked Peter. "I think it would make a great early Christmas present for my bride."

Agnes's exclamation of delight was cut short when Peter shook his head. "I'm not so sure it's mine to sell. I doubt very much the person who sold me the trunk knew a quilt was hidden inside. What if it's a cherished family heirloom?"

"Seller beware," Joseph quipped. "Who crams a cherished family heirloom beneath the false bottom of a chest and forgets about it?"

Peter inclined his head, acknowledging the point. "Even so, my conscience tells me I should contact the person I bought the chest from and confirm that they meant to sell the quilt too."

"Only if you want to do the ethical thing," said Joseph, but Agnes knew that for all his teasing, he too would insist upon doing whatever was right and fair.

While Peter withdrew to his office to search his files, Agnes and Joseph lingered over the quilt, admiring its handiwork, speculating about its origins. They agreed that it would have been impossible for the quilt to have become wedged beneath the plywood by accident. Someone must have hidden it, but why, and why had it never been removed? It seemed likely that the person who had hidden the quilt and the person who had sold the chest to Peter were not one and the same.

Twenty minutes later, Peter returned carrying an index card. "According to my records, I bought the chest eight years ago at an estate auction in Port Allegany, about one hundred miles northeast of here," he said, glancing at the card. "I have the original owner's name and address, but I confess my memories of the day are a bit vague. I attend dozens of auctions every year, and nothing distinctive about this one comes to mind."

"That's perfectly understandable, after so much time," said Agnes.

"I do recall meeting the former owner's son, Henry Frieberg, the executor of her estate. He had moved to Harrisburg years before. He seemed rather unsentimental about parting with his childhood home and his mother's belongings, but that might have been a stoic mask to conceal profound grief." Peter handed the index card to Joseph, who read it over before passing it on to Agnes. "I've listed his address and phone number as well."

drawing near. In the old days she would have driven the long way around the barn, parked behind the manor, and entered through the back door like one of the family, but the manor was no longer her home. She took the first fork instead, crossing the stone bridge and emerging from the forest at the edge of the broad front lawn, overgrown and browning with the season.

She instinctively slowed the car as she approached the front of the manor, where the driveway encircled a statue of a rearing horse, the old symbol of Bergstrom Thoroughbreds. As she parked the car, shouldered her purse, and took out the muslin-wrapped bundle and the cookie tin, she thought she felt eyes upon her, and yet after she climbed the stone stairs and sounded the heavy iron door knocker, several long minutes passed in silence except for the murmur of the wind in the trees, the scuttle of dried autumn leaves on the driveway, and the hoarse, distant caw of a crow. She knocked again, glancing to the windows visible from the veranda, certain she had glimpsed the flicker of a light within. Still no one answered her knock. Shifting her burdens to ease the pressure on her midsection, she was just beginning to wonder if she should try again when she heard a deadbolt slide back. The right-hand door slowly opened.

Claudia stood on the threshold, her expression drawn and suspicious until it gave way to recognition and surprise. Though she was only thirty-six, her shoulders had acquired a slight stoop, and coarse, steel gray threads dulled her once glossy chestnut brown hair, which she wore in an old-fashioned coil on the back of her head. Deep vertical creases framed her mouth, and two more appeared between her eyebrows as she looked Agnes up and down, her gaze alighting on the bundle and tin in her arms before returning to her face.

"Hello, Claudia," said Agnes warmly, genuinely glad to see her again. "It's been a while, hasn't it?"

"We'll call him," said Joseph as Agnes slipped the card into her purse. "If he wants the quilt, I'll return it to him on your behalf."

"Please do. If he doesn't want it, you can make him a fair offer with a clear conscience. I hope he'll simply let you keep it."

"But what about you?" said Agnes. "Shouldn't you get your cut?"

"I paid a fair price for an exquisite maple chest, which I still intend to sell at a profit," said Peter. "If you hadn't found the quilt, I never would have known it existed. As far as I'm concerned, the rule of finders keepers applies."

"Let's hope Mr. Frieberg agrees," said Joseph.

"I think you're being more than generous," Agnes told Peter, smiling, "but I'm not going to argue. Why put another obstacle between me and proper legal ownership of this gorgeous quilt?"

As soon as Agnes and Joseph returned home, she called the number on the index card, but no one picked up. She tried again an hour later, but it was not until her third attempt later that evening that Henry Frieberg finally answered. He seemed surprised to receive a call about his mother's estate auction, and he became keenly interested when she explained that she had discovered a false bottom to the maple chest, which he remembered well. His excitement diminished, however, when she told him that the plywood board had concealed a quilt.

"Is that all?" he asked. "Why would anyone go to so much trouble to hide a quilt?"

"I was hoping you could tell me," said Agnes. "It's an exceptional piece, not only because of its exquisite needlework, but its artistry." She described the quilt briefly, sensing that he was losing interest. "Could it perhaps be a long-lost family heirloom?"

"No, it doesn't sound familiar to me at all."

"Was your mother a quilter?"

He let out a harsh, abrupt laugh. "She was, but she never made anything that anyone would describe as 'an exceptional piece.'"

"I see." His derisive tone surprised her. "Are there any more talented quilters in the family?"

"I can't think of any who were worse, but I'm sure I never saw a quilt like the one you've described lying around my childhood home. You seem quite taken with it. Why don't you just keep it?"

It was the generous response she had hoped for—almost. "Don't you think you should see the quilt before you make a decision?" she asked. "We're willing to offer a fair price for it."

"Mrs. Emberly, let me be frank." His voice took on an edge. "My mother was a difficult woman. She was selfish, judgmental, and cruel. Even if she were capable of making a masterpiece quilt, which she wasn't, I wouldn't want it in my home. As far as I'm concerned, it belongs to the man who bought the chest."

"I'll let him know," said Agnes, taken aback, "but just in case, may I send you a photo of the quilt? It would ease my conscience to know you've made an informed decision."

He hesitated, but she wheedled a bit more and he eventually agreed. She hung up the phone and hurried off to fetch the camera she and Joseph had bought for their third anniversary, which they had celebrated with a weeklong excursion to Yellowstone. She spread the quilt upon the bed, took several shots, took a few more of the lovely autumn colors of the Waterford College arboretum to use up the film, and dropped off the roll with the developer. When she picked up the photos a few days later, she chose one of the entire quilt and one close-up of a single block and mailed them to Mr. Frieberg. A week passed before he called to confirm that he had never seen the quilt and did not consider himself the rightful owner.

"Maybe the quilt was already hidden in the chest when my mother inherited it from my grandmother," he said. "She passed on more than forty years ago, so I'm afraid we'll never know."

"I suppose not," Agnes replied. She thanked him for his help

and hung up, curiously disappointed. Shouldn't she be thrilled? She had done her due diligence but had reached a dead end. Mr. Frieberg did not want the quilt, and had in fact urged her to keep it. Why shouldn't she do exactly that?

Perhaps because in mentioning his grandmother, he had inadvertently suggested another possible quiltmaker, and Agnes believed the anonymous artist deserved to be acknowledged. Perhaps because Mr. Frieberg's certainty that they would never know the quilt's provenance seemed rather defeatist, considering how little time she had spent searching.

Perhaps because she knew that every quilt offered glimpses into its own history as well as the character of its creator, from the choice of pattern and color, to the type of fabrics available, to the quality of stitches—if one knew what to look for. And she knew someone who did.

In the four years since she had left Elm Creek Manor, Agnes had glimpsed Claudia from a distance a few times in downtown Waterford, but had never approached her. They exchanged Christmas cards every December, but never a lengthy letter, nor a phone call, since the Bergstroms had never installed a line. Agnes considered writing ahead of time to ask if they might meet, but she was afraid Claudia would refuse. So one Sunday afternoon in the second week of December, she filled a new tin with homemade spritz cookies and gingersnaps, loaded the tin and the quilt into Joseph's car, and drove out to Elm Creek Manor to meet with her erstwhile sister-in-law, unexpected and possibly unwelcome.

She almost missed the turnoff from the highway, but she spotted the unmarked forest road and hit the brakes just before she would have passed it. The winding way through the forest was as narrow and rough as she remembered, if not more so, but when she glimpsed the creek through the trees, she knew she was

"It has." Claudia drew herself up and pursed her lips. "What's wrong?"

Instinctively Agnes understood that Claudia assumed she had brought bad news from Sylvia. "Nothing's wrong," she quickly said, smiling and shaking her head. "I'm fine, Joseph's fine, and—well, I come bearing an early Christmas gift—" Cradling the quilt in one arm for a moment, she handed Claudia the red cookie tin with her free hand. "And a mystery. A mysterious quilt, to be precise. I hoped that with your expertise, you might detect some important clues that I've overlooked."

Claudia hesitated, glanced over her shoulder, but then nodded brusquely, opened the door wider, and beckoned Agnes inside. The foyer's marble floor looked as if it had not been swept in months, and several overstuffed cardboard cartons were haphazardly stacked in the corner where the walls of the ballroom and the banquet hall met. When Claudia led her to the parlor, Agnes hid her dismay to see more cardboard boxes stacked in a corner opposite the fireplace, newspapers and magazines scattered on every seat and tabletop, and a thin layer of dust covering all. Agnes had never seen Elm Creek Manor in such disarray. The Claudia she had once known never would have tolerated it.

Quickly Claudia began shifting piles of newspaper from the sofa to the coffee table. "I haven't had time to clean recently," she said, avoiding Agnes's eyes. "I've been terribly busy with the last of the harvest."

"The harvest?" Agnes echoed. "Do you mean—apples?"

"What else?" With her hand Claudia brushed lint and bits of thread from the sofa cushions to the floor. "The orchard is thriving. I hire students to pick and sort, and I sell the fruit to grocery stores and the cider mill in Grangerville."

"Claudia, that's wonderful."

"I wouldn't go that far. The orchard won't earn me a fortune but it pays the bills." Giving the arm of the sofa one last firm pat, raising a faint cloud of dust, Claudia straightened and regarded her expectantly. "Shall we take a look?"

Agnes removed the muslin wrapper and together they spread the quilt upon the sofa. Claudia's gaze sharpened and years seemed to fall away as she inspected it, first taking it in from a distance, then drawing closer, and then bending closer yet until her eyes were mere inches from the cloth. "You've discovered quite a treasure," she said at last, straightening. "The block pattern is called Christmas Cactus, and I'm sure even a novice like yourself can tell that it's quite challenging. Whoever made this was an expert with the needle. Her appliqué stitches are nearly invisible, the curves smooth, the points sharp. Her hand quilting is equally accomplished, twelve stitches per inch. The colors are harmonious, the balance of white space pleasing to the eye." She fixed Agnes with a shrewd look. "Where did you find it?"

Quickly Agnes explained. "The man who sold his mother's chest insisted that she wasn't skilled enough to make such a masterpiece," she added. "He thought that perhaps the quilt was hidden away before his mother inherited the chest from her mother."

"Did he mention when his grandmother passed?"

"Forty years ago, I believe he said."

"She can't be the one who hid the quilt, then. A quilt can't be any older than the newest scrap of fabric in it. Do you see these prints here, and here?" Claudia indicated a green Christmas Cactus in the upper right corner and several of the red buds. "These clear hues and small prints weren't available until the 1930s. This quilt could have been made last week, if the quiltmaker had pulled older fabrics from her stash, but it definitely could not have been made in 1914."

"So his mother must have hidden the quilt."

"Or someone else who used the chest did."

Mr. Frieberg had not mentioned anyone else, so it was safe to assume that the late Mrs. Frieberg was responsible. "Does the choice of the Christmas Cactus block tell us anything? Is it unique to a particular region or era?"

"Not especially. I've seen it in photos of quilts made as far back as the 1850s, and there are many variations. These fabrics too could be found in shops throughout the United States in the thirties." Claudia fell silent for a moment, thinking. "We could learn something from the batting, whether it's factory-made synthetic or hand-combed cotton or a wool reused from an older, worn-out quilt. That could tell us what region of the country the quilter hailed from, whether she was poor or well-to-do. But that would require us to remove part of the binding and pick out some of the quilting stitches to take a sample, and I assume from the look of horror on your face that you wouldn't want to do that."

"Definitely not," said Agnes emphatically.

"Perhaps it won't be necessary. Quilters often sign and date their work, writing with a pen and embroidering over the ink." Grasping one edge, she inclined her head to indicate that Agnes should take hold of the opposite side, and together they turned over the quilt. "Often quilters will add other information, such as where the quilt was made, for whom, and what special occasion it was made for, if any. These details can be worked into the design of the quilt top, but often they appear on the back."

Following Claudia's example, Agnes knelt and examined the quilt closely, running her fingertips gently over the back in search of an embroidered message from the artist. Perhaps she had modestly chosen thread that matched the backing fabric rather than draw attention to herself, or perhaps she had chosen a contrasting thread, but the color had faded over time. Agnes had worked her way down one edge and around a corner when her thumb brushed against a small, rigid bump. Peering closer, she saw that it was a knot, a small scarlet circle tied too firmly to pick out with a needle. Scarcely a half-inch to its right was another. In the same area, Agnes spied several tiny frayed threads of the same hue. When she pinched one between her thumbnail and forefinger and gently tugged, it would not pull free, as if a knot on the other side of the backing fabric held it in place. All around were many holes not much larger than pinpricks.

"I think I found something," she said.

When Agnes showed Claudia the knots, the frayed threads, and the pinprick holes, she studied them intently and nodded. "Something was certainly embroidered here at one point," she said. "But what? And why would she pick the stitches out afterward, or at least as many as she could without damaging the quilt itself?"

"I imagine she didn't," said Agnes. "My first thought was that one person put the stitches in, and another removed them."

"I suppose that's equally likely. Either way, we circle back to the same questions: What was taken out and why? The quilter used scarlet thread on a beige background, so she wanted the embroidery to be seen. Someone else erased it later."

"The late Mrs. Frieberg?"

"That seems most likely." Claudia closed one eye and held the pinpricked section close to the other, but after a moment, she sighed and shook her head. "I can't make out anything. My guess is that the knots were meant to be periods after initials or dots over two letter i's, but that's very little to go on. Perhaps if I had a magnifying glass—"

"Or we could shed some light on our subject," said Agnes, inspired. "Could you help me hold this in front of the lamp, the one on top of that table?"

Together they gathered up the quilt, rolling the other edges toward the center and lifting the formerly embroidered section so that it was suspended between themselves and the lamp. Light shone through the tiny holes where the embroidery threads had been removed, illuminating what once might have been three lines of writing, now illegible.

"I can almost make it out," said Claudia, squinting. "We need more light."

They set the quilt on the sofa, removed the lampshade, and tried again. In the brighter light, more holes were visible, as well as three lines of writing, the ink faded to the faintest of shadows. Claudia widened her eyes, squeezed them shut, looked again, but then drew back, shaking her head. "I can't read it. It's impossible."

"Why don't I try?" said Agnes, tactfully refraining from noting that she was ten years younger and might have better vision. Claudia shrugged and stepped aside, and as Agnes peered closely at the pattern of small holes, she noticed a distinct space between two light patterns on the first row. "Two words," she murmured, and as she spoke, she understood. "The quilter's first and last names."

"Can you make out any letters?"

"I think the first name begins with an E or a C. The last name . . ." Agnes blinked to rest her eyes and tried again. "The first letter looks like an H, but it could be an M. The surname looks about twice as long as the first name."

"That's not much but it's a start. What about the second line?"

"The first letter looks like a W or a V. Capitals are larger," she added, almost to herself. "Of course they'd be easier to read. But this looks like a capital R, right in the middle of the word, immediately following . . . a straight line. Perhaps a crossbar for a capital H, or a lowercase t? Then there's a space, then another capital letter, perhaps an O, right before the first of the two scarlet knots." Insight struck. "Not an O. It's *P.A.*, for Pennsylvania. The long word that preceded it was surely the quilter's hometown."

"You said the first letter looks like a W?"

"Or a V. Or perhaps a U."

"That straight line could be a hyphen. Wilkes-Barre. What other town in Pennsylvania has a hyphenated name that begins with a W?"

"That seems about the right length," said Agnes.

"Now we're getting somewhere." Claudia's voice rang with new energy. "This last line must be the date. Can you make out any numbers?"

"Only the very last. It's either a five, an eight, or the letter S."

"An S wouldn't make any sense, not at the end of the line." Claudia nudged Agnes aside in her eagerness to examine it more closely. "The line begins with a long word—'November' or 'December' would be my guess. As for the year, judging by the fabric and that last digit, if the number indicates the date she completed the quilt, it is almost certainly 1935 or 1938."

"Not 1945 or 1948?"

"I suppose that's possible," Claudia acknowledged. "Our quilter might have purchased the fabric in the 1930s but didn't use it until much later. I myself occasionally use fabric that my mother, aunts, and grandmothers added to our family fabric stash decades ago."

Agnes's eyes were beginning to water from gazing into the lamplight through the tiny holes, and her shoulders ached from the strain of holding up the quilt. With a sigh, she let her arms fall to her sides, careful not to let the quilt touch the unswept floor. Claudia helped her spread it upon the sofa again, and they both stood back to admire it once more in silent wonder. "I never would have thought to search for an artist's signature," Agnes said, breaking their reverie. "I'm indebted to you for suggesting it. Thank you."

"It's not much to go on, but I suppose it's better than nothing.

Your mystery quilter is someone with the initials EH or EM or CH or CM, and considering her evident skill, she was a mature woman, not an ingenue."

Agnes nodded, but even as a vague sketch of the mysterious quiltmaker began to take shape in her imagination, she realized just how difficult, impossible, even, it would be to find her. "I admit I have no idea what to do next."

"I'd send photos of the quilt to every fabric shop and quilt guild in Wilkes-Barre, Pennsylvania," said Claudia. "Your quilter bought her fabric and notions somewhere, and she surely showed the finished quilt to a friend or two. Someone will recognize it, even if they only glimpsed it from across a room twenty years ago."

Agnes fervently hoped she was right.

She rolled up the quilt—Claudia made her promise never to fold it, which would strain the delicate fibers—and returned it to the muslin wrapper. The energy and excitement that had flowed into Claudia as they examined the quilt seemed to drain from her as she escorted Agnes to the front door. "Please come and visit anytime," she said as Agnes put on her coat. "Promise to let me know what your search uncovers."

"Of course I will." On a whim, Agnes added, "We spent our entire visit talking about the quilt. Why don't we meet for lunch on Friday so we can catch up on the other news?"

"What other news?"

"Well . . ." Agnes resisted the impulse to rest her hand on her abdomen. "I haven't told you anything about my job at the Rare Books Archive, and I'm dying to know about your apple orchard adventures. You must be quite an entrepreneur to have launched your own business. I'm impressed."

"Don't be. Mostly I just renewed contracts with merchants my father had worked with for years." And yet for all her scoffing, Claudia looked pleased. "All right. Friday lunch."

"Let's meet at my place. Our entire house would probably fit inside your foyer, but we have a nice dining room and Joseph says I'm a fine cook."

"He says that, does he?" said Claudia, skeptical, but she agreed to come.

Agnes drove home with a light heart, pleased that she had renewed ties with her sister-in-law, intrigued by the clues they had uncovered about the mysterious quilter. Although it was true that the search would be difficult and Claudia seemed unhappy in her isolation, Agnes had every reason to hope for progress on both fronts with a bit of time, patience, and effort.

The next day on her lunch break, Agnes took her negatives to the photography shop and ordered reprints of the photos of the Christmas Cactus quilt. After work, she went from the Rare Books Archive to the reference section of the library, retrieved a phone book for Wilkes-Barre, and wrote down the addresses of every quilt shop and dry goods store listed. She could not find a category for quilt guilds, unfortunately, not even under "Clubs and Service Organizations," but she hoped the quilt shop owners would spread the word to their customers.

That evening after supper and whenever she could find spare moments throughout the next day, Agnes wrote several copies of a letter briefly explaining her search and asking for help tracking down the elusive quiltmaker, who may have lived in Wilkes-Barre around 1935 and may have had the initials EH, EM, CH, or CM. She included full-length and detail photos with each letter, but at Joseph's urging, she omitted a few significant details from the description to ward off unscrupulous characters who might falsely claim to be the rightful owner. She hoped such precautions would prove unnecessary.

She sent off a dozen letters with photos, then turned her attention to her lunch with Claudia. Since Elm Creek Manor was unreachable by phone, she sent Claudia a friendly note reminding her of their plans. On Thursday she shopped for groceries and made a pretty centerpiece of autumn foliage, pine cones, and ribbon to adorn the kitchen table. She took Friday morning off work so she could clean the house and prepare a lunch of chicken breasts with wild rice stuffing, Brussels sprouts salad with toasted almonds, and acorn squash. Then she set the table and waited in her favorite chair by the front picture window, eager to tell Claudia about the letters—and about the little bundle of joy she was expecting in early summer.

The bells at Good Shepherd Church a few blocks away rang out the noon hour as Agnes was checking on the acorn squash, and again at quarter past when the oven timer buzzed to announce that the chicken was done. Agnes turned the oven low to keep the chicken and squash warm and returned the salad to the refrigerator, wondering why Claudia had been delayed, wishing she could call Elm Creek Manor and see if she was on her way. At quarter of one, she suspected Claudia wasn't coming, and by one o'clock, she was sure of it.

Disappointed, she ate some chicken and half of an acorn squash alone at the kitchen table, put away the leftovers, and whiled away the afternoon knitting baby booties and debating whether she should drive out to the manor to make sure Claudia was all right. She decided against it. If Claudia had responded to her note and Agnes knew for certain she had meant to come, her absence would be cause for worry. As it was, it only meant that she had changed her mind.

Agnes had heard nothing from Claudia by the time the first responses to her letters arrived a week later. A quilt-shop owner wrote to say that she had posted the photos on her bulletin board, and one of her customers recalled seeing a quilt like it at a state fair many years ago. Unfortunately, she could not remember which year or even which state, but she was sure it was either Pennsylvania, New York, or West Virginia, because those were the only state fairs she had ever attended. The following day, two more letters arrived. The first writer claimed that she had made the quilt and would appreciate it if Agnes sent it to her by return post.

"I just bet she'd appreciate it," said Joseph dryly, reading over Agnes's shoulder.

"She signed the letter Janice Whitfield," said Agnes, indignant. "Her initials don't match at all. Honestly. The nerve of some people."

The second letter was more intriguing. The writer recalled from childhood that her family's next-door neighbor displayed two quilted throw pillows in her living room every holiday season, and the appliqués seemed to be a perfect match for the Christmas Cactus pattern in Agnes's photos. She vaguely recalled overhearing the neighbor tell her mother that she had made the pillows using blocks that were not quite perfect enough to be included in a holiday quilt she had made and had entered in a quilt contest. The quilt had gone missing somehow, but if the writer had ever heard the story, she had been too young to remember it. "My neighbor retired and moved away," she concluded, "but I'll get in touch with her and have her call you if you've found her long-lost quilt. If it isn't hers, she could give you the source of the pattern, and that might lead you to your missing quilter."

"This one sounds very promising," exclaimed Agnes, and after she read it aloud, Joseph agreed. She only wished the writer had provided her former neighbor's name so she could compare the initials.

The next day Agnes was tempted to call in sick so she could wait by the phone and meet the postman when he arrived with the day's mail, but honesty prevailed, so off she went to the library. No news from Wilkes-Barre waited in her mailbox when she returned home that afternoon, but the next day, she found a large, white cardboard envelope on the front porch half tucked under the welcome mat. It was too large for the opening to their mailbox, and their postman was too conscientious to bend things to fit.

Her excitement rose when she read the return address—Osterhout Public Library, Wilkes-Barre. Hurrying inside, she opened the envelope quickly but with care and spread out the contents on the kitchen table. There were two photostats of newspaper articles—one larger, folded in half, and the second a long, narrow news column—as well as a letter. The headline of the column drew her gaze, and she gasped to read LOCAL WOMAN'S PRIZE QUILT DISAPPEARS FROM STATE FAIR. It was dated July 1, 1936.

Eagerly she turned to the letter, which was from Marigold Johnson, a reference librarian and a quilter. Although Marigold explained that she had never seen the quilt in person, she recognized it immediately from the newspaper photo, a copy of which she had enclosed, and from the heartbreaking tale that still came up from time to time in the Wilkes-Barre quilting community.

In 1936, Edna Hachmeyer, a local quilter of great renown, had submitted her most recent masterpiece to the Pennsylvania State Fair. It had won first prize in the appliqué division and had earned a gold ribbon for Best of Show. On the morning after the fair, when Edna went to the tent to retrieve her quilt and collect her ribbons, they were gone. At first the officiants assumed that a worker had moved the quilt for safekeeping, as the tent was going to be dismantled soon, but all of the other quilts were accounted for and a thorough search turned up not a single thread of her Christmas Cactus quilt. The police were summoned, and they soon concluded that Edna's prizewinning quilt had been stolen.

"I'm convinced you've recovered it," Marigold wrote. "The photos are too similar for there to be any other explanation. After all this time, I'm sure Mrs. Hachmeyer has given her quilt up for lost. She moved to Harrisburg years ago to be closer to her family, but I have her youngest daughter's address and I'll write to her as soon as I finish this letter to you."

Agnes set the letter aside and unfolded the larger photostat. There, beneath a headline declaring WILKES-BARRE BEST OF SHOW QUILT STOLEN FROM STATE FAIR, was a photo of the Christmas Cactus quilt, unmistakable even in black and white. Below it appeared columns of text and a second photo of a woman standing in front of the quilt, smiling shyly as she shook the hand of a man in a three-piece suit and straw hat. Another man stood nearby just within the shot, looking on and beaming as he waited to hand her two ornate ribbons.

"Edna Hachmeyer," Agnes murmured as she sank into a chair, her gaze fixed on the woman in the photo. She was petite compared to the men, with bobbed, wavy light brown hair and glasses. She wore a pale, short-sleeved floral day dress with a tiered skirt and three bows on the bodice, one each at the neck, bosom, and waist. The photostat was not clear enough for Agnes to be sure, but she looked to be in her early to middle forties, which would put her in her early to mid-sixties now.

Mrs. Edna Hachmeyer of Harrisburg, Pennsylvania. With a name and a city, it shouldn't be too difficult to find the elusive quilter. Tomorrow on her lunch break, Agnes would look her up in the reference department's Harrisburg phone book, and when she returned home, she would call.

But after supper that evening, just as she finished washing the dishes and while Joseph was still drying them, the telephone rang. Agnes picked up, and when the caller asked for her by name, some instinct compelled her to reply, "This is Mrs. Emberly. Am I speaking to Mrs. Hachmeyer?"

"Please call me Edna," she said, her voice thin and warbling. "An old friend called me with exciting news, but I hardly dare believe it's true. Have you found my long-lost Christmas Cactus quilt?"

"I'm very sure that I have," said Agnes warmly, gesturing excitedly to Joseph, who set down his dish towel and hurried over. Agnes held up the handset between them and they both leaned an ear close.

"I wouldn't expect you to trust the word of a stranger on the telephone," said Edna, "but if you look on the back of the quilt, in the lower right-hand corner, you'll find my name, my hometown, and 'December 1935' embroidered in dark red thread."

Happy tears rose in Agnes's eyes. She had not mentioned the embroidery in her letters, the better to identify the true quilt-maker. "Most of the embroidery is gone, but I believe you."

"Why—I hardly know what to say." A chair scraped, and Edna breathed heavily as if she were easing herself into it. "Where has my quilt been all this time?"

"In an old maple hope chest I discovered in an antiques shop," Agnes replied. "I'd love to tell you the whole story, or at least what I know of it, in person, when I return your quilt to you. Are you free on Saturday?"

Flustered, Edna said that she was, and after a quick discussion of convenient hours and an exchange of addresses and phone numbers, they settled on two o'clock.

"You didn't make her an offer for the quilt," Joseph remarked after Agnes hung up the phone and seated herself at the kitchen table.

"How could I have?" Her voice caught in her throat. "She was so happy to know that it was found at last, and she's so eager to see it again. She wouldn't want to sell it, not at any price. I could hear it in her voice. Couldn't you?"

Nodding, Joseph sat down in the adjacent chair and took her hand. "You have a kind and generous heart, and I adore you for it."

She managed a smile, although that heart ached a little. She had grown very fond of the quilt and had hoped it would adorn their own bed throughout the festive season. "I would never keep something that didn't belong to me if the rightful owner could be found. Besides," she added lightly, waving a hand, "there are probably laws about keeping stolen property."

"There are," he said, leaning forward to kiss her, "but you can't fool me. You didn't think of that until this moment."

He knew her too well.

On Saturday, she and Joseph drove through a light flurry of snow two hours south and east to Harrisburg, the quilt carefully rolled and wrapped in muslin on the buckseat. A few minutes before two o'clock, they pulled onto a tree-lined, snow-dusted street and soon arrived at a charming redbrick colonial house with black shutters and an evergreen wreath on the front door.

They knocked, and the door swung open so promptly that the woman who answered must have been watching for them through the window. Agnes recognized her immediately as a grayer, stouter version of the woman from the newspaper photo.

She greeted them brightly and welcomed them inside, her eyes darting between their faces and the bundle in Joseph's arms. She invited them to sit down and offered them coffee and cake, but her eagerness was so contagious that Agnes laughed and said, "Thank you, we'll gladly accept, but first, why don't we reunite you with your quilt?"

Together they removed the muslin cover and unrolled the quilt. Tears filled Edna's eyes as she gazed upon it, her face bright with joy and wonder. "It's my quilt," she said, running her hand over the nearest Christmas Cactus block. "I never thought I'd see it again." She flipped over a corner of the quilt and ran her fingertips along the pinpricked space where her embroidery should have been. "Do you suppose someone picked out my stitches to cover up the theft?"

"That would be my guess," said Joseph. "Maybe the thief hoped to pass the quilt off as her own, but after the photos appeared in the newspaper, she panicked."

"That would also explain why she hid the quilt in the chest," said Agnes.

Nodding, Edna unfolded the corner and resumed studying the top. Sunlight streaming through the windows glinted on her glasses so Agnes could not read her eyes when she said, "You seem to have a good idea who the thief was."

Agnes and Joseph exchanged a look. "We think we do," said Agnes. "We know who the previous owner of the chest was, and it seems only logical that she was the one who hid your quilt within it. She passed on several years ago, and her son sold the chest at auction. He never knew about the quilt until I contacted him."

Edna looked up and held Agnes's gaze. "Who would do such a thing?" she asked, voice quavering. "Who would steal another woman's quilt and hide it away for decades? If a guilty conscience plagued her, she could have found some way to return it to me anonymously."

"I don't know," said Agnes, but she had a few theories. According to her son, Mrs. Frieberg had been a difficult woman, and she had never become an accomplished quilter. Perhaps she had seen Edna's quilt at the state fair, featured in the center of the quilt exhibit with its ribbons, and had been seized by envious greed. Somehow she had stolen it, perhaps minutes before Edna arrived to reclaim it, strolling into the tent and removing it from the wall and carrying it off with such nonchalance that no one thought to question her. Later, at home, perhaps she had been overcome by shame for what she had done. Perhaps she had realized that no one who saw the quilt in her home would believe that she had made it. Terrified that she would be caught and punished if she tried to return the quilt, she had instead hidden it away, taking it out only rarely, and only when she was alone to admire it, to wish that she were as gifted as the quilter she had wronged; then putting it away again when the shame and remorse became too much to bear.

But Agnes would never know for sure.

"We think we know who was responsible for the theft," she said. "We don't know the circumstances, not really."

"We could give you her name," said Joseph, "if you want to know."

Edna thought for a long moment in silence. "No," she finally replied. "What good would that do? You said she passed on, so I'll never get my questions answered. I have my quilt back, perfectly unharmed. Let her rest in peace."

Agnes sighed and nodded, relieved.

They admired the quilt awhile longer, but eventually they draped it over a sofa out of direct sunlight, and Edna led them to the dining room for the coffee and cake she had promised. They were chatting pleasantly about quilting and the upcoming holidays when Edna suddenly gave a start. "My goodness," she exclaimed. "I was so overcome with recovering my quilt that I forgot it belongs to someone else now. You must allow me to buy it from you."

Joseph shook his head, and Agnes said, "There's no need. It doesn't belong to us."

"The antiques shop owner, then."

"He wouldn't accept a penny from you," said Joseph. "You are the rightful owner. You don't owe anyone anything."

"And yet I do owe you two a debt of gratitude." Edna turned to Agnes, smiling faintly. "You mentioned that you've had some misadventures learning to quilt."

"I chose a far too challenging pattern for my first attempt," Agnes admitted. "Since then, I've started over from the beginning, with simple pieced blocks, and I think I'm making rather good progress."

"She's almost finished a quilt for the baby," said Joseph proudly. "A Nine-Patch, she calls it."

"Congratulations," said Edna. "For your little blessing, I mean, but the quilt too. You're going to be very busy after the baby arrives. Since you have more free time now than you will for the next eighteen years or so, would you like me to teach you how to make a Christmas Cactus quilt?"

"Would you?" exclaimed Agnes. "Do you think I could learn? The pattern looks so intricate, so difficult."

"Appliqué is very different from piecing, and you might find that you take to it much more quickly. And yes, I believe you can learn. I see how much you admire my quilt, and how it pains you to part from it. Wouldn't it be lovely to have one of your very own?"

Agnes agreed that it would be, and she accepted Edna's offer with a grateful heart.

Over the next few months, Edna taught Agnes the fundamentals of appliqué before moving on to the more advanced techniques required for the Christmas Cactus pattern. They met once a month at Edna's home for a daylong lesson, which they supplemented with frequent letters and phone calls. Week by week Agnes's skills improved, and by the time her daughter was born in June, she had finished all sixteen blocks and had almost completed assembling the quilt top. The demands of early motherhood required her to take some time off, but by autumn she and Edna had layered and basted the finished top, batting, and backing fabric. Whenever she could find a spare moment, Agnes quilted the layers, held snugly in a wooden hoop on her lap, with painstaking stitches, embarrassingly large and awkward until with practice she mastered the smooth, rocking motion she had first seen Sylvia and Claudia perform at Elm Creek Manor.

How far she had come since those sad and lonely days. She wished she knew that her erstwhile sisters-in-law had found happiness again as she had.

Agnes did not complete her quilt in time for Christmas, but she put the last stitches into the binding a few days before Thanksgiving the following year. When she proudly unveiled it for her teacher, Edna embraced her and praised her, pointing out one section of the quilt and then another to show her progress. "If you keep this up," she remarked, smiling, "I can only imagine the masterpieces you'll be creating when you're my age."

Agnes had fallen in love with appliqué, thanks to her wise, patient teacher, and she made more complex and intricate quilts in the years that had followed, but the Christmas Cactus quilt would always be precious to her, not only because she had discovered a new artistic path by mastering appliqué, but also because Edna's generosity of spirit inspired her to live her own life free of judgment and bitterness.

How fitting it would be for her Christmas Cactus quilt to adorn one of the walls of Elm Creek Manor, extending the holiday spirit of generosity and kindness to all who visited the Christmas Boutique!

Humming a Christmas carol, Agnes rolled up the quilt, slipped it back into its protective cover, and carried it downstairs to the living room, where she placed it on the sofa to await her next trip to Elm Creek Manor. She was walking through her home gathering up a few other holiday quilts she had already set out for the season when the phone rang. Leaving the quilts on the sofa with the Christmas Cactus, she hurried to the kitchen to answer.

It was Gretchen, calling from Elm Creek Manor. "Anna and I have arranged the dining tables in the banquet hall, but we still need some pretty centerpieces," she said. "Do you want to help me make them?"

"I'd love to," Agnes replied. "Just let me grab my coat, my purse, and my glue gun, and I'll be ready to go."

"Do you need a ride? Anna and Jeremy could pick you up in the Elm Creek Quilts minivan. They're out now collecting donations of food and supplies for the boutique buffet. I'm sure you could reach Anna on her cell."

"No need to trouble them when they're so busy. I'll call Gwen. Yesterday she mentioned that she's planning to come to the manor this morning to work on the layout of the market stalls with Sylvia, and I'm sure she wouldn't mind giving me a lift."

"See you soon, then."

"See you soon," Agnes echoed, and then hung up and dialed Gwen's number. She had quilts to deliver and centerpieces to make, and not a moment to waste.

# 6

## *Gwen*

 ON TUESDAY AFTERNOON, Gwen and Sylvia finished revising their plan for the arrangement of the Christmas Boutique booths, while Andrew and Joe put away the last of the sewing machines, irons, rotary cutting mats, and other quilt-camp tools and equipment. The tall white partitions and tables remained in the middle of the ballroom, ready to be moved into position to form spacious aisles and market stalls. On Wednesday afternoon, as soon as Gwen finished proctoring her last final exam of the day, she drove to Elm Creek Manor to get started.

It was a bright, sunny day, clear but bracingly cold, with capricious gusts of wind that blew clumps of snow from the treetops onto the road and the hood of her car as she drove through the forest from the highway to the rear parking lot of Elm Creek Manor. Gwen had been monitoring the weather forecasts closely ever since Nancy and Melanie had asked the Elm Creek Quilters to take on the Christmas Boutique, and thus far, all indications were that they could expect seasonally cold temperatures blessedly free of blizzards. A few inches of snow were expected to fall on the Elm Creek Valley late Saturday night, but as long as the snowplows cleared the roadways by Sunday morning, the weather should not interfere with their plans for a successful fund-raiser.

Or, of greater significance to Gwen personally, with her daughter's flight home.

About 575 miles to the west, Summer was finishing up her first semester of graduate school at the University of Chicago. As far as Gwen could tell from her frequent phone calls and occasional emails, she was thriving there. Her classes were challenging but fascinating, her professors exacting but fair. She had made new friends, and was especially close with the three graduate students with whom she shared an apartment in Hyde Park near Kenwood and Fifty-Sixth. In fact, Summer was so engrossed in her studies and so happy in her new surroundings that she had not come home for Thanksgiving. Gwen had been horribly disappointed when Summer hesitantly broke the bad news over the phone, but having survived a grueling graduate program herself, Gwen knew how difficult it was to get away from campus, how precious those four-day weekends were when one had sleep to catch up on, reading to plow through, and papers to write.

"You should do what you need to do," Gwen had bravely replied, forcing cheerfulness into her voice. "I'll see you in December." Summer, clearly relieved, had thanked her for understanding, but as soon as they hung up, Gwen burst into tears.

She and Summer had never been apart so long. Summer had earned her undergraduate degree at Waterford College, so even though she had lived in a campus dorm during her freshman year and had shared an apartment with friends after that, she had come home for dinner at least once a week and they saw each other frequently at Elm Creek Manor. All that had ended when Summer departed for Chicago. Since then, Gwen's Sunday evenings had seemed empty and lonely, no matter how determinedly she had packed them full of work, quilting, and dinners out with friends. But the autumn quarter was nearly over, Summer would soon be on her way home, and Gwen would enjoy three blissfully happy weeks with her daughter before she had to return to school in early January. Gwen meant to make the most of every hour.

When she pulled into the rear parking lot, she spotted the Elm Creek Quilts minivan and Andrew's motor home in their usual places in the far corner, while Diane's gleaming white BMW and Jeremy's modest brown compact were parked closer to the back door. When Gwen climbed the stairs and entered the manor, she nearly bumped into Diane in the foyer.

"Now that we've narrowed down the list of suspects," Diane declared, forgoing the usual salutations as she deftly tied a black-white-and-red-tartan scarf around her neck, "we can investigate their motives. Who would benefit from ruining the Christmas Boutique?"

Gwen muffled a sigh. "The group running that competing Christmas Boutique up in Summit Pass, obviously."

Diane gasped, eyes wide. "I didn't know there was a competing boutique."

"That's because there isn't one. I made it up. You're being ridiculous, you know, more so than usual. Whoever turned off the power did it by mistake. They surely feel terrible about it and don't need any more grief from you. Just let it go."

Diane planted a hand on her hip. "You're willing to let the culprit get away with it?"

"No one's getting away with anything. Nancy and Melanie know who was responsible, and if they don't want to disclose the person's name to spare them embarrassment, we should accept that." Shaking her head, Gwen stamped her boots on the mat and unbuttoned her coat. "I don't know why you're wasting your time on this silly investigation when we have so much to do to get ready for the boutique."

"I've been doing my job," Diane protested. "I've sent out hundreds of emails and I've personally spoken with the leaders of community organizations throughout the Elm Creek Valley. And there's my publicity coup number one: a feature article on the front page of the Arts and Leisure section of tomorrow's *Waterford Register*, followed by a prominent listing in the weekend calendar."

"Really? That's fantastic!"

"I know, isn't it? Publicity coup number two: an interview with WPSU." Diane quickly buttoned her red wool coat and pulled on her black leather gloves. "Airing live in exactly two hours, right before *All Things Considered*. They'll rebroadcast it Saturday and Sunday morning right after *Weekend Edition*, and they'll mention the boutique during the *Folk Show* calendar on Saturday at noon." She picked up a sleek red travel mug from the floor and shouldered her purse. "Want to come along with me to State College? Hippies like you love public radio. We could solve the mystery on the way."

Gwen rolled her eyes. "I'd love to, but as much fun as it sounds to be stuck in a car with you while you contemplate the sinister motives of our neighbors, I have too much to do here."

"Thought so. The rest of the setup squad has been hard at work in the ballroom all morning. Coffee's hot, so grab some before it's gone." With that, Diane gave her a cheery wave and hurried off.

Gwen hung up her coat and hat and went to the kitchen, drawn by the enticing aroma of a rich Italian roast. She found Anna at the center island, paring apples and sharing a laugh with Jeremy, who sat nearby at the long wooden table, a steaming mug at his right hand and books and papers spread all around. Anna jumped when Gwen walked in, nearly dropping her knife. "Hey, Gwen," she said, inclining her head toward the coffeepot. "I just brewed a fresh pot, but I can't promise that Diane left you any."

"She so rarely does," said Gwen, with an exaggerated sigh. To Jeremy, she added, "How's the dissertation going?"

"Slowly but steadily." He eyed his research materials and notes with a mixture of affection and distaste. "I still love the subject and I'm proud of my work, but at this point, I just want to have it done."

"I hear you." Gwen's struggles with her own dissertation were indelibly seared into her memory. She still had nightmares in which she was frantically typing the index mere minutes before her deadline, but somehow the words vanished from the page every time she hit the carriage return.

She wished him good luck, poured herself a cup of coffee, and carried it carefully to the ballroom, where she found all the partitions in the proper places, and nearly all the tables too. Gretchen and Joe were setting the last dozen or so in place, while Sylvia and Andrew were hanging quilts high upon the walls. Sarah moved from one group to the other, one hand pressed to her lower back, directing the operations and pitching in with the less physically demanding tasks as needed.

Gwen took a swift gulp of coffee, set her mug aside, and hurried to help Gretchen and Joe arrange the last few tables. When they finished, she and Sarah took dust cloths in hand and wiped them clean. Whenever Gwen moved from one table to the next, she paused to admire the lovely holiday quilts already adorning the ballroom walls. She recognized Agnes's Christmas Cactus, which she displayed in her home every holiday season, but not the traditional Log Cabin or the charming Christmas Star, although the appliqué borders suggested that they too were Agnes's creations. Gwen still needed to bring in quilts from her own collection. Between finishing up her teaching obligations for the semester and working on her academic research, she had not found time to pull them out of storage. Most of her seasonal quilts focused on the solstice rather than Christmas, but years before, when Summer was still in middle school, they had collaborated on a lively green, red, and white quilt that was as holly and jolly as any Christmas quilt ever made. She figured both quilts would suit Agnes's decorating theme well.

Just as Gwen turned her attention to another table, the clatter of metal on carpet startled her. A hanging rod had fallen from the wall hooks to the floor, and a quilt lay in a heap beside it.

"We could use an extra pair of strong arms," said Andrew wearily from halfway up a ladder, "and a few more inches in height."

"Sounds like you're describing Matt," said Sarah, pressing the back of her hand to her forehead. "Unfortunately, he's not available."

Gwen and Sylvia exchanged a wary look. When Sarah started brooding about Matt's absence, it could be very difficult to pull her out of it. "That's all right," said Gwen. "Jeremy's in the kitchen, and he's almost as tall as Matt."

She hurried off to summon him. When she found him still chatting happily with Anna as she chopped apples and deftly swept them from her cutting board into a mixing bowl, she suddenly understood why he was struggling to make progress on his dissertation. "Jeremy, can you give us a hand in the ballroom?" she asked. They both started, apparently so engrossed in their conversation that they had not heard her enter. "We need someone with a bit more height to hang some quilts."

"Sure," he replied, rising from the table. "I could use a break."

To Gwen it seemed that he could use a break from taking breaks, but she needed his help, so instead of giving him a good professorial chiding, she smiled and gestured for him to follow her. "What's Anna cooking up?" she asked as they turned down the corridor. "She seems a little jumpy today."

"It's a surprise for Sylvia," he replied. "Whatever you do, don't mention apples to her, and try to discourage her from visiting the kitchen for the next few hours."

"I'll do my best," said Gwen. "By the way, I've been meaning to ask you if you have any plans for winter break. Are you heading upstate to visit your parents?"

"I'm planning to stick around campus and work on my dissertation. I took the first week of December off to spend Hanukkah with my family, so they're not really expecting me back so soon."

"In that case," Gwen said as they crossed the grand front foyer, "you'll have to come by for dinner soon. Summer and I always celebrate the solstice with a midnight feast. You're welcome to join us."

As they entered the ballroom, he gave her a curious, sidelong look. "I think maybe you should check with Summer first."

Gwen was so surprised that she laughed, but before she could ask him to explain, Sylvia waved to them from across the room. "Jeremy to the rescue!" she called out. "And none too soon."

"Coming," he called back, breaking into a jog.

Bemused, Gwen resumed wiping down the tables while her friends hung the quilts, and she finished just in time to join them as they were hanging the last. "This is an excellent start," Gretchen remarked, hands on her hips as she turned in place to admire the display, "but that wall is still bare, and we need more quilts to fill in these empty spaces between the windows."

"I'm afraid I don't have any suitable quilts," said Sarah. "I don't know why I've never made a quilt from Christmas fabrics or in Christmas colors. Even the quilt I'm making for my father-in-law's Christmas present is blue, tan, and burgundy."

"I might have a few more holiday quilts in the attic," mused Sylvia. "If I had a few months to search, I might even find them."

"Anna said she's planning to bring one in," said Jeremy. "I think she called it a sampler."

"I have two still at home," said Gwen. "I promise to bring them tomorrow."

"Including your *Winter Solstice Star?*" asked Sarah. "I love that quilt."

"Yes, that's one of them. I don't think any of you have seen the other."

"That will help," said Gretchen, studying the walls, "but we'll need a few more to make this a proper quilt show."

"How about a Hanukkah quilt?" asked Jeremy. "I have one you could borrow."

Sarah's eyebrows rose. "Since when have you become a quilter?"

"You've been holding out on us," Sylvia teased. "If we had known, we would have put you on our substitute teacher list."

Jeremy grinned. "I didn't make it. It was a Hanukkah gift from Anna. It's really amazing, all these blue-and-gold six-pointed stars."

Now that he mentioned it, Gwen remembered seeing Anna cutting stout rhombuses from blue and gold fabrics on the Friday after Thanksgiving, during the Elm Creek Quilters' holiday quilting bee that had turned into an overnight stay, thanks to an unexpected blizzard. A handmade quilt was quite an impressive gift, even for someone that Anna often referred to as her best friend. If memory served, not even Summer had ever made Jeremy a quilt.

Gwen felt a faint stir of unease. Jeremy's quilt, his odd response to her dinner invitation, Anna's nervous behavior whenever Gwen came upon her and Jeremy together—

"We'd love to borrow your Hanukkah quilt, Jeremy," Sylvia declared. "Supporting the food pantry is an ecumenical enterprise, and all faiths are welcome at Elm Creek Manor."

Sarah threw Gwen a teasing grin. "This is where you usually add a remark about honoring the goddess."

"Diane isn't here," said Gwen. "What's the point, if I can't offend her?"

But even if no one else noticed, she thought her jollity sounded forced. Were Summer and Jeremy having problems? Long-distance relationships were challenging, of course, but Gwen assumed things were fine between them, since Summer had not said otherwise.

Wouldn't she have told Gwen if things were otherwise?

She knew Summer and Jeremy were in touch, because occasionally each passed along a bit of news to her that the other had shared, although it had been a while since either had done so. Although Summer had not been home since she had left for Chicago, Jeremy had driven out to see her for a long weekend in late September. He had intended to visit her for Thanksgiving too, but he had been turned back by the same storm that had kept the Elm Creek Quilters snowbound.

It *was* the storm that had compelled him to turn around, wasn't it?

Since their work in the ballroom was complete until they had more quilts to hang or the boutique merchants arrived with their goods, Gwen bade her friends goodbye. "I have a stack of exams to grade," said she apologetically, resisting the impulse to dig into her tote bag for her cell phone. "I'll see you all tomorrow afternoon."

"Bring your quilts," Gretchen called after her as she hurried away.

Gwen did not stop by the kitchen on her way to the rear foyer, but threw on her coat and scarf and slipped quietly out the back door. She waited until she was halfway to her car before calling her daughter. But what if Summer had no idea what was going on with Jeremy and Anna? What if nothing *was* going on? Gwen didn't want to sow doubt and mistrust where none were warranted, and she didn't want to nag her daughter about trouble in her relationship if Summer didn't want to discuss it.

And that, of course, was what bothered her most—not that Summer and Jeremy might have broken up, but that Summer had not confided in her.

Weighing her options, she climbed into her car and started the engine, shivering until heat began to waft from the dashboard vents. She could not simply blurt out her suspicions or come at her daughter with a barrage of questions, not if she wanted a calm, reasonable conversation. She must be more circumspect.

Summer picked up on the third ring. "Hey, Mom," she greeted her cheerfully. "You caught me at a good time. I just finished my Contemporary Issues of Human Rights exam, and I'm on my way to the library to work on my Historical Geography project."

"How did the exam go?"

"Very well, I think. I'll know for sure when I get my grade."

"Grades aren't always the best measure of comprehension," Gwen said, slipping into professor mode for a moment. "How's everything else going?"

"Fine, I guess. I'm a bit worn out and I'm looking forward to resting over break." She hesitated. "There was this one thing—"

Gwen pounced. "What? What is it? You can tell me anything."

"I know, Mom. It's not an emergency." Summer's voice faded for a moment as she lowered her phone to greet a fellow student in passing. "A few weeks ago, before registering for winter quarter classes, all the first-years had to meet as a group with the chair of the graduate program. Among other procedural things, she told us to write a paper, a statement of purpose to explain our intentions for graduate study—the intellectual problems and issues that interest us, the historical stories that intrigue us, our preferred analytical or narrative approaches—and why, given the declining number of academic posts in universities throughout the country, we've decided to enter this profession."

"That's quite a lot to throw at you all at once," said Gwen.

"Didn't you have to write a statement of purpose for your application?"

"Yes, but the application left out that part about the rapidly diminishing number of assistant professor positions that will be available when I finally have my doctorate."

"Oh, kiddo. You just got started. You won't be sending out CVs for years. It's almost impossible to predict how the academic job market will ebb and flow over time. Focus on learning and doing good work now. Everything else will fall into place."

"I hope you're right."

"Is that . . ." Gwen chose her words carefully. "Is that really all that's bothering you?"

"You mean that's not enough?" Summer laughed lightly. "Yeah, that's really all. Listen, I just got to the library. Was there some reason you called, or were you just checking in?"

"I just had one quick question. Would you mind if I included our *Christmas Garland* in the Christmas Boutique quilt show? The ballroom walls still look a bit bare."

"I'd love that. Why would I mind?"

"Well, it's a special quilt."

"All of the quilts we've made together are special. I'll be happy to see that one displayed at Elm Creek Manor when I come home. It won't be much longer, you know."

"I do know," said Gwen. "I've been counting the hours."

Summer laughed. "I'll see you soon, Mom. I love you."

"I love you too. Wait," Gwen blurted, before Summer could hang up. "There's one more thing."

"What?"

"Just now, I invited Jeremy to join us for our winter solstice feast. He gave me a cryptic look and said I should check with you first."

"Oh." Summer hesitated. "That's probably because we're not together anymore."

"What? Since when?" Without giving her time to explain, Gwen said, "You broke up over Thanksgiving, didn't you? Why didn't you tell me?"

"I didn't want to tell you over the phone. I wanted to tell you in person, so that you could see for yourself that I was fine, that I wasn't devastated, moping around the apartment with a broken heart." Summer forced a laugh. "I didn't want you abandoning your students so close to the end of the semester so you could hop on a plane and fly out to Chicago to check in on me."

"I would never do anything like that," Gwen protested.

"So you say, but I didn't want to test that theory."

Gwen muffled a sigh. "Are you sure you're all right?"

"I'm fine, just very busy. And I really do need to get back to work. I love you, Mom. I'll see you Friday."

"I love you too." Gwen waited for Summer to hang up first, then hung up and returned her phone to her tote bag.

She drove home, lost in thought. Summer's explanation was implausible and, to be frank, a little insulting. Gwen had never been the sort of overbearing, oppressive parent who demanded that her child account for every moment of her time or put aside everything else for a scheduled weekly phone call at a particular day and hour. If Summer needed her to come to Chicago, whether due to heartbreak or illness or whatever, Gwen would rush to her side if asked, but she would never disrupt Summer's life by showing up uninvited. Surely Summer knew that. And while Summer was very busy and preoccupied with school, they had chatted on the phone at least twice since Thanksgiving. Summer could have squeezed a few words about the breakup into one of those conversations without sacrificing any study time.

The only logical conclusion was that Summer didn't want to discuss it, at least not with Gwen. But why, when Summer had freely shared every sorrow and joy with her from the time she was a young girl?

Gwen brooded all the way home, and once there, she went to the kitchen to make herself a soothing cup of ginger tea. The stack of exams from her Women and the American Experience course awaited her attention in the spare bedroom she used as a study, but something far more enticing beckoned her to the spacious room over the garage she and Summer shared as a quilt studio. Gwen's father had built the custom-made shelves and bins in which they stored their quilts and fabric, but she had hired a contractor to install the skylights, which let in lovely, diffuse natural light, ideal for viewing the colors of fabric and thread.

Gwen knew exactly where to find the *Christmas Garland* quilt: on the center shelf near the front, just below eye level. One of her and Summer's favorite winter traditions was to snuggle up together on the sofa beneath the quilt, sip hot cocoa and nibble cookies, and watch holiday movies, two or three back-to-back for every night of their respective schools' winter breaks, unless they had company or were invited to a gathering elsewhere. They knew their favorites so well—not only the classics like *It's a Wonderful Life*, *Miracle on 34th Street*, and the animated Santa Claus stories from the sixties, but newer films like *A Christmas Story*— that they could and often did recite the lines along with the characters. Every year Gwen wondered aloud why the cartoons, in particular, often depicted Santa Claus as a curmudgeonly diva, and Summer found new plot holes that she had not noticed as a child.

"They are *flying* reindeer," she had pointed out at seventeen during *Rudolph the Red-Nosed Reindeer* after the toothless Bumble plummeted over the edge of a cliff, taking Yukon Cornelius and his sled dogs with him. "Rather than assume Yukon is dead, couldn't they spare two minutes for a flyover just to make sure he isn't lying on the ground injured?"

"Of course not," said Gwen, feigning astonishment. "They have to get the women back to Christmas Town!"

Jeering at the blatant sexism of some of the older movies was another favorite tradition.

Gwen smiled as she took the quilt down from the shelf and draped it over the worktable in the center of the room, her worries momentarily forgotten in the warm glow of happy memories. And yet like the quilt itself, its disparate shapes swirling in a circular pattern of bright and dark, other memories of the season when she and Summer had made the quilt were fraught with disappointment, uncertainty, and anger. What holiday was complete without a bit of angst?

Summer was thirteen then, an eighth grader, excelling in her classes, a star forward on the middle school soccer team, beloved by many friends. They had moved to Waterford from Ithaca two years before, after Gwen completed her Ph.D. at Cornell and accepted a job as an assistant professor in the Department of American Studies at Waterford College. Although Gwen had not learned to quilt until she was in her mid-twenties, she had begun teaching Summer when she was ten years old. Summer had made several quilts in the years since, not only simple beginner patterns but designs of remarkable complexity, and she held the record as the youngest official member in the history of the Waterford Quilting Guild. The previous July, she had taken third place in the machine-pieced, machine-quilted division of the Waterford Summer Quilt Festival—not in the children's division, but right up there with adults who had begun quilting long before she was born.

In late autumn, as the leaves changed hue and the winds blew colder, Gwen and Summer decided to collaborate on a quilt with a holiday theme. They knew they were starting a bit late in the year for that, but they refused to impose an artificial deadline upon themselves. So what if they didn't finish before New Year's Eve or even the Feast of the Three Kings? As nice as it would be to admire a finished Christmas quilt on Christmas morning, it could be even more fun to work on a holiday quilt throughout the festive season.

On afternoons after school and on weekends, they paged through quilting magazines for inspiration and browsed for fabric at Grandma's Attic, a marvelous quilt shop in downtown Waterford across the street from the college. Gwen envisioned a silvery white, midnight blue, and rich gold color scheme to represent the solstice, the longest night of the year and the welcome return of the sun, but Summer was drawn to more traditional Christmas fabrics—bright holiday prints, reds and greens with images of Christmas ornaments and snowflakes, and graceful, whimsical designs that resembled German paper-cutting art. Surprised, Gwen nonetheless promptly jettisoned her original plan. She would find more joy in pleasing her daughter than in imposing her own artistic vision upon their quilt.

While their fabric and color preferences needed some reconciliation, from the start they were in absolute agreement regarding the style. They both wanted to avoid blocks with "Christmas" in the name; such blocks were the obvious choice for a holiday quilt and they didn't want their quilt to resemble anything countless thousands of other quilters had already made. They also thought it would be fun to break free of the standard square blocks in a straight grid layout and opt for something more distinctive, even if it would be more difficult to make.

In early November, they were sitting together on the sofa studying Gwen's encyclopedia of pieced quilt patterns, the book open on Gwen's lap, Summer snuggled up to her side. They turned the pages, considering and rejecting one block after another, when suddenly they both spotted the same pattern at the same time and exclaimed, "That's it!"

Jack's Chain was marvelously simple to piece and yet complex in appearance. At the center of each unit—for the term "block" did not seem to fit—was a hexagon, with a Nine-Patch attached to each of the six sides. An equilateral triangle filled the spaces between each pair of adjacent Nine-Patches, one vertex touching a corner of the hexagon. The bases of the triangles added to the remaining sides of the Nine-Patches to create a dodecagon. When several of the twelve-sided pieced segments were arranged side by side and the empty spaces filled with more triangles, the quilt seemed to spring to life with movement as the viewer's eye followed the line of one arc of Nine-Patches and triangles to the next, traveling over the surface of the quilt.

Eager to begin, they sketched a layout, calculated sizes, and made templates, debating whether they should assign one color to each shape or mix them up for a vibrant, unrestrained, scrappy appearance. The pattern seemed to demand the latter, and so they cut hexagons, squares, and triangles alike from the same mix of green, red, and winter-white fabrics. They sewed together every evening after supper and homework, sometimes listening to the radio in companionable quiet, but more often talking. They discussed anything and everything—school and work, movies and books, personal dramas among their neighbors and acquaintances, who liked whom at Lydia Darragh Middle School, who was collaborating with or conspiring against whom in the corridors and offices of Kuehner Hall.

"We need to give our finished quilt a name, as any work of art has a title," Gwen remarked one Saturday morning shortly after they had cut out their pieces and were preparing to sew. "Jack's

Chain isn't very poetic, and it certainly doesn't evoke the holiday spirit."

"We should use a girl's name, not a boy's, since we're girls and it's our design." Summer frowned thoughtfully, then brightened. "*Jill's Chain*! You know, like Jack and Jill?"

Gwen liked the sound of it, so for a week they called their quilt *Jill's Chain*. They were never entirely satisfied with the title, though, because they didn't know anyone named Jill. Also, while a chain could evoke the ties that connected loved ones to one another or links between one brilliant idea and the next, the word also suggested restraints, a heavy burden, like the iron chains that bound Jacob Marley when he terrified Ebenezer Scrooge on Christmas Eve. That was not the mood they were going for.

"You know what this reminds me of, with its bright colors and circles?" Summer said one Sunday afternoon after they had placed their first few completed units on the carpet and had stood back to examine them. "Those construction paper chains we made in elementary school. We always put one on our little Christmas tree back in Ithaca, remember?"

"I do." Gwen slipped an arm around her daughter's shoulders and pulled her close for a side hug. "*Christmas Garland* would be a nice name for our quilt, don't you think?"

Nodding emphatically, Summer agreed.

One evening a week before Thanksgiving, they were working on segments of the *Christmas Garland* quilt while sleet pelted the windows. After an animated discussion of their plans to travel to Kentucky to spend the four-day weekend with Grandma and Grandpa Sullivan, Summer fell silent, a pensive frown on her lovely face.

"What's up, kiddo?" Gwen asked, glancing up from her work. "Are you going to miss school? I could ask your teacher for extra math worksheets if it would make you feel better."

"Don't you dare," said Summer, wincing. "I'm going to miss my friends, but not *school*."

"Sure, I believe you, Miss Straight-A Class Vice President. You loathe that place."

Summer allowed a smile. "Fine, school isn't that bad. That doesn't mean I want to do worksheets on vacation."

"Fair point." Gwen studied her daughter as she lowered her gaze to pin a triangle to a Nine-Patch, her long auburn hair veiling her expression. "So . . . what's with the frown?"

"It's no big deal." Summer kept her eyes fixed on her sewing. "It's just . . . there's this dance at school in January. For the eighth grade. It's supposed to be this revered tradition or something." She looked up, flipped her hair out of the way, and rolled her eyes.

The show of indifference did not fool Gwen. "Sounds like fun. We'll get you a great dress—"

"I'm not going."

"Why not? You love to dance."

"Because it's the Eighth Grade Father-Daughter Dance."

Summer had enunciated each word precisely for maximum impact, and the meaning struck Gwen like a punch to the stomach. "I see," she said carefully. "Well, they must make exceptions. There must be other girls in your class who don't have a father around."

"There aren't. Even the girls whose parents are divorced still see their dads, or they have a stepdad. Lisa even has two dads."

"Maybe you can borrow one of hers."

"*Mom*—"

"Sorry. Not funny." Gwen sighed, thinking. "Okay, kiddo. I'll speak with your principal. I'm sure they'd let me take you instead. I know it won't be the same—"

"It'll be even better," said Summer, dropping her sewing and hurrying over to hug her. "I know it's just a stupid dance, but all of my best friends are going and I really want to too."

"It's not stupid," said Gwen, stroking her hair, although as soon as she said the words, she wanted them back. What was an archaic, sexist throwback like a father-daughter dance doing in a public school anyway? Not only did it exclude girls whose fathers weren't in the picture, but also every eighth grade boy, as well as their mothers. How hard could it be to host an Eighth Grade Student-Parent Dance instead?

First thing in the morning, Gwen called and made an appointment with the principal. The following afternoon, their conversation began cordially enough, with Mrs. Braun praising Summer as one of their most gifted pupils. According to her teachers, she was not only bright, hardworking, and intellectually curious, but kind and inclusive, the type of young woman who led by example, and an utter joy to have in class. Gwen had heard similar reports before, but her heart still swelled with pride.

"So, what brings you here today?" Mrs. Braun asked. "Are you thinking of having Summer skip a grade?"

"No, I wasn't," said Gwen. "Childhood is too short already. Why rush her through it? Actually, I wanted to speak to you about the eighth grade dance. As you may know, I'm a single mother, so despite the dance's official title, Summer and I decided that I would escort her. I assume that you must make exceptions for girls in her situation, because it would be terribly unfair to exclude a child due to circumstances beyond her control."

"I'm sorry," Mrs. Braun said, and she sounded like she meant it, "but the only exception we could make would be for another male relative to take her father's place."

Gwen waited for the principal to break into a smile and explain that she was only joking. When that did not happen, she said, evenly, "To be clear, a stepfather, elder brother, uncle, or grandfather would be fine, but not a mother?"

"That's right."

"Why not?"

"At the beginning of the third quarter, the eighth graders will be learning basic partner dances in phys ed class. The dance in January is an opportunity to perform their new skills. Therefore, the girls need a male partner."

"Why?"

Mrs. Braun spread her hands. "How would it look if we had girls dancing with girls?"

"How would it look to see girls dancing with their mothers?" Gwen paraphrased, every word distinct. "Charming and heart-warming, I would think. I hope you're not suggesting the sort of intolerance it sounds like you're suggesting."

"I'm not suggesting anything." Mrs. Braun shifted in her seat. "Have you considered that you might embarrass your daughter if you escorted her? All of the other girls will have a male dance partner. Summer will stand out."

Gwen inhaled deeply, determined to control her temper. "Surely we can come up with a reasonable solution. What have other girls done in the past, girls who don't have a father around or an acceptable male proxy?"

"Usually those young ladies stay home."

"They stay home from a dance that all the other eighth grade girls will attend and will talk about at school for weeks." Gwen shook her head, incredulous. "*That* would embarrass my daughter. *That* would make her stand out. You see that, don't you?"

Mrs. Braun interlaced her fingers and rested her arms on the desk. "It's not my policy, but the school board's. You can take it up with them."

"We both know that won't resolve anything in time for this year's dance."

"Probably not." Mrs. Braun sighed. "Perhaps Summer would like to invite her grandfather."

"Summer already invited me."

"I'm afraid that's not an option." Mrs. Braun offered a sympathetic frown and rose from her chair. "I'll mention your concerns at the next school board meeting."

"You do that," said Gwen, rising, her tone brittle. She left the office before the principal could reach across the desk to shake her hand, or wish her a good day, or offer any other perfunctory niceties that might incite her to explode with rage.

Aggrieved and indignant, she returned to her office in Kuehner Hall and tried to settle down to work, but to no avail. The principal's refusal to make a reasonable exception for an excellent student like Summer utterly astonished her. She saw little good that could come of such punitive inflexibility, and a great deal of potential harm—not just for Summer, but for all children whose fathers played no active role in their lives.

Gwen had resolved long ago that Summer would never suffer unhappiness or shame because of her father's voluntary absence, and for more than thirteen years she had made sure of it, even when teachers assigned essay topics like "My Daddy's Job" or had the students make Father's Day art projects. Summer's grandfather had been a loving, nurturing presence in her life from the day she was born, and although from time to time Summer expressed curiosity about the father she had never met, she had never seemed to miss him, or to feel she had been abandoned. What if this unwittingly cruel eighth grade dance overturned all that?

Conflicted, Gwen considered keeping Summer home from the dance as a matter of principle, striking a blow for other single mothers and same-sex couples and their children, but Summer wanted to go to the dance, and she deserved that chance. Rather than plant her flag on a hill she could not hold, Gwen reluctantly conceded defeat and called her father.

Later, as she and Summer were enjoying supper at home—their favorite vegetable lasagna from the Italian deli near campus and ciabatta fresh from the bakery—Gwen explained that she could not take Summer to the dance. "But I called your grandpa and he'd be happy to escort you," she added. "He's a great dancer, so you're in luck."

"That's weird that they won't let you take me," said Summer, puzzled. "But I'm glad Grandpa wants to go. That'll be fun. Will Grandma come too?"

"She'll drive up with Grandpa and stay with us, but it will be just you and Grandpa at the dance."

"Oh, okay." Summer finished her lasagna and dabbed the corners of her mouth with her napkin. "If I finish my homework before eight, can we work on the quilt?"

"Sure thing," said Gwen, marveling at her daughter's resilience. Her own anger and indignation still smoldered, but if Summer was content, that was good enough for her.

But in the days that followed, she realized that Summer was not as content as she seemed.

"Mom?" she asked on Saturday morning as they were settling down in their quilt studio with triangles and octagons for *Christmas Garland*. "Who is my father, anyway?"

Gwen's heart thumped. "Kiddo, you know who your father is. His name is Dennis McAlary, and he was born in Topeka, Kansas, and he's about three years older than I am. He was a student at UC Berkeley when we met."

"But you weren't a student there."

"No, I was living in a commune nearby and . . . studying independently."

"And protesting and doing flower child stuff."

"Yes, exactly," said Gwen dryly.

"Do you have a picture of him?"

"No, I'm sorry, I don't."

Summer gave a little shrug as if it didn't matter and held a spool of thread up to a triangle of fabric to see how well they blended. "Do I look like him?"

"Obviously you got your auburn hair from me," Gwen replied. "As well as your brains and extraordinary beauty."

Summer glanced up, allowing a smile.

"But Dennis was tall and slender, like you, and he played the guitar well and sang, so you probably got your musical abilities from him too."

"Grandma has a beautiful singing voice."

"That's true." Her gift had evidently skipped a generation. "Then you must have inherited talent from both sides, lucky girl."

"Cool." Summer held out two spools. "Should I use the darker thread or the lighter for this triangle?"

"I'd go with the one in your left hand." Gwen braced herself for more questions about Dennis, but Summer threaded the sewing machine needle and turned the subject to a book report she had due before Thanksgiving.

Gwen's relief was short-lived.

"So, I have two more grandparents, right?" Summer asked abruptly at breakfast the next morning.

"Yes, you do," Gwen replied, rising to pour herself a second cup of coffee, then returning to the table. "I've never met them, and Dennis rarely spoke of them, but as far as I know, they lived their entire lives in Topeka. He owned a shoe store and she was a homemaker."

"*Lived* their *entire lives*'?" Summer echoed, wide-eyed. "You mean they're dead now?"

"Sorry. Poor choice of words. I honestly don't know." Gwen hesitated, unsure whether she wanted to prolong the conversation, not knowing where it might lead. "Your father had—has—a younger sister too."

Summer absorbed this. "So I have an aunt—and maybe cousins too?"

"It's possible."

"Wow. That's crazy." Summer toyed with her fork, her whole-wheat waffles growing cold on her plate. "If I ever go to Kansas, I could walk past them on the sidewalk, and we wouldn't even know we were related."

"I suppose that's true."

"Does my father live in Kansas?"

"I wouldn't think so. He loved California. I'd be surprised if he left."

"But you don't know for sure."

Gwen shook her head. Summer nodded, broke off a piece of waffle with her fork, but only held it, her gaze fixed on the window over the sink. Eventually she excused herself and cleared away her dishes, and she said nothing more about her father for the rest of the day.

The following evening, as Summer was loading her books and her completed book report into her backpack in preparation for school the next morning, she blurted, "Does he even know I'm alive?"

"Of course he does," said Gwen. "I've sent him pictures of you. I've given him our change of address every time we've moved."

"So you *do* know where he lives."

"I have an address. I wrote to him there to tell him we had moved to Waterford, and my letter wasn't returned, so I assume—"

Summer's cheeks flushed with anger. "He's never written back? He's never even asked about me? He never sent you any child support?"

Gwen shook her head.

"What a total jerk."

"Oh, kiddo." Gwen rose and embraced her, and Summer rested her cheek on her shoulder. "I'm so sorry."

"It's not your fault," said Summer, her voice muffled.

Perhaps not, but Gwen still felt wretched.

She saw Summer off to bed, kissed her good night, and returned to the kitchen to fix herself some chamomile tea. Carrying her cup into the living room, she curled up in a chair beneath a quilt and began reviewing her next day's lesson plans, but soon her notes lay forgotten on her lap. She had never regretted leaving Dennis, and she had never wanted a dime of his money, but should she have done more through the years than send him change of address postcards? Should she have insisted that he play some role in Summer's life, if only from hundreds of miles away, even though he consistently demonstrated no interest whatsoever?

A lifetime before, when she was just starting out as a freshman at the University of Kentucky, she told new friends she was from Louisville rather than admit that she actually hailed from Brown Deer, population 1,200, west of Lovely and about halfway between Kermit and Pilgrim, home to six churches and no movie theaters. Since kindergarten, Gwen had stood out as the class brain, and in high school she had earned a reputation as a troublemaking nonconformist by refusing to join the Future Homemakers of America and by being the only girl to enroll in auto shop instead of home ec. For as long as she could remember, Gwen had longed to escape that dull, stifling, provincial backwater, and pretending that she was from a city on the opposite side of the state was the first step in putting it behind her.

Enthralled by her new freedom, she threw herself into college life. Passionate professors shook her slumbering social conscience awake, fellow students taught her about fighting for justice and making her voice heard, and more worldly friends invited her to expand her consciousness in ways that she never would have imagined back in Brown Deer, where sneaking nips from parents' liquor cabinets was the dizzying height of audacity.

At first, Gwen worked feverishly to make up for the unexpected deficiencies in her education. Although back home she was considered the most brilliant student Brown Deer High School had ever matriculated, within her first few days on campus she had made the jarring observation that she trailed behind her peers from better school districts. Her sharp intellect, quick wit, and competitive streak soon helped her to gain an equal footing, and once securely there, she was eager to cast off her reputation as a grind interested in nothing more than top grades. Classes became a drag, visits home to Brown Deer, unbearable.

At the end of her sophomore year, Gwen decided to leave school and find herself. She had been stuck in a square little town for too long, chafing against her parents' and neighbors' expectations. She had no idea who she was or what she was meant to do with her life. College would always be there, if and when she decided to return. She only had a brief moment to be young, to love freely, to live as she pleased, and to discover who she was meant to be.

She set out with two friends, hitchhiking across the country, crashing wherever she was offered a bed, sampling whatever was passed to her, watching the days slowly unfold as if through a rosy warm haze. She parted with her friends in Denver and hooked up with another group headed out to California; she left them in Los Angeles and made her way north alone, hitchhiking up the coast. A casual invitation led to a lengthy stay in a commune in Berkeley, where she cooked for a changeable group of twelve perpetual students in exchange for a foldout sofa and access to their collective library, shelved on wooden planks stacked on milk crates in a converted detached garage. She wandered the campus, joining in antiwar protests and occasionally sitting in on lectures. Knowledge was meant to be free, and her attendance wasn't preventing a tuition-paying student from occupying an otherwise empty chair.

On one such day, she met Dennis, yelling epithets as he burned an effigy of the president on Sproul Plaza. Her mother would have said Gwen was instantly smitten—that is, if her mother would not have fainted dead away at the sight of the longhaired, strung-out, unwashed pale young man with his arms around her daughter. Gwen was certain she had discovered her soul mate.

After their barefoot wedding ceremony on the beach—it was too cold to go barefoot in February, but Dennis insisted they have unencumbered contact with the earth—they traveled the country with two other couples in a van plastered with peace signs and antiwar slogans. They bartered for gas money and worked occasional odd jobs for food. They went where they chose, with nothing to hold them down, nothing to bear them up but each other.

The carefree times ended when Gwen realized she was pregnant.

Suddenly it mattered where their next meal would come from, where they would live, what kind of mother she would be. When she gave up pot, Dennis's drug use, once a minor irritant, began to worry her. When she tried to persuade him to quit, he told her she was jealous, uptight, and square—that same old small-town-girl characterization he knew she hated. "Relax, baby," he said, blowing smoke in her face. Then he bent over to speak to her abdomen, still as flat as the day she had left Brown Deer. "That goes for you too, baby."

When he threw his head back in a fit of helpless giggling, Gwen felt nothing for him but shame and disgust. How could she ever have imagined that he was the love of her life? How could she bring a child into the world and expect him to help her raise it? Dennis could barely look after himself. How would they afford diapers and clothes and toys? She couldn't raise a child in the backseat of a van, a constantly shifting cast of unreliable traveling companions filling the front seats.

The next time they stopped for gas, Gwen left her wedding ring on the dashboard, stuffed her few possessions into her backpack, announced that she had to use the bathroom, and left without saying goodbye. She walked along the highway in the opposite direction the van was traveling, hoping to get a good head start before Dennis and the others realized she wasn't coming back. She considered returning to the commune in Berkeley, where the kind, gentle residents might welcome her back, forthcoming infant and all. But after an hour of trudging along on the shoulder of the road, the only driver who pulled over was heading east. After a moment's hesitation, she accepted the ride. A week later, she walked the last mile into Brown Deer, filthy, hungry, and desperately anxious that her parents would leave her standing outside on the doorstep, abandoning her as she had once rejected them.

Instead her mother burst into tears and brought her into the house, calling for her father, who came running to embrace her. Generous and kind, expecting nothing in return, they saw her through the rest of her pregnancy and the birth of her beautiful daughter. When Summer was fifteen months old, Gwen returned to college, knowing that she could make a better life for them both if she completed her education. In the three years it took her to earn her degree, Summer lived with her grandparents in Brown Deer, and Gwen drove home to be with her on weekends and school breaks. It grieved Gwen to spend so much time away, but Summer was a happy, affectionate child, the light of her grandparents' lives, and as hard as it was, Gwen knew she was doing what was best for them both.

Her mother cried tears of joy at Gwen's graduation, and even her father's eyes shone when he saw her in her cap and gown at long last. A few months later, they put on brave faces and sent her off with their blessings when she and Summer left for Cornell, more than six hundred miles away, so she could pursue her doctorate. Gwen knew she owed her parents everything. Without them, she never could have seized her second chance, could never have built the joyful, fulfilling life she and Summer now enjoyed.

Perhaps Dennis deserved a second chance too. Gwen had changed, matured, learned from her mistakes; he could have as well. After all, *she* had left *him*. Perhaps he had kept his distance because he assumed she wanted it that way.

She knew his name, birth date, place of birth, and last known address. After she saw Summer off to school the next morning, she dialed directory services, requested a reverse lookup of his residence, and took down the phone number. Given the three-hour time difference, it was much too early to call, so Gwen went to work, but throughout the morning, even when she was teaching and writing, her thoughts were elsewhere, mulling over what she would say.

At noon, she closed the door to her office and called the number the operator had given. Her heart pounded as the phone rang and rang, then flew into her throat when someone picked up.

"Hello?" a woman spoke.

Gwen cleared her throat. "Good morning. My name is Gwen Sullivan. I'm trying to reach Dennis McAlary. Is he available?"

"Oh, no, sorry, but he moved away years ago."

"Really? How many years?"

"We bought the house from him in eighty-five."

"I see." Then Gwen's last letter would have arrived in the interim when the post office would have forwarded his mail instead of returning it to the sender. "Do you happen to have a current address for him?"

The woman hesitated. "I'm sorry, but . . . I don't have one I could give you."

Gwen understood the subtext. "That's fine. Could you at least tell me if he's still in California?"

"Yeah, in fact, he's still in Santa Cruz. He owns a coffeehouse and surf shop near Steamer Lane."

"Great." Gwen jotted down notes. "I hate to put you on the spot, but I'm calling long distance. Could you please give me the name and phone number?"

"I guess that would be fine. It's called Java Surf. Hold on and I'll look it up." She set down the receiver and a moment later Gwen heard the faint sound of pages turning. A few moments more, and she was back on the line reciting the number.

Gwen thanked her and hung up, and after collecting her thoughts, she called Java Surf.

The phone rang on and on until a cheerful young-sounding man with a laid-back drawl picked up, promising to get Dennis on the line as soon as he was free. Gwen waited, tapping a pen on her desktop, listening to the muffled sounds of milk frothing and cash register drawers slamming, laughter and conversation. Then there was a scramble and a scratching and a mellow tenor voice said, "Java Surf. Thanks for holding. This is Dennis."

"Hey, Dennis." She forced casual friendliness into her voice. "This is Gwen. Gwen Sullivan. How are you?"

"Whoa, Gwen." He inhaled and blew out a long breath. "Gwen. Well, at the moment, I'm totally surprised."

She laughed lightly. "It's been a while."

"For sure. Hey, can you hold on? I'm going to transfer you to the office."

Another brief wait, a few clicks and muffled sounds, and then

Dennis was on the line again, but the background noise had diminished to a faint murmur. "So, what's up?" he asked.

"I thought a conversation was long overdue."

When he did not disagree, she told him, briefly, about Summer, her favorite school subjects, outstanding grades, and favorite activities—soccer, singing, playing guitar, and quilting. Dennis hung on every word, occasionally interrupting with a question, an unmistakable undercurrent of delight and pride in his voice. "She clearly takes after you," he said when she had finished. "Obviously you've done a wonderful job raising her."

Gwen was unexpectedly touched. She only wished he had expressed some remorse that he had missed all of it.

She considered her next words carefully. "As Summer grows older, she's had more questions about you," she said. "In mid-December, I'll be speaking at a conference at UC Santa Barbara. Santa Cruz is only a short flight or a four-hour drive away, an hour longer if I take Highway 1 up the coast to admire the scenery. Would you be willing to get together? I'd like to talk, and, if you're interested, we could consider arranging for you and Summer to meet."

There was a long pause.

"You caught me off guard," he admitted. "I should've known when you called out of the blue that you had something on your mind."

"I'm not trying to put you on the spot," she said, a slight edge to her voice. "I just thought since I'm going to be in California anyway—"

"No, no, I get it." He drew in a breath, exhaled slowly. "Okay. Let's meet. But I'll drive down to Santa Barbara instead of making you come all the way to Santa Cruz. It's only fair that I meet you partway, considering that you're flying across the country."

"That sounds good." Before she could change her mind, Gwen

gave him the details of where and when she could meet—one o'clock on the Saturday of the conference at a small café near her hotel. She had never been there, but it had been recommended in the conference paperwork.

"I'll find it," Dennis said. "See you then."

"See you," she said, and they hung up.

The next week, she and Summer drove six hours southwest through the rolling Appalachians to Brown Deer, where her parents came outside to the front porch to welcome them in from the rain. On Friday, after the sun had come out and Summer was outside playing with the dogs, Gwen divulged her plans to her parents, but she asked them to say nothing to Summer in case Dennis failed to show.

They regarded her somberly and agreed, but Gwen sensed their underlying alarm. They had never met Dennis and had no reason to approve of him. From their perspective, he was a drug-addled hooligan who had seduced their innocent child into a sham marriage before impregnating and abandoning her. Her father urged her to meet Dennis in a public place, in daylight, and under no circumstances should she get in his car and allow him to drive her to a secondary location.

"Someone's been watching cop shows on cable," Gwen teased, managing a shaky laugh. "Mom, Dad, I'll be perfectly safe. Dennis was never dangerous or violent."

"You said he used drugs back in the day," her mother said. "He was a criminal."

Gwen had to concede that point, but she reminded them that he had become the owner of a successful business, so apparently he had his life on track. And of course she would never let him anywhere near Summer if he was using.

"I'd prefer it if you never let him near Summer regardless," her father grumbled.

"That's going to be up to the two of them," she said. "If Dennis is willing to meet Summer, I'll ask Summer if she's willing to meet him. If either of them says no, that will be the end of it."

Her parents exchanged a look that told her they would pray for a swift and decisive refusal from Dennis. The odds were in their favor. Dennis had been silent so long that it was difficult to imagine him suddenly metamorphosing into an involved parent.

A week after Gwen and Summer returned home after the Thanksgiving holiday, her parents drove up from Kentucky to look after their granddaughter while Gwen flew out to Santa Barbara for the conference. The forested hills of the Elm Creek Valley had lost their brilliant autumn foliage weeks before and the stubbled farm fields were often thick with frost, so when she emerged from the plane and descended the stairs to the tarmac, the warm California sunshine felt like an embrace. She closed her eyes and lifted her face to the sun, flooded with memories of her younger self, hitchhiking up and down the coast, singing protest songs around a bonfire on Venice Beach, watching the sun set over the Pacific from a cliff in Monterey. She loved the life she had made for herself and for Summer in Pennsylvania, but California would always be the home of her heart.

She took a cab to the hotel, settled into her room, changed from her warm winter clothes into something lighter and brighter, and returned to the lobby to check in for the conference. The program began that evening with a supper and keynote address, and the next two days passed in a whirl of lectures, papers, seminars, lunches, dinners, coffee with colleagues and potential collaborators, and lengthy debates about the state of academia over drinks long after she should have withdrawn to her room for some solitary yoga and a good night's sleep. Her own lecture on Saturday morning was a smashing success, if she did say so herself—and she did soon thereafter, over the phone with Summer and her parents.

Her mother lingered on the line after the others had said goodbye and hung up. "Good luck," she said simply, not needing to name the source of her concern. "Be careful."

Gwen promised she would.

She felt as if she were moving in slow motion as she walked the few blocks to the café, the benevolent California sunshine suddenly seeming too perfect, like a caricature of itself, falsely bright and cheery even for the festive season. That was it, she told herself, trying to shake off her growing apprehension. Palm trees and ocean breezes rang false in December, the season of snowmen and Santa Claus. That was all.

She arrived first and claimed a table outside with a gorgeous view of the ocean. She ordered an iced tea and gazed at the distant waves, no more than a gentle murmur at this distance, and waited. Just as the server brought her drink, Dennis arrived, lanky and smiling through a scruff of beard, clad in khaki hiking shorts, sandals, and a red Java Surf T-shirt. His hair was thinner, his face tanned and lined, but his grin was the same, and with a jolt Gwen realized that Summer's eyes were exactly the same shade of denim blue. She had forgotten the color of his eyes.

Instinctively Gwen rose, heart thudding, as Dennis wrapped her in a bear hug. "Gwen!" he cried out, almost lifting her heels off the ground. "Man, you haven't changed a bit!"

She knew she had put on weight, but he seemed sincere. "Thanks," she said, pulling free and easing back into her chair. "It looks like California agrees with you."

"I've been here so long I feel like a native," he said, "but since I'm not, I appreciate this all the more." He swept an arm to indicate the sunshine, a nearby palm tree, and the ocean view. When he glanced at the menu, Gwen did too, and since the server was still standing nearby, they gave him their orders.

"I brought pictures," Gwen said after the server left, taking a thick envelope from her tote bag. One by one, she placed them on the table in front of Dennis, adding a few details for context. They ranged in chronological order from a few days after Summer's birth through Thanksgiving dinner the previous week, a brief history of the life of an extraordinary girl.

She had just shown him the last one when their meals arrived, but Dennis was so engrossed in the pictures that he did not notice and the server had to set his mushroom burger and zucchini fries off to one side. Gwen thanked him and moved some of the photos aside to make room for his plate, but she halted at the sudden memory of having done that many times before, long ago, making sure everything was just right for him since he was too distracted to take care of himself.

"You can keep those," she said, nodding to the photos as she placed her napkin on her lap. "I have copies at home."

He thanked her, but his smile faltered a bit. "Thanks," he said, an odd note in his voice. "I'll keep them somewhere safe."

"So, you know all about Summer and me, but what about you?" she asked, cutting her fajita chicken wrap in half. "How's the coffeehouse and surf shop business?"

"Couldn't be better," he said. "We struggled a bit when Starbucks came to town, but our customers are loyal and you can't get a board or a wet suit at Starbucks. Not yet anyway."

Gwen laughed lightly. "You seem happy." She remembered him as perpetually outraged and defiant, unless he was stoned, and he didn't seem high at the moment.

"I am." He paused to take a bite of his burger, chewed slowly, swallowed. "I'm married."

She hadn't expected that. "That's wonderful. Any children? Any other children, I mean?"

"Three. A girl and two boys, twins." He hesitated, then

reached into a pocket for his wallet and took out what were obviously standard school photos. "That's Ashley, and this is Guthrie and Dylan."

Gwen studied the photos and murmured the appropriate compliments, but she was struck by their ages. The eldest could not have been more than two years younger than Summer. "I don't suppose you have extras?" she asked, handing them back with a smile. "I know Summer would be thrilled to see them."

"I'm sorry. I didn't think to bring any."

"That's fine. Maybe you could mail some later."

"You know what?" He passed the photos back to her. "You keep these. I'm sure we have more at home. And we'll get more next year."

Gwen thanked him and tucked the photos into her tote bag, faintly light-headed, overwhelmed by the realization that Summer had siblings. Half-siblings, but still. Somehow she had never considered the possibility.

They chatted carefully as they ate, about parenthood, about the few mutual acquaintances who had kept in touch. When they had finished eating and were sipping refills of their drinks, Gwen stoked her courage and zeroed in on the subject she had been circling for the better part of an hour. "Have you given any more thought to what I suggested over the phone? Would you like to meet Summer?"

He held her gaze for a moment, looked away, wiped the palms of his hands on his shorts. "It's not that I don't want to meet her," he finally said. "It's just that it isn't possible."

"How so?" she asked. "If you're concerned that Summer will be angry or resentful, don't be. She's a loving, forgiving child."

He shook his head, his mouth pressed in a tight frown.

"Why don't you start with a phone call?" Gwen persisted.

"Get to know each other that way, and then we can talk about meeting in person. You could come visit us in Waterford, or we could come out to Santa Cruz—"

"No," he said vehemently, holding up a hand. "Whatever you do, don't come to Santa Cruz. Never do that."

Gwen stared at him, astonished. "Why not?"

"Because Susan and the kids don't know about Summer."

Gwen's heart plummeted, and then it began to burn. "You never told your family that you have another daughter?"

He pressed his mouth closed again and shook his head, cheeks flushed.

She kept her voice low, but her tone was cutting. "Don't you think your wife deserves to know?"

"How could I tell her now, when I've kept it secret so long?"

"Throw yourself on her mercy and hope for the best. Eventually the truth will come out. Better Susan hears it from you than from—"

"From you?"

"I'm not going to tell her," said Gwen, recoiling. "That's on you."

"You don't understand." He shifted in his chair, glanced over his shoulder, and leaned forward to rest his arms on the table. "After you walked out on me, I fell apart. I didn't know what had happened to you. I thought you'd been kidnapped, run over, worse. We looked for you. Did you know that?"

She shook her head. How could she have known?

"We backtracked all the way to Berkeley. We put up posters, passed out flyers. Then Katie thought of calling your parents."

Katie. Gwen searched her memory and drew forth the blurry image of a petite, copper-skinned girl with a reddish Afro and a gift for biting satirical poetry.

"Katie called and asked for you, pretending she was calling from the UC Berkeley library about an overdue book. Your mother said you were out and asked Katie to send her the bill, she would pay it."

Gwen inhaled deeply. "I'm sorry I made you worry. I never thought of that." Hadn't he noticed her wedding band on the dashboard? That should have been enough to convey that she hadn't gone missing, but had left him. Why make them both suffer through a maudlin parting speech?

"So you were gone, and my child with you. I took it bad. I hit bottom. Some guy dragged me half starved and raging with fever into a mission. Susan worked there. She pulled me out of it. She must have seen something worth saving in me." He clutched his hands together, rubbing the palm of his left with the thumb of his right. "So. Long story short. We married, started a family. I haven't had so much as a beer in all that time. We go to church every Sunday. She says I'm a good man. What will she say if she finds out I've been lying to her all this time?"

"She'll probably be angry. She has good reason. But from the sound of it, she'll forgive you."

"I can't take that chance." Suddenly he reached across the table and seized her hand. "Promise me you'll never tell her."

"I already said I wouldn't." Gwen snatched her hand away. "Listen to me, Dennis. Summer is not your dirty little secret. Her right to know her father and siblings transcends your privilege to bury the truth."

"If I see her, or call her, or contact her in any way, my wife will find out."

"Then tell her the truth."

"I just told you, I can't."

"No, you can. You just don't want to." Furious, Gwen signaled to the server to bring separate checks immediately. "Someday Summer will be old enough to seek you out on her own, and I won't pretend I don't know where you are, nor will I ask her to keep your secret. If she asks, I'm going to tell her about you and her half-siblings, as well as how to reach you. If she doesn't ask, when she turns eighteen, I'll tell her anyway. What she does with the information will be up to her." The server hurried over with their checks. Gwen took hers, dug into her purse, and gave him enough cash for her meal plus a generous tip. "You have five years, Dennis. Make good use of the time."

She rose, yanked the strap of her tote bag over her shoulder, and strode away, tears of rage blurring her vision all the way back to the hotel.

The conference ended that evening with a dinner and an open bar, but Gwen merely put in an appearance to speak with a few colleagues before retreating to her room. When she returned home the next day, and Summer greeted her excitedly with hugs and kisses and news from school, Gwen seethed with indignation that Dennis could ever believe that their daughter was something to be ashamed of, not a person, but a symbol of his youthful indiscretions.

She really saw no reason why she should ever contact him again.

Her parents stayed on a few days longer. On the second night when Summer was fast asleep, Gwen finally told them what had happened. Her father muttered euphemisms for curses and her mother grew pale with indignation. "He doesn't deserve to know her," she said, voice shaking, "and I hope he never does."

Gwen nodded, but in the end, that would be up to Summer.

As snow fell softly upon the Elm Creek Valley and Christmas approached, Gwen and Summer put up a tree, decked the halls, wrapped gifts for the family, and worked on their *Christmas Garland* quilt. They took the segments with them when they drove down to Brown Deer on the morning of Christmas Eve, and in quiet moments when the house was not full of friends and neighbors cheerfully celebrating the festive season, they set out their cut pieces and took turns at Gwen's mother's sewing machine, attaching Nine-Patches to hexagons, triangles to Nine-Patches. To their delight, Gwen's mother often joined in, sharing stories of Christmas joy from her childhood as she pressed seams flat, offering sage advice that improved their stitches or helped them avoid straining their wrists and fingers.

Gwen and Summer finished the quilt top back home in Waterford in the second week of January. They layered and basted the top, batting, and backing, fit it snugly inside a lap hoop, and traded off quilting and reading aloud from their favorite classics—*Jane Eyre*, *Wuthering Heights*, *Anna Karenina*. They had made quite good progress by the time Gwen's parents drove up to the Elm Creek Valley so that Summer's grandfather could escort her to the Eighth Grade Father-Daughter Dance. They had a wonderful time, but in the days that followed, Summer resumed her queries about her absent father, sometimes angrily, sometimes merely curious. Gwen always answered truthfully, but she volunteered no information beyond the boundaries of Summer's questions.

By the time they finished the quilt in early March, Summer's inquiries had become far less frequent, and by her fourteenth birthday, they had ceased altogether.

Four years later, Gwen brought out the photos of Summer's half-siblings, told her about her encounter with Dennis in California, and gave her a small card with his contact information. "You can reach out to them if you like," Gwen told her. "I can help you figure out how best to do it, especially since it's possible your half-siblings don't know they have another sister."

Summer fingered the card, studied each of the photos in turn, and set them down on the table. "Maybe someday," she said, rising, leaving the artifacts behind. Gwen waited, but when

Summer did not return, she put the photos and card in an envelope and left them on her daughter's dresser.

The next time Gwen passed through her room, the envelope was gone. She hoped Summer had put it away for safekeeping, but she did not ask.

In all the years that had passed since then, Gwen had not heard from Dennis, and neither had Summer. She would have mentioned it if she had. Gwen was often tempted to ask her if she had thought about getting in touch with her half-siblings, but she refrained. That was Summer's path to follow, if she wished. Perhaps someday she would.

In all those years too, *Christmas Garland* warmed them as they ate popcorn and watched holiday movies side by side on winter nights as snow fell softly outside their home, the cozy room fragrant with evergreen boughs and cinnamon, as the world turned and they awaited the return of the light.

# 7

# *Diane*

AFTER SEEING TIM off to work with a kiss at the door, Diane tidied up the breakfast dishes, put a chicken and some vegetables in the slow cooker for supper, and ironed the slacks, blouse, and jacket she planned to wear for her *News at Noon* interview with Nancy Reinhart later that day. It was just a three-minute segment on a local affiliate, but the program had a very large following of stay-at-home parents and retirees, an excellent target demographic for the Christmas Boutique.

Once that interview was over, Diane's publicity campaign would be essentially complete. She had sent out emails to every relevant campus group and community organization she could think of, had contacted all the local papers and radio stations, had put up flyers downtown and on campus, and had scored the one television news program that featured human interest stories from the Elm Creek Valley. As far as she could tell, she had exhausted every available form of publicity except for skywriting, which was impractical and cost-prohibitive. She would know soon enough how successful her efforts had been.

Much work remained, however, if the vast throngs of eager shoppers she hoped to inspire to come to the manor that weekend would indeed find the wonderful Christmas Boutique she had promised. Leaving her freshly pressed, camera-ready outfit on hangers, she changed from her yoga pants and hoodie into business-casual slacks and a sweater, snatched up her purse and phone, and set out for Elm Creek Manor. The last she had heard, Anna and Jeremy had food services well in hand, while Gretchen and Agnes were nearly finished decorating the ballroom and banquet hall. That morning, volunteers from Good Shepherd Church were scheduled to bring over the handicrafts, preserves, and baked goods they had been collecting over the past few weeks. Stragglers who had not yet turned in their pledged items had been asked to drop them off at Elm Creek Manor at their convenience throughout the day. Sarah, Sylvia, Gretchen, and Gwen had offered to greet the volunteers, collect the remaining contributions, and help arrange the merchandise attractively in their market stalls. Diane assumed her friends would welcome an extra pair of hands, even though she would have to leave by late morning for the interview.

Although the roads were clear of snow and ice, traffic was relatively heavy, the sidewalks bustling as people of all ages bundled in coats and scarves hurried off to work and school. The congestion eased as Diane left the downtown behind; she passed only a few cars on the rural highway, and none at all on the forest road leading to Elm Creek Manor. When she pulled into the rear lot, she spotted Gwen's car and Andrew's motor home, but to her surprise, Jeremy was emerging from the driver's seat of the Elm Creek Quilts minivan instead of his own car, a few spaces away.

She parked nearby, and by the time she approached, Jeremy had slid open the side door and was reaching inside for a wide, shallow carton decorated with illustrations of garden vegetables. "Do you need some help?" she asked.

"Sure, thanks. Careful with those paper bags. They're very full, and I doubt the handles will hold."

As he loaded another carton atop the stack in his arms, Diane reached for two paper bags overflowing with baguettes, sandwich rolls, and croissants, taking care to lift them from the bottom. "This is quite a haul," she remarked, eyeing the many other bags and cartons still waiting to be unloaded.

"Best of all, everything was donated," Jeremy said as he led the way to the rear entrance of the manor. "I had to make a lot of stops, but it was worth it. The merchants didn't give us their marked-down, past-expiration-date goods either. Anna will have everything she needs for a fantastic buffet this weekend."

"Anna could create a feast out of stale bread and a bag of frozen peas," said Diane, pausing at the foot of the back stairs while Jeremy balanced his cartons on the railing and opened the door. Grinning in agreement, he held the door open and lifted his chin to indicate that she should precede him inside.

The kitchen was warm and fragrant with savory aromas and spices. Anna bustled about in her white chef's toque and apron, smiling and humming a Christmas carol. She greeted them eagerly, her eyes widening at the sight of the cartons and bags in their arms. "Would you leave all that on the table?" she asked, glancing through the window of the lower oven at whatever culinary masterpiece was baking inside. "I'll help you unpack in just a moment."

They did as she asked, then headed back outside for another load. "It's funny how much this reminds me of how Anna and I met," Jeremy remarked, smiling.

"I thought you met because your apartments are in the same building," said Diane, quickening her pace to keep up with his bounding stride. "Don't you live across the hall from each other?"

"True, the first time we met was a few years ago when some of my mail ended up in Anna's mailbox and she brought it over to me. But we didn't really get to know each other until the Waterford College Key Club held a food drive." He opened the side door to the minivan, but instead of unloading more boxes, he leaned against the frame and folded his arms across his chest, tucking his hands beneath his elbows for warmth. "They left a carton in the lobby of our apartment building near the mailboxes and posted a sign requesting nonperishable food items to make Thanksgiving baskets for needy families. They did the same at all the apartment buildings and fraternities near campus. The day before the drive ended, our carton held nothing but a box of pasta, a canister of raisins, and a package of granola bars. That was kind of pathetic, so I went around the building asking for donations."

"So you knocked on Anna's door," Diane interjected, "she gave you some gourmet delicacies, because what else would she have in her pantry, and the rest was history."

"More or less. She also told me that she had seen a guy from the first floor take a box of cereal and a gallon of apple juice from the box a few days before, which explained our neighbors' ostensible lack of generosity."

"The nerve of some people." Diane reached into the minivan for a paper bag full of winter squash. "It was a food drive, not his own personal pantry."

"Exactly. So after Anna donated, she offered to help me finish my rounds of the building. By the time we were through, we had filled a second carton." Jeremy took two more boxes from the van and hefted a third on top. "After that, we went back to her apartment and she made us some whole-wheat chocolate cappuccino brownies to celebrate. They were amazing. We ate them right from the pan and watched *A Charlie Brown Thanksgiving*."

"Sounds nice." Diane studied him from the corner of her eye as they returned to the manor. "Sounds cozy."

"Best brownies I'd ever tasted."

"I bet they were," she said archly, but she fell silent as they entered the kitchen, where Anna's face lit up at the sight of them, or the donations they carried, or maybe just Jeremy.

Something was up with those two.

They needed three more trips to empty the minivan, but eventually the last carton was safely inside out of the cold. They hung their coats in the foyer closet and began unpacking the donations, storing perishables into the massive, stainless-steel refrigerator and setting the other items wherever Anna directed, in between checking on the oven and stirring the pot simmering on the stovetop. When they finished, Diane glanced at her watch and announced that she was overdue in the ballroom, for the volunteers and contributors could begin arriving at any moment.

"I'll come with you," said Anna, wiping her hands on her apron. Making her way around the granite center island, she removed both apron and toque, set them on the seat of the farthest booth, and picked up two folded quilts from the adjacent table. "Jeremy, could you please listen for the oven timer and stir that pot every so often? I need to deliver my quilts to the decorating team."

"Sure." Jeremy had just settled down in the booth by the window with a book, but he promptly closed it and stood. "Glad to help."

Diane felt a twinge of chagrin. "The deadline for quilts hasn't passed yet, has it?"

Anna smiled, a deep dimple appearing in her right cheek. "I think you still have the rest of the day. I won't tell on you."

Diane almost joked that she wouldn't tell on Anna either, but she held the words back just in time.

When they entered the ballroom, they found Sarah, Sylvia, Gretchen, and Gwen already sorting merchandise into categories and arranging items artfully in the market booths. "Earlier this morning, Melanie and Nancy dropped off the donations they've collected at Good Shepherd," Sylvia explained while they marveled at the vast array of items. "We might receive half again as much as this, if all the prospective donors meet their pledges."

"We should raise a tidy fortune for the food bank," Gwen remarked, "as long as Diane didn't get distracted by some other project and neglect her job."

Diane nudged her. "I defy you to find a better Christmas Boutique publicist in central Pennsylvania. I've checked off every item on my to-do list except for today's *News at Noon* interview— live television, thousands of viewers. Did I forget to mention that part?"

"You've mentioned it once or twice. Just don't forget to show up."

"I've got this. You focus on partitions and tables, and whatever other minor, menial tasks you can be trusted with."

"I don't have anything to sell at the market, but I do have two quilts for decorations," Anna broke in, indicating the bundle in her arms. Diane and Gwen came forward to take the one on top, which they unfolded and held up for all to admire. A dazzling array of gold, six-pointed stars were scattered upon a rich blue background ranging from azure to indigo. "It belongs to Jeremy now, but he said we could borrow it."

"We'll hang it up right away," said Gretchen, gathering it up and draping it over her arm. "I think that spot between the two windows would be perfect."

"This quilt is more traditional," said Anna, holding one edge and looking to Diane for assistance. Diane took hold of the opposite side, and between them they unfolded the second quilt and raised it high. It was a charming sampler made in jewel-tone greens, reds, purples, and golds, twenty-five six-inch blocks, each a different star pattern, with Celtic knotwork appliqué adorning the sashing and outermost border.

"How lovely," Sylvia exclaimed, drawing closer to inspect the intricate machine quilting. "This doesn't look like your usual style, Anna."

"I wouldn't have recognized it as your work," said Diane. "It doesn't look like food at all."

Gwen groaned, Sarah shook her head, and Sylvia sighed quietly. Gretchen alone looked baffled.

"What?" said Diane. "You all know what I'm talking about."

"We're aware of your assessment of Anna's particular style, dear," said Sylvia mildly.

Gretchen looked around the circle of quilters. "I'm sorry. I'm utterly lost."

"That's because you weren't at Anna's job interview." Sarah rested one hand on her abdomen and winced. Either one of the twins had just delivered a strong kick to her rib cage or Diane's remarks pained her. But why should they? Everyone, Anna included, knew that her abstract designs always ended up reflecting her beloved profession whether she intended it or not.

"You recall, of course, that as a test of their skills and creativity, each candidate for our faculty was asked to create an original block representing Elm Creek Quilts," said Sylvia. Gretchen nodded. Of course she remembered; she had made one herself. "I'm afraid that when Anna unveiled her quilt block, Diane declared that it looked like a tossed salad."

Gretchen gasped. "She didn't."

"Of course she did," said Gwen. "This is Diane we're talking about."

"But it *did* look like a tossed salad," Diane protested. "Anna said so herself at the time. Remember?" She threw Anna a beseeching look. "You agreed with me, right?"

"You weren't wrong," said Anna ruefully. "Somehow everything in my life ends up being about food. Like that quilt I finished when I first came to Elm Creek Manor? I intended it as an abstract arrangement of circles of varying sizes and hues set against two contrasting forms in brown and white, but in the end, it looked like a cascade of ripe blueberries falling from an overturned bucket into a pool of rich cream."

"I love that quilt," said Sarah.

"I do too, but the thought of it is making me hungry," said Gwen.

"At least it complements my strawberry pie quilt," said Anna, sighing, "and my eggs Benedict quilt, and my chocolate soufflé quilt. If anyone asks, I'm going to tell them that the resemblance is intentional. They're a series—'Quilts from the Kitchen.'"

Everyone laughed, Diane a bit sheepishly.

"What accounts for this departure from your usual style?" Sylvia queried, studying the sampler. "Was it your first quilt? A project designed by a teacher, perhaps, to help you learn the basic techniques before you went off to experiment?"

"It wasn't my first, but it was a fairly early project," said Anna. "When I was in high school, I worked part-time in my aunt's quilt shop. She asked me to make this to test a pattern for a class she wanted to teach."

"It's simply lovely," Sylvia declared, and everyone chimed in, in agreement. "As for where to best display it, I think that empty spot to the right of the doors would be perfect."

"We're still about three quilts short," said Gretchen, glancing around the walls. "And to think, when we first took on this project, I hoped we might have enough to decorate the banquet hall too."

"What about you, Diane?" asked Sylvia, peering at her over

the rims of her glasses. "I don't see any of your quilts gracing our walls."

Diane tried not to squirm beneath her knowing gaze. "I'll bring some in soon."

"Very soon, I hope," said Sarah. "You're running out of time. The boutique opens tomorrow morning."

The reminder sent a frisson of anticipation and anxiety around the circle of friends. "I'll deliver mine later today, after the interview," said Diane. "I didn't forget. I just wanted to see what the rest of you were bringing in first, so I'd know which of my quilts would best coordinate with them."

"Sounds plausible," said Gwen. "Barely."

Diane prepared a retort, but at that moment three women entered the ballroom, their arms full of bags and boxes. Diane and her friends hurried forward to welcome them and help them unpack their donations for the boutique. They had not yet finished when a young man and woman arrived together, each carrying one flat, heavy box full of jars of preserves, delightfully colorful in the sunlight that streamed through the south windows.

The next hour passed in a flurry of activity—welcoming Nancy and Melanie's team of volunteers, accepting donations for the sale, arranging merchandise in market stalls, helping the volunteers set up signs and affix price tags. Anna had returned to the kitchen long ago, but when Andrew and Joe arrived to hang up her quilts, Diane noticed her bright smiles and shining eyes, and recalled Jeremy's fond reminiscences and above-and-beyond helpfulness. Her curiosity rekindled.

With all the bustle in the ballroom, it took Diane a while to catch Gwen alone. "Is it just me," she mused, "or are Anna and Jeremy very friendly?"

"Of course they're friendly," said Gwen, her attention on the table of hand-knit scarves she was arranging. "That's a good way to go through life. You should try it."

"I'm not referring to ordinary friendliness. I mean, they seem very friendly, for people who are just friends."

Gwen sighed. "So you're saying friends shouldn't be friendly? Wouldn't that make them enemies?"

"Would you put down that scarf and listen?" Diane glanced over her shoulder, drew closer, and lowered her voice. "Let me spell it out for you: I think Jeremy and Summer have broken up, and now Jeremy and Anna are seeing each other. Or is it just me? Am I seeing drama where none exists?"

Gwen inhaled deeply, turned away from the table, and regarded Diane grimly. "It's not just you. I've noticed it too."

"When did Jeremy and Summer break up? Why didn't you say anything?"

"Because I just found out myself." Gwen planted a hand on her hip and looked away to the ballroom doors, where they had last glimpsed Anna walking back to the kitchen, a happy bounce in her step. "They broke up over Thanksgiving. Maybe Jeremy didn't turn around because of the storm that weekend. None of us knew his visit was supposed to be a surprise. Remember when we were taking turns talking to Summer on the phone, and Sylvia mentioned that he was on his way? Maybe afterward Summer called him and told him not to come."

"What's with all the 'maybe's?" asked Diane. "Summer hasn't told you?"

"Not in great detail."

"But you're always bragging about how well you two communicate, how Summer tells you everything."

"Exactly," said Gwen. "Why is she shutting me out? And what about Jeremy and Anna? Summer probably has no idea what's going on with them, if anything is, and I'm going to have to tell her."

"Oh." Diane mulled it over. "That's going to be a very awkward conversation when Summer comes home tomorrow."

Gwen gave a wry laugh, shook her head, and resumed folding scarves. "Don't I know it."

Diane could think of nothing reassuring to say, so she too got back to work, sorting items into categories and placing them on the appropriate tables, until it was time to drive home and prepare for her interview.

As she left the ballroom, Gretchen called after her, "Diane, don't forget your quilts. We're counting on you."

"I'll see what I can do," she replied, glancing over her shoulder, forcing a smile, and giving a jaunty wave.

There was no getting out of it now.

Pensive, a bit abashed, Diane drove home to change clothes and freshen her makeup. She deliberately turned her thoughts away from quilts—those she had promised but might not actually have—to her talking points about the Christmas Boutique. By the time she was back in her car on her way to the television studio, anticipation for the interview had chased away her lingering worries. Nancy met her in the lobby, and they had a few minutes to confer before they were summoned onto the set during a commercial break.

The interview went brilliantly. Nancy was knowledgeable and enthusiastic, Diane was clever and charming, and together they were so lively and interesting that the reporter gave them five minutes on air rather than the scheduled three. Afterward, they were so pleased and proud of themselves—as well as ravenous, since they had been too nervous to eat beforehand—that they decided to get lunch downtown. Over soup and salad, Diane updated Nancy on her publicity efforts, and in turn Nancy gave her some last-minute, minor logistical changes she wanted her to pass on to Sarah and Sylvia. "No problem," Diane assured her. "I was planning to head back to the manor after lunch."

But first, she would have to stop at home to change out of her interview outfit—and to search her sewing room for something, anything, that might qualify as a holiday quilt suitable to display at Elm Creek Manor alongside the works of the master quilters she called friends.

Back home, clad once again in casual clothes, she strode into her sewing room, planted her feet, and glowered as she scanned the shelves and closets, certain she was wasting her time but determined to search, just so she could say she had tried. "Quilt inventories," she echoed Sarah grimly as her gaze took in the bookcases of pattern books and magazines, full of inspiration that had led her blithely from one project to the next: the shelves of fabric in every hue, each yard and fat quarter purchased with a specific pattern in mind, and yet unused; the plastic zipper bags full of incomplete blocks and the carefully cut pieces needed to complete them; the boxes of finished blocks yet to be assembled into tops; and the tops that would be finished as soon as she attached the borders.

None of these would do.

At last her gaze came to rest on the only part of her so-called quilt inventory that offered her any hope in her current predicament: a small stack of finished tops, ready for layering, basting, and quilting as soon as she got around to it.

And she did, absolutely, mean to get around to each one someday. She never began a quilt she didn't sincerely, wholeheartedly intend to finish. It was just that life got in the way sometimes, or her interest waned, or the exigency for a particular quilt diminished, and a project just fell by the wayside. Diane was unique among the Elm Creek Quilters in that she did not have a vast collection of gorgeous finished quilts, each one a future heirloom destined to be cherished by her descendants for generations. What she had was an embarrassingly large stockpile of UFOs—Unfinished Fabric Objects—fated to earn a few bucks at the inevitable estate auction of her worldly goods, hopefully sometime in the far-distant future.

It wasn't that she never finished *any* quilts. She had made quite a few in her quilting career: cozy scrap quilts the family used around the house for warmth and comfort; gifts for relatives and friends; samples for her Beginning Piecing classes at Elm Creek Quilt Camp; and several especially cherished works she had entered in Waterford Summer Quilt Festivals, now given pride of place on the walls of the Sonnenberg home. But she had not learned to quilt until she was a thirty-something mother of two, whereas her friends had taken up the art as teens or even as children. That, combined with her preference for piecing and quilting by hand—an emotionally rewarding but time-consuming process—meant that she had very few finished quilts to her name. Of those she had not given away, none had been made especially for the holidays, in holiday colors or with a holiday theme or from blocks with "Christmas" in the name. Considering how much Diane adored the festive season, it was an astonishing oversight, one she could not possibly correct in time for the opening of the Christmas Boutique.

As for all of those unfinished projects, including several that would have fit Agnes's holiday decorating theme perfectly if only they were quilted and bound, Diane had a very valid excuse for why she had set each one aside. But the Elm Creek Quilters could not adorn the ballroom walls with pretty excuses.

She especially regretted abandoning the appliqué Advent calendars she had begun the day after Thanksgiving. Years before, one late November day when Michael and Todd were young, Diane had impulsively added an Advent calendar to her shopping basket when she was buying Christmas cards and wrapping paper. The double square of sturdy card stock had an attached, fold-out stand and was whimsically decorated with colorful symbols of the season—a snowman, a cardinal perched upon an evergreen bough, a candle, a golden bell with a red bow, a gift wrapped in striped paper, a reindeer, and more, one illustration for each pocket, all encircled by a plume of ivy and holly with bright red berries. That December and for years thereafter, she had filled the paper pockets with coins and small pieces of candy, and the boys took turns opening them and enjoying the prizes discovered within, one pocket each day from December first until Christmas. The boys had delighted in the daily surprises, and Diane and Tim had enjoyed watching their anticipation for Christmas grow as they counted down the days.

Every January, she had tucked the Advent calendar into a rigid cardboard folder and put it away with the other holiday decorations, but it was only card stock, and time took its toll. One by one the pockets fell off until only half remained, and then the foldout stand tore so they had to prop the calendar against the wall or leave it lying flat on the counter. By the time Michael started high school, it had become so dilapidated that Diane winced when she removed it from the cardboard folder, having forgotten how faded and forlorn it had looked the previous year. "It may be time to send this to the Island of Misfit Toys," she had told Tim ruefully as they packed up the ornaments and garland after New Year's Day, but she had saved it all the same.

Several years passed, and one Christmas after another, the once-cherished decoration had remained at the bottom of the storage carton. This year, when the Elm Creek Quilters had gathered at the manor on the day after Thanksgiving for their annual quilt-ers' holiday, Diane had spotted a pattern for a quilted Advent calendar in one of Sylvia's magazines. Inspired, she immediately began choosing fabrics and cutting out pieces for two calendars, one for each of her sons. She couldn't wait to see their reactions when they unwrapped them on Christmas morning. They would remember the old card-stock version that had brought them so much joy, fondly reminisce about Christmases past, and implore her to revive the once-cherished tradition, a request she would happily grant.

The thought of it brought a warm glow to Diane's heart, but Gwen soon doused it with a bucket of cold reality. Diane had started too late and would never finish in time for Christmas, she pointed out. "And to get the most out of the calendars," she added, "you really ought to give them to your boys on the first day of Advent, right?"

Diane was perturbed for a moment, but then she shrugged. "So they'll have them for next year's Advent rather than this one. I'll tuck something special into the last pocket to make up for any disappointment they might feel at missing out on the other surprises."

"Like what, a hundred-dollar bill? It would take something on that order to get most college kids I know interested in an Advent calendar."

"Gwen," Agnes had admonished, and Sylvia promptly chimed in that she thought Diane's project was a lovely idea. But doubt had crept in, and as Diane rearranged the appliqués on the snowy-white background fabric, she wondered why she bothered. Folk art Advent calendars for college men? What a stupid idea. Her sons wouldn't remember the Advent calendar from their child-hood. When they unwrapped their gifts Christmas morning, they would study them in bemusement and offer her perplexed thanks. By early afternoon of their quilting marathon, she concluded that Gwen was right. She was wasting her time in a futile effort to continue a tradition that meant nothing to anyone else in the family.

Feeling very sorry for herself, she abandoned the project. Then the blizzard struck the Elm Creek Valley, and her misguided attempt to drive home left her car stuck in a snowbank on the forest road. She had to trudge back to the manor and might have gotten frostbite if not for Jeremy, who had given up on his trip to Chicago, had come upon her struggling through drifts on the forest road, and had driven her back to the warmth and safety of the manor.

However, the event and the forced overnight stay had given her time to reconsider her choice. Maybe folk art appliqué Advent calendars weren't such silly gifts after all. If Michael and Todd didn't appreciate them this year, they might someday, when they had children of their own and were nostalgic for the Christmas traditions of their childhood. In the meantime, Diane could make one for herself to replace the dilapidated paper version she would always remember fondly.

The following day, after the roads were cleared and she finally made it home, her family greeted her as if she had been trapped on an arctic ice floe for a week rather than overnight at one of her favorite places with her closest friends. When she set down her tote bag and a few appliqués spilled onto the coffee table, Todd picked up a piece of brown fabric that was meant to be the side of a log cabin. He found a few others and quickly assembled the cabin and the red, snow-covered barn beside it.

Michael found a green piece cut in the shape of a pine tree, matched it to a brown trunk, and slid it in place beside the cabin. "This looks like that Advent calendar we used to have," he said, studying the scene. "Remember, Mom? You'd put candy or money in the pockets and we'd open one for each day of December leading up to Christmas."

Diane felt a thrill of delight. "You remember that?"

Michael shrugged. "Well, yeah. You never let us have candy except for Halloween, Easter, and Christmas. It was kind of a big deal."

To her astonishment, when she explained how dilapidated the old calendar had become, her sons offered to repair it. "We should start using it again," said Michael. "I can fix the pockets, and instead of candies and quarters, you can put tens and twenties in them."

"Inflation," Todd explained. "You know how it is."

"Yes, I think I'm catching on," said Diane, smiling.

She retrieved the old calendar from its cardboard folder, and while her sons repaired it, she gathered up the appliqué pieces and quickly put them out of sight in her sewing room. If she sewed a few hours a day, she was certain she could complete the new Advent calendars in time to give them to the boys on Christmas morning. And in the days that followed, she had kept to her plan—but then someone had ruined the floor of the community hall, the Christmas Boutique had moved to Elm Creek Manor, and she had not had time for anything but publicity and other preparations for the fund-raiser. Next Christmas, she told herself ruefully whenever she passed her sewing room and thought of the appliqué pieces abandoned on the desk between her thread bin and basket of sewing tools. She would finish them next year for sure.

Never before had she begun, abandoned, resumed, and reluctantly set aside a project in such rapid succession. Unfortunately, good intentions and great excuses did not bring a quilt one day closer to completion.

Sighing, she took the stack of finished tops from the shelf, set them on the daybed, and began sorting through them, first a crib quilt in bright primary colors originally intended for a baby, who had recently started the fourth grade, then an English-paper-pieced Grandmother's Flower Garden in pastel florals that she had put away when removing the papers became too tedious a chore to endure.

Then she came upon an unquilted top that made her cry out softly in fond recognition. It was exactly what Agnes was looking for, and if only it were finished, it would have complemented Gwen's *Winter Solstice Star* beautifully—as one might expect, since Gwen's superb quilt had inspired it.

That was in September of Michael's senior year. To Diane it seemed as if her eldest son had always struggled academically, not because he wasn't bright, but because he was bored—which, when he was younger, had led to numerous discipline issues that had driven her to distraction. For someone who intensely disliked high school, however, he seemed strangely indifferent to what might follow. While his classmates were applying to colleges or considering different trade schools or enlisting in the military, Michael refused to discuss any options, not with his school counselor and not with his parents.

"What about computers?" Diane had asked the previous spring, after a lunch with friends had enlightened her to the apparently obligatory gauntlet of standardized tests and campus visits that her son had not even begun. Two years before, his obsession with video games had led him to enroll in a computer programming class, where he had discovered a passion and an extraordinary gift for computer sciences. He had even joined the computer team, his first and only school club. "You could study programming or computer engineering. You'd be so good at that."

He shrugged. "If you do something for work, it isn't fun any-more."

"That's not true," Diane protested. "Your father loved chem-istry when he was your age and he's very glad he made it his career. I love quilting, and I've enjoyed it even more ever since we launched Elm Creek Quilt Camp. Being on the computer team hasn't taken the fun out of computing, has it?"

Michael frowned thoughtfully. "I guess that's true."

He said nothing more about it, resisting her careful attempts to pry information out of him all summer. Then, just a few days into his senior year, he came home from a computer team meet-ing and announced that he had decided he should probably go to college and major in computer programming or engineering or something. Diane and Tim refrained from jumping up and down and cheering, joyful tears streaming down their faces. Instead they calmly replied that it sounded like a good plan and they would help him however they could.

After signing him up for the SAT and doing a bit of research, they soon discovered that Michael lacked the grades and breadth of extracurricular activities expected of applicants to the top pro-grams in the country. It was too late to join a bunch of sports and run for student council, so he would have to find another way to make a good impression. A few teachers promised to write strong letters of recommendation, and Michael toiled over his personal statement, explaining with a frankness that alarmed Diane that he had made some bad choices when he was younger but he had figured it out and would not repeat the mistakes of his past. He admitted that school had never been his thing until he discov-ered computers, but ever since, the hard work he had put into mastering difficult concepts in his computer classes had taught him how to do better in other subjects like history and English.

He concluded with a few paragraphs describing his theories about how he believed computer technology would evolve in the future and what aspects especially fascinated him. It made absolutely no sense to Diane, but, guardedly hopeful that he knew what he was talking about, she resisted the impulse to suggest he delete them.

She did encourage him to ask Gwen, a college professor, for her professional opinion of his essay. "Dad's a professor too and he said it's great," said Michael.

"A second opinion is always helpful, and Dr. Sullivan will be more objective," she replied. "She may have some useful insights."

At that, Michael agreed. He printed out a clean copy of his personal statement and delivered it to Gwen at home, but he was in Harrisburg competing in a tournament with the computer team when she finished reviewing it, so Diane stopped by to pick it up. "It's a strong, well-crafted essay," Gwen told her after inviting her inside to wait while she hurried upstairs to her study for the corrected draft, "I noted a few typos, but otherwise I wouldn't change a word."

Relieved, Diane nonetheless asked, "You don't think he's too forthcoming about his checkered past? Shouldn't he accentuate the positive?"

Gwen shook her head. "His candor is refreshing. With some admissions officers, that will compensate quite a bit for the low GPA."

Diane thanked her and added that Michael would be in touch to thank her himself soon. As they passed the living room on their way back to the front door, Diane noticed a quilt draped over the sofa. "What do you have here?" she asked, drawing closer. It reminded her of a Lone Star quilt in that it was based upon an eight-pointed star design and that a single "block" comprised of smaller geometric shapes formed the entire surface of the quilt. But whereas a Lone Star was a single star with eight points made up of many smaller rhombuses, the points of Gwen's star had been constructed Log Cabin style, with a rhombus at the center and rows of strips sewn in a concentric pattern around it. Another distinctive feature was that the single eight-pointed star in the center was framed by four three-quarter stars in the corners. The colors and the shading of the rhombuses gave Diane the impression of gazing up into a starry winter sky.

"It's gorgeous," she said, but couldn't resist teasing, "It looks like you tried to make a Log Cabin quilt but you couldn't quite square it up."

"That's exactly what happened," said Gwen dryly. "Let's keep it our little secret."

"The star points are based on the Log Cabin, obviously, but how did you come up with this arrangement?"

"It's a Snow Crystals block, not my own ingenious invention. Don't you see it?"

When Diane admitted that she was not familiar with that particular block, Gwen led her upstairs to her quilt studio, pulled a mid-century index of traditional blocks from a bookshelf, and showed her an illustration. Diane liked the block even more in its original incarnation, standard-size with solid rhombuses. Borrowing paper and colored pencils, she carefully sketched it, already imagining how beautifully it would sparkle when multiplied across the surface of a quilt.

Later, taking a cue from Gwen as she browsed the shelves of Grandma's Attic, she selected rich blue, warm gold, and shimmery silver-white fabrics evocative of a frosty midwinter night. She made templates, cut pieces, and stitched them together with small, even stitches, imagining how cozy it would be to snuggle up with Tim beneath the finished quilt on New Year's Eve. With every block she completed, her anticipation for the finished quilt grew.

Unfortunately, she had picked the busiest time of the year

to begin such a substantial project, and other obligations persistently demanded her attention. She and Tim hosted their extended families for Thanksgiving, and Diane lost a week of sewing time to cleaning, cooking, decorating, feasting, and recuperating after the whirlwind. Then came the last-minute rush of helping Michael finish his college applications before the December 1 deadline. Soon thereafter she had to bake scores of cupcakes for the reception following Todd's winter band concert, and the very next day the family piled into the car and drove out to Schoepke's Christmas Tree Farm to cut down a gorgeous blue spruce, which they set up in the living room and decorated over the weekend. After that, it was a busy, wonderful, hectic season of baking cookies, decking the halls, attending holiday parties with friends, writing annual letters to include with their Christmas cards, shopping for gifts, enjoying holiday concerts at the college, and making religious observances, with very little time left over for quilting.

After the holiday merriment subsided, Diane frequently sat by the fireside with a hot drink and a few blocks to stitch, enjoying the stolen moments she had all to herself. But the snow she had found so picturesque and romantic on Christmas Eve seemed tedious and oppressive by the end of January, and by mid-February she never wanted to see another flake. The wintry hues of her Snow Crystals blocks steadily lost their appeal. She longed for spring florals, warm pastels, and patterns like Carolina Lily and Posies Round the Square. The Snow Crystals blocks often sat in her sewing room untouched for days at a time, but in rare, intermittent bursts of determination, she finished the last few blocks, sewed them into rows, sewed the rows together, and attached borders of midnight blue. All that remained was to press the finished top, lightly mark her hand-quilting lines, layer, baste, quilt, and bind. But that was a considerable amount of work, and after Diane finished ironing the seams smooth and flat, she never quite found the time for the next step.

March brought gusty, warmer winds and melting snows, meetings at the manor to plan for a new season of Elm Creek Quilt Camp, and college acceptances and rejections for Michael. When he decided to attend Waterford College as a computer sciences major, Diane and Tim were delighted and proud. Tim's status as full professor meant a nice tuition break; Diane had a very dear friend in the department, fellow founding Elm Creek Quilter Judy Nguyen DiNardo, who would look out for him; and although Michael firmly insisted that he intended to move into a campus dorm rather than live at home, he would be close enough that they would surely see him more frequently than if he had chosen a college hundreds of miles away. Things could not have worked out better for Michael, and Diane was thankful.

By then it was June, warm and sunny, with flowers blooming in the yard and Elm Creek Quilt Camp in full swing. Diane had no time for making winter holiday quilts, nor any inclination either. And when months passed and winter came once more, new blocks and fabrics and styles captured her imagination. She folded the Snow Crystals top and tucked it away on a shelf, and eventually all but forgot it.

If she acquiesced to necessity and quilted the top with her sewing machine, she could possibly finish it in time to hang it in the ballroom before the doors to the Christmas Boutique opened in the morning. Her machine quilting skills were a bit rusty since she almost never used them, but desperate times called for lowered artistic standards. Unless—

She carefully folded the Snow Crystals top, set it aside, and resumed sorting through the pile. If she found another top, equally suitable for the holiday decorating theme but smaller, she would be able to quilt it more quickly, increasing the likelihood of meeting her deadline.

Halfway through the stack, she came across a red-and-white quilt top she had pieced during a brief phase when red-and-white quilts were all the rage. When had she made it, and why? Probably just to follow the popular fad, although she had broken from the trend a bit by reversing the lights and darks, so that her blocks were white focus fabrics on a red background rather than the other way around. As to when she had begun . . .

She closed her eyes and ran her hand over a block, one of twenty-five arranged on point with red sashing between. A vague memory stirred, a faint certainty that she had assembled the top during the one year when both of her sons were in middle school.

On a day between Christmas and New Year's Eve, when the boys were home for winter break and were driving her absolutely crazy with their roughhousing and arguing and incessant beeping and chirping of video games, Tim had suggested that she get out of the house for a while to preserve her remaining sanity. She called Agnes, whose children and grandchildren had already returned to their own homes after Christmas, and gratefully accepted her invitation to come over for tea, quilting, and quiet conversation. As Diane sewed borders to her red-and-white quilt, she told Agnes about her plan to take advantage of post-holiday sales, for she needed a pretty new dress to wear when she accompanied Michael to the Eighth Grade Parent-Student Dance in late January.

The event had caught her a bit by surprise. Although Diane had been born and raised in Waterford, she had attended the district's second, more recently constructed middle school, and after she graduated from the University of Pittsburgh, it was there she had taught sixth grade until Michael was born. Abigail Nelson

Middle School also held a dance in late January, but it was called the Winter Round-Up and featured a delicious barbecue supper and square dancing to a live band for all grades, and all parents.

"Michael let me teach him a few basic dances, the waltz and swing, but he acts like it's sheer torture," said Diane, pinning a narrow red strip to the edge of the joined rows of blocks. "He doesn't want to go, but his friends will be there with their mothers, and apparently they've made a pact that if one of them has to suffer, they all will."

"Suffer?" Agnes echoed as she peered through her pink-tinted glasses at a small leaf appliqué that she was sewing to an Oak Leaf and Reel block. "Some might say they're lucky they get to attend at all. When my girls attended Lydia Darragh Middle School, the event was known as the Eighth Grade Father-Daughter Dance."

"You mean the eighth grade boys didn't go—and their mothers couldn't either?"

"That's right. A few years ago, though, a single mother complained to the principal when she was forbidden to escort her daughter. The girl's grandfather took her instead, but the following summer, the mother launched a petition drive to change the rules. The next year, after her own daughter had moved on to high school, all eighth grade students and any parent or important adult in their lives were welcome to attend the dance."

"I'm glad the administration saw reason," Diane declared. "I'd hate to sit home while half of my son's classmates and their dads were dancing the night away." Shaking her head, she reached for another pin. "My compliments to that persistent mom, whoever she is."

They sewed into the afternoon, pausing for a lunch of tasty leftovers from the Emberly family's Christmas Day feast. At twilight, Diane returned home calm and refreshed, with a completed quilt top to her credit. Why had she put it away unfinished, when it would have made such a lovely Valentine's Day gift for Tim or her mother? She honestly could not recall. A red-and-white quilt might not fit a strict interpretation of holiday decor, but Santa's suit was red and white, as were candy canes. It might be just Christmasy enough to be acceptable, especially if the alternative was a blank wall. How unfortunate it was that the block name—Dolley Madison's Star—did absolutely nothing to evoke the holiday spirit.

Diane decided that this one minor deficiency wasn't enough to disqualify it, so she folded it carefully, lay it on the Snow Crystals top, and returned to the stack, hoping something ideal awaited discovery. She found tops pieced from autumnal hues, samples for classes she had taught only once, and a Wedding Bouquet quilt for a couple who had called off their engagement a month before the wedding. Diane lingered over that top, sighing with regret. It truly was beautiful, perhaps one of her best, but it seemed bad luck to bestow it upon another couple, so off to the UFO pile it had gone.

She had almost given up the search as hopeless when at the bottom of the pile she discovered one of her early works—a red, green, gold, and white quilt of twenty-four ten-inch Providence blocks framed by a border of sawtooth triangles. Inspecting it, she was pleased to see that although it was only the third or fourth quilt she had attempted, her stitches were small, strong, and even, and her piecing accuracy had been consistently good, if not flawless. Of the three tops in contention, this one best suited Agnes's decorating scheme. It was larger than the Dolley Madison's Star, but if she started quilting it right away, she might be able to finish it by morning.

As for the teasing she would endure if her friends knew what had inspired her to make it—well, she could only hope that enough time had passed since she'd made the quilt and no one would ever suspect. Agnes might, but she was kind and discreet, and she would never dream of exposing a friend to ridicule, especially a friend whom she herself had taught to quilt.

Diane's mother had quilted, and her mother before her, as well as several aunts and great-aunts. Yet although she had grown up surrounded by quilts and the women who made them, she had never felt the slightest inclination to learn to sew. Why should she invest months or years into making a single quilt when so many other people were happy to make quilts for her?

She was grown, married, and the mother of two before the urge to learn seized her. One summer day, Agnes, a childhood babysitter who had become a dear friend, invited Diane to accompany her to the Waterford Summer Quilt Festival. Michael and Todd, eleven and nine, were off at day camp, so she was free to accept.

In the sunny atrium of the Waterford College library, quilts of all descriptions hung in neat rows from tall wooden stands. Quilters and quilt lovers alike strolled the aisles, admiring patchwork and appliquéd pieces both large and small, in every attractive color combination imaginable, and a few that Diane thought should have been left to the imagination. She and Agnes paused before nearly every quilt on display, reading the program for the artists' names and their thoughts on their work. Docents wearing spotless white gloves mingled with the crowd, ready to turn over an edge of a quilt so onlookers could examine the backing, where the fine quilting stitches appeared more distinctly than on the patterned top.

Agnes, a master quilter herself although she was too modest to say so, had accumulated an impressive store of knowledge about her beloved art, and whenever Diane admired an especially striking work, Agnes provided a tactful, quiet analysis of its pattern, design elements, and construction techniques. With her help, Diane learned to distinguish between a truly challenging pattern that tested the maker's skills and one that merely appeared difficult, but could be assembled rather easily if one knew the technique. Diane discovered how subtle variations in color and contrast added intriguing complexity to relatively basic patterns, and how uninspired fabric choices detracted from otherwise technically masterful quilts.

As they were turning the corner into a new aisle, Diane suddenly stopped short, captivated by a stunning quilt given pride of place at the end. It was a simple arrangement of twenty-four blocks in six rows of four, with a narrow blue inner border framed by a scrappy-pieced outer border. She did not recognize the pattern, which resembled a star with a square in the center overlying a cross. The horizontal and vertical crossbars seemed to create a woven net that captured the sparkling stars. What charmed her most were the quilt's colors, which at first glance appeared to be true reds, blues, and greens, but actually ranged in a narrow spectrum around the pure hues. The subtle variations of the colors were restful to look upon, as if the quilt knew a reassuring secret that it meant to share.

"It's simply gorgeous," said Diane, soaking in the peaceful feelings of contentment the quilt inspired.

"It certainly deserves that ribbon," Agnes remarked.

Diane tore her gaze from the quilt and let it fall upon the purple "Viewer's Choice" ribbon affixed to the tall post supporting the quilt stand. Above it was the placard announcing the title and maker of the quilt.

*Springtime in Waterford* by Mary Beth Callahan.

Diane felt her breath catch in her throat. "You've got to be kidding me," she croaked.

"What?" Agnes peered at her, concerned. "What's the matter?"

Diane could only shake her head. How could the world's most annoying next-door neighbor have created such a warm, charming quilt? "Someone mixed up the signs," she managed to say. It was the only explanation that made any sense.

"Don't be ridiculous," said Agnes. "They take good care to make sure mistakes like that don't happen. Even if they had, by now someone would have noticed and corrected it."

Diane stared at Mary Beth Callahan's name for a moment in utter disbelief before stalking off down the next aisle. "She only won that ribbon because she's popular," she muttered, even though she knew it wasn't true. "Notice how the quilt didn't win any technical awards?"

Agnes hurried to keep up with her. "That's quite enough," she said, her voice barely above a whisper. "The artist or her best friend or her mother might have been standing right behind you. You sweeten your sour temperament or we're going home."

Diane was tempted to remind Agnes that she wasn't her babysitter anymore, but she hated to see her longtime friend so distressed, so she promised to keep her editorial comments to herself. But the lovely quilt lingered in her thoughts, baffling her with the incongruity of its beauty and its maker's unpleasantness.

A few days later, Diane was in her backyard moving the sprinklers when Mary Beth stepped out onto her deck to refill her bird feeders. "Hello," Diane called after sparing a moment for risk assessment.

Her neighbor eyed her warily and offered a nod in reply.

Emboldened, Diane shut off the hose and drew closer to the invisible but inviolable line that marked the boundary between their yards. "I saw your quilt at the Waterford Summer Quilt Festival. It was beautiful. Congratulations on winning a ribbon."

"Thanks," said Mary Beth warily, as if waiting for the punch line of a nasty joke.

"What's the name of the block you used? I never saw my mom or her friends make anything like it. I wish I could."

"You?" Mary Beth burst out laughing. "Oh, Diane. If your mother quilted, you must have learned from observing her what it takes to be a quilter. You must realize that you aren't cut out for it, no pun intended."

"And why is that, exactly?"

"It takes patience and perseverance to be a quilter. Attention to detail too, and let's face it, you're practically allergic to details. But it's more than that. Those things can be learned with practice and willpower. You also need . . ." Mary Beth gazed speculatively somewhere past Diane's shoulder. "The soul of an artist."

"And you think I don't have one," said Diane tightly. "That soul-of-an-artist thing."

Mary Beth fixed her with a sorrowful, condescending smile. "Exactly."

Dumbfounded, Diane stood there gaping as Mary Beth walked around the side yard and disappeared into her garage. She was jarred out of her stunned outrage only when a gust of wind dashed her with cold spray from the sprinkler. Storming into the house, she kicked off her wet shoes in the foyer and padded to the phone in her bare feet. She dialed Agnes's number, and before her friend could begin the usual exchange of pleasantries, Diane begged her to teach her to quilt. She'd show Mary Beth who had the soul of an artist. She'd learn to sew circles around that wretched woman. She used to teach sixth grade. If she didn't know patience and perseverance, she never would have made it through a single semester.

Agnes was so delighted by Diane's request for lessons that she didn't ask why she suddenly, urgently needed to learn to quilt. Agnes probably assumed that she had been inspired by the glorious display at the quilt show, and in a manner of speaking, that was true. Diane didn't dare reveal her true purpose. Agnes strongly disapproved of the ongoing battle of wills between the two neighbors, and she might have ended the lessons rather than contribute to the tension.

Diane soon discovered that anger could sustain her only so long. Under Agnes's gentle but steadfast tutelage, Diane's hunger to prove herself better than Mary Beth disappeared, to be replaced by a genuine love for the traditional art form. The infinite possible combinations of color, pattern, and arrangement appealed to her craving for variety, and Agnes charmed her with folk tales about block patterns and their intriguing names. As she gradually mastered piecing and quilting by hand, she finished a small sampler wall hanging and one quilt apiece for the boys' beds.

One September day two years after she had begun her quilting lessons, she was contemplating her next project when she remembered Mary Beth's gorgeous quilt. While paging through Agnes's quilt books, she had stumbled upon the block her neighbor had chosen—Providence. A traditional pattern based on a five-by-five grid, it was comprised of simple geometric shapes assembled with a basic running stitch, with no curved seams or setting-in of pieces required. Wouldn't it be the ideal test of Diane's skills to attempt the pattern that had inspired her to take up quilting? And by completing it, what better way to disprove Mary Beth's disparaging assessment of her character?

The leaves had only just begun to turn and the days remained pleasantly mild, but Diane looked ahead to the holidays and decided to make her own Providence quilt in colors and prints suitable for the season. She chose reds of varying shades for the narrow pentagons that lay along the horizontal and vertical centers, green for the wider pentagons that fell on the diagonals. For the star points and the central squares, she selected rich golds and bronzes.

As autumn waned and winter approached, she finished twenty-four blocks, and by Thanksgiving, she had sewed them into six rows of four blocks each. She added an inner border of ivory, and then an outer border of the same width comprised of half-square triangles. When she put the last stitch in the top on a snowy day in mid-December, she was so pleased and proud of herself that she almost laughed aloud. She had done it. It had taken her two and a half years, but she had proven to herself and to her spiteful next-door neighbor that she too could create a masterpiece.

But had she?

Doubt crept in as she draped the finished top over the daybed and stepped back to study it as objectively as she could. For a novice, it was indeed fine work. The blocks seemed all the same size, the points met properly, the quilt lay flat and even. And yet, when she looked closely, she detected small variations in the width of one red pentagon and its counterpart in an adjacent block, several triangles that were a degree or two off from a perfect right angle, and something about the sawtooth border that seemed out of balance, as if it were too narrow for the proportions of the quilt blocks it surrounded. She was sure Mary Beth had used a border exactly like this one, but Diane had worked from memory and might have gotten something wrong.

She frowned, thinking—and suddenly she realized exactly what was missing.

There was almost nothing of herself in the quilt.

She had chosen red, green, and gold focus fabrics instead of red, green, and blue, but otherwise she had put none of her own preferences or personality into the quilt. *Christmas in Waterford* was pretty, even striking, but it was a mediocre imitation of the original work of a more accomplished quilter. Even the title was derivative.

It was some consolation to know that only someone with the soul of an artist would have perceived this fatal flaw.

Blinking away tears, she folded the pretty quilt top and clutched it to her chest, a hug that failed to comfort. She told herself that it was better she had figured this out now rather than after she quilted and bound it and showed it off to her quilting friends. Mary Beth's quilt was too breathtaking, her "Viewer's Choice" triumph too recent, for any local quilter not to immediately guess where Diane had found her inspiration. Her heart plummeted when she realized that everyone who had seen both quilts could not help comparing hers unfavorably to her rival's.

That was the realization that had compelled Diane, years before, to put the unfinished *Christmas in Waterford* quilt on a shelf in her sewing room, the first of a pile that had accumulated slowly and steadily through the years. She had hoped that it would remain her secret, but it was a lovely quilt, if not as perfect as the one that had inspired her. The Elm Creek Quilters needed holiday quilts, and Diane had one. Perhaps enough time had passed and memories had faded sufficiently that no one would ridicule her for essentially copying another quilter's pattern. Didn't apprentice painters learn their craft by imitating the works of the great masters? Diane had done much the same thing, but with variations to the borders and colors. As long as she did not attempt to pass the quilt off as her own original design, it would be unfair to accuse her of plagiarism, or whatever the sewing equivalent was.

But Diane would go one step further. If she spotted a Christmas Boutique customer admiring her quilt top, she would approach them and explain that it was an adaptation of an original design by Mary Beth Callahan. Better yet, she would post a small sign on the wall identifying Mary Beth as the designer.

But she could do that only if she finished quilting and binding the top in time for the opening of the boutique, scarcely eighteen hours away. That was impossible, she knew. Even if she quilted at top speed through the night, she would never finish in time.

She sat down on the daybed and rested her hand on the quilt top, heart heavy. She had promised her friends she would contribute to the decorations. They were counting on her and she was about to let them down. It would not be the first time and they would forgive her, but she hated to seem irresponsible or indifferent when the truth was that she cared very much. She was sorry to disappoint the other Elm Creek Quilters, and sorrier still that she had not finished her projects, but she would never regret starting them. Each was a milestone on her journey, a measure of her progress as a quilter and a person.

Incomplete was better than never attempted—and her friends would understand that more than anyone.

Quickly she rose and wiped her eyes with the back of her hand. Taking scissors from the basket of tools on her desk, she carefully trimmed loose threads from the unfinished edge of *Christmas in Waterford*, rolled it up, and tucked it neatly into a tote bag. After a moment's hesitation, she did the same with the red-and-white Dolley Madison's Star quilt and the Snow Crystals. So they weren't quite finished. What did it really matter? They were still pretty, and they still evoked the spirit of the festive season. She would take them to Elm Creek Manor and let the decorating crew decide if they were good enough to display at the Christmas Boutique. After they were hung high upon the ballroom walls, perhaps no one would notice that they were still works-in-progress.

Her remorse dissipated as she pulled on her coat and boots, slung the strap of her tote over her shoulder, grabbed her purse, and headed out to the garage. As she backed out onto the driveway, she saw the Callahans' garage door rising. Something compelled her to pause with her foot on the brake, and as she watched the house next door, she observed Mary Beth loading three large shopping bags into the trunk of her car. She closed it and turned around, and when she did, she spotted Diane watching her through the windshield. Mary Beth hesitated, wrung her gloved hands, and seemed to steel herself before crossing her own driveway to meet Diane in hers.

Diane rolled down her window. "Hey, how are you?" she asked warily. Mary Beth looked like she was on a mission, and that could mean anything.

"Will you be stopping by Elm Creek Manor any time soon?" Mary Beth asked.

"Yes, in fact, I'm on my way there now."

Mary Beth heaved a sigh of relief. "Would you be willing to drop off my contributions for the Christmas Boutique?"

"I'd be happy to." Diane popped open her trunk, shut down the engine, and got out of the car. "I'll help you load."

Mary Beth thanked her, and within minutes they had transferred her bags of quilts for the market to Diane's car. "I really appreciate this," said Mary Beth, strangely agitated, as Diane closed the trunk. "I can't bear to show my face at Elm Creek Manor, not with all the Christmas Boutique volunteers working so hard."

"Why not?" asked Diane, bewildered. "You've been to the manor twice since the end of summer, and Sylvia said you were welcome back any time. Is this because of what Brent and his friends did? Bonnie forgave them, and she's in Hawaii so you don't have to worry about seeing her—"

"No, no, this has nothing to do with all that." Mary Beth shook her head, distressed. "They don't blame me but I blame myself. Nancy and Melanie and the others have been so nice, so understanding, but I still can't face them. I quit the facilities committee. I can't even bring myself to go back to church."

"You mean—" Understanding struck so suddenly that Diane took a half-step backward. "You were the . . ." She paused, thoughts racing. "Listen, everyone knows you didn't do it on purpose."

"I certainly hope so. What kind of horrible person would deliberately destroy a church hall and jeopardize a fund-raiser for a
food pantry?" Mary Beth laughed a bit frantically, her eyes shining with unshed tears. "I'll tell you who. The mother of a boy
who vandalized a quilt shop. I know what everyone is thinking:
It runs in the family."

"No one is thinking that."

"I feel so stupid, and after trying so hard to do everything
right, to make up for—" She closed her eyes and shook her head
again. "I volunteered to work at the boutique throughout the
weekend, but I can't do it. I just can't. Will you tell Nancy I'm
sorry?"

"Mary Beth, listen to me." Diane grasped her by the shoulders.
"You have to stop blaming yourself. No one else does. Anyone
could have made that mistake. We need you at the boutique.
You have to work your shifts."

Mary Beth sniffled and eyed her, taken aback by the urgency
in her tone. "What if . . . what if people tell me to go away?"

"No one would, and I dare them to try. Sylvia would send
them packing instead. She doesn't tolerate bullies." Diane held
her gaze, determined, and even gave her a little shake. "Promise
me you'll work your shifts. This is an all-hands-on-deck situation. We need you. And there's something I want to show you at
the manor."

"What?"

"I'm not going to tell you *now*. What other leverage do I have
to get you to show up tomorrow?"

Surprised, Mary Beth choked out a laugh. "I—I guess—I'll
think about it."

"Think fast. Friday morning will be here before you know it."
Diane climbed back into her car. "I'll see you tomorrow, if not
sooner."

She shut the door. Mary Beth nodded bleakly, turned away, and trudged back across the driveway and the strip of snow-covered lawn marking the property line, and disappeared into her garage.

Diane took a deep, shaky breath, started the car again, and headed off to Elm Creek Manor. It had been Mary Beth all along, but it was clear she felt deeply remorseful. The damage done to the community hall had resulted not from malice but from a stupid mistake, of the sort Diane made all too often. She or any of her friends could have made the same careless error in a moment of stress, and she knew how she would want them to be treated in the aftermath.

She felt a wave of shame wash over her, so intense it hurt to breathe. How could she have treated a neighbor's unfortunate mistake like an amusing intellectual puzzle? It was one thing to eagerly pursue an anonymous villain, quite another to look into a neighbor's eyes and find guilt and regret there. She wished she had not been so eager to hunt down the person responsible. Mary Beth had suffered enough.

# 8

## *The Elm Creek Quilters*

 GRETCHEN WAS JUST setting the last centerpiece on the last dining table in the banquet hall when the door near the butler's pantry burst open and Diane swept in, breathless, a tote slung over each shoulder and a third clutched in her arms. "Anna said I would find you here," she said, hurrying over, setting the totes on the floor between them one by one.

"My goodness, you've been busy," Gretchen exclaimed, stooping over to peer into the nearest bag. "Are all these for decorating the ballroom?"

"Only this one," said Diane, indicating the bag nearest Gretchen. "These hold Mary Beth Callahan's donations for the boutique."

"I want to see everything, but let's start with your quilts." Gretchen reached in and removed the first, a lovely unquilted top made up of Snow Crystals blocks in blue and gold on a silvery-white background. She admired it for a moment, but Diane was fidgeting, so Gretchen draped it upon the nearest table and took out the second, a stunning red-and-white unquilted top, an Ohio Star variation with the focus fabrics and background reversed, a simple artistic choice that made a traditional pattern seem entirely new. "This is very striking. What do you call this block?"

"Are you sure you want to know? It's not very Christmasy."

Gretchen smiled. "Yes, please do enlighten me."

"It's called Dolley Madison's Star, but I changed the shading a bit."

"Of course. I recognize it now. Well, the block name isn't as merry and bright as one might wish, but the design still evokes the holiday spirit, and you can title the quilt whatever you like."

Diane threw her an odd look. "So you *do* consider this a holiday quilt? It officially passes inspection?"

Gretchen laughed. "There's no inspection, and I'm no more official than you are." She set the red-and-white quilt top upon the Snow Crystals. "Come on, show me what else you brought."

It seemed almost reluctantly that Diane reached into the bag and took out a larger bundle. When Gretchen helped her unfold it, she drew in a breath, captivated by the lovely Providence blocks arranged in a straight setting, resplendent in warmly cheerful red, green, gold, and ivory fabrics. "Diane, this is absolutely gorgeous."

"Do you really think so? It was my fourth quilt, and when I look at it, every mistake leaps off the fabric at me. I know how it's supposed to look, and I can see all too clearly how it falls short."

"I think you're being a little hard on yourself, especially if this was one of your first quilts. Although you chose a traditional holiday color scheme, the subtle variations of hue add wonderful depth and dimension. The layout too is very nice."

"I can't take full credit for that." A faint flush rose in Diane's cheeks. "I actually based my quilt upon one I saw at the Waterford Summer Quilt Festival years ago, Mary Beth's *Springtime in Waterford*. I changed the colors slightly, but otherwise I just duplicated her quilt. Except that I added lots of mistakes not present in the original, to make it my own."

"So you're saying your mistakes were intentional artistic choices," Gretchen teased, but then something else struck her.

"Is the Mary Beth who designed the original Providence quilt the same Mary Beth who donated these quilts for the boutique?"

Wincing slightly, Diane nodded.

"Is something wrong?" Gretchen queried. "You keep making faces . . . Oh, I understand. This is your neighbor, the one whose son served out part of his sentence here this summer."

Diane's wince turned into a grimace. "One and the same. We haven't always gotten along, which is why it's especially important to me to acknowledge her as the designer of this quilt. I didn't ask permission, but I'm hoping that apologetic flattery will help make amends."

"It probably wouldn't hurt."

"I was thinking I could make a placard to post on the wall beside the quilt, with the same information one would see at a quilt show—the title of the quilt, the maker's name, the source of the design, and the year."

"That's a wonderful idea. Perhaps you should do that for all of the quilts on display."

"You're right, I should. That would also make it clear which quilts are for sale in the boutique, and which are for display only." Diane glanced at her watch. "I have plenty of time to collect the information and whip up some signs, if I can use the computer and printer upstairs in the library. But first . . ." She hesitated. "I think you've overlooked a rather obvious problem."

Gretchen studied her, puzzled. "Could you give me a hint?"

"My quilts aren't quilts. I mean, they're not finished. They're just unquilted tops."

"Oh, I don't think that's a problem, do you? Quilts, unquilted tops—for our purposes, I don't think it matters."

Diane gaped. "Are you serious? Unquilted tops were perfectly fine all along? If you had any idea how I've agonized over this—"

"Please tell me you're exaggerating." Diane's woebegone expression gave Gretchen her answer. "Oh, Diane. You should never agonize over anything that could easily be resolved by one conversation with a friend."

"Lesson learned."

"I should certainly hope so." Gretchen smiled and hugged her reassuringly. "Now, let's have a look at Mary Beth's donations for the boutique and decide which market stall to put them in."

"Do you mind taking care of that yourself? I'd like to find Jeremy and any other tall person who isn't too busy and ask them to help me hang these quilt tops so I can get to work on the signs."

"Go right ahead," said Gretchen, waving her off. "I can handle this. You'll probably find Jeremy in the kitchen and most everyone else in the ballroom."

Looking more cheerful than she had all day, Diane thanked her, picked up her quilt tops, and hurried off.

Alone, Gretchen opened the other bags and removed Mary Beth's three quilts—fully finished quilts—of different sizes: one bed quilt, one lap quilt, and one wall hanging. All three were beautifully made, but the smallest moved Gretchen so deeply that she lingered over it much longer than the others. It was a Dove of Peace, intricately appliquéd and pieced, rendered in fabric but resembling a stained-glass window image of a dove in flight, holding an olive branch.

She could not think of any symbol that more perfectly represented the spirit of the Christmas Boutique.

THE ELM CREEK QUILTERS, their husbands and friends, and the volunteers from Good Shepherd worked late into the evening finishing their preparations for the grand opening of the Christmas Boutique, but eventually the visitors departed. The manor's permanent residents complimented one another on a challenge well undertaken and they all went off to bed. Sylvia hoped for sweet dreams and a sound rest, for the next day was sure to be as busy and full of unexpected turns of events as any in the peak season of quilt camp.

On Friday morning, although the sun had not yet risen, so close were they to the longest night of the year, Sylvia and Andrew woke before their alarm. Soon they were on their way downstairs to the kitchen for their scheduled breakfast debriefing before the volunteer sales crew arrived. Not long after that, Sylvia would throw open the front doors to welcome what she hoped would be a steady stream of eager shoppers willing to pay fair prices for fine handcrafted goods in support of a worthy cause.

The delicious aromas wafting from the kitchen told Sylvia and Andrew that Anna was already awake and hard at work, and probably had been for quite some time. "You mean like a tip jar?" they overheard her say as they entered. Sylvia guessed even before she spotted him setting platters of bagels and scones upon the long wooden table that Anna was speaking with Jeremy.

"I was thinking something larger, like a barrel," Jeremy replied, but he broke off at the sight of Sylvia and Andrew. "Good morning. Sleep well? Ready for opening day?"

"Good morning to you, yes, and I hope so," Sylvia said with a smile as she went to the cupboard to find her favorite mug and fill it with Anna's freshly brewed coffee. "What's this about collecting tips?"

"Jeremy thought that maybe we could collect donations for Good Shepherd during the boutique," said Anna as she deftly stirred up a yogurt sauce for the delectable fruit salad sitting on the counter nearby. "We could set up a container and a sign near the food cashier and invite people to leave their change to help pay for the repairs to the community hall."

"They'll inevitably have to pay some of the repair bills before the insurance check comes through," said Jeremy. "I think we can take up a collection to help them in the short term without detracting from the boutique sales."

"Sounds like a great idea," said Andrew, helping himself to a cup of coffee. He sighed gratefully between sips as he seated himself at the table and admired the continental breakfast taking shape before his eyes.

"I agree," said Sylvia, "but first let's ask Nancy and Melanie and have them consult with their pastor."

"Good morning," Sarah said, entering the kitchen bright-eyed and alert, having given up caffeine during her pregnancy and not needing the bracing beverages the rest of them depended on to get their day started. She eased herself onto the bench beside Sylvia and gazed longingly at the cranberry-orange scones. "When is everyone else due to arrive?"

"Any moment" was the answer, but those already present could not resist digging in to such a tempting breakfast right away. Soon their other friends and colleagues joined them around the table and in the nearest booths, and when everyone had filled plates and mugs with enough delicious food and drink to sustain them through the morning, Sarah reiterated everyone's assignments and ran through the most important details of the day. The volunteers were due to arrive an hour before the doors opened; Nancy and Melanie were responsible for their shifts and schedules, so the Elm Creek Quilters could concentrate on other duties. The workers had been instructed to park in the rear lot, enter through the back door, and use the foyer closet for their belongings. Food and beverages would be available for them throughout the day in the kitchen. Jeremy had posted a sign by the first bridge across the creek so customers would take the route to the front of the manor and park in the circular drive.

"I'm still concerned that there won't be enough space for parking out front," said Andrew. "I'll remind you, there never is for the first day of quilt camp. That's why we valet park for them."

Sylvia mulled it over. "If the circular drive becomes full, customers can park along the road. It's at least a quarter mile to the edge of the forest, and Matt cleared the snowbanks from the shoulders during his last visit."

"It's too bad he's not here to go over it once more before we open," said Sarah wistfully.

"A quarter mile might be a long way for some people to walk," said Gretchen, "especially if they'll be carrying lots of purchases back to their cars afterward."

"We definitely want to encourage that," said Agnes.

"Why don't we go with our original plan for now," said Sarah, "but let's monitor the situation and keep a few designated valet parkers on deck just in case."

Andrew, Gwen, and Joe volunteered, but when Jeremy raised his hand too, Anna said, "Jeremy, I really could use you in the kitchen instead, if you don't mind." To Nancy and Melanie she added, "If you can spare some volunteers around lunchtime and dinner, I'd be grateful."

Melanie nodded, and Nancy asked, "Do they need to have any particular culinary skills?"

Anna smiled. "No, I just need a few people to bus tables, keep an eye on the buffet, and carry food from the kitchen to the banquet hall to replenish it."

Sarah finished covering her agenda with about fifteen minutes to spare before the volunteers arrived, so they all pitched in to clean up the kitchen and set it up as a rest and relaxation space for the workers.

"Before you go," said Anna, raising her voice over the din of conversation as they prepared to report to their stations, "I want to give you a little something to look forward to at the end of the day."

"You mean besides a chance to sit down and rest?" asked Joe.

"Yes, besides that," said Anna over her friends' laughter. "Sylvia, you stay seated right there." She disappeared into the pantry and emerged carrying a jelly roll pan lined with parchment paper.

Sylvia smelled apples and cinnamon, and when Anna set the pan before her, she gasped in recognition. "Apple strudel," she exclaimed, clasping her hands together as she admired the four perfectly rolled and lightly browned pastries lying side by side.

"I used your Great-Great-Aunt Gerda's recipe," said Anna. "This is my special good-luck gift to you, Sylvia, and a reward we can all enjoy after our customers leave, to celebrate our first successful day of the Christmas Boutique."

"Hear, hear," said Andrew, and everyone chimed in their agreement and applauded.

"And when we get a bit closer to Christmas," Anna continued, smiling, "I'm going to fill up your Santa Claus cookie jar with *Lebkuchen*, *Anisplätzchen*, and *Zimtsterne* baked from your Great-Aunt Lucinda's recipes."

Sylvia blinked away tears. "Thank you, dear," she said warmly. Anna nodded, her own eyes shining.

How could the Christmas Boutique fail when it was driven by such affection, determination, and goodwill? Sylvia was certain they would have good reason to celebrate their success at the end of the day. She intended to enjoy every morsel of Anna's delicious strudel, as well as all the fond memories of childhood Christmases the familiar flavors and aromas evoked.

SARAH AND HER friends and colleagues had barely taken their places when the first group of volunteers arrived, chatting excitedly, eager to get to work. Sarah's task was to welcome them

in the rear foyer, assist them with their coats and scarves, show
them where to find refreshments in the kitchen, and direct them
down the corridor to Melanie, who waited just inside the front
foyer with a clipboard and the master schedule. It was a bit chilly
back where Sarah was stationed, since each newly arrived group
let in frosty gusts of air when they opened the door, but she had
prepared well for that, layering a long cardigan over a soft, warm
turtleneck and adding a scarf for good measure.

By half past nine, all but one of the morning shift's volunteers
had checked in, so Sarah left her post and made the rounds of
the kitchen, banquet hall, and ballroom to make sure that everything was in order. The rooms were decorated so beautifully that
her heart rose with joy as she took in the scene, and the bustle
of anticipation as the volunteers made last-minute adjustments
to their market stalls sent a thrill of anticipation through her.
The quilts displayed on the walls of the ballroom set a warm,
cozy, festive mood that Sarah hoped would inspire shoppers to
take some of that holiday spirit home in the form of handcrafted
treasures.

She and Sylvia had arranged to meet at the front entrance at
ten minutes to ten to welcome early arrivals, who could gather
in the foyer, hang their coats on the portable wardrobe racks,
and admire the decorations until Gwen and Gretchen opened the
ballroom and banquet hall doors to mark the official start of the
Christmas Boutique.

Sarah arrived five minutes early, and while she waited for her
friend and mentor, she drew back a curtain from one of the windows flanking the tall double doors and steeled herself for what
she might glimpse outside. She hoped to find two or three cars
parked in the circular drive with several customers waiting in
each, but she told herself it would be fine if she saw only one
waiting there, or even none at all. Friday was a workday for most

people, after all, and according to Nancy, tomorrow's attendance was what really mattered. Saturday was traditionally the boutique's busiest day, when the crowds were largest and sales the briskest. Sarah should not jump to any conclusions about the overall success of the Christmas Boutique based upon the first fifteen minutes of opening day.

"Procrastination by analysis," she murmured, and forced herself to peer outside.

The circular drive was already full, and more cars were parked along one side of the driveway at least a quarter of the way across the lawn toward the forest. Clusters of people stood on the veranda or climbed the curved stone staircases, chatting in small groups, sliding back gloves and coat sleeves to check watches, their breaths faint white puffs in the crystalline cold.

Sarah let the curtain fall and stepped back from the window. "Okay," she said aloud. "No problem." They should have heeded Andrew's warnings and planned for valet parking from the beginning. But it would be fine; this was not a crisis. She would just pull Andrew, Gwen, and Joe from their posts and reassign volunteers to cover their roles. It might take a bit of wrangling, but once the traffic jam was cleared, arrivals and departures would be quick, smooth, and convenient for their visitors.

She turned away and set out to alert her designated drivers, but halfway to the ballroom, she halted in the middle of the foyer at the sight of a familiar figure entering from the west wing.

"Matt," she said, stunned. "You're here."

"Morning, sweetheart." He swiftly crossed the black marble floor and swept her up in a gentle hug, releasing her to rest his hands upon her abdomen. "How are you feeling? How are Harry and Hermione?"

"Oh, that's good," said Sarah with a laugh, placing a hand on top of his. "We might have to seriously consider those names."

"Your mom would have a fit."

"My mom probably wouldn't get the reference." Sarah gave her head a little shake. "Matt, what are you doing here? I wasn't expecting you until late this evening. You said your dad needed you to hang drywall all day."

"It sounded like you need me more."

"I do," she said, a catch in her throat. "I really do. Not just today but every day. That's what I've been trying to make you understand."

"I do understand." He drew her close. "Sarah, honey, I'm always going to be here when you need me. Not just today. I promise."

She rested her cheek on his chest and closed her eyes, her heart swelling with love and relief. "I believe you." For the first time since he had announced his decision to spend the winter working for his father, she did believe him.

He smoothed her hair back from her face and kissed her forehead. "You looked like you were on a mission when I interrupted. What's going on? Can I help?"

With a gasp, she remembered the crowd gathering outside and the parking lot forming in the driveway. "Yes, you can," she declared, rising up on tiptoe to kiss his cheek. "I hope you're not too tired of driving, because that's your first assignment."

MARY BETH GAZED out the living room window, a cup of coffee cooling in her hands. Roger had departed for State College earlier that morning, and Brent was scheduled to finish his last final exam at one o'clock. Allowing for time for Brent to pack his bags and Roger to load up the car, by now her husband and son must be almost home. Mary Beth had a thousand things to do, but she found herself unable to focus on any task long enough to complete it, not with the clock measuring each passing hour and the sound of cars passing on the street drawing her to the window, one false alarm after another. How could she leave home when her beloved son would soon walk through the door after so many long weeks away?

That was the excuse she would give Nancy and Melanie if they asked her why she had skipped her shifts at the Christmas Boutique. In the excitement of her son's homecoming, she had completely forgotten. That was why she had not told them ahead of time; she could not have known that she was going to forget.

As excuses went, it was pretty pathetic, but Nancy and Melanie would pretend to believe it. Diane, on the other hand . . . Mary Beth sighed, sipped her cold coffee, and winced, and not only because of the unpleasant taste. Diane would see right through her. She would know that Mary Beth had stayed away out of shame and embarrassment, and after her pep talk in the driveway, she would consider Mary Beth a coward. That stung, but better to endure the accusing stares of one disgruntled neighbor than the cold disdain of dozens of church ladies, studiously ignoring her as they sold handicrafts and baked goods together.

Dispirited, Mary Beth went to the kitchen, poured the cold coffee down the sink, and put her mug in the dishwasher. She hated seeming timid in front of Diane, she hated backing out of her volunteer commitments without a word of explanation, and she hated to miss out on all the fun and, yes, the hard work too, of the Christmas Boutique. She wanted to do her bit, to be a part of a grand, ambitious event that would benefit the community— not only because it was the season of giving, not only to atone for her past mistakes, but because the world was a mess, and no effort to make things better, no matter how small, was ever wasted. Roger and Brent weren't even home yet. She could have spent all morning and half the afternoon raising essential funds for the county food bank without missing a single minute of her son's visit.

Just then, she heard the electric rumble of the garage door opening. Pausing to wipe her fingertips on a dish towel, she hurried to the mudroom to meet them. "Brent," she cried when the door opened, reaching out to embrace him, but she quickly backed out of the way when he entered with a bang and a thud, hauling an extra-large duffel, an overstuffed laundry bag, and a backpack so full it looked likely to burst its zippers.

"Hey, Mom," he said, grinning, letting his burdens fall every which way to the floor. He wrapped her in a bear hug, and for a moment her feet left the floor. "It's good to see you. I'm so glad to be home."

"He says he passed all his classes," Roger declared proudly as he followed his son into the house carrying a suitcase. "Possibly with straight As."

"I won't know for sure until my biology exam is graded," Brent explained.

"I'm sure you aced it," said Mary Beth. "Come into the kitchen. Are you hungry? Dinner won't be ready for a few hours but I could make you a sandwich."

"Sorry, I don't have time. I've got to go." He regarded her quizzically. "Wait. Why are you here? Why aren't you at Elm Creek Manor? You always work the Christmas Boutique."

"I wanted to be here to welcome you home, of course." She felt her smile trembling. "What do you mean, you're leaving? You just got here. Where are you going?"

"To the Christmas Boutique. Michael Sonnenberg texted me this morning. They didn't count on such a huge turnout, and they're understaffed. His mom asked him to help out, and he asked me." His brow furrowed. "I'm sure they could use you too, Mom. You're great at this stuff."

Her heart glowed. "Do you really think so?"

"Of course."

"I second that," said Roger, smiling at them both.

"But . . ." Mary Beth looked from her husband to her son, basking in their confidence, and yet uncertain. "It's your first day home. You just finished your exams. Not even that judge would expect you to do community service today."

"Mom." Brent put his hands on her shoulders and leaned down to look her in the eye. "I'm not going for the community service hours, although, yeah, I know I still have to do the time. I'm going because they need help, and I'm proud they knew they could ask me." He glanced over his shoulder at his father. "We should all go help. After spending my whole summer there, I know there's always work to be done."

"But what about dinner? I was going to make a casserole—"

"Mom. Trust me. They have awesome food there. The casserole can wait. You won't be sorry."

"Well . . ." Her doubts were no match for her son's eagerness. "Let me freshen up first."

Brent grinned and said that he should probably do the same, so they parted with promises to meet back in the mudroom in fifteen minutes. In the meantime, Roger would get Brent's laundry started.

As she changed clothes and ran a brush through her hair, Mary Beth felt a curious mixture of dread and hope milling through her. She had no idea how she would be received at Elm Creek Manor, but Brent made her proud. Over the past few months, it seemed that his perspective had altered dramatically. No longer was toiling at Elm Creek Manor a grueling punishment simply to be endured, but a tangible way to make up for the harm he had done. Best of all, he seemed eager to do so.

Her son had turned his life around, she realized, pressing a hand to her lips as tears of thankfulness gathered in her eyes. If Brent could come so far so swiftly, there was hope for her too.

*    *    *

WHAT GWEN HAD referred to as an opening rush only increased throughout the day, peaking in the mid-afternoon and steadily diminishing as visitors left to meet children headed home after school. Many especially clever shoppers purchased supper to take home to their families from Anna's marvelous buffet, which her kitchen crew had kept well stocked with delicious entrées and tempting desserts throughout that hectic, busy, wonderful day. The cold spread for staff and volunteers was equally delicious, as Gwen could personally affirm, having sampled both.

After the parking debacle was sorted, the Christmas Boutique had run remarkably smoothly, with only a few spills in the banquet hall, a run on singles and five-dollar bills that had sent Gwen racing to the bank for change, and one superficial injury when a woman carrying an oversize purse took a corner too sharply, knocked a ceramic vase off a market table, and cut herself trying to pick up the broken shards. The wound hadn't required more than a wash, a dab of ointment, and a bandage, and the mortified shopper had insisted upon paying for the vase, so even that mishap ended tolerably well.

From what Gwen could see, sales were brisk and steady, the banquet hall was always at least a quarter full with satisfied diners, and the quilt display attracted many admirers, several of whom remarked that seeing the beautiful quilts truly put them in the holiday spirit. "They should have a quilt show with the Christmas Boutique every year," Gwen overheard one gray-haired woman tell a companion.

That was an intriguing thought, which sparked two more in Gwen's mind: Would the Elm Creek Quilters remain involved with the Christmas Boutique when the calamity that had brought it to the manor was resolved? Should Nancy and her team consider a permanent change of venue to Elm Creek Manor?

Gwen knew it was too soon to say—they had not even counted the first day's earnings yet and had not received a single evaluation form—and it was not her decision. Still, it was something to consider, and she wished she could be talking it over with Summer instead of ruminating alone. But Summer was still in transit. She had texted on her way from her apartment to Chicago O'Hare, and again when her flight was boarding and when it landed in State College. Not long ago, she had texted, "In the home stretch! On the bus to the ECV!" Gwen stared at the initials for a moment, smacking herself on the forehead when she figured out "ECV" meant Elm Creek Valley. She had been working too hard. It was time to stop by the kitchen for one of those amazing chocolate cappuccino brownies everyone was talking about, just a small sliver, so she would not spoil her appetite for apple strudel later that evening.

"Let me know when you arrive at the bus station and I'll pick you up," Gwen reminded her daughter via text as she left the ballroom. It was nearly closing time, and most of the volunteers had finished their shifts and had gone home, but a dozen or so shoppers still browsed the market stalls, looking for the perfect gift for loved ones or perhaps for themselves. Crossing the foyer, Gwen stopped short at the sight of Brent Callahan, one of the juvenile offenders who had worked quilt camp the previous summer, as he bounded in the front entrance and handed a set of keys to a woman carrying several large shopping bags. Brent gestured to the bags and spoke, the woman nodded, and the next thing Gwen knew, he was carrying the bags outside to her car while the woman followed along. Surprised, Gwen lingered a moment, watching until the door closed behind them, shutting out the cold. Apparently Brent had been drafted for the valet crew, and he had learned some manners and had developed a stronger work ethic during his first semester of college. Gwen looked forward to telling Bonnie the next time she called from Hawaii. She would be thrilled to hear that her plea for leniency had inspired at least one of the young offenders to make the most of the opportunity to redeem himself.

Gwen turned the corner into the west wing, smiling to herself, when suddenly the back door opened and into the rear foyer stepped her daughter, radiantly beautiful even in her long winter coat, a knit cap with a pom-pom perched jauntily upon her long auburn hair, which, if Gwen was not mistaken, glistened with melting snow.

"Mom," Summer cried out, letting her bags slip to the floor and launching herself down the hallway toward her.

"Kiddo," Gwen exclaimed, opening her arms, sighing as if relieved of a heavy burden the moment she embraced her daughter. "How did you get here so fast? I was supposed to pick you up at the bus station."

Summer hugged her tightly. "I knew the bus was going to pass the forest road, so I asked the driver ahead of time if he would let me off at the junction. I walked the rest of the way."

"At night? In the dark? At this time of year?"

Summer laughed. "It wasn't that bad. A car passed every once in a while on its way back from the manor, and the headlights lit up the road."

"And any one of those cars could have struck you and knocked you into the creek." Gwen hugged her again, fiercely. "I need to know you're looking out for yourself when I'm not there to do it."

"I'm careful, Mom. I promise." Summer patted her on the back and pulled free of her embrace. "At the moment, I'm also ravenous. I smelled something delicious the moment I walked in. Is that supper, and dare I hope there's enough for one more plate?"

"The buffet closed down at seven, but I'm sure we can find some leftovers for you in the kitchen." Gwen linked arms with her and steered her toward the closet so she could put away her coat. "And for dessert, Anna made apple strudel."

"From Great-Great-Aunt Gerda's legendary recipe?"

"The very same." Abruptly Gwen halted. "But first, there's something I need to tell you."

"The buffet didn't include a single vegetarian dish for me?"

"No, actually, there were several, and they were all fantastic." Gwen inhaled deeply, bracing herself. "I think Jeremy is interested in Anna."

Summer's eyebrows rose. "Really? That was fast. Thanks for the warning." She continued on down the hallway, unbuttoning her coat.

"Hold on." Gwen placed a hand on her shoulder to bring her to a stop. "That's it? You're taking this rather well."

"How else should I take it?" Summer glanced down the hall in both directions as if concerned that another Elm Creek Quilter, perhaps Anna herself, might come upon them suddenly. "Jeremy and I had been drifting apart for months—you must have noticed—but it took us a while to finally have the conversation that made it official. We're still friends. If he's found happiness with someone else, it would be petty and spiteful of me to resent him for it."

"But to find someone else so soon?"

Summer shrugged wryly. "I admit that stings a bit, but I'll get over it."

"Oh, kiddo." Gwen sighed. "Could I ask you a favor? The next time anything like this happens, tell me right away. Don't leave me wondering what's going on in your life, sifting our conversations for clues and struggling to ignore Diane's rumors."

"She's spreading rumors?"

"Not many," Gwen quickly replied. "More like . . . questions. And only to me. As far as I know."

"Lovely." Sighing, Summer tugged off her hat and ran a hand through her long auburn hair. "Promise you won't take this out on Anna, okay? It's not her fault. If they are seeing each other, I'm certain it didn't start until after Jeremy and I broke up."

"I would never do such a thing."

"Could you make sure no one else does either? I think Diane might be a problem."

"She won't be," Gwen assured her. "You know Diane. She has a sixth sense for drama. But if you show her you don't bear Anna any ill will, she won't either."

Summer nodded and agreed. "There's something else, for future reference," she added as they continued on to the kitchen. "I want you to know that I couldn't possibly tell you *everything* that's going on in my life, but I can promise to tell you every *important* thing. Is that good enough?"

"That's better than good enough, kiddo," said Gwen. She put an arm around her daughter's shoulders and led her off to the kitchen to find her something good to eat.

ON SATURDAY MORNING, Diane and Michael rose early and drove straight to Elm Creek Manor, looking forward to starting the second day of the Christmas Boutique with the delicious breakfast Anna had promised. Tim stayed behind to finish scoring exams and lab reports so he could submit his students' final grades before the deadline, but he would take an intermission to pick up Todd from the airport. They both promised to stop by the manor on their way home so that Diane would not have to wait until later that night to see her youngest son again.

Michael had taken charge of the valet parking, so he joined the breakfast debriefing, where he suggested a few improvements to the car-retrieval process that were quickly approved. Then it was time to clear the table, set up the refreshments for the volunteers, and hurry off to their posts. Diane gave Michael a quick kiss on the cheek in parting and reported to the ballroom.

Soon the volunteers arrived and took their places at the market booths, and before the doors opened, Diane passed through the aisles making sure they had everything they needed— change, bottles of water, receipt paper, or help rearranging merchandise so that it would better catch a shopper's eye. Halfway along the center aisle, Diane came upon Mary Beth folding lovely hand-knit sweaters and laying them out neatly upon her table. "Good morning," Diane greeted her, surprised. "I'm glad you came. I didn't see you yesterday."

"Good morning." Mary Beth offered a brief flicker of a smile as she picked up another sweater. "Yesterday I didn't arrive until mid-afternoon, and I worked both of my shifts in the banquet hall."

"Then you haven't seen the quilt show."

"Not much of it." Mary Beth glanced around, but from where they stood, most of the quilts were at least partially obscured. "I'll see it during my break."

Diane checked her watch. "We have a few minutes before the crowds arrive. Can I show you something?"

Mary Beth hesitated, but she nodded, set down the sweater, and followed Diane down the aisle. Diane's heart thumped as she led the way to a corner of the room where *Christmas in Waterford* was displayed on the wall to the left of the doors leading into the banquet hall. Mary Beth halted before the quilt top, recognition slowly dawning on her face. Her gaze went to the placard beside it, and then, sharply, to Diane.

"When I told you that I admired your prizewinning quilt, I meant it," said Diane. "I wanted one of my own, but I should have asked permission to copy your design. I hope you don't mind."

When Mary Beth leaned forward to study her handiwork,

Diane winced inwardly, certain she would note every flaw. "The Providence block is in the public domain," Mary Beth said, straightening. "I think you're well within your legal rights to make your own version, especially since you chose a different color scheme and a slightly different border."

"Maybe, but there's legality, and then there's simple courtesy. I should have asked, and I'm sorry I didn't."

"There's no need to apologize. Isn't imitation the sincerest form of flattery?" Mary Beth gestured to the placard. "You did give me designer credit. That's all I would have requested."

"Really?" Diane heaved a sigh of relief. "Thanks for understanding."

"It's no problem, but the next time you want to copy one of my quilts, let me know and I'll help you. Your borders are a bit out of whack."

"It was only my fourth quilt," Diane protested, but when Mary Beth grinned, she knew she was being teased.

Just then Sylvia called out that she was about to open the doors, so they hurried off to take their places. Soon the ballroom was full of customers browsing the aisles, admiring the array of handcrafted goods, and, Diane was pleased to see, filling shopping bags with purchases.

Shortly before noon, Diane was walking around the perimeter of the market booths, keeping an eye out for volunteers in need of assistance, when she noticed a woman lingering before her red-and-white quilt, her gaze intent and admiring. She looked familiar, and as Diane approached she recognized Katherine Quigley, the county judge who had officiated at Sylvia and Andrew's Christmas Eve wedding the year before.

"Good morning, Your Honor," Diane greeted her, gesturing to the bulging tote hanging from the crook of her elbow. "Thanks for coming out to support the food bank."

"Oh, I have only just begun to shop." Judge Quigley smiled and indicated the placard with a tilt of her head. "You're the artist who made this lovely piece?"

"I am, thanks."

"And this one—" The judge indicated the Snow Crystals quilt top, a short distance away, and then gestured across the room to *Christmas in Waterford*. "And that one, in the corner?"

"Yes, they're all mine."

"You have quite an eye for color." Judge Quigley stepped back and gave the red-and-white star quilt a long, appraising look before turning again to Diane. "How much do you want for them?"

"How much—" Diane caught herself. "I'm sorry, but the quilts on the walls are for display only. They aren't for sale."

"Aren't they? This is the Christmas Boutique, after all. I'm willing to pay extra to support a worthy cause."

Bemused, Diane asked, "Of all the quilts for sale in the market booths, and all the masterpiece-quality quilts hanging here, you're interested in *my* work?"

"Are you telling me I shouldn't be?"

"That's not at all what I'm saying, but . . ." Diane hesitated. "You do see that they aren't quilted, right?"

"That's part of their appeal. I'd like to frame them and display them in my office." Judge Quigley glanced over her shoulder at *Christmas in Waterford*. "Except, perhaps, for that one. I might ask my sister-in-law to finish it for me so I can use it in my hearth room during the holidays."

Diane thought quickly. She would almost certainly never finish those quilt tops herself, and she liked to think of them going to good homes where they would be appreciated. As the judge pointed out, the money would support a very worthy cause. But only a few days before, when the idea of a quilt show had first been proposed, Diane herself had warned her friends that people would assume the quilts displayed on the ballroom walls were for sale too. At the time, she had considered that a serious problem, but with a potential buyer standing before her, she wondered if she had been too hasty in her opinion. If she decided to sell her quilt tops, that didn't mean the other Elm Creek Quilters would be obliged to sell theirs as well.

"What exactly would you consider a fair price?" Diane asked, and when the judge offered a substantial amount for each one, her misgivings vanished. She accepted the offer gladly, and as the judge wrote out a check, they agreed that they would not spoil the display by taking down the quilt tops immediately. Instead Judge Quigley would collect them Sunday afternoon as the Christmas Boutique drew to a close.

"Be sure not to sell them to anyone else in the meantime," the judge advised, handing Diane the check.

"Don't worry," Diane replied. She still found it hard to believe that anyone wanted her unquilted tops.

But just in case, in the unlikely event that another prospective buyer with unusual tastes came along, after turning the check over to Nancy, she hurried upstairs to the library to make a few more signs so that everyone knew the judge's quilts were off-limits.

AT THE PEAK of the lunch rush at half past noon, the banquet hall was so full of hungry customers that Agnes barely had time to direct her crew to clear and wipe down a recently vacated table before another group hurried over with their trays to claim it. On the buffet, the platters and deep stainless-steel warming dishes emptied almost as quickly as Anna could replenish them. Of all the mishaps that could have befallen the Christmas Boutique, Agnes would not have put running out of food near the top of the list, but perhaps she should have.

"Excuse me," said a woman pushing a stroller, craning her neck to read Agnes's name badge, "are you Agnes Emberly?"

"Yes, dear," said Agnes, quickly taking in the two shopping bags dangling from the stroller's handles and the restless toddler in the seat, yawning and tugging fiercely at his left shoe. "I see you have your hands full. Would you like some help going through the buffet line?"

"Oh—thank you, maybe later. Actually, I wanted to talk to you about your quilt, the Christmas Cactus?" She gestured over her shoulder toward the ballroom doors. "It would be the perfect Christmas gift for my mother. How much are you asking for it?"

"I'm afraid it's not for sale," said Agnes, smiling apologetically. "We Elm Creek Quilters hung up some of our favorite holiday quilts in the ballroom in order to create a festive atmosphere. There are many lovely quilts for sale in several of the market booths, however. Would you like me to show you?"

The young mother's brow furrowed. "None of the quilts hanging on the walls are for sale?"

"I'm sorry, no."

"Then why do some of them have 'Sold' signs pinned to them?"

"I beg your pardon?"

The toddler succeeded in pulling off his shoe, and with a crow of delight, he flung it as hard as he could in front of the stroller. "Fro away!" he shouted gleefully.

Agnes went to fetch the shoe, and when she returned it, the young mother thanked her and asked, "Do you want me to show you?"

"Lead the way, please," Agnes replied, bemused. Perhaps the woman had been distracted by her son and had misread the placards.

But when the stroller halted in front of Diane's Snow Crystals quilt top, Agnes saw for herself that a small sign about the size of an index card had been pinned to the bottom right corner. A single word, in all caps and boldface, announced **SOLD**.

"I don't understand," Agnes murmured, studying the sign.

"So, does this mean that the quilts on the walls are for sale after all?" the young mother asked hopefully, pushing her stroller back and forth to amuse her little boy.

"Not the Christmas Cactus," said Agnes firmly, shaking her head. She looked around the room for Sarah or Sylvia, but just when she spotted Sarah engaged in fervent conversation with several shoppers who had gathered around Anna's sampler, she felt a touch on her arm.

"If this quilt is for sale, I'd like to place a bid, please," said a fifty-something woman she vaguely recognized from the Waterford Quilting Guild.

"It's not for sale," Agnes repeated. Sylvia had joined Sarah and the group of shoppers, which seemed to be growing exponentially as the minutes passed. "My apologies. Would you excuse me, ladies?" Without waiting for a reply, she hurried off to join her friends.

She arrived just as Sylvia was calmly explaining that only the quilts in the market booths were for sale; all others were decorations. In the clamor of voices that followed, Agnes picked out a few rumors—some of the quilts on the walls had already sold, there was going to be a silent auction of the quilts on Sunday morning, the Elm Creek Quilters were selling raffle tickets for the wall quilts but no one knew where to buy them.

"Everyone, please," Agnes called out above the din, raising her hands. "Clearly there's been a misunderstanding. There is no auction, silent or otherwise, and no raffle." A moan of disappointment went up from the crowd. "As Sylvia said, the only quilts on sale are those in the market booths."

"Judge Quigley told me that she bought three quilt tops from one of the show organizers, and she's picking them up after the Christmas Boutique closes," said one particularly grumpy woman at the front of the pack, scowling, fists planted on her hips. "She said she paid the blonde— Her, there!"

The woman pointed, and in unison Agnes, Sylvia, and Sarah followed her line of sight until it led them to Diane, who was smiling and chatting with a pair of shoppers as she directed them to the banquet hall.

Agnes sighed. She should have known Diane would be involved. "I'll talk to her," she told Sylvia and Sarah, and slipped off through the crowd.

She managed to corner Diane near her red-and-white Dolley Madison's Star quilt, where another "Sold" sign was pinned to the bottom corner. "Are you selling your quilt tops?" Agnes asked, incredulous. "After the fuss you made about confusing the customers?"

"Apparently so," Diane replied, beaming. "Judge Quigley wouldn't take no for an answer. Wait until you hear how much I earned for the food pantry, and they aren't even quilted—"

"Diane, you've really stirred the pot. Since word got out that you sold your quilts, people have been making offers left and right for the others on display."

"That's fantastic!"

"No, it isn't, not when we don't want to sell."

Diane frowned, then shrugged. "Just tell everyone they aren't for sale."

"No one believes us. Judge Quigley set a precedent for not taking no for an answer."

"Oh." Diane winced. "I'm sorry, I guess?"

Exasperated, Agnes sighed and took Diane's arm. "Come

along, publicist. We need you to make a statement before we have an angry mob on our hands."

Diane's eyes went wide, but she dutifully followed Agnes back to Sylvia and Sarah. Gwen and Summer had joined them too, and were fielding questions, pleading for calm, and trying their best to quash spontaneous bidding wars. Agnes maneuvered Diane to the front, gave her a little nudge, and murmured, "You're on."

Diane drew in a breath, put on a smile, and explained that while she had sold her quilts from the display—to benefit the food pantry, of course—the other quilts belonged to private collections and were not available for purchase. A chorus of lamentations and protests met her remarks, and she held up her hands to silence the crowd, to no avail.

"A riot at the Christmas Boutique," remarked Nancy, who had appeared at Agnes's side while Diane was speaking. "That's a first."

"That's our Diane," Agnes said wryly. "Never a dull moment."

"But my mother would really love that Christmas Cactus quilt," a voice rang out, one that could only belong to the young mother with the stroller.

"Well, my grandmother would too," someone replied sharply.

As other voices rose in argument, Agnes drew herself up to her full five feet two inches, raised her hands for peace, and called out, "Everyone, please! My Christmas Cactus quilt is not for sale. Please understand, it's very special to me and I simply can't part with it."

A murmur of disappointment went up from the group, and in that moment, Agnes remembered Edna Hachmeyer.

"However," she continued, smiling, "if you would like to learn how to make one of your own, I would be very happy to teach you."

Someone squealed in delight, and someone else cried out, "Sign me up, please!"

Catching Sylvia's eye, raising her eyebrows in a question, and waiting for Sylvia's answering nod, Agnes added, "I'll hold a class here at Elm Creek Manor, and your tuition will benefit the food pantry."

"I want to make that lovely quilt hanging in the foyer," another woman called out.

"I'll teach you," said Sylvia and Sarah in unison, then turned to each other and laughed.

The next twenty minutes were barely controlled chaos as the other Elm Creek Quilters were enlisted to teach, a week in January for a special day camp was selected, sign-up sheets were passed along, and aspiring students went away satisfied that they would receive official registration information soon.

When the crowd at last had mostly dispersed, Gwen folded her arms and regarded Diane with amused exasperation. "Look what you did, when everything was going so smoothly."

"Yes, look what I did," said Diane proudly. "I just arranged to earn a small fortune for the food pantry."

"Excuse me," a voice broke in.

The Elm Creek Quilters turned to find nearly a dozen members of the crowd regarding them expectantly.

"Yes?" Sylvia asked. "Can we help you?"

"We'd like to make *Christmas in Waterford*," a second woman said, gesturing to Diane's quilt top. "We couldn't find the sign-up sheet."

Agnes turned to Diane, perplexed. "You don't want to teach your quilt? Why the other two, but not this one?"

"It's complicated," said Diane, a faint flush rising in her cheeks.

"Uncomplicate it," said Sylvia, peering at her knowingly over the rims of her glasses. "We'll wait."

*     *     *

AFTER DIANE EXPLAINED the provenance of her quilt design, Sylvia realized there was only one thing to do. She conferred briefly with her friends and colleagues, and when they promptly reached a unanimous decision, Sylvia asked Diane to accompany her to deliver the proposal.

Somewhat abashed—and with good reason, considering the commotion she had caused—Diane led Sylvia through the aisles to the market booth where Mary Beth was selling beautiful hand-knit sweaters of every style and color and type of yarn, made by many pairs of hands. "Can I interest you in a Fair Isle pullover for your husband or a cable-knit cardigan for yourself?" she asked tentatively as they lingered in front of her booth, regarding her expectantly.

"Perhaps later, dear," Sylvia replied. "I do need to purchase Christmas and first anniversary gifts for Andrew. But first, I wonder if you're aware of the brief controversy about our quilt display?"

"I haven't left my booth in a while, but I did overhear some odd conversations." Mary Beth looked from Sylvia to Diane and back, her expression guarded. "Someone wasn't supposed to sell a quilt, but she did anyway, and chaos broke out until you stepped in?"

"I wouldn't call it *chaos*," said Diane.

"You have the basic facts correct," said Sylvia. "As it happens, in order to satisfy the many would-be owners of the quilts in our holiday quilt show, we decided to offer classes so they could learn to make their own instead."

"If they're sufficiently motivated," said Diane, "and if they have some basic skills. Those quilts are more difficult to make than they look. Speaking from personal experience—"

"Thank you, Diane," Sylvia broke in. To Mary Beth, she added,

"We were hoping that as the designer of *Christmas in Waterford*, or rather, the quilt upon which it was based, you would be willing to teach the classes for that quilt. It appears to be one of the most popular."

Mary Beth's eyes widened. "You want me . . ." She paused to draw in a breath. ". . . to teach here, at Elm Creek Manor?"

"If you're available during the last week of January. We're all working pro bono to benefit the food pantry, so you won't be paid, but I can promise you an excellent lunch every day."

"I'll do it," said Mary Beth, bolting to her feet, grasping Sylvia's hand and shaking it firmly. "If anything is on my calendar, I'll clear it. You can count on me."

"Thank you, dear," said Sylvia, smiling and patting her hand, which trembled slightly in her own. She pretended not to notice the tears welling up in Mary Beth's eyes. "I'll be in touch after the boutique with all the details for our winter quilt day camp." She smiled and released Mary Beth's hand. "Back to work, everyone. Nancy tells me that even without our anticipated quilt lesson revenue, this Christmas Boutique is on track to be the most successful ever. Let's not spoil our chance to break some fund-raising records."

Lighthearted and satisfied, Sylvia parted company with Diane and Mary Beth—neighbors, former rivals, and perhaps future friends. Why not? It could happen. Unlikely friendships were forged almost every day at Elm Creek Manor. She and Agnes were one example, she and Sarah another. Diane and Gwen. Drawn together by their love for the art of quilting, they had discovered that they had much more in common than superficial differences implied.

By any measure, the Christmas Boutique was already an overwhelming success. With all her heart, Sylvia believed that the true mission of Elm Creek Quilts was not only to pass on the heritage of quilting, but to nurture friendships, encourage service to the community, and inspire students, faculty, and visitors alike to undertake new challenges with courage and hope. What better time than the holiday season to renew her commitment to that mission? As long as Elm Creek Manor stood, compassion and generosity would infuse every class taught, every meal shared, and every story told within its gray stone walls, not only at Christmas, but every day, year after year.

# Acknowledgments

I AM VERY grateful to the friends, family, and colleagues who contributed their time and talents to *The Christmas Boutique*, especially Maria Massie, Rachel Kahan, Alivia Lopez, Lauren Truskowski, and Molly Waxman. Geraldine Neidenbach, Heather Neidenbach, and Marty Chiaverini were my first readers, and their comments and questions about early drafts of this novel proved invaluable, as ever. Nic Neidenbach generously shared his computer expertise to help me in crucial moments; I honestly don't know what I would have done without him.

I was inspired to write *The Christmas Boutique* by the many Elm Creek Quilts fans who have told me through the years how much they adore and miss the Elm Creek Quilters, and how they longed to return to Elm Creek Manor through the pages of a new novel. I hope this story, which I wrote especially for you, brings you joy.

Most of all, I thank my husband, Marty, and our sons, Nicholas and Michael, for their steadfast love and encouragement. You make every season merry and bright!